# A Beautiful Couple

Leslie Wolfe

# BOOKS BY LESLIE WOLFE

## STANDALONE TITLES

*A Beautiful Couple*
*The Surgeon*
*The Girl You Killed*
*The Hospital*
*If I Go Missing*
*Stories Untold*
*Love, Lies and Murder*

## TESS WINNETT SERIES

*Dawn Girl*
*The Watson Girl*
*Glimpse of Death*
*Taker of Lives*
*Not Really Dead*
*Girl With A Rose*
*Mile High Death*
*The Girl They Took*
*The Girl Hunter*

## DETECTIVE KAY SHARP SERIES

*The Girl From Silent Lake*
*Beneath Blackwater River*
*The Angel Creek Girls*
*The Girl on Wildfire Ridge*
*Missing Girl at Frozen Falls*

# A Beautiful Couple

A  N O V E L

Leslie Wolfe

ITALICS PUBLISHING

$\llap{I}\mathbf{I}$ **ITALICS**

Italics Publishing Inc.
ISBN: 978-1-945302-76-3

*A special thank you to my New York City legal eagle and friend, Mark Freyberg, who expertly guided me through the intricacies of the judicial system.*

# 1

# AMANDA DAVIS

*I killed a man.*

The surreal words fill my mind, echoing in tremors that weaken my body. Wide-eyed, I stare at the body lying in a motionless heap at the bottom of the stairs, disbelief clinging to me in scattered thoughts and anxious breaths. As reality starts setting in, I gasp silently, covering my mouth to stifle a sob.

*It can't be true. He can't be dead.*

But I can see it's all too real. In his neck, twisted and crooked sideways to an impossible posture. In the sickening crack of broken bones that sounded just as he landed on the hardwood floor after bouncing down the steep flight of stairs. In the pooling blood that's slowly seeping from his head, gleaming burgundy under the yellowish light coming from the floor lamp by the door.

A noise outside startles me. Someone's coming. I freeze in place at the top of the stairs, my fingers white-knuckled on the handrail as the footsteps draw closer. Then, in the dark frame of the living room window, the profile of a woman appears, her face dimly lit as she passes by. Without turning her head to look inside.

I breathe.

But I also realize someone could've seen what happened. A passerby. A neighbor. Anyone.

I force some air into my lungs to steel my fraught nerves. Still holding on to the handrail for support, I climb down the stairs, careful not to slip, as if his fall could repeat somehow and seal my fate in vengeful symmetry, my body next to his. I hold my breath as I approach, senselessly hoping he's still alive, yet fearing it. When I breathe again, the metallic smell of blood invades my nostrils, filling me with dread.

I rush to the window and close the blinds, then peek outside between two slats. The street is eerily deserted and still. For now.

Crouching by his side, I feel for a pulse with frozen fingers. Touching his skin sears me, prickling the back of my head as if he could snap out of death and grab my shaky wrist.

There's no pulse.

His golf shirt is soaked with blood at the collar and smells faintly of aftershave, although his face shows a two-day stubble. His skull is fractured where it must've hit the edge of a step, the indentation clearly visible through his buzz-cut hair, despite the bleeding laceration. Reluctantly, I slip my fingers sideways and trace his neck, wincing as I find the protruding vertebra—a sign of a fractured cervical spine that resulted in a fatal spinal cord injury.

He died the moment he hit the floor.

I'm more than qualified to come to that conclusion. It doesn't change how I feel, though. Unsure of myself. Scared. Unsteady. My heart is racing, and my chest tightening, as if the walls of the room are drawing closer and closer, about to squeeze the life out of me.

The sound of an approaching car makes me rush to the window. It doesn't slow down until it reaches the corner and turns, tinting the darkness of the small, suburban street with hues of bright taillight red.

I turn on my heels and stare at the body, unsure what to do.

His eyes are still open, as if looking straight through me with hypnotizing, dilated pupils. It chills the blood in my veins. I crouch down and close his eyelids swiftly, barely touching him with the tips of my shaking fingers—eager to put some distance between me and him. I stand quickly and step back, unable to take my eyes off of him. Part of me still expects him to get up and grab me, slam me against the wall, then put his hands around my throat and squeeze until my world goes dark. Just as his is now.

But he doesn't move. He's dead.

*I* killed him.

The enormity of what I've done weighs heavily on my heart. How could I let this happen?

It seems I had no choice, and yet, the truth is that I *had* a choice, and I made the wrong one. That life-altering choice didn't happen a few moments ago, when I pushed him down the stairs.

No.

It happened earlier. Much earlier.

And now, I have to deal with the consequences of what I've done.

My first thought is to run, to put as much distance as I possibly can between me and the body lying on the blood-soaked floor. But there's no running away from this. Not right now. Not without a plan.

Walking backward, my heel stops against the bottom step of the staircase and I nearly trip. I let myself slide down and sit on a step. For a moment of respite, my elbows rest on my shaky knees and my face lands in my hands, hiding from the grim sight.

Perhaps I can stall things for a few days before they come for me, because I know they will. Clinging to that glimmer of hope, my mind starts working. I raise my weary head and look around, looking for anything I could use to buy myself some time. There isn't much.

One thing's certain: I have to get rid of the body.

I need help.

He's massive, at least six-three and well-built, weighing perhaps two-forty. It's what I liked about him...the strength, the agility, the apparent stamina and self-confidence. However, I'm not nearly that tall, and I'm one-forty at the most, on a bad, bloated day. I reach for his leg to test my strength, but stop before touching his ankle. It's pointless to even try. At work, it takes six of us to transfer a patient of his size from a stretcher onto a bed.

I take out my phone and turn it on. The bitten apple lights up white on the black screen, then vanishes, making room for a picture of my son. Tristan just turned nine; we took this pic last summer on the Santa Monica Pier. Seeing his piercing blue eyes touched by his enchanted smile brings the threat of tears to my own eyes.

What if I lose him? What if they lock me up and I never see him again?

I can't bear the thought of that. A hollow, burning ache opens up in my chest, swallowing everything. *No... I can't lose my son. That won't happen. Whatever it takes.*

I push the grim thoughts away and breathe deeply while typing in my phone's passcode. Tristan's face disappears off the screen.

*It will be all right.* But the words I've told myself fail to reassure me.

As the screen fills with apps, I realize there's only one person I can call for the kind of help I need. The one person I'd rather never call or see again. My fingers falter while retrieving the name from the contacts list.

Hesitating, I give the fallen body another look, desperately wondering if there's any other way.

There isn't.

I brace myself for the questions that are about to come my way like machine gun bullets, merciless and cold and ripping through me in rapid-fire sequence.

Then, I make the call, knowing that as soon as I share what I've done, there will be no turning back. My entire existence will be at the mercy of someone else. Someone I know I can't trust.

As the line rings in my ear, I reflect bitterly on the last few weeks, and on everything that's happened.

I never wanted any of this.

All I wanted was a damned divorce.

# 2

# PAUL DAVIS

*Two weeks ago*

*Hot damn. Tits like those should be illegal.*

I touch my tie knot briefly, wishing I could loosen it a little. Instead, I end up straightening it—a reflex when I know I'm directly in camera view. Only, there's no camera trained on me. Not yet.

The cameras are all huddled outside the ballroom, where the guests keep arriving in their fancy cars and rental limos to attend the annual *Citizens Against Impaired Driving* fundraiser I'm chairing. Even so, I should be focusing on the people seated at the table with me, including my wife Amanda. But no...I can't focus on any of them.

Only on her, the stranger who captured my interest the moment we arrived at the venue. She's walking across the atrium with a sway of her hips, so rhythmic and smooth that it's as if she's dancing her way through to the light music in the background. Her satin gown hugs her perfect shape, taut over her perky, little breasts. A high leg slit lets me put eyes on more of her skin than my wife would appreciate. Good thing Amanda's not looking at me right now. She's chatting with an older woman seated next to her while I get to feast my eyes on the unsuspecting stranger.

The woman doesn't look my way, and I'm not used to being ignored. To feeling invisible. I hate how it makes me feel. I almost want to shout, "Hey, I'm here," but there's no point. I'd make an ass of myself. As she makes her way to the open bar, she turns away, and I can see that gown is a backless wonder, seemingly clinging only to her shoulders...and so lightly, I could make it fall off of her with the touch of a finger. The thought unsettles me. I shift in my seat. And keep watching.

Her back is just as perfect as everything else she's strutting. The dress, a deep shade of red, shimmers under the dim lights, generously draped and still tight over her ass. It dips daringly below the small of her flawless back. I can't keep my eyes off her.

I bet she's not wearing anything underneath that thing. For a moment, I imagine how it would feel to touch her smooth, glowing skin. How that perfectly shaped back would arch when I took her from behind. How she'd look at me after, laying spent on crumpled sheets, with her wavy, chestnut hair spread on my pillow.

She disappears from sight as a couple of men trail after her and block my view. They're probably sucked in by her wake, empty drink glasses in hand and following her like panting dogs on the prowl. I'm about to down my drink and give myself a reason to visit the open bar where she's headed, but my glass freezes in mid-air when I notice Amanda's eyes, drilling into me with barely contained rage.

She leans toward me until her breath touches my skin. "Really, Paul?" she whispers in my ear, faking a smile for whoever might be looking at us just now. "With me here? With all these people watching?"

My teeth grit as I set my glass down. I hate being scolded like I'm four. "I didn't do anything," I growl back in a low voice, hating myself for saying it, for making excuses. She doesn't reply. Just sits there smiling, pretending everything is okay, but her chest is heaving, and her lower lip is trembling slightly.

But I'm still angry.

I'll admit I can get pissed off easily.

I take a sip of bourbon to hide the emotion, and pretend to pay some attention to what an overly bejeweled, middle-aged woman across the ten-person table is telling me. But it's pointless; I'm too frustrated to care. She goes on and on about a nephew of hers who died, and I'm forced to sit here, nod, and take it. She makes sweet eyes at me, and I fear I'll be throwing up in my mouth soon. I wash away the bad taste with more bourbon, then continue to smile and nod every now and then as she tells her endless story. Soon enough, she'll write me a check.

That's why I'm here, for the *Citizens Against Impaired Driving* annual fundraiser, gracefully hosted in the university atrium. The vast room is lavishly decorated with cascading white flowers set on every ten-person table, placed at the center of fine, white table linen. We're seated on dressed-up chairs tied up with satin ribbons. The myriad lights are dimly shining above us from chandelier-like, modern LED fixtures featuring intricate layers of crystal-clear prisms that glimmer in flickers of rainbow. These are not the drab, fluorescent university atrium lights I remember from my prior visits. They must've had them replaced for tonight. They really went over the top this time. I'm impressed.

The sound of my wife's laughter catches my attention. She looks beautiful tonight, with her long, blond hair done perfectly so, and she captures the undivided attention of at least two men. And I'm supposed to be okay with that. As if she can read my mind, her hand lands on my forearm. I pull away, instinctively, the thought of being seen as my wife's attachment bothering me on a deep level.

The air hums with low-key chatter and the occasional drunken burst of laughter. Because, of course, what's more fitting for a sobriety organization event than an open bar?

The event is sponsored generously and advertised for free by Golden State Broadcasting, the TV station I work for. They make sure that all invitation-only attendees can afford to fork out at least a couple grand for the four-course gourmet meal and said open bar. And the privilege to mingle with television people and the few Hollywood stars in attendance, and perhaps get a selfie with someone famous.

And as the president of *Citizens Against Impaired Driving* for the past few years, I'm at the center of all of it, soon to take the stage for the final speech of the evening, as soon as the guests finish their desserts.

Yet, I'm annoyed as fuck.

My boss, Raymond Cook, the president and CEO of Golden State Broadcasting, is a balding bundle of blundering ego. This year, the fourth in the pained history of his favorite event, he decided that the most prominent people in the station be seated with random donors, to engage them in conversation and have them imbibing and star-struck by the time they sign those checks. For what it's worth, he was fair; he's seated with donors, too. But he doesn't have unfuckable women drooling all over him while his wife is seated by his side. And that's not because he's not married. It's because no one really knows who Raymond Cook is. And no one cares.

But Paul Davis? That's a different story.

# 3

# PAUL DAVIS

I'm the face of the evening news and the brains behind it. I'm the lead anchor, and there's a reason for that. On the evenings I'm working, the Nielsen ratings go up, ad revenue climbs by at least ten percent, and viewership and engagement both spike. Yes, I'll admit that the spike is mostly reflecting women, and I'm secretly pleased with it.

With ratings like that, I got my own show two years ago. It's a fifteen-minute interview attached to the end of the news program, called *The Final Question*. There's no co-anchor involved; just me and whomever I choose—carefully—to skewer or commend that evening, dealer's choice. The show's been quite successful, further increasing the station's ratings. That's why Raymond Cook decided I should report directly to him. It was an actual promotion and came with more money—lots more money. Unfortunately, it also came with a closer working relationship between Raymond and me.

I'm not that happy about that part.

I hate his guts, and I'm sure he envies my popularity, although his bottom line loves it. Regardless of how I might feel about it, though, he's still the boss. He gets to call the shots. All of them. And never lets me forget it.

But that's not the only fly in my bourbon.

My former co-anchor, Carly Crown, is seated at my right. She's stunningly elegant in a sapphire blue dress with a plunging neckline that draws the immediate attention of every male in the room. Some females, too. Her blond hair is styled in loose waves and, tonight, looks disturbingly like my wife's. Perhaps she didn't intend it to, but I wouldn't put it past her. Every now and then, her knee rubs against my thigh.

I usually like the seemingly casual interactions, the not-so-accidental touching, the innuendo coloring our conversations at work. But not tonight. Not with a pissed off Amanda seated at my left. I don't want trouble on the home front.

Pulling away, I shoot Carly a warning glance. She veers her eyes toward the empty stage, but there's a certain tension in her lips that tells me I'm going to hear about my distance real soon. And I'm not going to like it. Carly is a death hazard dressed in Pierre Cardin.

The woman across the table stops speaking mid-phrase as the lights in the atrium grow brighter. Raymond climbs onto the stage and grabs the microphone. The light music in the background fades. He clears his voice and coughs into his fist—thankfully, before the mic goes live.

"Thank you all for being here with us tonight in beautiful Malibu. What a fantastic setting for such a noble cause! I hope you enjoyed the delicious meal as much as I did—though I must admit, the dessert might've been a bit too good. If I don't fit into my tux tomorrow, I'll know who to blame!"

The room regales him with a roar of laughter. I can tell the open bar made a difference this year.

"But before the evening comes to an end, there's the moment you've all been waiting for." He pauses for a moment, and the audience stills.

*About fucking time.*

We've been doing this for four years, and this is the first time he's letting me speak. I straighten my tie knot once more, but refrain from smoothing my hair with my hands. I'm ready.

*No, I'm not.* I take another sip of bourbon. *Now, I am.*

"She saves lives for a living," Raymond says, gesturing at and looking in Amanda's direction. The limelight follows his lead and finds us. My wife smiles shyly and bows her head. "As a critical care nurse working the endless battlefields of impaired driving, she's the first one to see the carnage. She will tell you that not everyone makes it, even if Sunset Valley Medical Center's Trauma Unit is one of the best in the nation. She has witnessed, time and again, the heartbreak a split-second bad decision can bring upon families."

He pauses for a moment, then shifts his focus to me. "He is a trusted voice in our community, bringing us the news with integrity and dedication. You know him well; you welcome him into your homes at dinnertime. And before you turn on the news to hear of yet another tragedy that has bloodied the streets of Los Angeles, he hears of it first. He investigates, uncovers the truth, and delivers it to you with all of the shocking details." It's my turn to smile and nod in acknowledgement. "Together, they are a beautiful couple, partnering to play a pivotal role in our organization's success and drive critical change in legislation, with your help. Please welcome Amanda and Paul Davis, ladies and gentlemen!"

My wife and I stand as the audience starts applauding. Beaming, Carly chooses that moment to step up into our limelight and hug me, as if we're at the Oscars or something. She lingers in the hug, filling my nostrils with her scent, grinding her hip against me. I pull away discreetly, knowing all cameras are trained on us. Then, I offer Amanda an arm that she quickly takes as we walk toward the makeshift stage.

She stands by my side at the lectern when I take the mic. The crowd quiets down looking at me, and I love it. "Thank you all for being here tonight. Before we get into the serious stuff, I wanted to share a little joke I heard recently: Why did the reporter sit on the teleprompter?" A pause for effect. "Because they wanted to stay on top of the news!"

The audience laughs heartily, and I bask in it. Then, as the response subsides, I continue. "Alright, now that we've had a laugh, let me tell you a story." I look at my wife, and she nods almost imperceptibly. "About how we started *Citizens Against Impaired Driving*, and, most of all, why. It was when we both realized that our jobs had too much death in them. For Amanda, it was the lives that the amazing team at Sunset Valley couldn't save. Senseless deaths that could've been avoided. For me, it was the litany of incidents I had to bring to you via the news I delivered, every single night. Not a day of respite in our lives and yours; not a day of not having to talk about yet another horrifying 'accident' happening here in LA." I allow a beat of silence to pass so my message can sink in. "It just has to stop. And you can make it happen. *We* can make it happen. Together."

As I say those words, the last of them being drowned by enthusiastic applause, my throat scorches for a drink. At a table close to the podium, the beauty in the backless red dress smiles at me.

I make eye contact and hold it for a moment. Her smile blooms, her head tilting slightly as she throws me a loaded look.

For a moment, I forget about Amanda.

Who knows what the evening might still bring? It's looking good for now.

# 4

# AMANDA DAVIS

My feet are killing me. I don't do high heels well, not after a full shift in the emergency department and an event that went on and on and on. Now, it's finally over and we're at the curb, waiting for the scrawny student working as parking valet to bring over Paul's Cadillac. I wish I could just sit on the concrete steps and take my shoes off.

We're among the last to leave, and I feel tense, anxious. I'm a nervous wreck, aching for everything to be over. Malibu's lights flicker in the distance, and the dark, ominous ocean reflects lightning flashes coming through the clouds. Moments later, thunder rolls, still sounding distant. And that valet takes a long time to bring a car around. I hope we won't get drenched waiting.

I'm dreading the moment Paul and I will be by ourselves in the car. We'll get into it again, my resentment toward his behavior aching to come out. Yes, I know I'm bitter and bitchy; most disillusioned women are. It's a side effect of having had your heart broken.

For now, I'm still on his arm, as it's expected of me, smiling and nodding and waving at the few remaining people who are yet to leave. They're mostly Paul's coworkers. His former co-anchor stops to say good night, and I pretend not to see what she's after when she's fluttering her mascara-heavy eyelids at my husband. She seems to be wasting her time, and I feel ridiculously relieved. Paul's mind seems to be elsewhere. Probably on someone younger than Carly. Younger than me, too.

When she finally gets the message, she leaves, her head held high, her perfectly styled curls bouncing with every step toward her red convertible Beemer idling a few yards down with the door open.

His new co-anchor, Latesha Jones—a woman he says he despises—shakes my hand in passing, then stops squarely in front of Paul.

"I wonder if there's a better way to engage these donors," she says with a tiny, shrewd smile on her full lips. I can't help but notice how pristine her makeup looks, after so many hours. Must be professional-grade, and not the department store variety I'm using.

"Really?" Paul replies. His brow creases briefly.

"I'll think of a few pointers. Audiences like this need something new. Something fresh. Perhaps different speakers next year?"

I sense my husband's arm stiffen, but he doesn't say anything. Just nods at her. Says nothing.

"Well, if you're not interested enough to hear me out, I'll take my suggestions to Raymond."

"You do that," Paul replies with clenched teeth. "Drive safe, Latesha, or better call a cab. You had a few."

Her car is already at the curb, a white convertible Benz. She laughs off Paul's comment and climbs behind the wheel. She doesn't drive off right away, though. By the way she's squirming in her seat and reaching under the steering wheel, I'm guessing she's kicked off her four-inch Manolos and slipped on something more comfortable.

And I'm looking forward to doing exactly that. I would've taken off my black pumps while seated at the table, if I weren't worried about all those cameras, hunting for the doubtful future "stars" of Saturday's supermarket tabloids. I can see the dreaded headlines in my mind. *Fashion faux pas or a savvy move? None other but Amanda Davis kicked off her shoes under the table at last night's glitzy fundraiser.* Or, my biggest fear of all: *Drama at the fundraiser! All eyes were on Paul Davis, caught on camera sneaking glances at other women throughout the night, even with his stunning wife seated right beside him. Is there a crack in the beautiful couple's façade?*

Disrupting my inner anguish, the recognizable headlights of Paul's Cadillac XT6 turn the corner, approaching the atrium stairs unnervingly slowly.

Paul sees it, too, and lets out a quick sigh. "At long last," he mutters, slurring a little. The smell of bourbon is strong on his breath.

"Let me drive, Paul. I only had club soda tonight."

He throws me a side glance. "There's no need. I'm fine. Let's go."

He's never liked me driving his fancy car, but doesn't say it. On his best behavior since there are a couple of tabloid cameras still rolling, Paul opens the door for me, and I touch his hand briefly. "We could call an Uber. Please. I have a bad feeling about this."

"This what, Amanda?" He steps in place, eager to leave and visibly frustrated with me. His voice pitches higher. "Huh? When was I not a safe driver?"

That doesn't warrant a reply. I give up. Instead of arguing pointlessly, I climb into the car and kick off my shoes right after he slams the door shut.

But the moment the Cadillac sets in motion, I can't help myself. "This entire thing, CAID, the fundraiser, it's all a sham for you, isn't it? I bet you do it for the ratings. You don't believe in it... You're just using it—and me—to prop up your career and get face time with influential people."

"Damn it, Amanda," he says, slamming his hand against the steering wheel. "What the hell is wrong with you tonight? Lay off my fucking back!"

"There's no real advocacy. No benefit. There's no legislation that was changed in the past four years since we started this. Honestly, I don't know where all the money is going."

"Oh, so now you want an audit?" The wheels squeal in protest as he takes the left turn onto Malibu Canyon, speeding up. "Just tell me if you do, and we'll have the books ready for you. 'Cause you're the boss here, aren't you?"

I roll my eyes in the darkness of the vehicle. Everything is about power and control with him. That's all he cares about. And people's perceptions of him.

Giving up for the second time in only two minutes, I let my mind wander aimlessly, trying to stave off the anxiety coursing through my veins. Trying to silence my screaming thoughts and make the right decision.

The sky flickers brightly with lightning over our heads, and thunder startles me, making me flinch. It sounds menacing, foreboding. For a while, I look out the window at the canyon walls rushing by under the car's powerful headlights as Paul drives faster and faster on the deserted, winding road.

*Won't be much longer.*

"You were ridiculous tonight," he says, shooting me a seething glance. "Your suspicions, your attitude, everything."

I shake my head and refuse to say a word in my defense. It's pointless; everything I try with him ends in defeat. I take out my phone from my purse, then type a quick message.

"Who are you texting at this hour? It's almost midnight." His suspicions of me would be hilarious if they weren't so hurtful. If his mind is on other women, he thinks I'm the same way. He doesn't know me at all.

"I forgot to tell Mrs. Higgins we're leaving," I tell him.

"Who?"

"The older woman at our table. I promised I'd meet her at the bar for a champagne nightcap and totally forgot."

Paul looks at me with suspicion. I keep typing. "I just left. So sorry…" There's no reply to it—just a notification that it was read by the recipient.

Then, I hold the phone's screen toward Paul. "There, want to see for yourself?" He keeps his eyes on the road.

"Whatever," Paul mumbles as I slip the phone back into my purse.

"So, did you meet with that woman?" I ask, unable to keep my mouth shut. I'm scratching this wound like it's an itchy scab, knowing quite well it's going to hurt worse, the more I do it.

"Jeez, Amanda... Which woman is that?"

"The one in the red dress you were ogling all night. Did you get her number?"

"For fuck's sake, Amanda! I told you again and again! That's what sells television, movies, fundraisers. Anything really!" His fingers are white-knuckled on the steering wheel. A few warning beeps come from the car's systems when the wheels bite into the double line separating the lanes.

"What? Good journalism?"

"Sex!" he shouts, glaring at the road in front of him. The loud voice in the enclosed space of the speeding vehicle rattles me into staying silent as he continues shouting. "That's what they want to see! They don't care about anything else but my face. That's what I have going for me, if you really have to know! Worth more than my journalism degree and all the investigative reporting I do!"

I never thought of it that way. Never thought he'd care, as long as he's the center of attention, getting what he wants.

"But must you act on it?"

The car beeps, and Paul swerves into the other lane as he approaches a tight curve too fast. "Son of a bitch," he mutters, resuming his high-speed drive across the Santa Monica mountains after re-entering the right lane. "What would you like me to do? Let the likes of Latesha Jones or Carly Crown eat our lunch? Become their producer and run their errands?"

Anger roils inside me. I just can't let go of it. "I'd like you to show me some respect! At least when I'm there with you and everyone's looking. You, they admire and they...lust over. But me, they look at with pity or disdain. Like I'm some sort of—"

A woman's silhouette appears out of nowhere, a dark shape against the flickering lightning. I shriek a split second before the car hits the thin body. The pedestrian is thrown against the windshield, cracking it. Then, she's bounced over the car to land on the road behind us. The vehicle brakes furiously, beeping all sorts of warnings, its tires screeching and grinding on the asphalt.

The car is now fully stopped, but Paul won't let go of the steering wheel. "What the hell just happened?"

# 5

# PAUL DAVIS

*"What the hell was that?"*

My voice is a strangled whisper. I open the door and get out of the car, but have to hold on to the doorframe for balance. I'm weak at the knees and shaky, and about to throw up all that single-barrel.

Barefoot and holding her long skirt in one hand, Amanda runs toward the downed pedestrian. Her silver gown flutters in the wind, making her look like a ghost. Shivers go down my spine. As soon as she reaches the pedestrian, she crouches by her side and starts doing her job, probably checking to see what's broken. Her hand feels for a pulse, then she lowers her ear close to the woman's face, probably listening for a breath.

A flicker of rage fires through me as I notice she's dressed in black. How was I supposed to see her in the dark?

Time slows to a standstill while Amanda remains crouched by the pedestrian's side, doing her thing in the faint light coming from her phone. She runs that light up and down the fallen body. A knot tightens in my gut, fear spreading from it like poison. There's no movement, no pained groan coming from the person. Nothing. Just silence, every now and then interrupted by ominous thunder.

*What the hell am I gonna do?*

I stare at the cracked windshield. It's stained with blood. My hand rushes to my gaping mouth instinctively. *What if I killed her? Oh, God, no.*

Amanda lifts her head and looks at me, urging me to go to her. I walk over, my hands shaking badly as I loosen the tie around my neck. But I stop a couple of feet away from the fallen pedestrian. I can't take a step more.

"She died on impact," Amanda announces clinically, but then wipes her eye. "You need to call the cops." She stands and looks at me, her gaze intense and unforgiving. "Now, Paul."

In a split second, I can see the future, and what that would do to me. To all of us.

"No!" I reply decisively. My fingers run through my hair, entangling then tightening around the strands and pulling hard, as if I'm about to rip them from my scalp. "I can't do that! Are you kidding me? I can't."

She's standing still, her eyes fixed on the victim for a while before drilling back into mine. "Paul, you can't *not* call them. Every moment we spend on this road, we risk someone plowing into us at sixty miles per hour. You need to make that call."

I'm pacing erratically, taking a few steps toward the car, then coming back, unable to get any closer to her. A battle of instincts is going on inside me. With every fiber in my body, I'm aching to run away from here and leave everything behind, but I can't. Not like this.

"Amanda, it was an accident. She looks like a homeless woman or something. Look how thin she is. And she's wearing a jacket in this weather… What was she doing out here at this time of night?" I look around, my hands propped firmly on my hips. "In the middle of Malibu Canyon Road?" Amanda just stares at me in disbelief. "No, I'm telling you, this wasn't supposed to happen. It was an accident."

"I agree," she says calmly. Sometimes, I envy her composure. It probably comes natural to her, with all of the emergencies she handles at the hospital. "You'll get a lawyer— a good one, someone you probably won't even have to pay that much, considering who you are and how much everyone wants to be on your show. They'll explain all that to the police and you won't be charged."

"What about my blood alcohol? You know that's the first thing they'll test for." The irony of that, of how it all happened and when, doesn't escape me.

There's an I-told-you-so slant to the thin line of her lips. "That's the lawyer's job. He'll make that go away. You know they can keep things on the down-low if you stay ahead of everything." She bites her lip nervously, constantly looking over her shoulder, checking for traffic. "You can't just drive off. You'll do serious time if they catch you. It's a felony."

"And I'm telling you, we can't call the fucking cops!" My anguished shouting bounces against the canyon walls, echoing strangely in the night. I'm tired of her logic, her pleading, and all the sensible arguments she's laying thick on me. Like this could somehow persuade me to throw my life away.

"You should lower your voice. You're drawing attention to yourself."

The woman drives me insane. She won't shut up for long enough to let me figure this out. We're on a deserted stretch of road, more than a mile away from the nearest house. Aggravated, I stomp my foot, then gesture at the canyon walls with my open arms. "Whose attention? There's nobody here!"

"That's what you thought before you hit her."

It takes a moment before her words sink in. When they do, the hairs on my nape tingle. I look around, trying to see in the deep darkness hued red from the taillights. What if someone saw us? Everyone's got a camera on their phone these days; they could've taken pictures of this whole mess. Of my tags. Of my face. *Oh, God.*

I have to do something. I pause mid-step, my chest tightening as I glance around, my hands clenching into fists. My breath catches, shallow and unsteady, as a wave of panic washes over me.

There's no moon, just occasional lightning zigzagging though a low and dense cloud cover. I turn on the flashlight in my phone and look around some more. The flashlight beam is too weak to reach far. I see a steep, barren rock canyon wall on the left side of the road, and a deep ravine on the other. I approach the right-side railing and look down. The ground and gorge below are covered in dense, tangled shrubs. There's no telling how deep the ravine really is, under all that greenery.

I think I know what to do.

I pick up a rock from the side of the road and throw it, my flashlight trained on it as much as possible. It falls straight through the shrubbery and rustles for a split moment more before it settles. The ravine is deep enough. It will work.

But before that, I try something else—a Hail Mary pass at staying on the right side of the law. "This was an accident, Amanda. You know it was."

She nods, looking at me curiously. "Yes. It was."

"Earlier, you offered to drive." Her eyebrow shoots up and her eyes drill into mine, colored in disbelief. "It could've happened to you just as well, right?"

"What's your point?" Her voice is ice-cold. Threatening.

I made a mistake bringing it up. "Never mind. I was just thinking, maybe you could—"

"Take the blame for you?" She chuckles bitterly. Her voice is filled with contempt. "I guess, yeah, you'd expect that, wouldn't you?"

I swallow hard, my throat constricting mercilessly. "Will you do it?"

"No, Paul, I won't." She looks me straight in the eye. "I'll give you one more minute to do the right thing. Then, I'll call the cops myself."

I believe her. She probably has a few cops on speed dial. Buddies from work.

But I can't believe she won't help me. She's made lots of useful friends in her line of work. I've only made enemies. And still, she doesn't care about me, about what's going to happen to us. Just her damn values.

"Listen, we can't call the cops if you won't—" I stop talking, seeing the way she looks at me. "We'd be the laughingstock of this entire town. Everything will be destroyed. My career... I'll never work again, not in television. I'll go to prison! You know I'm over the limit." She doesn't flinch, as if she's not hearing a word I'm saying. "I'll be happy if they let me work in construction with a criminal record. And CAID? Can you imagine what that will do to the organization? We *built* this! You and me, together! We can't just let it burn. Over what? Some homeless woman who stepped in front of my car? Come on, Mands, be reasonable." I reach for her hand, but she pulls away angrily.

"Don't you dare touch me!" she hisses. "Right now, I don't know who you are."

Withdrawing my hand quickly, I look at her, then at the body, trying to decide. It's only a matter of time until another vehicle drives by. Senselessly, I try to remember if anyone still left at the event lived across the canyon. It doesn't matter. Someone *will* come, sooner or later.

It's obvious there's no real choice here.

I walk back to crouch by the woman and look at the gaunt face covered in blood. Only for a brief moment, though, before I have to look away. I consider lifting her frail body to carry it over to the side railing, but that would destroy my tux. Then, I'd stain the car seat with blood, the steering wheel... everything. There'd be no end to it. Not a forensically sound end, anyway.

Grabbing her ankles, I start dragging the body towards the side of the road, leaving behind streaks of dark red blood, uneven and smeared. "Son of a bitch," I mutter, knowing there's no way I could clean that. Maybe, by sunrise, it will be all dried up and unnoticeable. Or perhaps it will rain. There's an atmospheric river coming that's supposed to dump six inches on us tonight. I need that to start happening already.

Amanda steps into my path, her eyes wide, unforgiving. "No," she says firmly, raising a hand to stop me. "I won't let you throw this woman in the ditch like she's garbage! That's not who we are."

Tension crackles between us like static electricity. Our eyes lock in a silent battle of wills.

*Hell if I'm going to let her ruin my life with her righteousness.*

I push her aside. "Try to stop me."

# 6

# AMANDA DAVIS

I've never been afraid for my life before. Not like this. Perhaps it's the fact that Paul is dragging a dead body. A frozen dread seeps through me and makes me take a step back. Or maybe the look in his steeled eyes...cold, merciless, tinged with insanity. A cornered killer's look.

But what did I see, exactly? How much can I trust myself here, in the dark, after all that's happened?

We've had our problems in the recent past, much like other couples, but I thought I knew who my husband is. What he's capable of. I no longer trust that to be true. Still, I keep trying to find excuses for him. Some kind of justification for what he's about to do. He's being pushed to the limit; I get that. He's reached his breaking point tonight.

And now, I'm letting him do this. I can't begin to understand how. Am I really letting him? I must be in shock. *Oh, God, I can't just let him...I can't.* And yet I'm not moving. The way he pushed me aside just now, brutally, nearly knocking me off my feet, still resonates throughout my body.

Arms crossed at my chest, I feel the chill of the night seeping into my bones. My feet are frozen. Barefoot, I'm stepping in place on the cold asphalt to keep them warm. The wind is brisk and gusting, raising dust and dead leaves from the side of the road and twirling them in the air. Thunder is now closer, louder, and lightning draws Paul's outline by the side of the road, painting an ominous picture that will haunt me forever. He's dragged the woman's body over to the edge of the ravine. Now, he pushes it under the railing, then rolls it a bit further down, it closer and closer to the edge, leaning forward over the railing, grunting with the effort.

I keep my distance, standing by the car. I can't be a part of what he's doing. My stomach riles up and I force some deep breaths of air into my lungs to keep it from lurching. This is not the place to unload my dinner and my nerves, leaving DNA behind at the scene of a hit-and-soon-to-be-run.

The brush branches crack and break loudly as the body falls. Paul lets out a loud groan and straightens his back, still looking into the ravine. His back is turned to me, but I can tell he's rubbing his hands together, probably to shake off any dirt or grime he might've picked up. Then, he switches on the phone flashlight and looks into the ravine for what seems like hours.

But it's barely been a minute.

When he finally approaches the car, he avoids my eyes. I can see how distraught he is, from his faltering gait, and the line of his tense shoulders and his lowered head. He's staring at the ground, probably ashamed of what he's done. "Let's go," he says. All the threatening chill is gone from his voice, replaced by fear.

I draw closer, my skirt lifted with my hand as I step around the blood smeared on the asphalt. I can't take my eyes off of it as I walk past. The sight of it tears through my chest like a blade, and I let out a stifled sob, my hand clasping my mouth.

Heading for the passenger seat, I walk in front of the Cadillac to examine the damage. The windshield is cracked and covered in blood, and partially caved in. The front grille is cracked, with pieces broken off to have fallen who knows where. If the cops find them, they'll match them to the make and model of our car. And from there on, it'll be easy to find us.

"How are we going to drive home like this?" I ask in a subdued voice.

He climbs behind the wheel and grabs it with both hands. "I don't know, all right? Come on, let's go."

I hesitate, but then realize I don't have much of a choice. What am I supposed to do? Walk all the way home, across the

Santa Monica Mountains? Argue with him in the middle of the road? No...we're in this together now.

Just as I make my decision, a heavy raindrop splashes on my face. I climb into the passenger seat and close the door, shuddering. As I rub my arms to warm them up, he turns on the engine and shifts into gear.

"If we run into a cop on the way back, we're done," I say, stating the obvious, which I know he hates. "The moment anyone sees the—"

"Don't you think I know that?" He drives off cautiously, no longer exceeding the speed limit. Within minutes, the rain turns heavy. He flips on the wipers, but then swears and shuts them off. "The glass won't take it. It might cave."

I stare at the place where the pedestrian hit the windshield. Just like a spiderweb, the cracks spread from a central point all over the laminated safety glass. Under the heavy rain, the blood starts to wash off. Some of it drips through the cracks inside the car, mixed with rainwater.

"Oh, shit," Paul mutters. "Put something under that. Don't let it spread all over the dash or get into the vents. We'll never get it out."

I open the glove box and rummage through the contents. Registration, a small flashlight, a car freshener, a pair of leather gloves... "There's nothing here I can use."

"Try the door pocket. There should be a piece of terry cloth in there." His voice is tinged with panic. His eyes dart from the road to the rearview mirror and back. The road remains dark behind us, and the rain has gotten heavy. No one's coming up the mountain from the city.

I find the terry cloth where he said and place it under the center of the crack, but it won't last long. There's too much water coming in.

He grabs it from my hand and pushes it against the windshield. "Here, hold it like this. Don't push too much—just try to keep it from caving in."

I have to pull myself to the edge of the seat to do what he wants. Releasing my seat belt, I place my right knee down on the car floor to reach. My hands are shaky, and my gut twists into a knot with fear, but I hold myself steady. It won't be long now.

As soon as we emerge from Malibu Canyon Road into Calabasas, we both look left and right. The streets are well-lit with yellowish lights as we drive on toward the house. Everything is deserted, which almost never happens in Los Angeles. It's probably the rain. And it's late, almost one-thirty in the morning.

But it won't be good enough.

"There are cameras at the lights, and the ATM—"

"Don't you think I know that?" he snaps. Funny how easy it is for him to shout at me whenever he feels like it. Sometime in the past couple of years, I've become his relief valve, his verbal punching bag. The effect is particularly bad in this enclosed space, where the loud, threatening sound of his voice is captive here with me.

"I'll take the back roads from here," he adds.

He takes a left turn after waiting for what seems an eternity for a red light to change, right under a traffic camera trained on our car. Then, he starts the intricate journey that will put us at our home in Deerhill Park, taking back streets where traffic light cameras aren't that frequent. Not that it matters much, when everyone in this city has some kind of security system with video surveillance—at least a Ring camera, if not more. I know for sure all of our neighbors do.

We're halfway through our drive home when he suddenly changes course. He pulls a 180 across the deserted, four-lane Kanan Road and starts driving back toward the freeway. "There's never going to be a better time to do this," he mutters.

"Where are we going?" My heart's racing, and I can't get enough air. I'm ready for it to be over.

"Car wash. There's an automated one that takes cash, a 24/7. I know it well." He pulls to a stop at a traffic light. The sound of the blinker is unusually strong against the muted sound of heavy rain falling. "I know where their security cameras are," he adds, sounding unconvinced.

*That's a really bad idea.*

But just as I wonder if I should voice my concern, an LAPD patrol car comes to a stop in the right lane, next to us.

# 7

# PAUL DAVIS

---

"Fuck," I whisper, trying not to turn my head and stare at the cop. Maybe he won't notice anything wrong. Maybe he won't look at us at all. If he does, he'll notice Amanda is sitting on the edge of her seat, no seat belt on, reaching far across to hold the cloth in place.

"What do I do?" Amanda asks, breathless. She's pale and shaky, but that's no surprise. I'm gripped by a fear so deep it leaves me breathless.

I reach to hold the terry cloth against the windshield in her stead. "Leave this to me and try to slide back in your seat slowly. No sudden moves."

As I take the terry cloth from her, I notice a blood stain on my cuff. I shift how I'm holding the cloth, so the jacket sleeve slides over the stain. I try to appear steady and composed, but my mind is racing. What do I do when the light turns green? How fast do I drive off? Is the cop looking at us?

"Paul?" my wife asks between gritted teeth. I turn to look at her, and see the cop has lowered his window and is about to tap on Amanda's with the butt of his long flashlight.

*Oh, fuck.* I lower the window on her side and gesture a greeting. "Hello, Officer."

He nods as he studies us with sharp, beady eyes. He's about fifty, with graying buzz-cut hair that attempts to make a deeply receding hairline less conspicuous. His neck is packed with muscle; he probably spends a lot of time at the gym, popping steroids. I wouldn't want him laying a hand on me.

"What happened there?" he asks, projecting the powerful beam of his flashlight inside the car at the windshield. He looks at both of us, then focuses his attention on the windshield and the towel I'm holding against it. "Crash?"

I nearly choke. "Um, no, just a stone on the highway. Thrown by an eighteen-wheeler. Made a hell of a mess."

He puts the beam on my face again. My blood turns to ice, but I try to stay perfectly calm. "I'll say," he grumbles, his lips pressed tightly as he continues to look at me. "Aren't you that news guy, Paul something?"

*Fabulous. He's recognized me. I am so fucked.*

"Paul Davis, yes." Saying my name in front of him somehow makes me find my stage legs, my public persona. For a split second, all is forgotten and I'm in the limelight again, albeit that the light's coming from a cop's Maglite this time. "That's me." I'm smiling, personable and seemingly relaxed. "Do you mind if I lift this window just a notch? We're getting flooded in here."

"No," he says, turning off that dreadful Maglite. Comfortable darkness surrounds us again, glimmers of yellow from streetlamps and green from the traffic light reflecting in every raindrop landing on the cracked windshield. "Go right ahead. One thing, though, before you go." He pauses for a moment, while my heart stops beating. "Ma'am, please take your seat correctly and fasten your seat belt."

Amanda nods. "Yes, Officer. I was just trying—"

"If your airbags deploy, even in a low-speed crash, and you're not wearing your seat belt, you could die." Pale as a sheet, Amanda nods. "All right," he says, taking two fingers to his forehead in some sort of abbreviated military greeting. "Drive safe. And have yourselves a good night."

With that, he puts his window up and drives off.

I breathe.

Amanda starts sobbing as she clicks on her seat belt. She's a mess. Rain has pasted her hair into clumps on her face. Her soaked, matted dress clings to her skin, revealing every shiver as the cold seeps through the open window.

I bring the window all the way up, but it still feels cold.

By the time I'm ready to drive off, the light is red again. "It's okay," I say quietly, looking all around me for traffic. Eager to disappear, I don't believe a word I'm saying, and yet I say it again, for both of us. "It's going to be okay."

"No, it's not," she replies. Her voice breaks up with tears and shattered breaths. "You just lied to a cop, and he knows who you are. He recognized you."

"But he didn't do a formal traffic stop. I won't be in any report." She looks at me as if I'm an idiot. I hate it when she does that. "Yeah, I know, I'll be the highlight of their little watercooler party. He'll tell everyone at the precinct that he met me."

"And that your windshield was cracked," she adds, annoying me as she always does when she's listing all the facts. I've asked her a couple of times to stop doing it. Seems it's something from her job, where they have to list symptoms quickly and precisely so that the emergency teams figure out what to do. Well, fuck that shit. I don't need it now. Or ever.

"When we get to the car wash—"

"Do you think this windshield can take the water pressure in a car wash?" Her voice is restrained, cautious even, as if she knows she's pissing me off. Yet, she still has to make her damn point. "I thought we were going home, you know. After running into that cop. I need us to go home, Paul. *Please*."

Her comments ignite a spark of frustration in me. "I don't think we have a choice. The rain washed some of the blood off the windshield and the hood, but the grille and front bumper are going to drip all over the garage floor. If there's blood caught in there... How would you like me to deal with that? It's not like I can wash the blood off our damaged car on our driveway with the garden hose."

I try to stay calm, but I'm about to lose it. I don't understand how this could've happened to me. Especially tonight. Shitty, fucked up luck...that's what it was.

But I can't think about it. Not now.

# 8

# PAUL DAVIS

As I was expecting, I find the car wash open and deserted. It's dimly lit by a streetlamp, the owner probably too stingy to pay for any additional lighting. Hooray for that. I stop alongside the building, out of camera view, grab the gloves from the dashboard box, and get out of the car in the pouring rain.

"Paul?" Amanda calls, just when I'm about to slam the door shut. "Where are you going?"

I groan with frustration. Where does she *think* I'm going? If she hadn't cut me off when I was trying to tell her, she'd know. "Just wait, all right?" I slam the door shut, giving it the brunt of my frustration.

Turning the one camera to face the wall is a quick bit of work. I look around briefly, to see if there are others, but don't glimpse any. I can't see much anyway through this rain, but that works both ways. Even if there's another camera and it catches us, the recording might well be completely unusable.

I rush back to the car, stepping in a few puddles on my way, but I don't care anymore. I'm soaked and tired and scared, and just sick of everything. I drive up to the pay station and select a full lather without dry, then insert a twenty using my gloved hand, and the machine obliges me with a tenner as change.

Amanda picks up the terry cloth towel and holds it against the windshield crack, bracing herself as if it's going to be boulders, not water, landing on the car. After I enter the automated touchless station, I set it the car park and let the machine take over.

Droplets of foam in three bubblegum colors drop onto the vehicle. With a push of a button, I fold the side mirrors and lean back into my seat, hating the feel of wet clothes on my back and what they're doing to the perforated leather seats of my brand-new Cadillac. I'd rather think of that than the agonizing fear that's twisting my gut into an unbearable knot.

As the power wash begins, water starts dripping faster through the windshield cracks. My tux is soaked as it is; I might as well use it. It sticks to my shirt as I take the jacket off. Then, I lay it down over the dashboard, covering the vents. It will hold some of the water back.

"I don't know how you're imagining you could still get away with this, Paul." Amanda gives me a quick, disappointed look. "I know traffic cops. I've seen how tough they get on people who flee the scene. Some of them land in the emergency department, you know. And those guys in Traffic show them no mercy."

"Well, they're also tough on drunk drivers who kill pedestrians." My hands tighten on the wheel, knuckles going white, as I process my own words. She probably didn't expect me to say it like that, and gasps when she hears it. I didn't expect to react so deeply to my own damning words, either. It's as if the despair and fear inside me have been stoked to unbearable levels.

The carwash's green light turns on, and I drive off, going around the building for another run.

"Again?" She shakes her head, then massages her forehead with trembling fingers. "How many times do you want to do this?"

"Two, three times, I think is enough. We can't have a single blood drop on this car. You know they'd find it."

"You're not being reasonable, Paul. You're backing yourself into a corner. Don't you realize they will still prove—"

"I didn't have a choice!" My voice reverberates in the car, making her flinch. She pulls away as if I'm about to hit her. Which is ridiculous. I've never laid a hand on her. "I've been advocating against drunk drivers for years, and now this? They'd skin me alive!" I shake my lowered head bitterly. "They'd make an example out of me."

"And how is this better? Did you think of Tristan? What will it do to him when you go to prison?"

"That's below the belt, and you know it." I breathe away my instant rage in quick inhales and exhales. "Don't use my son like that."

"*Our* son, Paul. Don't you fucking forget that." Her eyes glint with rage in the soundproofed darkness of my lather-covered car. "You should've thought of him when you drove off. When you pushed that poor woman's body into the ravine. How will you explain that?"

I hate what she's doing to me, chipping away at every bit of self-confidence I still have. Destroying me from the inside out. We sit in loaded silence until the wash is done, and then I start the engine, drive around, and re-enter the car wash again.

For the first time since the accident happened, I'm starting to doubt I made the right call when I fled.

"Maybe I won't have to," I mutter. "Who's going to find her in that ravine, huh? They won't catch me unless you tell on me, and I swear to God—"

"I'd never do that," she says calmly. Coldly. But I believe her. "A coward or not, you're still Tristan's father. Unlike you, I think of him before making my decisions."

A new layer of tricolor foam sets on the car like snowflakes. Her words leave me speechless for a moment. She seems so determined in her contempt for me, so final and judgmental, as if only her ruling matters and there's no appeal.

"Don't you understand? Even if they catch me tomorrow, they won't be able to prove I was over the limit. It won't be that I killed someone; it will just be the accident that it really was, and a moment of weakness, of panic when I fled. That, I can manage. But not..." My voice trails off under the weight of my shame. I wouldn't survive the public humiliation that would ensue being caught.

She looks at me without another word, but I can see her wheels spinning. I need her on my side—working with me, not against me. I need her to believe in me the way she used to do, to love me as much as she used to.

"So, you've got it all figured out, haven't you?" The contempt in her voice is searing. "How we're going to live like fugitives, hiding in plain sight, afraid whenever we hear a police siren. How it could strike us down at any moment and tear our lives apart?" She pulls a loose strand of hair off her face and tugs it behind her ear with unsteady fingers. "Haven't you?"

"Amanda, I'm—"

"I won't call them, but they *will* come. And you expect me to take your side in this, lying to the cops about everything, and for what?"

The silence is heavy and loaded between us for a long moment. The light turns green at the end of the wash, but I don't start the engine. I stare at my hands, pale and frozen where they grip the wheel.

Winning Amanda back will take work and time that I don't have. "For Tristan," I eventually say. My words are barely a whisper.

"Damn you, Paul. Damn you to hell."

# 9

# AMANDA DAVIS

*The nerve on this man.*

I can't believe he's using our son like this. But why am I surprised? He figured out a while ago that I'd do anything for my little boy. He must be really desperate to hold Tristan over my head like this. Just like he was the day I asked for a divorce.

A shiver rattles my body, and I rub my frozen hands together. My sleeveless dress is wet, clinging to my legs unpleasantly. I can't shake the nausea and painful pit in my stomach. Since it happened, my stomach has been lurching. It's nerves. Understandable after what happened tonight. But it's the memory of that other day that twists my gut into a knot of anger and fear and heartbreak.

Paul drives out of the car wash slowly and takes the back roads home while I think back on the worst day of our marriage.

It happened almost a year ago.

***

When I married Paul, I knew perfectly well what I was getting myself into. I was desperately in love with a handsome, intensely charismatic man. Someone who routinely turned heads at the mall or the grocery store, and everywhere else he went. Women fawned over him shamelessly, from waitresses to neighbors and even some who called themselves my friends. He didn't seem to care about it, and I didn't feel too threatened by the attention he got. I knew some of it came with the territory of him being a face on television. I was choosing to ignore it, and trusted that he'd stay true to me.

For years, I didn't want to imagine what his days were like, if there were any kind of special coworkers or friends or acquaintances that might be too irresistible to him. No...I had my own life, a full and satisfying one, raising Tristan and working at Sunset Valley in the emergency department. I was sure that Paul enjoyed the same kind of contentment in his life, between his sky-rocketing career in broadcast news and our life together raising our son.

That day proved just how wrong I was. About everything.

It started with a patient being brought to the medical center with a drug overdose, more than halfway through my evening shift. The man, a rather large truck driver, had already been given a dose of Narcan by the EMTs, but after checking his vitals, Dr. Grant—the emergency department's attending physician that day—decided to administer another dose. The patient awakened directly into a state of agitation while I was trying to poke his vein to get IV fluids going. His unexpected flailing caught me off guard.

I didn't pull back fast enough, and his fist clocked me in the eye. I lost my balance and fell. On the way down, I hit my head against the ultrasound cart.

It wasn't a big deal, but Sunset Valley is big on procedure. Dr. Grant performed a quick exam, then sent me home, although my head laceration didn't require stitches. I drove myself home that evening, feeling perfectly fine except for some swelling starting to crop up below my eye. Nothing an ice pack wouldn't fix.

I got home at about eleven, instead of my usual one or one-thirty in the morning when I work the evening shift. I was smiling when I pulled into the garage, thinking I might still catch Tristan awake to tuck him in. He refuses to go to bed before his dad gets home, and Paul's car was in the garage.

The first thing I noticed as I walked into the house was the smell. It wasn't too strong or distinctive, but it was foreign, a scent of something I didn't recognize. It was present even in the laundry room, where I stopped briefly to hang my keys on the wall rack.

Then, the sounds. Hushed whispers, frantic shuffling, clothes rustling. When I opened the door to the living room, I froze, blood draining from my heart and leaving it barren.

A pair of high-heeled, red-soled shoes were discarded on the rug, one close to the door to the laundry room where I stood, the other by the sofa. In a poorly faked appearance of casual conversation, Paul was seated at one end of the white leather three-seater, and a woman I didn't recognize sat at the other. Her lipstick was good-quality, but smudged off her full lips. Her flawless skin was reddish around her mouth. My husband's eleven-o'clock shadow can do that to a woman; I know that firsthand.

"Hey, you're home early," Paul blurted out. He looked flustered, his cheeks on fire, like a teenager caught making out behind the school building.

Still frozen in place, I scoffed at his statement.

He cleared his throat nervously. "This is Emily Parker, my research assistant. We've been going over—"

"Save it," I replied coldly, looking at the woman's feet, and how she was trying to hide the fact that she was barefoot, covering one perfectly pedicured foot with the other and curling her toes. The rest of her seemed just as uncomfortable. Her eyes darted across the room as if looking for a way to vanish. Then, after a long moment, she settled. I saw her chest heaving when she took a deep breath of air. She'd given up trying to escape her situation; she was bracing herself.

Unnervingly beautiful, Emily was a classic stunner with perfectly styled blonde hair and hazel eyes, and a body to die for. And she looked younger than me, rested and ready for romance, for adventure. Not coming home after a shift in the ED, punched in the face by a cokehead. Of course, she was younger. My husband never compromised on anything. Why would he?

Paul sprung off the sofa and walked toward me. I put my hand up in the air, and he stopped. "We're working," he said, sounding pathetic. It made me sick; the first time I'd seen my husband as a coward. That day, he fell off the pedestal I'd raised him onto, in more ways than one. "We have to finish the list of show guests—"

I stopped his excuse-making tirade with a dismissive gesture. An immense wave of weariness washed over me, filling me with dread. My life, as I'd known it until that moment, was over, and a new era was about to begin. An era of heartbreak and resentment. It couldn't be avoided.

But there was no time to think about that. I needed to stay strong. "Emily Parker, right?" She nodded, turning pale. "Please be so kind as to pick up your shit and get the hell out of my house."

She did exactly as she was told, with rushed, tiptoed sprints to gather one shoe and then the next, and a moment's hesitation before finding the front entrance and making a beeline for it. She must've arrived in Paul's car and entered through the garage. That explained the scented wake she'd left behind in the laundry room.

In less than a minute, she was gone, the door she closed on her way out the only sound between us for a while.

I don't know what happened in that long moment of loaded silence. Some people struggle for years before giving up on a dying marriage. Perhaps my ED experience kicked in. At work, we're trained to rapidly and accurately assess situations, determining the most effective course of action to ensure the best possible patient outcomes. To know what will work and what won't, in a matter of seconds.

"I want a divorce." My voice was calm and factual. No emotion left, no pain seeping from my wounded heart. There would be a time to grieve over what I'd lost. It would come; I knew that.

Paul stood a couple of feet in front of me, ashen. He looked sick, about to fall apart, but that only lasted a moment. Then, splotches of red started coloring his face and neck as rage built up inside him. I'd never seen him so mad.

"Over this?" He gestured toward the empty sofa. "We were working, for fuck's sake! You're being ridiculous."

"Where's Tristan?" I asked, my voice barely a whisper.

"He's upstairs, sleeping." Paul turned his face away briefly.

He always does that when he lies to me. When I surprise him with a question and he doesn't have time to cook the lie, to carefully think it through.

"You son of a bitch," I whispered. I'd still been hoping he'd arranged a sleepover with Tristan's best friend, or that maybe Dad had returned early from his voyage and taken him out. "What if he saw you?"

Paul turned his head and looked over his shoulder, but Tristan wasn't sitting on the steps, peeking his head between the banisters. "He's asleep, Amanda. And there was nothing to see. We were working."

I crossed my arms over my chest. The man I'd thought was my soulmate was showing his true colors. A liar and a cheat and a coward. "Yeah, sure. Lipstick always gets smudged when women work. They always kick off their shoes and pull out their wrinkled silk blouses from their pants. Buttons come undone, too. It happens."

Paul instinctively looked down at the buttons on his shirt. I laughed, sarcasm and humor my only armor against the pain slicing deep into my heart.

"Baby, let me explain." He took a step forward and raised his hands as if he was going to put them on my shoulders. I hated that. Male dominance at its best, disguised as compassion and warmth.

"Don't you dare touch me," I said. His arms dropped, hanging inert. "You're leaving tonight, so pack whatever you need and get lost. Tomorrow, I'll get a lawyer and be in touch."

The pallor returned to his face, but my eyes were drawn by the crackles in his joints as he clenched his fists. Instinctively, I took a step back and locked my eyes onto his. The rage glinting in his blue irises chilled my blood. I didn't recognize him anymore.

"I'll make sure you won't get custody of Tristan. How's every other weekend going to work out for you?" His whispered voice was accompanied by a defiant smirk.

The enormity of the threat broke me. In an instant, just like that.

Could he do that? Absolutely, even if I got the best lawyer in town. Because everyone who's anyone in Los Angeles secretly dreams of getting invited onto his show. And that list includes judges, lawyers, and even cops.

I felt a chasm opening right under my feet, threatening to swallow me.

"Remember two years ago? The Christmas party at the station?" he asked, drawing closer to me, his voice still a whispered threat. "When you had a little bit too much to drink? I have video of that. It would give any custody hearing some color, wouldn't you say?"

I choked and gasped for air, remembering how I'd thrown up in the parking lot that night, holding on to the front wheel of Paul's car and mortified with shame. The threat of tears burned the corners of my eyes. I had no choice, no way out. I could see that clearly, and so I did the only thing I *could* do.

I backtracked.

Even if it killed me, I had to pretend I was willing to forgive him. So that I could still be with my boy. It took everything I had in me to fake it, when I wanted to scream and shout and scratch his eyes out.

"You're breaking my heart, Paul. I'm still in love with you, but coming home to you making out with this—"

He gave me an inquisitive stare, and then he breathed, visibly relieved. The red blotches on his skin started to fade. He put his hands on my shoulders, and I let him, even if it made my skin crawl. "Baby, for the last time, we were working. I swear that's all it was." He lifted my chin with his fingers and kissed my lips.

I could taste her strawberry lipstick on his mouth. It made me sick.

Later, when he found me under the sheets, I dug my fingernails into my flesh to make my body welcome his, knowing this way he'd be done with me quicker.

Then, after he was done with me, the most desirable man in LA broadcast television wrapped his arms around me and whispered, "No one takes my son away from me, sweetheart. Get that into your head."

# 10

# PAUL DAVIS

---

The entire drive home, Amanda gives me the silent treatment. She keeps looking out the window, head turned away from me, lips pressed together in a tight, unforgiving line. I'm sick with fear, and I wish she'd talk to me—show some support, some empathy. I deserve that much, for crying out loud, after all these years. This stupid accident could've happened to anyone, including her.

Her words linger in my mind.

The more I think about it, the more I realize there had to be someone else out there with that woman. Someone who saw what I did, all of it, and has probably saved it in their phone. That pedestrian couldn't've been walking there by herself. I remember clearly that when I grabbed her ankles to drag her to the side of the road, they were so thin and seemed so frail that I was afraid they'd give out and tear off in my hands.

The thought makes me shudder. In my weary mind, I see myself pushing her body off the edge of the ravine, grunting with effort, then rubbing my hands together and breathing deeply, relieved. Fear hits me in waves as I relive the details.

*What have I done?*

Did someone see me? If they did, have the police been called already?

I need Amanda to be by my side on this one. I groan as the next thought takes shape in my mind. She'd do anything for her son, I know that much, but will she do *this*? Lie for me to the cops? Risk her own freedom over something I've done? Things have changed between us over time; she isn't who she used to be.

*Needing people...ain't that a bitch.*

I turn onto our street and notice the babysitter's red Civic is still parked at the curb. *Fuck.* I completely forgot about her. She'll see the state we're in and ask questions. And remember everything. Gossip about it with her girlfriends at the mall.

I check the time. It's a little after three-thirty in the morning.

I hope she's asleep in front of the TV by now, half-spilled popcorn bowl in her lap, with kernels littering the Persian rug. If Amanda would let me make her vacuum one time, she'd remember what to do with that bowl when she feels like napping. But I guess anything's better than her looking out the living room window right now and seeing us drive home in a damaged car.

Once on the driveway, I align the car with the garage on the right. Our house has three garage spaces, one with a single door and the other two sharing a larger door. Amanda's Subaru takes the middle garage spot, and I usually take the far right. The other spot's been empty since I sold the Beemer.

The moment my hand reaches up for the garage door opener, Amanda stops me. "Take the left one," she says. "The smaller door is quieter."

Of course, it is. I pull back, then align with that garage. When the door opens, it sounds as if it could awaken the entire neighborhood, but it's only loud for my fraught nerves. Nothing moves on our street, no dogs are barking, and no bedroom lights are being turned on to check about the noise we're making. Thankfully, the houses on our street have decent-sized yards.

I wait for the door to close behind us before getting out of the car, and so does my wife.

Amanda sneaks between the Cadillac and her Subaru, and finds the light switch on the wall by the door to the house.

When the powerful lights are turned on, I squint, blinded, and shield my eyes with my hand as I inspect the damage.

*Fuck, it's bad.*

The honeycomb mesh grille is broken in a few places, and pieces of it are missing. They're probably scattered on Malibu Canyon Road where the accident happened. If the cops ever go looking for evidence at the scene, they'll find some. The badge is hanging loose, about to fall off. The left headlight frame is broken. The bumper is cracked and detached from the left fender, hanging crookedly to the side. The hood has a large, irregular dent in it.

But there isn't a drop of blood visible anywhere. Rainwater still drips from the car all over the garage floor, but it looks clean.

When I look up, I see Amanda standing there like a disapproving statue.

"What will you do now?" she asks. Her voice sounds tired. In the bright lights, I can see she's drawn, pale, and that her mascara is a little smudged. "We need to fix this somehow."

Raising an eyebrow, I look at her with suspicion. Is she really trying to help me? Or carefully waiting for the right opportunity to do me in? Under my gaze, a crooked smile touches her lips. As if she's read my mind.

"What's done is done, Paul. We can't undo it, and we're in it together, for the sake of our son. I suggest you start figuring things out."

Her words erase the fight left in me. I lower my eyes, sagging against the car. I'm unbearably scared...for my life, for my future, for every moment of this new day. "Thank you," I manage to say, hating her in this moment for making me feel so small and weak and powerless. But I cling to the hope that some of the love she used to have for me is still there. "I'm glad you see it like that. It's the best way, for all of us."

She doesn't reply. Just looks at me as if she's never seen me before, with a mix of curiosity and something else—something I instinctively know is not good. But I'm too tired to delve into it now; perhaps I'll never have to. Maybe I'm imagining it, paranoia infecting my mind like a virus. She might be my wife and the mother of my son, and I might still love her, but she's also a witness to what happened tonight. A witness who could, one day, decide to turn against me. I can't afford to forget about that.

"We need to sleep," I say, not sure why she's still standing there. "I'll shower downstairs; you take the master bathroom. Then, I'll go straight to bed. I'll leave a voicemail for Ray and tell him I'll be in later today. He won't be surprised."

She rolls her eyes at me, not even trying to hide it. "You can't do that, Paul. You can't afford to make any changes in your known routines. You always show up early the day after these fundraisers to make thank-you calls and get ready to feature them on the news. You announce the total amount raised and parade through all the muckety-mucks who were there, remember?"

What she's saying sounds only vaguely familiar, as if it's something I used to do in another life. Maybe it is. In a life when I wasn't scared of being arrested and thrown in jail.

"Yes, you're right." My legs feel too weak to hold me, and I lean against the Cadillac's fender. I'll be lucky if I get a few hours of sleep. My workdays don't usually start until three in the afternoon, but this time I'll have to get there way before lunch.

"I'm going in, too," Amanda says with a bitter sigh. "I'll take a shift." I know she wasn't planning to; she told me that much when we made arrangements for the event. She touches her chest briefly, putting her palm there as one would to steady the rhythm of a racing heart. "I'll be right on time for work, with a smile on my face, and so will you."

I nod, unable to find the strength to say anything. I'm shattered; that's the word that comes to mind. My entire life is falling apart, becoming something I don't recognize. Something surreal.

It takes effort to leave the support of my car's fender and stand, but I'm eager to get out of the wet clothes that are making me dismally miserable. As I walk toward the door, Amanda turns her back to me and says, "Unzip me." She pulls her long hair out of the way and waits.

I lower her zipper, a slight frown creasing my brow. With a quick move, she lets the dress fall off her shoulders. It lands in a heap of shimmering silver at her feet. She's almost naked now, wearing only a black thong, and she wraps her hands around her body for a moment, shivering. Seeing her like this stirs me up—quite unexpected after such an ordeal. It must be the alcohol.

Strange how I never envisioned her wearing a thong tonight, or being braless under that dress. I didn't even look her way much. I just knew she was there, as she should be. Her beauty makes me proud, despite my grim disposition. She's gorgeous and sexy and smart, and she's all mine. I chose well.

She steps over the fallen dress and walks over to the laundry hampers. Crinkling her nose a little, she rummages through the linens and fishes out a large bath towel she quickly wraps around her body. Then, she finds another one and drapes it around her hair after tilting her head forward, then securing the ends into a twist, forming a snug turban.

"What are you doing?" I finally ask.

She takes a finger to her lips. "Stay put until I come for you."

# 11

# AMANDA DAVIS

---

*That kid better be asleep.*

Making that wish, I open the door to the laundry painfully slowly, knowing how badly it squeaks. I've been meaning to spray some WD40 on the hinges, but never got to it. Until now, it's been quite low on my endless list of chores.

Once inside the laundry room, I close the garage door with a soft click, then stop and listen. Nothing moves inside the house. No TV sound in the background, and no sliver of light making its way under the door. I take a couple more steps and open the next door, the one leading into the kitchen.

Still nothing. Except the smell of dirty laundry that's clinging to me like stink on a wet dog. *She better have a cold, too,* I'm musing while slowly closing the laundry door. The moment that thought crosses my mind, I remember Mona's nose ring. Why do people do that to themselves? I'll never understand.

Our sitter is the sixteen-and-a-half-year-old daughter of a gossipy and always-curious neighbor down the road. She's a good kid, smart, if a bit of a slob like most teenagers are, but she's kind, and I've seen how good she is with Tristan. She likes to help him with homework, and I think my nine-year-old son is a little taken with her. When she rolls her eyes at him, which she seems to do so frequently that I'm afraid she might set a record, he falls quiet. That doesn't happen with me lately.

Once I'm in the kitchen with the door closed behind me, I stop by the counter and breathe, listening intently for the tiniest sound in the silence engulfing the house. Nothing. Faint silver light flickers against the living room walls. The TV is probably on, but with the sound muted. Holding my breath, I tiptoe into the living room and find Mona fast asleep on the couch, her head propped high against the cushions. The TV remote is still in her hand, about to fall off the couch. I can tell she and Tristan enjoyed some ice cream tonight. The dirty bowls are still on the coffee table, because why would any of them bother to take them to the sink? I'm just hoping that ice cream wasn't consumed *instead* of the dinner I left for them in the oven.

Back in the kitchen, I breathe deeply. No one heard me come in. My fingers hover over the light switch, trembling slightly. I stop for a moment, overwhelmed with all the feelings swirling inside me.

How did we get here, Paul and I? We used to be so good…so much in love. My aching heart still remembers those times. The laughs we had when were young, walking hand in hand on the Santa Monica Pier with the ocean breeze tousling our hair, the setting sun warming our smiling faces. How it felt when we were together—overwhelming and addictive at the same time, a rollercoaster ride of exhilarating emotions. And now? When he touched me to unzip my dress tonight, I flinched with both desire and aversion, in a maddening and senseless mix of yearnings I can't make sense of.

Now is not the time to dwell on that, though. I straighten the towel wrapped around my body and turn on the light, like I do every morning, only it's about two hours too early. Then, I pour water into the coffee maker, add a new filter and a couple of scoops of my favorite grind, and switch it on. It beeps loudly, as always. I nod, satisfied, and whisper to myself, "Uh-huh." That should do it.

Surely enough, the noise awakens Mona. I know she's up when the TV remote hits the floor with a muted thump. She drags her feet into the kitchen, squinting and rubbing her eyes. "Ms. Davis?" Her voice is a bit raspy, and her question ends with a hearty yawn. Then, she pops some gum into her mouth and starts chewing it lazily. The smell of peppermint fills the air.

I smile widely. In passing toward the fridge, I stroke her cheek with the tips of my fingers. Just like I always do. "Good morning, sunshine."

She frowns at me, then at the digital clock on the microwave. "It's four," she says, visibly confused and a bit reproachful. She rubs her eyes just like a child. She still is one.

"I have an early start this morning. Got to show up for work two hours earlier than usual. Some issue with hospital staffing. I'm sorry I woke you. How was everything last night?"

She stares at me as if I'm a recently landed alien. In a way, I am. "When did you get back? I didn't mean to—"

"Nah, you're fine," I reply, hiding a frown and dismissing her concerns with a wave of my hand. I don't like her asking questions, but it's what smart people usually do. "We got here at about one. You were sleeping. I didn't have the heart to wake you. Just gave Tristan a kiss and went to bed. You can sleep some more, if you want."

"No, Ms. Davis, I don't want to impose." She runs her fingers through her tangled hair and attempts to straighten her pink sweatshirt. "I'll just go." She shifts her weight from one foot to the other, waiting. "I just don't know how I didn't hear you come in. I usually do. I pay attention, I swear."

Tension returns to my chest, trapping my breath inside my lungs. Was she awake until late? Does she know I'm lying? "It's okay, Mona, don't worry about it. We tried to keep it quiet." I open the drawer where we keep some cash and pull out a hundred and fifty dollars.

Her eyes widen. "That's too much, Ms. Davis. I can't." She takes a tentative step back.

"No, it's not. Paul and I appreciate you very much. We have peace of mind when you're watching Tristan, and that's worth a lot to me. To us." And hopefully, she'll go home and tell her mother we returned at one in the morning.

She takes the money with a hesitant hand and shoves it quickly into her jeans pocket. "Thanks," she says cheerfully. When she smiles, her septum nose ring moves. I shift my eyes away and decide to examine the coffee maker instead. It's almost done brewing. I've never needed a cup so badly in my entire life.

"You okay to drive at this hour? It's still dark. I could drop you off," I say, nudging her a little to be gone already.

She takes the hint. "Oh, no, Ms. Davis, I'm okay. It's just down the street." She walks toward the door, then stops and turns toward me. "Call me whenever you need me. For you, I'll make time."

I nod, still smiling, and hoping I seem relaxed to her, not frozen into a grimace like I'm actually one pull away from a Jenga crash. "Bye, sweetie."

She pulls the front door shut behind her, and I let out a long, pained sigh. For a few moments, I stand in the middle of the kitchen, giving myself some time to find my bearings before I invite Paul in.

# 12

# AMANDA DAVIS

When I return to the garage, I find Paul standing close to the door, arms crossed at his chest, sullen. His brow is furrowed when he glares at me.

"Sure took you long enough," he mutters, walking past me. He drops his soaked shoes onto the laundry room floor and moves to go into the kitchen, but I stop him with a raised hand and a quick no.

"Everything you have on you goes directly in the washer, but don't start it yet. I'll add my own things and some peroxide to burn through any remaining blood stains." He doesn't argue. Just stares at me for a moment, as if he's wondering why I'm helping him.

I honestly don't know.

I've asked myself that question obsessively since the crash. Yes, I'm doing it for Tristan, but really, is it only Tristan I'm thinking about? Or is it also that I can't envision myself walking away serenely while Paul gets thrown in prison?

One by one, soaked garments make it into the washer. He's still wearing his underwear, but I ask for it with a beckoning finger. "Everything." His eyes glint with something dark, and yet there's a hint of the old sensual playfulness I remember so well. Or perhaps it's defiance, and I'm getting my signals crossed. Whatever it is, I don't welcome it anymore. "Just in case there's blood transfer."

Those words have a chilling effect. He throws his shorts into the washer angrily, glaring at me. Then, he props his hands on his hips, flaunting his nakedness. "There. Happy?"

Our eyes are locked like swords in the dim light of the laundry room. "I'm fucking thrilled, Paul. I'm living every wife's dream." I bite my lip and force myself to stop, refusing to let this turn into a shouting match that would lead nowhere. I'm the first to break eye contact and breathe off my anger. "Why don't you go take a shower? Take your time in there. I'll finish here, then go upstairs for mine."

"Okay," he says with a shattered breath. He sounds tormented, and suddenly depleted of energy. The events of the day are catching up to him, but upstairs, they're about to hit like a freight train. Showering has that effect on people; it cleanses the mind just as much as it does the body. It brings wisdom and perspective, and a bit of clairvoyance, too. It's eye-opening.

*Good.* He needs that, even if he doesn't know it.

"While in there, try to figure out how you're going to drive the Cadillac to work today. Perfectly intact." I look into his dilated pupils and mercilessly twist the blade. "In about five hours or so."

Stunned, he stares at me for a moment, raising his arms and then letting them drop in a gesture of consternation. I don't believe I've ever seen him so vulnerable, so lost. It triggers me, and I find myself feeling sorry for him. I press my lips together, doubting my sanity once more...and all of the choices I'm making, knowing quite well they're wrong.

"I'll take care of it," I eventually say, my words carried on a long breath.

"You'll drive me?"

He's standing naked and helpless in the middle of the laundry room, caving under my cold stare. I'm not thinking of how to use this to my advantage to free myself of him. Even though this is what I've been hoping for, an opportunity to get divorced while keeping custody of Tristan. I could twist his arm and make him sign everything over today.

Yet, I'm just thinking of him, of the hell he must be going through, of his fear. And at the same time, I realize there are dark, dangerous parts of him I've never seen before, and that scares me. I'm shaken from witnessing him dragging a woman's corpse across the road and shoving it down into the ravine without any hesitation. Of feeling his hand push me aside like I was nothing. I've been petrified since he threatened me when I tried to stop him. I thought he could've shoved me down into that ravine just as easily as he pushed her lifeless body out of sight.

For the life of me, I can't understand why I'm not running for the hills right now. Instead, I say like I would to Tristan, "Get your shower done. Then, we'll talk."

# 13

## AMANDA DAVIS

I sit at the dining room table and stare into thin air, thinking through my next steps. Exhaustion has hit me hard, even if I'm accustomed to long night shifts in the ED. This is an entirely different situation.

After what happened, I'm hypervigilant. Reluctant to let go, my mind follows Paul's every step through the noises he makes. The closing of the bathroom door. The flushing of the toilet. The water running steadily in the shower. I can visualize him in there, his hands pressed flat against the tiles, his head bowed under the stream of hot water, standing still, not moving a muscle, hoping the jets will wash off the memory of this horrifying night.

It takes a lot of effort to ignore him and focus on the task at hand. I pull my phone out of my purse and start searching for car rental companies nearby. There are a few, mostly clustered around Hollywood Burbank Airport. I browse their available inventory after choosing luxury as the type of vehicle I'm looking for. We might be in luck; there's a location by the airport that has Cadillacs. Black ones.

Rubbing my forehead for a moment, I decide not to get sucked into the obsessive questions swirling in my mind. Like, why am I doing this? I damn well know why; it's a decision I'm making. I hope it's a good one.

After a quick glance at the clock on the wall, I tap the number listed under the rental company and make the call. It's a little after six in the morning; they should be open.

"Airport Car Rental," a chipper female voice greets me on the phone. "How can I help you?"

My throat is dry and tight. "Um, hi, I have a problem. I screwed up something," I say, sweetening my usually assertive tone to match the character I'm impersonating. "I need a black Cadillac XT6. Do you have one? My boss is going to kill me; I made the wrong reservation, and now—"

"Um...yes, we do have one. I can hold it for you, if you're picking it up today."

"You saved my life!" I reply cheerfully. "I'll pick it up in an hour."

When Paul comes out of the shower, he finds me still clutching the phone, although the conversation ended a few minutes ago. My mind drifts easily. I wish I could call my dad. I miss his strength, his uncompromising logic. He's out at sea, working, and I can't unload my troubles on him just to make myself feel a little better. And plus, I know what he'd tell me to do... Call the cops. *"Right now,"* he'd say. *"Don't waste any more time, Mandy. Get it over with."*

But I can't.

"Who did you call?" Paul asks, frowning. His hair is still wet, loose strands dripping water down his forehead. He's wrapped a towel around his hips and didn't waste any time drying himself off, showing no concern for the wet footprints he's stamping all over the hardwood floor.

"I found a car rental location and reserved the exact same model as yours. Same color."

He raises his arms in the air, frustrated. "Why the hell did you do that?"

*Why did I expect a sliver of gratitude?*

I'm disappointed in myself. I'm oh, so tired of being delusional.

I exhale slowly, reining in a sigh of frustration. "Because you need to show up for work today in your black XT6 as if nothing happened." He stares at me, his mouth slightly open and his frown deepening, as if he's not getting it. I find it strange, but explain. "Cops will investigate at some point, Paul. We need to act like nothing happened."

"And going to work in a rental achieves that?"

I close my eyelids for a moment, hiding an eyeroll. He's probably too tired to think straight. He's smarter than this.

"Who will know? You'll switch the tags."

"Ah," he replies, barely a whisper. "I see." He paces the floor slowly, his eyes throwing daggers at me. "I would've appreciated a heads-up before you started calling people. Before leaving a paper trail. Because, you know, *cops will investigate at some point*, and all that."

I bite my lip, deciding I need a shower more than I need to rip him to shreds. "You're welcome," I say coldly. "Get yourself together, and get dressed for work. Remember, you were a success last night, the life of the party. Get ready to act like it, the whole damn day."

"You're unbelievable," he mutters, but I pretend not to notice as I walk into the downstairs bathroom and close the door behind me. Then, for the first time since we've been married, I turn the lock.

When I breathe, the air leaving my lungs washes off the tense mask I've been keeping on my face for Paul's sake. I don't recognize the pale, drawn face in the mirror. My wide eyes still reflect the shock of the night's events. My lips tremble slightly, as if I'm unsure whether to speak or cry or remain silent, not with the secrets buried inside me forever. A sheen of sweat glistens on my forehead, although my skin is covered in goose bumps and I'm freezing. My expression is one of disbelief and fear, as though the weight of what happened hasn't fully sunk it.

Moving mechanically, I turn on the water in the shower, welcoming the steam that engulfs me. I let the towel wrapped around my body fall to the floor and take off my panties. Stepping under the hot jets, I bite my quivering lip to keep the sobs locked inside my chest.

It's my turn to spend time standing completely still, letting water run over me while painful memories flood my mind and make me gasp quietly, unheard. I'm not thinking about the crash, though. No, I'm recalling a business trip I took to Palma de Mallorca to attend a two-week conference and training seminars on emergency care practices.

I remember how thrilled Dr. Grant was to add me to the list when I asked him to. He's my unofficial boss, one of the department's attending physicians, and a handsome man who I suspected was—and still is—a little attracted to me.

I didn't tell him the real reason why I wanted to go.

The conference opportunity appeared a few weeks after I'd asked Paul for a divorce, and his threats were still resonating in my mind. "How would every other weekend work out for you?" Paul had asked, talking about access to my son. That was why I'd wanted to go to Palma. To test my own ability to bear two weeks without seeing Tristan. To see if I could survive it.

And it was horrible.

I'd thought that the day I asked Paul for a divorce was when he broke me. But in truth, it was the stay in Palma. I was restless, snapping at people, locking myself in my room every night and crying myself to sleep until reality became crystal clear.

Life without Tristan wasn't an option. I know that now.

But life *with* Paul isn't one, either.

Lathering my long hair slowly, unwilling to leave the confines of the bathroom for another round of battle with life, I realize there's no better moment than the present to get Paul to sign the divorce papers. When he's vulnerable and needs me.

Rinsing my hair with my eyes closed, I see him in my mind, with that look on his face when I tried to stop him, on the side of the road by the ravine. In my imagination, the threatening glimmer in his eyes turns into words he speaks in a low, tense voice, barely above a whisper.

*I've already killed one woman today. I could easily make that two. I've got nothing left to lose.*

My eyes pop open and I shudder, terrified. Would he really kill me? Until yesterday, I would've sworn it was impossible; Paul would never do something like that. He's not a violent man.

He's not a killer.

# 14

# PAUL DAVIS

The bathroom door opens, and I'm rattled by the sound. As if I wasn't in my own damn house. I watch Amanda as she walks across the Persian rug, a large, white bath towel draped around her body, her hair wrapped in a perfectly neat towel turban. Everything about her is so fucking proper, it makes me want to smash something.

She walks straight past me without as much as a glance my way. As if I'm not even there. She stops at the coffee machine and pours herself a cup, then holds it with both hands, inhaling the scent with her eyes closed.

As she usually does.

As if today is just any other day.

It drives me crazy.

I should've crashed the car into a lamppost or something, after hitting that stupid woman. I wouldn't be in this situation right now. Needing her help. Being afraid. *I fucking hate that.* I can't remember the last time I was afraid of anything. Things usually go my way, because I *make* them go my way.

Amanda slurps a bit of hot coffee and lets out a satisfied sigh.

I should've let her drive last night. I'm such a cliché...the man who should've listened to his wife. *Fuck.* This would've been her problem now, not mine. I would've offered my moral support for five minutes, and then she would've called the cops and taken the blame for the crash, because that's who she is. Righteous to a fault. Rigorous. Insanely strict. I bet a slew of cops would've rushed to her rescue, already hard and blue-balled just from the thought of her smiling their way. And the whole thing would've been forgotten by six or seven in the morning.

And I could've spent the morning getting some damn sleep.

I take one last swig of coffee, then drop the empty mug in the sink. It clatters loudly, but doesn't break. Amanda doesn't even look my way. I walk over and stop next to the table, where she's sitting with her legs crossed, the towel slipping off her thighs inch by inch. I wonder if she's doing it on purpose, teasing me when I'm down, about to fall apart.

"I'm not entirely comfortable with this whole car rental idea," I say as calmly as I can. "I have to admit it's got some merit, but—"

She looks at me with cold, clinical eyes. "But?"

"I could say the Cadillac is in the shop if anyone asks."

"No one will ask today," she replies, taking another sip of coffee infuriatingly slowly. Meticulous, as if testing me. "When they eventually ask, it will seem very suspicious that you put your car in the shop—which you won't be able to verify with receipts or evidence, by the way—right after a hit-and-run happened."

"How do you know so much about cops and what they'll do? Are you fucking one?" I can't help but ask, just because I've noticed how men look at her. It didn't use to bother me so much before, when I still believed she was in love with me. Funny how the word *divorce* threw an ice bucket over the whole romance thing. She must be getting it elsewhere, because she sure as hell doesn't want me anymore.

She presses her lips together in that gesture of silent disapproval I've seen so many times. "They're in the ED all day long interviewing victims, staff, taking statements, and talking to other injured cops. I listen."

"And the rental?" I ask, propping my hands on my hips. "How will you explain that?"

"They won't think to ask," she replies flatly, staring at her fingernails with a critical eye. Then, she flicks her eyes at me for a split second. "The typical drunk driver isn't too intelligent. He'd crash the car again against a tree, to hide the damage, then show up for work in his wife's Subaru with no plausible explanation."

I choke on hearing her dismissive statement. She senses nothing, or just doesn't care about how I feel. I thought she had empathy...too much of it actually, for her own good. I've seen her come home all shattered after a bad case at work. But there's none of that bleeding heart available for me. She says she wants to help me now, but what will happen when she goes to work and runs into her favorite cop? Will she tell him? Ask him for his help? I grit my teeth so badly they start hurting.

*Motherfucker.*

"Leave the car rental to me," she adds, standing up after finishing her coffee. "It will be in my name, charged to my card." She stops squarely in front of me and points her index finger at my chest, without touching me. "You figure out how to fix *your* car. Or what to do with it."

Then, she walks up the stairs slowly, swaying her hips. My eyes stay riveted to where the towel barely covers her butt. For an unnerving moment, way after she's gone into our bedroom, I see myself climbing those stairs three steps at a time and taking her right there, on the landing. She'd fight me off, scratch and claw at me, curse my name, but I wouldn't—

"Good morning, Daddy!" Tristan squeals, rushing downstairs.

I step behind the counter, giving things a moment to settle down unseen, and swallow an oath.

"Morning, champ," I say, ruffling his hair with affection, all the while hoping he won't notice how different things are today. My attire. My hand, trembling slightly. The scratchy, grating sound of my voice.

He doesn't. He rubs his eyes as he pushes himself up on a chair, propping his elbows on the table and bouncing his feet. This time, I'm not going to ask if he's brushed his teeth. It's okay to let one slide.

Like he usually does in the morning, Tristan watches me move through the kitchen. Routine takes over, and I seem to know what I have to do.

"Cereal or eggs?" I ask. "Your choice."

# 15

# AMANDA DAVIS

---

The traffic is starting to jam badly when I reach the airport, driving my Subaru with the radio on. I turn up the volume, forcing the music to spill some good cheer into my darkened soul. To scatter the shadows nestled in there, threatening to invade my wavering conscience. It's not working.

*Oh God... What have I done? What am I doing?*

I pull into one of the parking spots in front of the car rental office, then walk briskly into the building using the side entrance. It's late already—almost nine. The busier it gets, the more I run the risk of being seen renting a car I shouldn't need.

I don't wait much; the man in front of me is just picking up his keys. He walks to the front of the building, where a Ford Escape is pulled to the curb.

"Hi, I called earlier about a Cadillac XT6," I say when the attendant beckons me with a professional smile pasted on her face. She's young and tall, and her long, braided hair is dyed pink.

"Ah, yes, I remember," she said. "We have it ready for you. I'll need your driver's license and a credit card, and we'll send you on your way."

I hand her the two items requested, looking at the remaining vehicles pulled up at the curb. None of them are black, but one is a Cadillac.

It's white. Covered in glistening water droplets.

I feel a pit opening in my stomach.

"Um, it has to be black, and an XT6," I say, painfully aware of the attention I'm drawing to myself with the unusual request.

"Oh?" She looks at me with surprise, as if I hadn't said that on the phone. "This one has just been detailed. It's a great vehicle; you'll love it."

I bite my lip for a moment, unsure what lie will work best. "It's not for me, I'm sorry. I don't want to be difficult. It's for this French actress who is very specific and entitled and," I lower my voice, "such an unbelievably bratty bitch. My boss will kill me if she yells at him again."

She raises her glance from the computer monitor with a spark of interest in her eyes. "You're from the studios?"

I nod vigorously. "MGM, yes. Please, can we make it happen?"

She looks at the screen, typing something slowly with long acrylic fingernails that click against the keys. "Um, let's see. We do have a black one, but it's not detailed yet. It will take a couple of hours—"

"Oh, no, please," I say quickly, putting my hands together in a pleading gesture. "I'll take it the way it is. I'll have someone wash it and whatever, but I can't be late."

"How long do you need it for?"

I'm drawing a blank. I should've thought of this. "Um, at least a week? Maybe two."

"All right." She stares at me for a long moment, as if she's trying to figure out what to do. Eventually, she agrees and calls a car jockey to bring the black Cadillac around.

I breathe a long sigh of relief. "You're the best. Thank you. Oh, and I'll leave my car here, if that's okay, until I can swing by later to pick it up."

Moments later, I drive off in a black Cadillac that looks just like Paul's. It smells different, and it feels strange for me to be driving it. My husband never lets me drive his precious car.

When I get home, I find Paul seated at the breakfast table with Tristan. He's dressed up and shaven, smiling, being his usual chipper, charming self. I stop for a moment, looking at the two of them interacting casually—at my son's deep, blue eyes smiling when he sees me, and at my husband's face, hiding the night's ordeal to perfection. Effortlessly.

As if it never happened. He killed that woman, rolled her body into a ravine, and now he seems perfectly fine.

*Who is this man?*

I thought I knew.

"Mommy, you're back," Tristan says. "You're not working today?"

I snap out of my daze and walk over to him quickly, then land a kiss on my little boy's forehead. "Yes, I'm working, and so are you." Another kiss, because I just can't help myself. "Your bus leaves in ten minutes."

When I raise my eyes, I see Paul looking at me and Tristan intensely, as if he's afraid of something.

Of me.

The thought freezes me. He's probably wondering where I've been, and if I called the cops. If I betrayed him.

I drop the Cadillac's key fob on the table. "It's done."

He gives the key fob a long stare. "Any issues?"

I rush to get Tristan's lunch ready. "No." There's no need for any more explaining. He should be happy and thank me for my help. I keep waiting for that to come, but it doesn't.

A few minutes later, Tristan is finished tying up his shoelaces. Schoolbag in hand, he's hurrying out the door to catch the bus that he's already late for. From the driveway, I watch him climb onto the bus, and then the door closes with a hiss and the bus departs.

The house is eerily silent in Tristan's absence. I lock the door behind me. Paul is standing by the breakfast table, dressed in a starched blue shirt that brings out the color of his eyes and a navy-blue tie with oblique stripes in silver.

Grabbing the key fob, he looks at me with a tense frown. "Let's see what we've got."

I lead the way to the garage, where I open the door and turn on the lights. I parked the Cadillac in the rightmost spot, leaving my Subaru's spot empty in the middle. Paul will have to drive me to Burbank to pick it up.

"Damn it to hell," Paul mutters, rubbing his chin angrily. "This isn't going to work."

"Why?"

"It's not the same trim. It's a different XT6. This is a cheaper one."

I feel the blood draining from my chest, leaving me weak and hollow. "How can you tell?"

"Look at the wheels. The rims are different. The tires, too."

My mind spins, desperately looking for a solution. "What else is different about it?"

Paul circles the rental carefully, sometimes glancing toward his own car. "Transmission, features, entertainment center, lots of things." He sneaks between the rear of the Cadillac and the closed garage door. "Uh-huh, that's good. The badge is the same."

"What badge?"

He touches something with his finger. "This chrome 400 here, on the tailgate."

"Okay. Is any of this different trim stuff visible on the outside?"

"Just the wheels."

I can't help a shrug. This is nothing. "So, swap them."

He stares at me for a moment, but I hold his gaze steadily. He's probably never replaced a tire in his whole life, but today he's going to learn how to do it. I'm not offering any more help.

For about an hour, he works on swapping the wheels, grunting at times, and swearing and sweating profusely as the temperature rises with the sun and I busy myself in the kitchen. When he's done with the wheels, he shifts his personal belongings from one vehicle to the other. Then, the tags are swapped. The transponder comes next.

When he's done, he comes into the kitchen to wash his hands. I step aside from the sink, making room for him. His presence so close to me is unbearable.

His jaw is tightened, his hands a little shaky. I look at him, wondering why I won't let myself ask him if he wants some coffee. I just can't.

"It's done," he says, throwing me a quick glance. "But the parking decal won't come off. It's not meant to be moved from one car to another. I'll need to get another one."

The small, square sticker pasted on the lower right corner of his windshield would be clearly visible in a security video. If the cops start looking at parking videos, they'll notice it's gone. I rummage through one of the drawers and find a roll of dental floss. "Use this."

I watch from the laundry room door as he manages to peel off the parking decal from his car, but it coils badly and won't stick to the rental's windscreen.

Eventually, he tapes it to the windshield with some packing tape. It's a little crooked, because the stubborn fool wouldn't ask for my help to paste it straight.

Oh well.

I'll take an Uber to Burbank. I don't want to be in the same car as Paul if I can help it.

Then, I'll go to work and try to stop thinking about what's going to happen to us when the police find that poor woman's body.

# 16

# AMANDA DAVIS

---

We call it an ambo tone, the loud alarm-like horn that announces the arrival of an ambulance, and it snaps me back into reality. I'm grateful for it. I spaced away for a brief moment, obsessing over last night's events. That terrifying moment when the cop put his flashlight on my face, then on Paul's. I thought I was going to die.

Grabbing a pair of fresh nitrile gloves, I rush toward the arriving ambulance and find myself running in lockstep with Dr. Grant. The emergency department's main doors slide open, and the EMT crew pushes a stretcher in.

"Christina Farren, 27, unresponsive, GCS 6, bleeding profusely," one of the EMTs announces, her voice a little uncertain. "BP 90 over 50, pulse 120, O2 sat 90. Lactated Ringer's in, one liter running."

Pushing the gurney as hard as I can, I wait for the rest, but she doesn't say anything about the source of the bleed.

"Station Three!" the head nurse's voice carries over the ruckus, assigning our space. I grab the side of the gurney and push toward the right, where trauma station three is the closest one open.

"Where's she bleeding from?" Dr. Grant asks impatiently.

"I don't know," the EMT replies, letting go of the gurney as we reach the empty trauma station. "We found her unresponsive, on the beach, lying on her back on a towel soaked in blood."

"Damn it," Dr. Grant mutters.

We position ourselves around the gurney and trauma bed, grabbing the sides of the slide board and waiting for Dr. Grant.

"On my count," he says, grabbing the slide board from the side. "One, two, three."

The patient's overweight body lands on the trauma bed, and the gurney is wheeled out. The woman's clothes are slick with blood and peppered with sand where her wet clothes touched the ground.

I hang the bag of Ringer's and grab a pair of scissors, starting at the hem of one pant leg.

"Give me CBC, ABG, type and cross, coag," Dr. Grant says. "And let's find that bleeder." He grabs another pair of scissors and starts cutting through her blouse while I focus on her jeans. They're so tight on her, it's impossible to pull them off, even with the zipper all the way down. They're caked in blood and sand is stuck to them like a crust. The blades of the scissors grind through it, making cutting a difficult task.

Sunny, a young, petite critical nurse recently transferred from San Francisco, draws blood quickly, filling the vials with the bare minimum required.

Dr. Grant gives up trying to cut through the woman's clothing and just rips her shirt open. There's no visible wound on her chest. "Help me turn her," he says. Sunny and I help roll the patient's body onto her side. There's no visible laceration anywhere to account for all that blood. The way it stained her shirt, I could tell she was lying in a pool of it, but it had to be coming from someplace else.

"BP's dropping!" Sunny calls at the same time the monitor starts beeping furiously.

"Get her out of these clothes," Dr. Grant says sharply.

Abandoning the scissors, I grab the fabric at the hem and try to rip it, but it's slick and slips from my gloved hands. Then, I notice something. One pant leg, the one I've been trying to cut, looks slicker than the other one, as if there's more blood there.

I run my hands up her leg, feeling carefully under her thigh, then on the side, until I find it. A tiny little hole on the inside of her pant leg. Slipping my hand under the soaked fabric, I feel with the tips of my fingers around the wound.

"Gunshot. Probably nicked the femoral," I call calmly. "She must've been lying down when she was shot."

Dr. Grant's eyes smile above his mask. "Good job. Get a tourniquet on that leg. Get me a trauma surgeon, stat."

While I tighten a tourniquet, Sunny picks up the wall phone and dials an extension. She speaks quickly into the receiver, then turns to us. "OR Two is available. They're waiting."

It's a short trip to push the trauma stretcher to OR Two, but I'm short of breath and dizzy when I reach the operating room and my colleagues take over. I bend over and force myself to breathe deeply. Sweat breaks at the roots of my hair, on my neck and on my back.

"You okay?" Dr. Grant asks. "You look a little pale."

I manage a smile. "Long day yesterday. Didn't get much sleep."

"Weren't you scheduled off for today?"

"Tentatively." I shrug and start walking back to our department. I need people to notice me here today, working, being my normal self as if nothing is wrong. "It was either this or clean the house."

"Excellent choice," he laughs, then holds the break room door open for me. "Coffee?"

I nod, although I probably shouldn't have anymore. I've been mainlining caffeine since four in the morning, and I can feel its effects in the slight, feverish tremor in my fingers. I fill up a mug and hold it tightly, as if my life depends on it.

"I've seen you on TV," Sunny says, catching up with us.

Her casual comment startles me. I freeze, my coffee mug mid-air. What does she mean?

"When?" I ask, painfully aware that my voice sounds choked and shaky. I take a sip of coffee.

"Last night, on the news." She grabs a cup from the cabinet and fills it to the brim.

I breathe out, relieved. Of course, it was about the event. I'm an idiot, a nervous wreck.

"That fundraiser event you went to—how does someone get invited to those things? I want to go next time!" she continues. "You looked gorgeous! Oh my...and that piece of arm candy of yours, to die for!" she says, her face reddening a little. "How does it feel to be married to someone like that?"

Dr. Grant's eyes meet mine. It feels as if he can see all through me, through my jitters and silence. I look away, smiling for Sunny's benefit. She's so innocent, this girl. Twenty-four years old, a promising young nurse, and she still believes everything she sees on television. I wish I could give her some advice—like, don't get married. Ever.

"They're kind of boring, those events," I say, but she's not buying it. She's still brimming with vicarious excitement. I know for a fact that she'll keep asking me questions about last night for weeks to come.

When I look at Dr. Grant again, a flicker of a smile flutters on his lips. He gets it. More than I'd like him to. "Listen, why don't I—"

The ambo tone silences me, and I'm grateful for it. We abandon our coffee mugs and rush out the door, grabbing fresh gloves on the way.

We have a new emergency.

# 17

# PAUL DAVIS

I stop at the studio parking garage barrier, just like I always do, and wait for the barcode on my crumpled decal to be scanned and recognized. It takes a bit longer than usual, or maybe I'm imagining that. By the time the barrier lifts, I'm gritting my teeth.

I have to get a new decal. This one's barely held in place with tape. HR will gladly accommodate the request, but I bet they'll ask me what happened with the old one. Did I change cars? Am I buying a new car and planning to use both for my commute? "Damn it to bloody hell," I mutter as I slip into my reserved spot. *Fuck.* I can't afford any questions. Not now.

Am I being paranoid? Probably. Nobody will give a shit about my parking decal.

Minutes later, I scan my keycard and access the studio building. A nod and a quick simper take care of the receptionist, who smiles and tilts her head, batting her eyelashes shamelessly and ignoring the woman waiting in front of her desk. The receptionist's a pretty little thing, not a day older than twenty, and I might hit that someday, but she's a bit too skinny for me. Wouldn't hurt her to binge on some chocolate for a month or so, to put some meat on those bones. On her tits, too; she's got nothing there.

A short elevator ride, another keycard scan, and I'm on the production level, walking steadily toward the control room.

The door to the green room, a large lounge reserved for show guests and production assistants on break, is wide open.

I hear whispers as I pass by, followed by gasps and giggles, the two female voices sounding young, but not recognizable.

"Oh, my God, that was Paul Davis! In the flesh! He's so fucking hot," one of the women breathes out, my step slowing as soon as I'm past the door. "It will be so cool to intern here." Her voice drops a notch. "I'd climb him like a tree."

Unable to resist, I stop and lean casually against the wall, listening and pretending to check my messages. A lopsided smile tugs at my lips. Too bad I walked by too fast and didn't notice if she's good looking. For a moment, I forget everything about last night, my wife, the parking decal, and all that shit. I feel alive again.

"Now, don't go doing anything stupid," the other one says. "I've been an assistant producer on his show for three years, and he doesn't even know I exist."

"What? No," the intern says, "I'll make sure he knows *I* exist, then introduce you."

"No, you can't do that, all right?" All the giggles are gone from her voice. "This is my job, and I happen to like it, okay? Don't mess with it." A moment of silence. "Anyway, people say Paul's got that whole 'perfect husband' thing down, but every now and then, he steps over the line. Flirts like crazy, sleeps around, but 'officially' stays loyal to his wife. Honestly, I think it's kind of hot."

A derisive snort. "Yeah, *real* commitment."

"Oh, but get this—last year's Christmas party? Total disaster for the perfect little wifey. Apparently, she got absolutely shitfaced, stumbling around, practically falling over people. He stood by her the whole time, though, like nothing happened."

"He hasn't met *me* yet!" The intern giggles. "One taste of *this*, and he'll forget he even met her."

A grin blooms on my lips, and I roll my eyes, but I'm curious. On Monday, when I'll be in a better mood, I must remember to check out the new interns.

"Oh, God, you're awful," the assistant producer says, and both women laugh.

"But it's true," the intern adds. "Come on, tell me more about my future lover."

"Never mind the wife. You should see their kid. Those blue eyes? To die for."

The loaded comment wipes the grin off of my face. I tense up, continuing to eavesdrop.

"That little angel could rake in millions as a child star. But nope. Daddy dearest won't let him near the cameras. You know how many directors would kill to get that kid? They'd crawl over broken glass if Paul just snapped his fingers. Just to land on his show, on prime-time TV. But, no, can't have a Davis dynasty in showbiz." A disappointed groan ends the woman's comment. "What I wouldn't give to have a kid like that."

"God, if I had the kind of power he's got..." the intern laughs. "Actually, I'd probably use it to get men. Lots and lots of men. *Him* first, and then—"

I'm no longer entertained.

Walking briskly, I enter the control room and stop in the doorway. More than ten people stop talking and turn toward me. It's standing room only, and most of them don't belong.

What are they doing here?

# 18

# PAUL DAVIS

About a dozen people are crammed into the control room, talking loudly. Among them, Latesha Jones—my backstabbing co-anchor, an ambitious little bitch—and Carly Crown, my producer, looking pristine and perfectly rested, as if they weren't more intoxicated than me last night. Then, there's Raymond Cook himself, rarely seen mingling with the plebeian production staff. The chatter dies when they notice me. Then, my research assistant, a young man by the name of Aidan Williams, starts clapping his hands, slowly at first, before he hoots loudly.

"Yeah," he says, clapping faster and faster as the others join in. "Let's give it up for the man of the hour!" He grins widely with perfectly white teeth, but my eyes are drawn to his hair, a tangled mess springing upward in every direction as if every curl has its own agenda. "Woot, woot!" he calls, until I make eye contact briefly and he stops with the hollering, but not the clapping.

Ray approaches me and shakes my hand, then turns to the team, his hand firmly on my shoulder. "Five million dollars, people! And he didn't even break a sweat. Still found the time to waltz with that beautiful wife of his."

"Thanks," I say, shaking his hand vigorously. "I believe we're ready for the next level. Ten million next year?"

"See me later, and we'll talk," Ray says in a low voice, meant only for my ears.

I nod in lieu of thanking him and take inventory of everyone's reaction to my arrival, including his. Ray is obviously happy as a clam at high tide, and the tide is indeed high. I'm curious to see how long his gratitude will last. I'll test the waters later and see where we land. I need to cash this in now, while he's still basking in a five-million-dollar afterglow.

Latesha's smile is as fake as her breasts. Although I suspect she went cheap on those tits of hers and just stuffed her bra with silicone padding instead. Her eyes are throwing poisonous darts at me, but she's groveling to Ray, trying to get his attention. She reminds me of a Chihuahua nipping at a German Shepherd's heels. I wish I could mule-kick her into oblivion. She's annoying as fuck.

Carly beams, bowing her head and thanking people as if the five mil were raised by both of us together, not just me. She walks toward me and plants a kiss on my cheek, and then her arm snakes around my waist and refuses to withdraw. She flips her hair and smiles for everyone, engaging loudly with Ray, telling him what generous people sat at our table and how glad she is to be a part of this amazing success.

I'm sick of it. Of everything. The bullshit, the fakery, the wasted time pretending to think and feel something other than what I actually do feel.

"Thank you, everyone," I say, raising my voice to cover the ruckus, "but we have a show to prepare."

My words have the effect of a fire suppression drill, extinguishing the excitement and chatter like ice-cold water sprayed from ceiling sprinkler heads over lively flames.

"I'll leave you to it, then," Ray says, heading out the door with his coffee cup still in hand. Latesha chases after him, struggling to keep up. Her tight skirt and high heels slow her down, but she's determined just as much as she's hilarious, at least to me.

Soon, it's just the control room people left, as it should be, and they're resuming their usual activities.

I check the time and let out a frustrated sigh. It's almost four. This day is spiraling out of control.

"Come on, people, we have nothing. Aidan, who do we have tonight on *Final Question*?"

His curls bounce around his head as he's checking his notes, but he remains stubbornly upright. "An LAPD cop, a Detective Al Jazinsky."

*A cop. Fuck.*

"And what's so special about this cop?" I ask, propping my hands on my hips, impatient and irritated. Why do I have to pry the information out of him? He's done this for me countless times; he knows the drill.

His eyes go back to his notes. "It's the third time he's been accused of excessive force during an arrest, leading to severe injuries. One of his prior victims died while in police custody, yet he was never reprimanded. I believe we have something there."

I feel rage surging through me, hot and searing. I run my hand through my hair, trying to control it. "You *believe…?* Why would the people of Los Angeles care about what you believe, Aidan?"

The control room is deathly quiet. The sound engineer puts on his headphones and pretends to be working. Aidan looks at me, his eyes wide, his mouth slightly open. I can't recall another time I shouted at him. I like the guy; he's about ten years younger than me, a talented journalism grad. He treats me like I'm the center of his universe. But today, I have zero tolerance for ineptitude and sloppy work. I stare at him until he lowers his eyes, defeated.

"I'm sorry," he says, shifting his weight from one foot to the other, visibly uncomfortable. "I thought this was—"

"I want some serious dirt on this cop, you hear me?" I take a step closer; he takes a small, shaky step back. "I want him skewered on the set, his career finished, trampled over, like the lives of the people he damaged. And do you know why?"

He doesn't dare to voice a reply. Just shakes his head, staring at his shoes.

I let out a frustrated sigh. The real reason cannot escape the confines of my mind. Since last night, I've become afraid of cops. Terrified, even. I don't want to have anything to do with them, but this man is already on the schedule, his mug on the show's weekly advertising banner. There's no escaping it now. But being afraid is new to me and I can't stand it. I see myself as one of Jazinsky's arrestees, brutalized and injured for no good reason, my life turned meaningless, crumpled in his hands like yesterday's newspaper. In a silent, unshakable oath, I promise myself I will bring this motherfucker down.

"Because this is what we do here, Aidan—we *deliver justice*," I say instead. "Not just stories, not just headlines—justice. Our viewers tune in after the news every damn Friday, when they could be out drinking, grilling, fishing, or doing whatever the hell normal people do, but they choose to sit down with us. Why? Because we're the ones who call out the bullshit that stinks up their lives. We're not just a show—we're the last goddamn stand. We're Robin-fucking-Hood, and we take aim at anyone who thinks they're untouchable."

Silence falls heavy for a brief moment. I notice Latesha is back, staring at me with a glimmer of curiosity in her eyes.

"Hear, hear," the video engineer says, without raising his eyes from his screens.

"Got it," Aidan says, taking a few steps toward the door, hesitantly, as if afraid to pass by me on his way out.

"Now, get me some real filth on this cop, Aidan. Something to end this abuse."

He stops a few feet from me and flips through his notepad. "Do you care that his wife's a drunk? She washed out of AA a couple of times."

I shrug, still fuming. "So what? Everyone in America has a drinking problem."

He taps his fingernails against the notepad. "Yeah, but not everyone in America gets away with driving while intoxicated."

A smile flutters on my lips. "Give me more."

"The missus was pulled over, way over the limit, but the traffic officer called good ol' Detective Jazinsky instead of booking her. They let her slide."

My smile turns into a bona fide grin as I pat Aidan on his bony shoulder.

"Now, you're talking. Double-check your info and have our distinguished guest sign the waiver before we go live. The show will be a doozy."

*I'll bury the fucker.*

# 19

# AMANDA DAVIS

The patient is crying in pain, curled up on her side and panting heavily between screams. The IV tube is wrapped around her forearm, but she doesn't seem to care. Her hands clutch her lower abdomen. Hollow, wide eyes are staring into empty space. The EMTs should've managed her pain; I'm not sure what happened.

"Female, 32, presenting with severe abdominal pain, possible ruptured ovarian cyst," one of the EMTs calls out. "BP 100 over 60, pulse 120, O2 sat 97. IV saline running, 500 ml in."

Dr. Grant snaps on a pair of gloves. "Pain level?"

"Ten out of ten," the EMT replies. "Started about two hours ago. She's been in and out of consciousness. We pushed eight milligrams of morphine on the ride over."

Dr. Grant's eyes widen, but he doesn't say anything. He's just as surprised as I am. "Alright, let's move. Trauma One!" he orders, leading the gurney down the hallway. The nurses follow, pushing the gurney into the nearest trauma bay. I'm the last one in, falling behind although I'm doing my best not to.

I watch as Sunny quickly sets up the IV, hanging another bag of saline while Dr. Grant leans over the patient, holding his stethoscope to her chest.

I stare at the patient's face, transfixed. Frozen. She looks just like her...just like Marisol. Her face, covered in sweat and twisted in agonizing pain. Those haunting eyes that I still see in my nightmares.

"Ma'am, can you hear me? I'm Dr. Grant. We're going to take care of you."

The woman's eyes flutter open for a second, her lips trembling as she tries to respond, but winces instead, her entire body curling in on itself with another wave of pain.

"Let's get a CBC, type and cross, coag, and metabolic panel just to be sure. Get an ultrasound to confirm the cyst rupture," Dr. Grant requests, not waiting for a response as he gently presses on the woman's abdomen. "Tell me where it hurts."

The patient lets out a sharp cry as he touches the lower right side. "Ow..." she wails, pushing his hand away. "It's...killing me."

"Alright," he mutters, glancing at me. "Morphine—5 milligrams IV. Let's get this pain under control."

I rummage through the cart drawer and pull out the preloaded syringe. I insert the needle into the port and push the plunger. The patient's breathing slows, her muscles unclenching as the drug begins to work its way through her system.

"We need an ultrasound in here!" Dr. Grant calls out again, his tone sharper now. I don't move, and don't get out of the way. As if living a nightmare, I realize I should've rolled in the ultrasound machine the first time he asked.

The tech rushes in—wheeling the machine around me, picking up my slack—then hooks it up. Sunny and I struggle to get the patient's clothes removed, while she adamantly wants to stay curled on her side.

"Hey, hey, I know you're in pain," I say softly, crouching down so I'm level with her tear-filled eyes. "We're trying to help you, but we need to see what's going on in there. The ultrasound is quick, I promise. You don't have to move much—just let us see your belly, okay?"

She nods, a look of distrusting despair in her eyes, but she tries her best to fight the pain that shatters her breath.

The tech applies gel to the patient's abdomen and hands the probe to the attending.

"Let's see what's going on in there." Dr. Grant shoots me an inquisitive, worried look.

As the probe presses against the woman's skin, an image forms on the screen in hues of pixelated grays. Dr. Grant studies the display closely, his eyes narrowing. "There it is. Right ovary. Cyst rupture, possible internal bleeding. Get the gynecologist down here. We need an OR, stat."

Sunny runs to the wall phone, dialing quickly. "Gyno on call, OR 3. Prep for surgery."

They wheel the woman out of there as I watch, my eyes riveted on her features. The morphine has taken the edge off her pain, and her face is almost relaxed now, her eyes barely open.

And she looks nothing like Marisol. I'm losing my mind.

My gloved hands fall inertly along my body. I shake my head as if to scatter the remnants of a bad dream. Last night did things to me...things I'm not ready to deal with or even acknowledge.

A gentle squeeze on my shoulder makes me flinch.

"Why don't you go home?" Dr. Grant asks. "You need some rest."

I smile with sadness, remembering the last time he sent me home before the end of my shift. I ended up asking for a divorce that night, and realizing I was trapped in my marriage with no way out.

"I'm sorry, Dr. Grant," I say instead. "It won't happen again. For a second, she seemed to—"

My phone chimes, stopping me from saying more. I peel off my gloves and drop them in the trash, then fish the phone out of my pocket. It's a message from Paul.

It reads, "Raised five million last night 👍 👍 Too bad that bitch fucked up my evening."

The message hits me in the chest like a punch. The letters dance in front of my eyes, blurry through tears. Not one word of remorse or regret, no apologies, nothing but the cold-hearted, self-centered man I married shining through in every word, his real colors painfully visible.

"Come on, let's get you another cup of coffee," Dr. Grant says, looking at me with clinical eyes I shy away from.

"Are you coming tonight?" Sunny asks, catching up and walking into the break room as only a twenty-four-year-old can, with a lively spring in her step.

"What's tonight?" I frown looking at her, trying to remember. Dr. Grant gazes at me with concern.

"We're all going out for beers, at the Irish Pub. It's Friday, right?" She stares at me, visibly disappointed. "Hello?"

*Oh. It's Friday.*

I can't. I just want to rush home, hold Tristan in my arms for as long as he'll have me, and then lock myself in the bathroom and cry.

"I'm too tired," I say instead. "I need some sleep."

Dr. Grant nods imperceptibly, but the scrutiny in his eyes is still intense. And there's something else in there, but it's something I can't really grasp.

"You gotta be kidding me!" Sunny pushes back, her arms raised in the air as if she's offended, but there's laughter in her eyes. "Are we not glamorous enough for the famous Amanda Davis?"

I sigh, a little frustrated, but also amused. I need youth like Sunny's in my life—her laughter, her naiveté, her optimism. "No, it's just that...I can't, Sunny. Not this time." There's a sadness in my voice that I hope no one notices.

She leans against the counter and stares back, then waves a finger at me as if I were a disobedient child. "Now, you listen to Mommy, Amanda. I know your life is like something out of a movie. Fancy galas, expensive dresses, rubbing elbows with people who fly private jets for brunch... I can't even imagine! I mean, while I'm here wondering if I should splurge on a venti latte, you're out there living like royalty. But some beers with me and the guys would be good for your soul." She makes a sweeping gesture as if she's brushing lint off her blue scrubs. "What do you say?"

I've rolled my eyes as she's spoken, but end up smiling. She's infectious. "If you think high heels is what I'm dreaming of after a long shift in the ED, you're so wrong. Those galas are seriously overrated." I reach out and squeeze her hand. "Next time, okay?"

The ambo tone ends her protests.

Seconds later, we're receiving a double-delivery. Two patients, with a police escort. Must be a bad one.

The first gurney has the EMTs running fast. "Male, 42, driver, T-bone collision, truck versus sedan. Airbag deployed, unrestrained. GCS 12, he's conscious but confused, complaining of chest pain and difficulty breathing. Suspected rib fractures, possible pneumothorax. BP's 100 over 60, pulse 110. We've got him on oxygen, O2 sat's at 92. IV's in, normal saline running."

"Trauma Two!" a nurse calls.

Dr. Grant looks at me intently. "Take the other one."

I wait for the second gurney, and the other attending, Dr. Sofia Martinez, joins me. She's still chewing a mouthful of her lunch, breadcrumbs clinging to her lips. The gurney is rolled in quickly, the body lying on it a child about the size of my son. My heart skips a beat.

"Seven-year-old female, backseat, booster seat, no airbag. She's alert, complaining of abdominal pain, likely seatbelt injury. BP 110 over 70, pulse 130, O2 sat 98%. No obvious external injuries."

"Take her to five!" someone shouts. Hearing the assignment call, I push the gurney that way. Then, I go through the motions, following the attending's directions, moving quickly, without thinking of how little she is. Without remembering Marisol.

"Where's the other driver?" I ask. I'm expecting another ambo, but the desk nurse shakes her head.

"It was a hit and run," a familiar voice says, chilling my blood as if the simple mention of the words could make the entire world see right through me.

The cop standing next to me is dressed in a worn-out uniform and looks grim. I've known him for a while. He works traffic investigations this side of the interstate.

"Hey, Danny," I say quietly, choked.

He looks at me, and, for a moment, doesn't say anything. His tense mouth is a little crooked, as if a corner is weighed down by constant disappointment. His eyes are bloodshot, glimmering with anger under his furrowed brow. After we hand him over, the father is being rolled out from the trauma bay toward the OR, while the restless six-year-old cries for her daddy.

"You're married to that TV hot shot, right? Paul Davis?" Danny eventually asks, already knowing the answer.

Fear twists in my gut. I nod and cross my arms at my chest, bracing for what he has to say. What if he somehow knows about last night? Cops talk with other cops, over actual coffee and donuts.

"He's such a force with his advocacy against drunk driving," Danny says. "Please thank him for everything he does."

I lower my eyes for a moment, then look at him and whisper, "Sure, Danny, I will." I can't stop myself from thinking what will happen when they come for Paul with an arrest warrant. How will I look these people in the eye again? How can I look Danny in the eye now, after what happened last night?

When I turn to leave the reception area, I find Dr. Grant staring at me from across the receiving area. His eyes are dark and too inquisitive. I find myself wondering what he knows.

Fearing it.

# 20

# PAUL DAVIS

---

Detective Al Jazinsky is sweating under the studio lights, and I haven't even started yet.

We're both seated in the cream-colored, plush armchairs at the center of the set, half-facing each other while my make-up artist applies final touch-ups. She struggles with the sweat breaking out on Jazinsky's forehead. Then shoots me an apologetic smile, and I shrug in response. There are things we cannot fix. Well, perhaps we *could* make him sweat less; I know a little secret he could use right now, but I'll be damned if I'll share it with a cop.

"Twenty seconds!" the stage manager calls. The makeup artist rushes off set.

I hold my thumb up for a second, then look at Aidan's scribbled notes in my lap. At the top of the page, he'd written WIFE, AA, and DUI in big, block letters, and underlined each one multiple times with forceful strokes. I stare at the notes scribbled underneath that—dates, events, all the details that will help me direct my interview. I shift in my seat and adjust my jacket, then smile encouragingly at Detective Jazinsky.

I'm ready.

Behind us, on the large digital backdrop, the background graphics start rolling. Studio lights turn brighter even, and my guest keeps sweating and fidgeting. He must know I'll go after his excessive force track record. The one thing I can't explain is why he's here. What does he stand to gain from letting himself be torn to pieces on my show? I know why politicians and attention hogs and celebrities want it; they'd risk everything for a bit of limelight on national television. But him? It just doesn't add up.

The stage manager holds her hand up. "In four, three—" and she finishes the count silently by showing two fingers, then only one. With that, she points at me.

"Good evening, ladies and gentlemen, and welcome to *The Final Question*. I'm Paul Davis. In studio with me tonight, we have one of LAPD's most senior detectives, Al Jazinsky. Welcome, Detective, thank you for joining us."

He swallows hard and clears his throat. "Thank you for having me."

I lean forward slightly and clasp my hands together. "How long have you been a detective with the LAPD?"

"A little over nineteen years," he says. His voice sounds choked, as if his teeth are clenched. "In fact, I'm coming up on my twenty in April."

"Ah, congratulations," I say, but the smile I paste on my face doesn't color my tense voice.

"Thank you," he says coldly, then presses his lips into a tight line. His hands are clasped in his lap, his knuckles white. Sweat's breaking at the roots of his hair. I'm tempted to fuck with him for a while longer, but that's not why I'm here. My viewers expect more from prime-time television on a Friday night than cheap, cheesy theatrics.

I let my smile wane and check my notes before continuing, letting the suspense build a little. "Detective Jazinsky, you were involved in three separate incidents where excessive force was alleged—one of which ended with a suspect dying while in police custody. These are not minor complaints. In fact, they've cast a shadow over your department and your work. How do you respond to those who say you've crossed the line?"

His eyes drill into mine. "Paul, you know the kind of people I deal with. High-risk criminals. Murderers. Rapists. These people aren't jaywalkers. We're talking about guys who would rather shoot their way out of a situation than be taken in. When things go south, I have to react—and fast." He shifts in his seat just a little, then settles, rigid and a little pale. He was definitely coached on what to say. No average cop talks like that.

"You're talking about high-pressure situations, no doubt." I keep my voice level, but pointed. "But, in one of these incidents, the man you arrested last month, Brandon Hill, wasn't armed. He died in your custody after what some are calling an unnecessary use of force. Can you walk us through why it ended that way?"

Jazinsky's eyes narrow. "Hill was no innocent. Entering that building, we knew he was a recently released ex-con who'd served time for murder. He had a record a mile long, all acts of brutal violence. And the day he was released from prison, his former wife was shot by a man matching his description." He pauses for a moment and shrugs. "He resisted. You don't always see that in the reports or headlines, but he put up one hell of a fight. Two other cops were injured that night; one has permanent brain damage from the incident. I had a choice—let a murderer get away or stop him. I stopped him."

How convenient. His responses are well-rehearsed and good, but fail to convince me. "But he died later, in the holding room. Hill was already subdued when things escalated. This wasn't a shootout or a life-threatening situation. How do you justify what happened in that holding room?"

The cop's eyes flash with frustration. "You weren't there, Paul. I was. Hill had been violent before, unpredictable. Even when a guy's cuffed, he can still be dangerous, and Hill was a big guy, six-four and weighing about three hundred pounds. You have to keep in mind, a man in his situation has nothing left to lose; he knows he's going down for good. When he lunged, I did what I had to do to protect myself and the other detective in the room."

"You snapped his neck while he was handcuffed."

His jaw tenses up and his nostrils flare. "I tried nothing more than to restrain him."

I pause for a moment, regrouping. "No one doubts that your job is dangerous, Detective, and that you're dealing with some of the worst situations out there. But when there's a pattern—three incidents, all with excessive force allegations— it raises questions about whether force is being used as a first response instead of a last resort."

Jazinsky stiffens in his seat. "You call it a pattern. I call it survival. Doing my job. Look at the latest such arrest with use of violence—a drug kingpin, armed, trying to flee during a raid. You think I had time to ask him nicely to come with me? These aren't clean, simple arrests where you knock on the door and serve a warrant. This is the real world. I don't have the luxury to sit back and second-guess in the heat of the moment."

"What about accountability?" I ask, my tone neutral. "There's no doubt your job puts you in impossible situations, Detective. But with three investigations and a man dead, do you ever wonder where the line is—between doing your job and going too far?"

For a while, he takes me down a rabbit hole of police procedure, explained in minute detail that's about to bore everyone to tears, and he knows that. I ask a few more questions, and he keeps on dancing until I hold my hand up in the air, stopping him.

"Detective, I believe everyone understands procedure, but where exactly is that line you have most likely crossed? I believe you're dodging my question."

His eyes shift from frustrated to determined. "As cops, doing our jobs out there is as simple as this: You go in, you handle it, and you get out alive. That's the job. Yes, there are rules, and we all do our best to follow them, but, ultimately, our job is to keep the public safe. That, sometimes, can turn ugly."

Now, he sounds genuine, not scripted. A little surprised, I cross my legs and lean toward him. The notepad slips from my lap and lands face up under the coffee table, closer to his side.

*Fuck.*

He could easily read Aidan's notes from where he's sitting.

"But you have, in fact, bent the rules before, haven't you?" I ask in a rush, hoping to distract him from seeing Aidan's underlined scribbles.

My strategy fails. Jazinsky's eyes land on the notepad. He turns ashen and leans forward in a threatening posture, scowling at me. I shoot the monitors a quick glance, waiting for the right moment to retrieve the damn thing.

The moment the camera shifts, I reach under the table and pick up the notepad, flipping the cover to close it.

Then, I lean back in my seat and smile, not giving him the time to answer. "Don't we all, really? It's in our DNA to bend the rules," I say calmly. "To defend what we love, what's most important to us. The safety of our families." My index finger taps against the notepad cover. His eyes are glued to it.

"That is correct," Jazinsky replies coldly.

"Then, the final question for you is this," I announce, pausing for dramatic effect. "Detective Jazinsky, considering your recent actions on- and off-duty, how far do you think you can stretch the limits before they snap?"

I see on the control monitors the camera zooming in on Jazinsky's stunned face. His eyes are flickering with tension. Before he can open his mouth to respond, the camera shifts over to me and finds me sitting straight in my chair, smiling, ready for the final line of tonight's show.

"We're going to leave Detective Al Jazinsky to ponder on that. Thank you for joining us on *The Final Question*." As I always do, I've cut my guest off before he could answer, leaving the pleasure of speculating exclusively for my viewers.

Credits cue, and the stage manager says, "Clear." The bright lights are turned off, and I spring to my feet. I shake my guest's clammy hand, pretending not to notice the smoldering rage in his eyes, then leave the set, rushing toward my dressing room.

Aidan catches up with me in the corridor, past the control room. "Why didn't you use it? It was double-checked. No—" he grabs my sleeve as I'm about to close my door in his face. "It was *triple*-checked."

I love the kid's ambition, but I'm about to deliver a harsh message on subordination and manners in the workplace. I can't afford to have my assistants challenge my on-air decisions. And then Latesha shows up. Seeing her makes me grit my teeth. This day can't be over soon enough.

"Raymond wants to see you." She grins at me wickedly. "Right now."

# 21

# PAUL DAVIS

"Bourbon?" Ray asks, holding the glass he's already filled and topped with ice. He's standing by the large window of his office, overlooking West Hollywood and its stunning nighttime skyline. In the busy streets below, traffic is slowed to a standstill, and a distant concert of honks barely reaches us, seeming distant and unreal from my top-floor vantage point.

I draw closer and accept the liquor with gratitude. My throat is scorched, aching for a shot. It takes everything I've got to not down the entire glass in one thirsty swig. Yet, the twelve-year-old Weller rises up in my throat, its taste kindling memories of last night.

"Latesha was in here?" I ask casually, setting the glass down. "In your office?"

Ray grins. "Well, of course, she was. She's in here every goddamned day." He sips a bit of bourbon, then puts the glass on his desk. I notice he's dressed spiffier than his norm, in a bespoke charcoal suit, and a shirt in bright white silk with its collar held in sharp place by a gold pin. He gestures toward the window and laughs, a quick, throaty giggle. "Privileges of the stratosphere, I guess. Wannabes come calling. She's angling to be lead anchor and take over *The Final Question*. She's quite adamant about it."

Anger rises through me, lighting my blood on fire. *The nerve on that bitch.*

Ray pats my back and returns to the abandoned bourbon glass for another quick nip. He's a cautious yet constant drinker, keeping himself slightly buzzed all day long. I don't mind; it makes my job easier.

"I watched the show tonight." Glass still in hand, he drops into an armchair and invites me to join him with a gesture. I take the opposing chair, bracing myself for his criticism. He's going to call tonight's show "a wasted opportunity to draw some blood" or "a mediocre job."

I give him a moment, but he's not adding anything. Just staring at me.

"What did you think?" I eventually ask, leaning against the seat and bringing my ankle over my knee.

"Latesha was quick to inform me you could've nailed that cop over his wife's skirted DUI. The entire building will be abuzz with that." Another taste of liquor, and Ray clears his throat quietly, leaning toward me as if he's about to share a secret. "Of course, she would've torn that cop apart on air and bumped our ratings. But you went mellow on the guy."

And I bet that backstabbing little bitch rushed upstairs to rat on me. "I did, yeah."

"Why did you do that, buddy?" Ray's eyes are no longer smiling. He seems keenly sober right now. "I go in front of the board on the twenty-seventh, to secure approval for the KCLA Channel 8 News merger. You know how important this merger is to me, right?"

I nod. "Yes, I do."

"And you, my trusted friend and cohort, let that guy slide when you had him by the short ones. I just don't get it."

"A last-minute thing," I say, taking a quick, reluctant sip of bourbon before abandoning the glass on the coffee table on a logoed coaster. "I thought it would be best if we didn't make an enemy out of this particular cop. There's something about him."

Ray frowns slightly, but nods. He's leaning into his elbows, as if I'm not speaking loud enough and he has to draw closer to hear me. Maybe he's getting old and hard of hearing.

"First off, I couldn't think of a reason why he was willing to be on the show. There's no upside for him; only risk, with his twenty coming up in just a few months. Why risk his pension over this?"

"Uh-huh," Ray says. "Interesting. So, that's why—"

I raise my hand briefly, casually. "There's something else. He's been promoted after three different excessive force incidents, as if those complaints never existed. One ended in the death of the suspect; another incident put the suspect in a coma for weeks. And nothing stuck to him, like he's Teflon. That means he's got backing, and we still don't know who that is. Until we do…" I shrug.

Ray stands and closes the distance between us with one large step. I stand, too, unsure what to expect. He shakes my hand enthusiastically, while with the other hand he pats my shoulder.

"And that's why your co-anchor will stay your co-anchor!" He laughs. "You keep your head level in the heat of the hunt. Latesha Jones doesn't. Once she smells blood, she won't stop." He raises his glass, and I pick up mine so that we can clink cheerfully as I breathe with relief. "Now, go home and celebrate with that beautiful wife of yours. Please give Amanda my best."

"Thanks, Ray, I will." Saying the words, I feel tiredness weighing my body down, weakening me.

"You made us shine last night," Ray adds, finishing up his drink. Ice cubes clatter when he sets the glass down. "Three members of our board were there, and all three sent me notes about you."

I can't help but smile. That's something. "Thank you," I say, noticing how Ray is gently leading me toward the door. "Please thank them for me."

Ray's grin widens. "One more piece of business before you leave."

"Sure."

"Make this KCLA merger happen for me, and you'll be my second-in-command. On top of your new national lead anchor job." He winks and nods, probably knowing exactly how well his offer lands with me. It's not just going to be fame... it's going to be power, too. Decision-making power. And I'll finally be rid of Latesha.

"For Golden State Broadcasting?" I ask, feeling my chest swell.

"For the entire network. We're going prime time. National television news, buddy. You and me."

# 22

# AL JAZINSKI

*He's probably got a stack of unpaid parking tickets a mile high,* I'm musing as I make my way to the visitor's parking lot. "Arrogant, entitled prick." Mumbling, I slide behind the wheel of my unmarked SUV.

Still pissed, I peel out and cut into the sluggish traffic. Moments later, my siren's blaring and my lights are flooding the streets with hues of red and blue. People move out of my way, but not fast enough. Some even jump the curb trying to clear a path, but I'm still leaning on the horn, impatient, boiling over.

I never should've done that goddamn show.

Because of it, the nosy assholes researched me and know about Maria's DUI, and they're gunning for me. I still don't get why they didn't nail me on air like they usually do to every poor schmuck that walks into their trap, but it's obvious Gabriela's gonna have to make some calls. And she better work fast.

This whole mess? It's on her.

She put me in front of those vultures. Had someone pull the strings. Played me like a fool, like she always does. And who the hell knows why? Maybe it's for her own political bullshit. *"Tell your side, clear your name before you retire,"* she said. *"Do this for me, and I'll take care of you. I promise."*

That's how it's been for years. Gabriela, my wife's aunt and now the mayor of LA, always scheming. Even back when she was a hungry policy analyst with her eyes on the governor's mansion and I was a green-as-hell rookie detective—forty pounds lighter, no beer gut, no gray in my hair, but just as cocky, if not worse. And Maria? She was a mess back then, strung out on pills. Now, it's wine, and God knows what else. I've thought about having her tested, but those days of being able to destroy test results are long gone. Everything's in the system now.

Computers. Can't rip those to shreds.

I might borrow a K9 unit one day and have the house sniffed good, just to know what to expect.

Maria's aunt opened doors for me, though. When she became a councilwoman, I became LAPD's liaison. Then, with her as LA's mayor, I've climbed those stairs at City Hall more times than I could count, always with a smile for the cameras. That's gotten me noticed. Moved up quicker than anyone else.

I kept waiting for someone to connect the dots. Some overzealous rookie sniffing around. But Gabriela long ago changed her name to something more palatable—Alcaraz to Agua—something that sounded good to voters in a state decimated by drought, instead of reminding them of a dreaded prison. No one's ever found the link between us. She made a smart move, even back then.

But all that? It's about to go to shit because of that smug bastard, Paul Davis. If this blows up, I'm not just losing my pension. I could end up behind bars.

"Goddamn it," I growl, slamming my hand against the steering wheel. The car in front of me scrambles onto the sidewalk. A few more horn blasts, even if they don't do much on top of the siren, and I hit the interstate. Forty minutes later, I'll be back home in Thousand Oaks.

The house is dark when I pull up. But it's not late enough for Maria to be asleep. Something feels off. I unlock the door, that old familiar knot twisting in my gut. I love my wife, but lately it's like waiting for a bomb to go off every time I walk through the door.

The TV is off, and the house is eerily silent. Maria never sits in silence. She hates it. Makes her lonely. Makes her drink. I call her name, my voice rough and low in the stillness. No answer.

I rush upstairs, but she isn't there, either. Not in the bathroom, not sleeping in our bed. The guest room's empty.

I rush back downstairs. "Maria?" I check the downstairs bathroom, the den, and even look behind the living room sofa in case she slipped and fell. "Maria?" I open the door to the garage. Both our cars are in there. Mine is always home when I drive the squad car.

I find her purse with her wallet and keys on the small table by the door. Running my fingers through my hair, I head into the kitchen, taking note of things. Her phone is on the counter by the coffee filter, and that never happens. The thing is practically attached to her, like a body part.

She cooked dinner, and she ate alone; there's only one plate and one fork in the sink. The oven's Keep Warm light is on; there's probably lasagna waiting for me.

I love her lasagna, but I'm not hungry; I'm sick to my stomach. Where the hell is she?

A faint whistling sound catches my attention. The backyard door is cracked open. I turn on the porch light and freeze.

Maria's lying face-up on the ground, her white nightgown fluttering around her body. She doesn't move. A fine trickle of blood stains her pale face coming from ber bruised temple. She must've hit her head falling.

"Oh, God, no," I whisper, rushing outside with my phone in hand to call for a bus.

Touching her neck with two fingers, I feel for her pulse. It's strong and steady, just a little fast. A whiff of wine carries over with her breath.

"Maria," I whisper, touching her face gently. "Wake up." I shake her shoulder gently. "Come on, baby, let's go."

Her eyelids flutter, but stay closed, as if stuck. "Mitzy got out," she mumbles, slurring badly.

Damn cat. "Okay, let's take you back inside," I reply, slipping one arm under her shoulders and another under her knees. As I lift her thin body, I grunt, breathing heavily with the effort. I'm badly out of shape.

"No, I have to find the cat," she mutters, but her eyes stay closed and her face is resting on my chest.

"Don't worry about the cat. I'll find her." Gently, I move inside and lay her on the sofa, propping her against some pillows, and then I turn on the TV and make some tea.

After the first cup, she can keep her eyes open and can speak a little better. There won't be a need for the nine-one-one call I was dreading making. Not tonight.

About an hour later, when she's sleeping in bed and I'm confident she won't throw up and choke on her own vomit, I walk out into the small backyard. Large cedars mark the two back corners of the property; the stupid cat is probably up in one of those trees.

"Here, kitty!" I call quietly, aware it's late and the neighbors are probably sleeping. Those old schmucks go to bed at sundown. "Come on, Mitzy, don't be a bitch with me tonight. Here, kitty, kitty!"

I don't give up easily; I know how much Maria loves that sneaky little silver tabby. But I do, eventually, give up. I head back inside, lock the patio door, and take the lasagna out of the oven. Too tired to carry it to the table, I eat some standing by the stove, stabbing it with the fork angrily, as if it wronged me.

Later, when I'm almost asleep in front of the TV with my feet on the coffee table, Mitzy jumps into my lap, startling me half to death.

"Motherfucker," I grumble, and then settle back with the purring cat in my lap. "Where have you been, you little shit?"

The cat mews, but my thoughts drift back to Paul Davis. For a while, I can't figure out why I hate him so much. Is it his power? His smug face? The fact that he could blow my life to pieces for the sake of ratings?

Then, it hits me.

It's knowing that, for the first time in my life, I can't do a damn thing to stop the man that's getting to me. I can't strong-arm, intimidate, shoot, or talk my way out of this one. And that's worse than fear—it's knowing I'm at someone else's mercy.

# 23

## AMANDA DAVIS

"Mom!" Tristan's annoyed voice is matched by the squirming of his thin body. He's eager to escape my embrace. Reluctantly, I let him go, and he settles in the passenger seat, red as a beet. In the back seat, my son's best friend Dylan is staring at his phone, pretending—or managing—not to notice anything. His freckled face is all scrunched, his fingers dancing on the phone screen, and muffled beeps come from the device as he scores points in whatever game he's playing. Meanwhile, my son stares dead-ahead through the windshield, probably still embarrassed to be hugged by his mother in front of the school, where everyone can see.

I smile as I shift into gear, blinking away the sting of tears. I took half a day off today, just to be here for him. I missed Tristan today, more than ever, and I can't tell him. He'd give me one of that tilted-head, are-you-crazy looks.

It's stop-and-go traffic, the usual speed of the afternoon pickup routine. It takes me about ten minutes to reach the light and turn into moving traffic. "You coming over, Dylan?"

"No, Mom," Tristan replies, a hint of his earlier annoyance still coloring his voice. "I *told* you. We're going to Dylan's today. It's Friday."

"Ah, yes."

"You always do that," he accuses in a sharp voice.

"Do what, hon?"

"Forget it's Friday. You're like Deadpool."

His words fade, lost in the maze of my racing thoughts.

Friday. It doesn't feel real, as if weekdays have lost any meaning since last night. For me, time is standing still, yet moving along at break-neck speed.

Part of me panics at the thought of spending two days alone with my husband, locked inside the house with our thoughts and the damning secret we share. But perhaps it's for the best Tristan will be at Dylan's for the night. Paul and I need to talk as soon as he's home.

When we arrive at Dylan's, Tristan opens the door before the car reaches a complete stop. I don't say anything; just smile and ruffle his hair quickly before he can pull away. "Have a good time!" I call behind the two boys, but I doubt either of them hears me.

Then, I'm alone, driving myself home in heavy silence. No music, no radio...just my shallow, fraught breathing as I remember things that haunt me. The thin, frail body at my feet, lying in a pool of blood on Malibu Canyon Road, lit by distant lightning and the red hues of our car's taillights. The patient from earlier today, the one with a ruptured ovarian cyst, who, in Dr Davis? Amanda? my mind, looked just like Marisol.

Arriving home is a sequence of familiar actions I perform on autopilot, yet differently, as dictated by my new reality. Opening the garage door. Pulling into the garage quickly, after making sure no one's there to sneak a peek at the damaged Cadillac parked inside. Rushing to close the garage door. Breathing with relief when the door clanks closed and the yellowish ceiling light engulfs me.

Once inside the living room, I kick off my shoes and let myself drop onto the sofa, too exhausted to get out of my hospital garb. With the comfort of solitude, my façade comes crumbling down. My chest swells, and I let out a shattered wail. I bury my face in my hands, giving into the grief and fear and pain that consume me. And, for a while, I lose track of time.

It's completely dark outside when I wake with a start. Tears have dried on my face, the stain barely visible on the couch pillows in the weak light coming from the reading lamp. I sit up, eager to put everything behind me. It's almost midnight. I was out for hours.

"Get a grip," I say to myself a moment later, rubbing my eyes with my hands and standing. I need a shower, to cleanse my mind of the horrors of the day and the night before it. To at least try.

A distant rumbling freezes me in my tracks. I close my eyes and press my lips tightly together, keeping things bottled up inside. The shower will have to wait.

Paul's home.

I can hear the wheels of his car squeaking onto the garage floor, and then the rumbling resumes as the garage door closes. With a sigh, I pull a chair and sit at the dining room table, turned a little sideways to face the door he's about to walk through.

Still, when the door opens, it gives me a start, as if in those few seconds that passed since he drove up, I forgot he was about to walk in.

"Hey, baby," he greets me with a smile. His face is composed, relaxed, and his smile touches his eyes. He looks unnervingly the same, as if nothing happened. As if it's just another Friday.

I stare at him, unable to speak.

"Where's Tristan?" he asks, loosening his tie and looking around for our son.

"At Dylan's. He's spending the night there."

"Oh."

The smile on his lips withers and dies. His composure is quickly replaced by an expression of agony. He walks slowly toward the couch and lets himself drop onto the cushions, just where I was sitting a few moments ago. His hands are clasping and unclasping restlessly. His head is bowed, his shoulders hunched forward and burdened.

I've never seen him so defeated and scared.

Meanwhile, I feel nothing but rage. It rises like fire—hot and sharp, clawing up my throat and burning behind my eyes.

My fists clench so tight I feel my nails bite into my palms, but the pain is nothing compared to what's surging inside me. I want to scream. Break something. Rip the universe apart with my bare hands for letting last night happen the way it did.

When he turns toward me, his eyes are hollow and tormented. "Look, I'm sorry—"

"Don't you even!" I snap, springing to my feet and walking angrily toward him. "I asked if you were sober enough to drive. I gave you every chance before—" I gasp, stopping as I'm about to say things I can't take back. Things that should never be said. "I gave you every opportunity," I say eventually. The shimmer of tears in his eyes fuels my anger. "You said you were fine. You shut me up, even if you'd been drinking all night and I'd had nothing but soda." Panting, I stop squarely in front of him, my hands propped on my hips. I can't breathe; I feel I'm suffocating, choking on my own words, my own tears. "Your stubbornness will be the end of this family."

I walk away, keeping my back turned toward him. I can't look at him right now.

"Not *my* stubbornness," I hear him say calmly. The low pitch of his voice sends a chill down my spine. I turn on my heels to face him.

His earlier weakness is gone. The look in his eyes is now defiant, piercing and merciless.

"What do you mean?" I ask in a low whisper.

"Everyone knows how much I love you, my sweet Amanda," he says, leaning back against the backrest and crossing his legs. His hands rest relaxed in his lap for a moment, and then he raises his arms slowly, clasping his hands behind his head. "You made a mistake... had a little too much to drink and hit someone. I begged you to call the cops, but—"

The shriek that leaves my chest sounds foreign to me, primal, like the death cry of a wounded animal. "You lying son of a bitch!" I say when I'm able to articulate words again. "You wouldn't dare."

He stands and draws close to me, his blue eyes cold as ice and locked onto mine. "Just watch me," he says, running the back of his fingers against my cheek.

I shake my head in disbelief. "No, no, there's video showing you climbed behind the wheel last night—"

He doesn't flinch. "Are you sure about that? There used to be, but…" His words trail off as he shrugs. "Things sometimes get lost. Misplaced."

I can't breathe. Dizzy and feeling faint, I walk backward toward the dining table and lean against it. I'm trying to think, but I can't, my thoughts a jumbled mess of panic and fear and rage.

"Everyone will understand that I couldn't turn in the love of my life, my beautiful wife who, as everyone remembers from last year's Christmas party at the station, has a bit of a drinking problem."

"Damn you to hell, Paul."

He laughs quietly. "This goes to show it could've happened to you just the same, baby—nothing else. I won't pin this on you, even if I could."

I stare at him, knowing I can't trust a single word that comes out of his mouth. "Then, what do you want?"

His attitude shifts again. His hands plunge into his pockets, his shoulders hunching forward a little. "Help me get out of this mess."

I breathe, feeling relief against my better judgment. I've been an idiot. I rented the other Cadillac under my name. My credit card. I covered for him when I should've called the cops. I lied to that cop, cleaned blood-soaked clothes, and destroyed evidence. All acts of a guilty person.

*Oh, my God.*

It takes everything I've got to get myself together. "In my work, I deal with families in crisis," I start, and then stop, unsure of where I was going with this.

"How do they manage?"

"One day at a time," I whisper, dying to be alone with my thoughts, to buy myself some time. "So...let's live through the day. Get some rest, make decisions with a clear head."

He leans against the wall to take his shoes off. A shoe hits the floor with a loud noise, and I flinch. Then the other. Paul comes toward me, and I fight the urge to pull away, to run.

"Tomorrow, we figure out how to get out of this mess." I run my hand through my hair, noticing how badly my fingers are trembling. "Actually, *you* figure it out, Paul," I add bitterly. "It's your mess."

A glint of rage touches his eyes. He walks over, abandoning his jacket on the side of the sofa. "We're back to this again?" he asks angrily.

"You know you need to get a lawyer and turn yourself in," I say, stubbornly refusing to accept who I'm dealing with.

A flicker of a crooked smile trembles on his lips. "You'd love that, wouldn't you?" He draws a step closer, and his hands land on my shoulders as he looks down on me. I feel their weight pinning me in place, squeezing harder and harder. "We're in this together, or I will call the cops on you, my dear. I thought you understood that already. Seems that you didn't. So, there, I'm spelling it out for you."

Tears well in my eyes, choking me. "Think of Tristan, Paul! You can't do this to him!"

"I *am* thinking of Tristan. How about you? You want him growing up with both his parents in prison, the laughingstock of the entire community? Just because you want to do what's right, by some twisted, fucked-up, and inconsequential moral code you deem more valuable than our life together?"

I stare at him, speechless, my throat parchment dry and my stomach revolting. I have no way out. I'm trapped in his lies, the only witness to his crime. A convenient scapegoat and loose end at the same time. The moment I lifted a finger to help him, I sealed my own fate.

Nothing escapes his cold scrutiny. It's as if he can read my thoughts. "Exactly," he says. "I'm glad we understand each other." He lets go of me and walks away toward the stairs. "Let's not have this conversation again. Ever." He climbs a few steps, then looks at me over his shoulder. "That is, if you want to see your son growing up."

# 24

# PAUL DAVIS

"Son of a bitch," I mumble, standing quickly and reaching for some tissue as the coffee stain seeps through the fabric of my pants, warm and sticky against my groin. I pat the stain, but it still shows like hell. Way to start a Monday.

With a long breath loaded with whispered oaths, I retake my seat at Ray's coffee table, while he laughs and laughs.

"Really?" I ask, frustrated with how much he's entertained by my one moment of clumsiness.

"Oh, come on, it's not like you don't have at least ten suits in your dressing room, paid for by the station, and dry-cleaning service at your beck and call. I *get* to laugh, seeing you standing there slapping your dick like it did you wrong."

His laughter is contagious, but all I can manage is an awkward, forced smile and a loaded sigh.

He waves off my frustration with a swat of his hand and stops laughing. "So, where were we?"

"You were saying Amanda and I—"

"Ah, yes. I need you two to be on call until this takeover deal is closed. You're one of Golden State's biggest assets, and your beautiful wife is part of your brand now. If the Channel 8 people want to meet you, or have you speak with their board, I need to know you can make it happen on very short notice."

I lean forward, mostly to keep the stain on my pants out of sight as I look straight into Ray's eyes. "We'll be ready whenever you need us. I know how important this merger is to you. You know how much I want to see it happen. I have plenty of skin in this game."

*And Amanda's schedule better not get in the way.*

He extends his hand, and we shake above the table, both grinning like we've just signed a major deal. As I leave his office, he says, "Give Amanda my best." I nod and smile, and the moment the door is closed safely behind me, I stop grinding my teeth and let out a long breath.

"Motherfucker," I grumble, heading for the elevators. How the hell am I supposed to get Amanda to walk the line with me? I'm not even sure she's committed to keeping me out of jail.

I haven't slept well since the accident happened, and haven't eaten much, and people are starting to notice. That nosy little bitch, Latesha, said earlier today that I look like an alley cat, a bit mangy. I can't afford that kind of static in my life, especially not at work.

I guess I'm learning what anxiety is...a crippling state of constant fear, so intense it twists my gut and makes me want to scream. All I've been thinking about since Friday night's fight with my wife is her good old friends, the cops she knows from the hospital. Who are they going to believe? Me? Or her? After so many years spent working together, she's almost like one of them. She's patched up their gunshot wounds, consoled their families, and taken care of their hurt partners. She's their family, and all that while she's stopped wanting to be mine.

Who's to say she's not on the phone with one of those cops right this moment, spilling her guts about last night?

I'm not sure she bought what I was saying yesterday, that the recordings from the venue are gone. They aren't. I'm not going to draw attention to myself without reason by going back there and snooping around. But she seemed scared enough by my threat to think twice before doing something stupid. She knows I'd do exactly what I said...if it comes to my choosing between me and her, I can't afford to be a gentleman.

But I'll send her flowers at the state prison.

And if it rates well on socials, I won't even divorce her. That much I can do for my dear wife.

Strangely, the thought of blaming everything on Amanda doesn't scatter my fears. It stokes them. It's not realistic for me to expect I'd get away with pinning the accident on her. People saw me drinking at the fundraiser. Getting behind the wheel of my car. Convincing them otherwise wouldn't work. But it might keep Amanda's mouth in line for a while.

Until I can get myself out of this fucking mess.

By the time I walk into the newsroom, I've forgotten about the coffee stain. When I sit in my chair, the cold, damp fabric serves as an unpleasant reminder. Thankfully, I have enough time to change into a new suit before I go on the air tonight.

Aidan rushes over with a clipboard in his hand and a wide grin pasted onto his face.

"Where have you been? We have to talk—"

I stare him down a little, enough to remind him of his place in the pecking order. He doesn't get to ask me where I've been. "Get me a cup of coffee, extra cream."

It takes him less than a minute to fill that order, but it's enough for me to gather my thoughts and decide on an action plan. I can't afford to sit and wait for shit to happen. That's not my style. Never was, never will be.

I take the hot paper cup from his hand and take a sip. It's just as I like it. I nod slightly, and he beams. Then, I point at the chair across from mine. Aidan sits, clipboard neatly in his lap and pen in hand.

"Who do we have on *Final Question* next month? Or are we asleep at the wheel? I haven't seen any names yet. Get me the list of candidates. We need the ratings plumped up nicely before the board votes on the merger."

"You got it." A little flustered, Aidan flips through the stack of papers clipped onto his clipboard. "We have a dentist who—"

"No." I wave my hand to entice him to move on. What the hell am I supposed to do with a fucking dentist?

"A dog groomer, but listen to this. She went to—"

"Nope."

The smile wanes off his lips and worry touches the glance he throws me. "A housemaid caught trying on her employer's lingerie and posing with it on OnlyFans. It could be good—"

I fake-yawn, and he moves on, flipping another page.

"A lawyer who—"

"Criminal law?" I ask, intrigued.

"Yes, Larry Chapelle's a litigator. But he's a crook." He hesitates for a split moment, fidgeting. "I think." He stares at the ceiling while I glare at him. "No, I'm sure. I really am."

I extend an impatient hand. "Let me see."

He detaches a sheet of paper covered in chicken-scrawled notes. I snatch it from his hand, still impatient. His style is completely disorganized. I'll need a GPS to follow his train of thought through all this scribbled mess. It still works for me, because the only tidbits that I usually need are always written in bold block letters and underlined or circled angrily.

It's possible that, this time, I'll have to actually read all of Aidan's notes.

"Is this Chapelle guy vetted yet?" I fold the paper and slip it into my pocket. I can work with this. It's just what I needed.

"Almost." Aidan shifts in his seat and sends his eyes away from mine. "I need corroboration. I couldn't get anybody to talk just yet."

I groan. Why is it so damn hard for people to do their jobs right? "Okay, we'll proceed with this attorney. Start working on it. Let me see the full vetting before booking him, though." I stand and throw the coffee cup in the trash. "Find me every bit of filth that's crossed this man's mind since he was born. I want him sobbing on air, alright? I want him destroyed."

Carly Crown, my producer and former co-anchor, raises her eyes from her screen and throws me an inquisitive glance I choose to ignore.

Aidan springs to his feet. "Where are you going?"

I give him a side glance that silences him. Then, I change my mind. "A late lunch. Call me if you need me."

From across the room, Carly's still staring at me, intrigued. A sly smile spreads on her lips. She knows me too well.

I leave the newsroom under Aidan's stunned gaze. He probably didn't expect me to tell him where I was going. I'm not exactly famous for being a nice guy. Being successful and being nice are not on the same life path, and I made my choice a long time ago.

But things are different now. I need friends. People to vouch for me, to think of me as family, the way Amanda's cop friends think of her.

*Damn that woman and the day I married her.*

I'm almost at my dressing room when Latesha's laughter snaps me out of my thoughts.

"What happened? Had a little accident?" she asks, cackling in the middle of the corridor, loud enough to get a few people's attention. "You couldn't hold it all the way to the boys' room?"

I frown and glare at her. "Huh?" I have no idea what she's talking about. Not until I see her purple acrylic fingernail pointed at my groin.

*Ah, hell.*

I draw close to her, staring. She doesn't flinch. Then, I smile, calm, and with an unspoken death threat in my eyes. Her pupils dilate ever so slightly.

"Don't make an enemy out of me, Latesha," I say softly. "I'm much more useful as a friend."

# 25

# AL JAZINSKI

It's the Monday from hell.

Maria had a seizure last night, and I had to call for a bus. The brain scan revealed a micro-bleed—as they called it. They asked me if I knew about any falls or fainting spells. I stood there and lied like a pro, like a guy who knows how good lying is done. At least I was home all day yesterday, and know she hadn't touched a drop.

But a seizure? She's doing way worse than I thought.

And Gabriela won't answer my calls. Her Honor, the mayor of Los Angeles, is too damn busy for a quick chat about her niece or the mess from Friday night's TV circus. But we need to contain this. Maria needs alcohol rehab, plain and simple. Those doctors aren't fools; they'll catch on to her drinking problem soon enough. Then, it will be on her record forever. It's bad enough those TV people know about her drinking and are fixing to use it to bring me down. The fuckers.

Now, I'm staring at the case file my boss dumped on my desk like it's last week's trash. Murders pile up in this town faster than we can shovel them into case files. But no, after that interview, the boss is keeping things close to the vest, playing safe until he figures out which way the wind's blowing.

I flip the file open and glare at the report. A hit and run.

Perry Eckhart saunters over, a Monday morning-grin plastered on his face the way only a thirty-year-old can manage. He's tearing into a muffin like it's his last meal, too, scattering crumbs over my desk. "What's the story?" he asks, mouth full.

"Hit and run," I say flatly.

"Seriously?" He takes another bite, trying to mask the disappointment. "How many dead?"

"Zero. A truck T-boned a sedan and sent two to the hospital. Minor injuries, but one's a kid."

My partner leans in, still chewing like he's got all the time in the world. "What gives? Did we piss off the brass? What's this really about?"

"No idea," I lie, waving him off. "Traffic must be swamped," I add, not ready to dig into the 'why' with him. He's too green, always eager to run his mouth before his brain catches up. The kid channels Liam Neeson every chance he gets, so working a traffic case must be killing him inside. He kind of looks like Neeson, too.

But he surprises me. He grabs the file, eyes lighting up like it's Christmas. "Let's find out why that truck driver was in such a hurry. I bet there's a story behind it."

"Put out a BOLO," I say, pointing at the report. "We've got his plates from the red-light camera. Already sent a unit to pick him up. No-show at work, and no answer at his place."

Perry's face falls a little. He unbuttons his jacket, deflating like a balloon. Liam Neeson is gone. "So, then, what are we really working on?"

I gesture at a stack of cold case files, at least ten deep. "Those. Unsolved murders from last year. Dive in and take your pick."

He rifles through the pile, muttering now and then. I can tell he's recognizing some cases from the news, probably eyeing the ones that got the most airtime. He'll pick one and daydream about his moment in the spotlight.

Meanwhile, I'd give anything to forget my own TV appearance Friday night. And the way that son-of-a-bitch Paul Davis looked at me.

I know the bastard's coming for me. I just don't know when. Or how.

# 26

# AMANDA DAVIS

It takes me a couple of hours to realize why I feel so energized in the emergency department. More so than I felt at home over the weekend, where I stepped on eggshells around Paul, dreading the long, loaded silences between us. Fearing his words.

It's because he's not here.

I can breathe freely, without feeling like I'm drowning under the pressure of his threats. I can think on my feet and act quickly, unafraid, knowing that my doing the right thing is good enough for everyone else. Without Paul here, I can be myself again, even if only for a few hours. It's refreshing.

As part of my Monday morning routine, I finish stocking up the crash carts, grateful it's been a quiet day so far and I can get it done quickly. On my way to the break room, I run into Sunny. She slips her arm under mine and smiles.

"Let's get seriously caffeinated, girl." She giggles. "Can you hook me up to the coffee machine? I need this so badly. I was out all last night with some friends, and I'm totally done for."

*Oh, to be young. And single,* comes the afterthought. I almost slip and urge her to never get married. "Sure," I reply instead. "One liter caffeine IV, large bore, coming right up!"

Dr. Grant is seated in one of the break room's armchairs, reading a magazine. A tall coffee cup rests on the table in front of him. He smiles when we come in. "Care to join me for a cup?" The question seems to be for the both of us, but his eyes are locked onto mine.

Sunny squeezes my arm discreetly and grins. "Absolutely," she replies while I busy myself with the machine, trying to hide my reddening cheeks. A moment later, Sunny takes her cup from my hands, filled to the brim, and throws me a long, meaningful glance.

"Thanks..." she says. "Oh, what do you know, I forgot to call my mom." Then, she vanishes. The door closes behind her, and I'm alone with Dr Grant, my attending. I'm tempted to leave, but at the same time, why would I? We work together, and I can't afford to make things weird. He didn't do anything. He's just sitting there, reading—

No, not anymore. He's looking at me with that clinical stare he sometimes gives his patients. I freeze under it, slowly veering my eyes away, hoping it's all in my imagination. Hoping he can't read my mind right now.

"I know you're married to this media darling," he eventually says, standing and abandoning the latest edition of *Harvard Health* on the table. "But he seems to be an asshole."

The comment surprises me. "Why do you say that?"

"I don't see you smile that much. You have a beautiful smile, and I almost never see it."

I look away, toward the door, while he draws closer, leaning against the counter casually, a few feet away. "In here?" I push back weakly. It's not the first time I'm surprised by how perceptive he is. "What's there to smile about in here, with all this suffering?"

He nods quietly, and, for a while, we're silent. I stare at my coffee cup, confused about the conflicting thoughts swirling in my mind. In the corridor, outside the break room door, people hustle back and forth without throwing us a glance.

"Have lunch with me today," he suggests.

I smile and look at him briefly before lowering my eyes. "It's such a bad idea...another cliché aching to turn into a disaster." And yet, I'm dangerously tempted.

His smile puts dimples in his cheeks. "Which cliché would that be? Doctor dating nurse?"

Our eyes meet for a brief, loaded moment. "No... Wife cheating on husband with boss."

"Ooh...that one," he replies, mock-frowning. "Dinner, then?"

The ambo tone interrupts my attempt to find the right words to decline. Our coffee cups find their way into the trash as we rush out of the break room and toward the entrance. The double doors slide open as paramedics storm in, pushing a gurney. Its wheels rattle noisily under the weight of the patient, a heavyset man who's flailing and gasping for air despite the mask held in place by an EMT.

"Male, mid-forties, collapsed in the street!" one of the paramedics calls out. "Presenting with pneumothorax; suspected cracked ribs. Unilateral breath sounds."

"Trauma Two!" the desk nurse calls loudly.

"BP?" Dr. Grant asks. I can sense his frustration. The EMT should've mentioned it. She's young, not someone I've seen before. Probably a rookie.

"Eighty over fifty, pulse 140," the paramedic says. Sweat lines her brow from the rush, and her voice is out of breath. "O2 sat is low."

"Well, how low?" Dr. Grant asks, then counts for the patient's transfer onto the trauma bed.

"Eighty-two percent," I reply, taking the read from the monitor I've already connected the patient to. The man's face is ashen, his breathing shallow and labored, and a cyanotic shade of blue is spreading on his lips.

I notice the attending's jaws clenching. "Chest tube," he orders, his stethoscope held firmly against the man's chest. "Unilateral breath sounds on the left," he confirms, his voice steady despite the tension. "Trachea deviation to the right."

I move to grab a sterile kit from the drawer while Sunny quickly preps the patient's side, swabbing it with chlorhexidine.

"Tension pneumothorax," Dr. Grant mutters, meeting my eyes. "Needle decompression, now."

My hands move with practiced precision. I grab the large-bore needle and position it above the third rib. The man's eyes flicker open briefly, glassy with confusion, before closing again.

"Here we go," I whisper, inserting the needle and feeling the sharp release of air. A hiss escapes, and the man's chest drops slightly as the pressure eases.

"BP's rising," Sunny announces, a note of relief in her voice as the monitor's beeping steadies.

I look at the man's face. It's still ashen, his lips bluish—color only marginally improving. The needle decompression bought us precious moments, but the chest tube needs to go in fast. Dr. Grant is already moving, eyes hard with focus.

"Chest tube, Amanda, let's go."

"On it," I reply, the urgency pounding in my veins as I reach for the tube. Dr Grant's scalpel makes the incision while I tear the sterile wrapping and hand him the tube.

"We're in," he announces after a moment, giving the monitor a quick, tense look. The patient's numbers are improving. "All right, get portable X-ray in here. Let's find out what caused this."

But I'm afraid I might already know the answer. As soon as I've seen the sternal fracture and cracked ribs, I know I'm right. I've seen wounds like this man's on too many occasions. It's what happens when a driver doesn't wear the seatbelt and gets into an accident. The steering wheel does this exact kind of damage when it hits a man's chest.

"Are we calling the cops?" Sunny asks.

"Why would we?" I ask, even as a shiver travels down my spine.

"This patient fits the new BOLO that just came in."

I freeze. My hands are stuck in mid-air above the man's barren chest.

"What new BOLO?"

# 27

# AMANDA DAVIS

---

*I'm going to be sick.*

The thought crosses my mind as I'm heading toward the break room, where they post the BOLOs safely away from the view of patients and their family members. I was just in there, but didn't see it. Didn't pay attention to much else except Dr Grant's lunch—and then dinner—invitation.

But it's there, pinned on the corkboard with a red thumbtack. My vision blurs as panic spreads through my body. My eyes are fixed on the words *HIT AND RUN*, but the letters are dancing in front of my eyes, frenzied. It takes every bit of willpower I have to keep on reading past that point. Even when I manage to read the words, their meaning escapes me for a while.

Red truck. Gray sedan. Two people in the hospital.

I breathe deeply as the meaning sinks in.

It's not us. The BOLO isn't about us.

Sunny catches up with me. Two steps behind her, Dr. Grant's worried eyes find mine. I've learned to fear his uncanny scrutiny.

"What's wrong, Amanda?" he asks in a gentle voice. His brow is slightly furrowed, and his hands are sunk into his pockets.

"You know how I feel about this," I say, pointing at the BOLO. "I've always said it. We have no right to call the cops on the people who come here looking for help." I'm breathing heavily, my chest heaving under the strong emotions I'm feeling. *Relief. Fear. Shame.*

Is this what my life will be like from now on? Feeling my gut turning into a knot whenever the LAPD sends over a hit-and-run BOLO? Shaking and sweating and fearing for my future every single day, terrified of losing Tristan? Lying to everyone around me?

"No, we don't have the right," Dr Grant replies in a low, troubled voice. "But we do have the legal obligation to do so, as unfortunate as that might be."

Sunny stares at me, then at Dr. Grant with curious, unsettled eyes. I just want the entire thing to go away.

"It's what keeps people from getting the help they need," I whisper, lowering my gaze to the floor to hide the mixed emotions that threaten to fill my eyes with tears. "It's why this man chose to risk dying in the street instead of coming here after his accident."

"I'm not saying it's right," Dr. Grant says, reaching for my hand.

I shy away from his touch, mostly because I'm still wearing gloves. Slowly, I peel them off and discard them in the trash can, wondering why I do any of the things I'm doing when he's involved. I shouldn't have left Trauma Two without throwing away my gloves; it's procedure. And I broke it.

"I'm saying we have to," he continued. "It's the law."

I look at him for a brief moment. "Based on this BOLO, he's a Mexican national. Might not be here legally. What will happen to him?"

Sunny comes closer to me and touches my forearm. "Remember that little girl last Friday? Screaming for her daddy? This is the man who put her there, who could've killed them both. The guy who didn't care about another human being's life enough to stop and give them some help or call them an ambulance. He just drove off like the piece of shit that he is. As far as I'm concerned, he deserves to die in prison." Her hand squeezes my forearm until I turn and look at her. "Like my mom would say, don't burn paper offerings at the wrong tomb. Let the cops deal with him. It's not our problem."

I nod silently. "I'll make the call."

"I can do that, if you'd like." Sunny says.

"It's my job," I say quietly, taking the BOLO down from the wall. Before dialing the number printed on the piece of paper, I notice how Dr. Grant's looking at me. As if he knows. As if he noticed how Sunny's words sliced through me like a blade.

*He deserves to die in prison.*

One day, they'll find out what I've done.

I don't know how I'll survive it.

# 28

# PAUL DAVIS

I didn't expect Larry Chapelle's office to be in a Wilshire Boulevard high-rise. I thought he might've been burrowed in a single-story, somewhat decrepit standalone on Main, or a B-mall location where the stench of deep-fried foods mixes in with the more sophisticated scents emanating from a hair salon next door. I also didn't expect his offices to be this luxurious, or his receptionist to look so damn fine in her red mini-skirt suit.

I *did* expect his law business to be more of a one-man show, and that part I got right. Several other glass-walled offices in his suite are only partly furnished and empty. Chapelle himself takes the corner office, and seems to be busy when his receptionist knocks on his matted glass door and sticks her head in.

"I have Paul Davis for you," she says, gesturing discreetly. An undertone of thrill colors her voice.

"Who?"

"Um, *the* Paul Davis," she says, lowering her voice to an excited whisper. "The news guy?"

I can't contain a smile. I don't go out in the field often enough. Turns out, it can be rewarding.

"What? Show him in," I hear Chapelle say. Then, he tells someone he'll have to call them right back and slams the desk phone receiver.

Beaming a megawatt smile, the receptionist invites me into Chapelle's office. He stands and walks around his massive desk to greet me with a handshake.

"Mr. Davis," he says, "what an honor! I'm a huge fan of your show."

His handshake is strong and enthusiastic, just as I like it. But that's where his appeal ends. At about forty, he has a polished look that's a little too slick in his off-white suit and light pink shirt. His hair, thinning at the temples, is dyed to hide the grays, and needs another treatment because roots are starting to show. The mustache, thick and perfectly trimmed, almost looks like a prop, part of a carefully constructed façade. His beady eyes are sharp but calculating as he sizes me up, with a faint, predatory glint that suggests he's always looking for an angle, a way to twist things to his advantage.

Just what I expected.

We take our seats at his conference table, and I don't waste any time.

"Mr. Chapelle, I've heard great things about your work."

He grins widely, showing two rows of white, slightly crooked teeth. "Thank you. Can I get you anything—"

"I'm impressed with your efforts to protect the rights of disabled people in our community. You're not allowing predatory businesses to get away with the abuse against the less fortunate, and that takes a certain kind of human being—a leader and a protector. A hero, if I may say so. Your recent class action against *Embers Steakhouse* was an eye-opener for us. They'll think twice before they cut corners on wheelchair accessibility."

"Oh, thank you," he replies, stuttering a little. "I'm doing my job the best I can."

The redness in his face is genuine, and so is the sweat that pops up at the roots of his thinning hair.

"I'd like to invite you onto my show, *The Final Question.* Perhaps you've heard of it?"

He can barely contain his excitement. He claps his hands together and grins widely. "Of course, I've heard of it. Who hasn't?" He's nervously wringing his hands, talking excitedly, out of breath. "I watch it every Friday." He clears his voice quietly and manages to slow his speech to a more professional level. "I would love to be on your show, Mr. Davis. I appreciate the invitation. Just say when and where," he adds, shifting in his seat.

We shake hands again.

"Good," I say slowly, leaning back into the cushy leather seat and staring straight at him. "This is what's going to happen on the show."

"Uh-huh," he says, nodding as I speak.

"We're going to introduce you, and talk a little about the latest cases you've won in defense of the rights of the disabled people of Los Angeles." I pause for effect, and I can tell he's holding his breath. "Then, I'll expose you for the complete fraud you are, right there on live television. I might even invite some of your victims onto the show—people you've pretended to represent, people who have no idea you exist. People whose identities you've used for your own benefit."

He gasps, turning pale and stiff. His jaw goes slack, and his hands fly to his throat as if he's chocking. For a moment, I'm afraid I might've pushed it too far, but he's not having a heart attack. He loosens his tie with trembling fingers, staring at me in shock.

"By the time they roll the credits, the cops will have you in cuffs."

"What—um, are you talking about?" He's trying to feign surprise, but fails miserably.

I cross my legs and fold my hands in my lap, and then I look at him silently for a moment, gauging the impact of my words. He's a wreck. His eyes are darting around the room as if he can barely keep himself from bolting out the door. He probably wouldn't stop until he got over the border, down Mexico way.

"At first, I didn't know if you're running a settlement mill or what. Turns out, everything was fake, even the doctors' notes you presented as evidence as part of your deal-making dossiers. I could end your scheming right now, and your freedom with it. With one phone call."

Chapelle stares at me, his eyes round and his pupils dilated. "What do you want, Mr. Davis? I can cut you in."

His offer makes me laugh. I reach into my pocket and pull out a five-dollar bill, then throw it on the table. "Or you could represent me."

He swallows with difficulty. His fingers tremble badly as he reaches out and grabs the fiver. The fear in his eyes is unmistakable. "Y-yes, sure. Anything you want."

"So, now I have attorney-client privilege?" I ask, watching him slip the bill into his pocket.

"Yes, sir."

It's a ridiculous question. I know that. What's to keep him from breaking this law on top of every other law he's trampled all over? But still, it means something to him. People like him—and me, for that matter—understand the value of a contract.

"Then, you'll send me someone I can trust with a certain car issue." My throat turns dry as I say the words. Once they're out there, my secret is no longer a secret. My future is in the hands of scum like Larry Chapelle and his cohorts.

"A mechanic?" he asks hesitantly, a confused frown on his face.

"Oh, you have to be smarter than this!" I snap. "I thought it took some brains to orchestrate the kind of scam you've been running, or perhaps I'm wrong? Any idiot can do it?"

He stares at me, seeming scared to even breathe.

I realize I'm wasting my time, kicking this dead horse in the balls, so I cut to the chase. "I need someone who can get me some car parts on the down-low, no paper trail. Someone discreet, mouth shut forever, someone I can trust. Someone I will fairly compensate for their efforts. I'll pay them double if they help me install those parts." I stop and stare at his stunned, ashen face. "Do you know a guy like that?"

He nods quickly, enthusiastically. He's probably dying to see me walk out of his posh office.

"Y-yes, I know someone. He's discreet. I helped him—"

I hold my hand up. "I don't need to know." I push a piece of paper over the table, with the number of my new burn phone. "Have him call me. Today."

"You got it."

I stand, but he remains seated, dumbstruck and breathing heavily. I find my way out of his office, even waving at him before closing the door behind me.

And as I smile at the fiery, double-D brunette seated behind the reception desk, all I can think about is how I might've made the biggest mistake of my life.

# 29

# AMANDA DAVIS

---

"I'm looking for Amanda Davis," the man says, flashing a badge. He walked in a moment ago, a bit hesitant, and managed to get in the way of an incoming emergency. Quick on his feet, he stepped aside, then stared after the gurney for a while as if the patient was someone he knew.

The nurse seated behind the reception desk throws me a glance, and I approach him, feeling a little weak at the knees. He's a cop, but someone I've never met before.

"I'm Amanda Davis," I say calmly. "What can I do for you?"

"Detective Eckhart," he says, flashing his badge again. He seems young. "You called about a BOLO."

"Oh. I spoke with a different detective...um, Jazinski, perhaps?"

The cop smiles. "He's my partner. He had something urgent to take care of and sent me instead." He shrugs and smiles.

"All right, then, please follow me."

I lead the way to Trauma Two, where the patient is sedated and intubated. "I'm afraid you won't be able to question him right now or any time soon, Detective."

"Please, call me Perry." He has a nice smile, but I still can't look him in the eye.

"Perry," I reply quietly. It's not unusual for cops and ED nurses to be on a first-name basis. It comes with the territory. "Danny usually handles these cases."

"Who?"

"Danny Bilger. He handles traffic cases south of the interstate."

He shifts uncomfortably from one foot to the other. "Well, I don't work in Traffic. I'm in Homicide."

I feel a chill. "Really? I didn't think anyone died—"

"Just helping with the workload is all," he rushes to explain, as if embarrassed. "Has anyone been to see him?" He's still standing in the doorway, somewhat hesitant to approach the patient.

"N-no, not that I know of," I reply, chocking on my words. "There was no wallet and no phone. We couldn't notify anyone. Is this the man you're looking for?"

He checks something on his phone, then looks at the patient's face. "Yes, that's him."

I plunge my hands into my pockets. "Well, then, we can notify you when he's regained consciousness, but I have to warn you, he's going to need surgery."

"What's wrong with him?"

I struggle over disclosing that information. I haven't seen a warrant or a subpoena. The best I can do is to keep what I reveal to the minimum.

"Cracked sternum, cracked ribs, and a small bleed in his lung. He'll be out of commission for a while."

The detective stares at the man for a moment, silently, then flips through the images on his phone. "A woman might come see him. She's blonde, mid-thirties, Caucasian. She might be his wife or partner or someone from his work. We don't know yet. But I'd appreciate a call the moment that happens." He hands me his business card.

Curiosity gets the best of me. "How do you know she's going to come here?"

"She was with him in the truck at the time of the crash." He shows me a traffic camera picture on his phone. "See here? Kind of blurry, I know, but she was there. We need to speak with her."

"About the crash?"

"About fleeing the scene. Amanda, is it?"

I smile weakly and nod. "Yes."

"This woman is just as responsible as he is."

"But she wasn't driving," I reply, my voice a little high-pitched, telling of my fears. "How is she to blame?"

"She isn't responsible for the crash itself, only for not reporting him for the hit-and-run. She could do some serious time for that. It's up to the DA and the judge." He shrugs again. "My job ends when I snap the cuffs on them."

I can barely hear his words. My heart's thumping heavily in my chest, drowning out the sound of his voice. The reminder that I could go to prison for not reporting Paul's crash slices through me, cold and sobering. *Oh, my God.* And everything else that I've done since.

It doesn't seem fair. Paul is my husband, for better or worse.

"Even if she's his wife? I thought wives—"

"Ah, you're talking about spousal privilege," he cuts me off. "She's got the right to not testify against her husband. It doesn't extend to covering his crimes. That's aiding and abetting, and it's a category C felony—and that's only because no one died."

My stomach churns. "Oh, I see. If someone would've died in the crash, she'd be in more serious trouble?"

"As in twenty-years-in-prison kind of trouble," the detective says coolly, whereas I grab the sliding door handle to steady myself. "It depends on the degree of her involvement, what she's done since the crash, if she had the opportunity to report the crime and all that. That's why we need to speak with her."

The beeping of the patient's monitor is all I can hear past the whirlwind of panicked thoughts in my mind. This is where they brought in Marisol last week. Here, in Trauma Two. That beautiful girl died here, while her mother sat by her side, her hand clasping her gaping mouth so she wouldn't scream.

"You'll call me?" the detective asks, then smiles. "If you see this woman, or if, you know, you have any questions? Or a sudden craving for a cup of coffee?"

I nod, unable to open my mouth and articulate words. I keep staring at the patient, but I don't see *him*. I see Marisol. As if the machine were still connected to her chest, I expect the beeps to start fading, then turn into the warning sound of a flatlining heart. And I know I wouldn't rush to resuscitate her... I'd let her go.

"Are you okay?" he asks. "You look pale."

"Um, yes, I'm okay," I say, managing a weak, apologetic smile. "I'm just thinking of the things people do." Unwilling to say more, I turn and leave.

"Don't even get me started on that one," he says, walking by my side toward the exit. "Good meeting you, Amanda." He shakes my hand and looks at me intently. "I think I know you from somewhere, don't I?"

I shrug and hide my hands inside my pockets, where he can't see them shaking. "I don't think so."

A tentative smile flutters on his lips for a brief moment, but then he nods and walks away. I return to the reception area. Sunny makes one of her usual comments regarding men's reactions to my charms, and I choose to ignore it. Spent and dizzy and torn inside, I lean against the wall.

The detective's words still echo inside my head.

*Twenty years in prison.*

# 30

# PAUL DAVIS

---

I'm so tense I could snap. Someone's neck, most likely.

Larry Chapelle's guy didn't call yesterday. I checked the phone—even called it myself to make sure it was working. But no call from the scumbag lawyer's man. I'm tempted to drive over to Wilshire Boulevard and tear the slimy bastard a new one. Or find he's long gone, his phone disconnected and his assistant sobbing on the unemployment line.

Either way, I told Aidan Chapelle wasn't a good fit for the show, and he should find someone else.

Then, my dear wife decided to give me the silent treatment all last night. I didn't mind it at first, but it got me antsy when I realized how out of the norm that was. She took care of Tristan, smiled and chatted with him, helped him with his homework...but she barely interacted with me. Side glances, scowls, and deep silences is all I get these days. When she locked herself in the guest bedroom as soon as she tucked our son in, I thought she might be on the phone with one of her precious cop friends. Then, I found her phone. She'd left it on the dining room table.

It took me a few attempts, but I eventually broke her passcode and looked at her recent activity. Nothing. She hadn't called or texted anyone since the car rental companies she went through on Friday morning. That is strange. Perhaps she, too, has a burner stashed somewhere safe. One she doesn't forget on the dining room table for me to find.

One thing, I know for sure. I can't trust her anymore. She wants me gone, out of her life, and wants full custody of my son. Not gonna fucking happen.

When I get to work on Wednesday afternoon, I have cops on my mind, along with crime scenes and my betraying wife selling me out cheap like I'm yesterday's news. I drive my car to its usual parking spot and start reversing into the spot, like I always do, but then I freeze. What if cops come by and check the VIN? It doesn't match the tags. Muttering oaths, I pull out, resituate, and then pull into the spot facing the wall.

But, I'm losing my mind. Why would cops troll the TV station's parking lot checking VINs?

I get out of the car and slam the door behind me. When I turn toward the elevators, I run into Latesha, remote-locking her car. She's with a young assistant producer, a young man whose name I can't recall. The bitch is everywhere, as if she's stalking me.

My blood chills at the thought. "Good afternoon," I greet them casually, as if I have no care in this world.

She smiles and nods, then gives my car a long stare. "Why the change, Paul?" she asks. "Something we should know about?"

"Like what?"

She chuckles, and her companion follows suit. "Well, I don't know. You tell me."

We're at the elevators, and the push of a button gets the doors to slide open. We climb in, and I check my reflection in the mirror, then straighten my posture and run my fingers through my hair, slicking it back.

"Nothing to say, I'm afraid. But I would suggest you find more meaningful hobbies than obsessing over what other people do."

The elevator dings and its doors slide open. "Not people, Paul. Just you." She shoots me a quick smile as she exits the elevator with her friend in tow.

I fall behind, struggling to swallow my anger while Latesha shamelessly talks on about me with that young assistant producer.

"He's something else, this guy," she's saying, her voice barely lowered. "Can you believe he dug up and affixed his mother's maiden name to his, when they were starting to make changes to the all-white cast of the show? He went by Paul Davis Gonzales for a while."

"What?" the man replies. "He claims to be Latino? He doesn't look it with those blue eyes."

"Yeah, half-blood, I guess, if it's even true. Didn't stop him from sleeping with his co-anchor at the time, Carly Crown. Everyone was talking about it. Apparently, she's a screamer."

"Get out," the man says, briefly touching her forearm before bursting into laughter. Then, they both disappear into the newsroom for the editorial meeting I'm supposed to be in.

A few moments later, I'm seated at the table with the entire crew, and Carly is distributing the day's rundown.

For a while, the only sound is that of papers rustling. No one speaks before I do.

I take a quick look at the rundown, but my mind is elsewhere. I pick on something at random. "This news block should come first," I say. "The lineup needs to be reworked. The wildfire court case is a headliner."

"I disagree," Latesha says. "We should open with the federal policy changes. That's national news."

I smirk at her and stare her down, but she defies me shamelessly. "They teach this in first-year journalism, Teesh. A-block is top stories and breaking news. National is B-block. You might want to read up on the rules of rundown, since you're a marketing grad and all that, no clue about journalism whatsoever."

Just as she's about to get nasty with me like she's done before, my burner phone rings. I leave the room in a hurry to take the call, rushing toward my dressing room.

"Hello," I say, sounding a little out of breath.

"What'cha need, bruh?"

"Excuse me?"

"My lawyer said you need some parts. Was he pulling my leg or something?"

"No, that's right, I need some parts. Can you get them?" He scoffs and doesn't answer. I take that as a yes. "I need the grille and the front—"

"Make and model?"

I close my dressing room door behind me and let myself drop into an armchair. "Cadillac XT6, last year's model."

"Trim?"

"Um, premium luxury. Black." My voice sounds a bit shaky, choked. What if this guy's a cop? What if that slimeball Chapelle sold me out? Cut himself a deal in the process?

"Gotcha. What d'ya break?"

I take a deep breath, steadying myself. "Front grille. Windshield. Bumper. Left headlight block. And dented the hood."

"Airbags?"

"No."

"On the inside? Radiator? Anything?"

*Fuck.* I didn't look. "Not that I noticed. Can you get all that?"

"They don't call me Fast Lane Foster for nothing." He laughs, a raspy cackle that irritates me like fingernails on a chalkboard. "But it'll cost you. Want just delivery? Or installed? That'll be double."

Something tells me bargaining or asking for a discount would not exactly get this job done. "Fine. As long as the parts are genuine, and the car looks like new when we're done."

"Alright, but don't say I didn't warn you."

"How long?"

"You'll have everything tomorrow." The call ends with a click, right after I give him my address. He's probably going to call again when he has the parts.

A soft click makes me look up and flinch. Carly is leaning against the dressing room door, smiling, her eyelids lowered, and her legs crossed at the ankles. Then, she locks the door with a quick turn of the deadbolt.

How long has she been standing there? How much did she overhear? *Motherfucker.*

She's watching me with that familiar spark in her eye. I know the look. Hell, I've seen it a hundred times on a hundred faces. But on her? It's got a different kind of charge. The one I've been dodging. Still, the memory of her body grinding against mine at the event last week stirs me below the belt.

"Some personal emergency?" she asks softly, walking over with her hips swaying just enough to remind me what I've been missing. She's close now...close enough that I catch the faintest hint of her perfume.

"Not really." I keep my tone light, watching as she slides onto the edge of my makeup table, her fingers playing with my tie like she has all the time in the world.

"We haven't really...talked in a while, have we, Paul?"

Since Thursday, really. Not that long of 'a while,' but she doesn't mean talking. I could play coy, but that's not what she wants. And hell, neither do I. If she overheard anything, what I'm about to give her will erase that memory.

I grin, leaning back just a little, giving her space to keep going. She pulls at my tie, her lips inches from mine, and yeah, this is definitely a bad idea. But that's never stopped me before. And she knows it.

"Careful, Carly," I whisper, just close enough to feel her breath. "You know what happens when you start things you can't finish."

She raises an eyebrow, challenging. "Who says I can't finish?"

That's all I need to hear. I close the distance, kissing her hard, pulling her against me. Her back arches, her hands in my hair and my hands on her waist, and there's no point pretending we don't both want this.

And I know I'm going to regret it, when she'll present me with the ask in return for her attention. But right now, I couldn't care less.

# 31

# AL JAZINSKI

Funny how a call from Her Honor restores my standing with the lieutenant. Just like that, like snapping fingers, we're pulled off that stupid traffic case and get assigned a homicide. It's always been like that. I do what she wants like a nice, little puppet. Then, things start happening for me.

I wonder what she's going to do about that asshat, Paul Davis. She said to give her time.

I'm about to grab the case file and leave when Eckhart comes in, a stupid grin on his face. I wave the file in front of him. "Body dump, partner. Saddle up."

His reaction is puzzling. I expected him to be thrilled and immediately start channeling his favorite actor. His voice goes lower-pitched when he does that, his phrases getting shorter. It's actually fun to watch. Instead, he's visibly disappointed.

"How about the hit-and-run? I found the guy. He's—"

"Traffic will handle that. Lieu gave it to their sergeant."

A deep breath and a quick shrug—him feigning indifference. He doesn't fool me for a second. "Alright, then, what do we got?"

I open the case file. Only one page is stapled there. The incident report. "That's all I got."

While I drive, he reads the hand-written notes. "Dog walker found the body. It's up on Malibu Canyon Road, in the ravine."

I know that already. As I make my way through heavy traffic, I shoot Eckhart a quick look. He's not bad-looking, and definitely not touched by old age yet. His abs are lean and ripped, his back is straight, and three-day stubble actually looks good on him. If I wore that, I'd look unkempt. Life isn't fair, but I bet I know why he's not so happy about letting that hit-and-run go.

"Did you meet anyone interesting at the hospital?" I ask as I take the left lane up onto Malibu Canyon Road and turn on the lights and siren. The right lane is completely blocked, but nothing comes down from the mountain. The road is probably closed by now.

"Damn it to hell, partner!" He laughs. "How did you know?"

"You have to ask?" I say, laughing hard as I pull over at the crime scene.

It's already taped up. A large section of the road has been secured. The Crime Scene Unit is canvassing, and the coroner's van is parked sideways, rear facing the ravine.

A couple of CSU techs crouch near the guardrail, collecting evidence in small plastic pouches. They seal those quickly, sign the dotted lines, and then drop them in a plastic container, one after another, a conveyor belt of evidence. Another CSU tech is taking pictures, placing yellow-numbered markers at various spots where new evidence is being found.

Eckhart and I get out of the car, walking toward the CSU team. The air is thick with the salty mist of the ocean and the dry, dusty smell of the canyon.

"Detectives." A CSU tech nods as we approach, gesturing to the evidence markers scattered around the road. "Looks like a hit-and-run with cover-up. Real messy." He points at something near the guardrail. "The roadway was clear, but there's debris from the crash here, stuck in the dirt."

With a groan, I kneel down near the guardrail, where fragments of plastic and chrome glint under the CSU tech's flashlight. It's a palm-sized piece of honeycomb car grille, cracked and scratched to hell. Eckhart crouches beside me, his eyes narrowing as he studies the debris.

"Looks like a recent model," the technician mutters, running his gloved fingers over the jagged edge. "Maybe a sedan. High-end. The plastic is new and good quality."

"Looks that way," I say, filing away the thought. "You'll give me the make and model?"

"Probably," he replies, two fingers at his forehead in a mock military salute. He can't be a day older than twenty-five, but I know him. He's really good, in the way modern forensics are done. It's all a big database now.

We stop by the edge of the ravine. It's not too deep, the bottom covered in shrubs. Some of the greenery was removed to expose the dump site.

A few yards down the road, near the edge of the ravine, the coroner, Dr. Evans, stands beside the body, her gloved hands on her hips. She's wearing some of those CSU coveralls in white plastic; she must be boiling. Ropes are still attached to the rescue gurney she's used to retrieve the body. I'm a little surprised she didn't wait for me before removing it from down there, but knowing her, she had her reasons.

Dr. Evans is inspecting the surroundings, her face impassive. She glances up as we approach, nodding once.

"Hello, Detectives. The vic is female, about fifty years old. She took a serious hit. Dead on impact, by the looks of it." She gestures to the body lying on the gurney. "She's got multiple fractures along the left side—neck, rib cage, arm, leg. And—" she points to the scalp, but I'm not close enough to see what she's showing me, "this little souvenir. I'll confirm it at autopsy, but I'd bet it's automotive glass."

Eckhart shifts his weight, his gaze fixed on the body. "What about blood?"

Dr. Evans nods. "These injuries would've bled a lot. CSU found a small, dried pool of blood under a rock. I'll have to confirm, so don't quote me on this, but there's evidence she was killed just before that heavy rain started last week. So, I can give you preliminary time of death quite accurately. Last Thursday night, sometime between midnight and one-thirty. I'll know with more precision once I confirm with the Weather Service."

Eckhart whistles. "That's amazing, Doc. But then, how is there blood—" Eckhart starts to ask, but she cuts him off.

"It was under the guardrail, *and* under a rock. And not too much of it, but enough to try and match DNA to our vic."

Eckhart crouches down to study the place the CSU tech is pointing at, a boulder clearly marked by a crime scene tag.

"Maybe she was thrown by the impact?" I ask, scanning the area. "As opposed to discarded over the guardrail on purpose?"

The CSU tech speaks up from behind us. "We found traces of blood under that rock and a few other places, like she was tossed or tumbled a bit before coming to a stop there, at the bottom of the ravine. Nothing on the upper road, though, so it looks like the impact happened right around here."

Eckhart stands and adjusts his jacket. "So, we've got a probable hit-and-run. No brake marks; no swerve. Driver hit her, panicked, and kept going."

The coroner frowns. "Listen, there's no way a person hit by a car would've landed so neatly straight and aligned to the side of the road like this one did. They had to have pushed her. Driver hit her, and she landed on the road. They tried to hide her body, and *then* drove off."

"Got it," I reply. "You'll confirm?"

Dr. Evans scoffs. "When have I not?"

I smile apologetically and hold my hands up in a pacifying gesture. "You're the best, Doc."

Eckhart still stares at the guardrail, scratching his head, then crouches again. "Or it rained and washed out everything on the main road, and they dragged her and threw her over the guardrail."

"Under," Dr. Evans says. "See here?" She points a gloved finger at the edge of the road, where asphalt meets compacted dirt. "The loose gravel here was disturbed. See this section, about the length of our victim, that seems as if it was broomed off? Her body was rolled under the guardrail and pushed into the ravine, right here."

I follow the direction of her glance. "Do I need to go down there?"

"Up to you, but if you don't mind, I'd like to move this along before it gets dark."

"Fine by me," I reply, after giving Eckhart a quick glance. He's still crouched down by the CSU tech, examining the blood that was found on the side of the road. "Any ID yet?"

The coroner shakes her head. "No wallet, no phone, no fingerprints in our system."

"Damn," I reply. "Anything else you can give me?"

"I'll know more after the autopsy. Time of death, exact injuries, her identity...hopefully. But I can tell you it was a high-speed collision."

A CSU tech walks up holding a small evidence bag with another piece of glass and a few flecks of black paint. Another bag holds a tiny speck of something red and shiny. "This was collected from the dirt underneath the guardrail. Looks like we might have a color match on the vehicle."

Eckhart gives me a knowing look. "Black paint, high-end vehicle, grille fragments. That narrows it down."

"What's the red stuff? Was there more than one car involved?"

"I'd have to look into it. It's not car paint. It seems to be covered in protective enamel."

I stare at him, unsure what that means.

"Like you'd find on a car's badge," he adds. "I'm not sure yet that it's from the same car, but if it is, this would help us narrow it down very quickly. Makes sense?"

Just what I wanted to hear. I nod, feeling the pieces starting to line up. "Yeah, it does. Smashed grille goes well with a damaged badge. Let's see if anyone saw or heard anything—car lights, a sound, anything."

As Eckhart starts talking to another tech, I look down the road, the evening air heavy around me. Beyond the crime scene tape, traffic is halted, and most of the cars have their engines off. I listen for a moment and don't hear much except for the occasional bird cry. As far as crashes are concerned, I'd say this is the ideal spot to hit someone and get away with it. Probably, no one saw or heard anything.

I look around and take in the surroundings. Steep rock on the left side of the road. A twenty-foot-deep ravine on the right, where the vic was found. At least a mile to the nearest dwelling. What was this fifty-year-old woman doing here? Was she alone?

This case just got a lot more interesting.

# 32

# PAUL DAVIS

---

"Bye, Dad," Tristan says from the door, dragging his backpack across the floor in that lazy, careless way that drives me nuts. His school clothes hang on him like he threw them on last minute, completing the look of a slob.

I wave at him without taking my eyes off Amanda. She stands impatiently, tugging at Tristan's hand, but he looks behind as if he forgot something. It can only be one thing.

"Did you take your lunch?"

"Uh-uh." He stares at the floor and plays with the backpack strap.

Amanda groans and rushes back into the kitchen. She opens the fridge, takes out Tristan's lunch bag, and then slams the door shut.

"Are you coming back before your shift?" I ask casually, taking another sip of coffee. I put the cup down and resume buttoning my shirt. Even if it's Friday, I still have about five hours until I'm due at work, and I'd love a few minutes alone with my wife. She and I barely talked this week, and I'm sure she's got a lot on her mind that I'd better know about.

"No," she replies coldly. "Going straight to work after I drop Tristan off. And we have to pick up Dylan, too."

The sound of the slammed garage door echoes in the silence. *Is she spilling her guts to someone?* It's all I can think about. I imagine her betraying me, selling me out, because it would work so damn well for her. If I'm convicted, she'd get her divorce, full custody, the house, and the whole shebang. Just like she'd like it. So, then, why am I not arrested yet? What's keeping her from calling the cops? What the hell is going on?

I finish getting dressed and start pacing the floor, staring at my burner phone. The parts guy didn't call back, and it's been two days. How long does it fucking take to get a few car parts these days? I tried calling him last night and got nothing. Something tells me the price goes up for every call he's not picking up.

Angry as hell, I slip the burner into my pocket and down the rest of the coffee, deciding to go into work early. Maybe Carly's in the mood for a quickie before the editorial meeting. I need that release. I know what she's after; she wants her co-anchor job back, but I'm not going to tell her it's not really up to me. Good ol' Raymond has no need for the kind of attention she's giving. Let her hope. They say hope is good for the soul. Definitely good for mine.

Once in my rental Cadillac, I hit the ignition, and the garage door whirrs open. I'm barely out when an old, beat-up Chevy truck rumbles onto the driveway, blocking my exit. I slam the brakes, gripping the wheel as I stop inches short of needing parts for yet another Cadi.

I step out and throw my hands up. "Hey!" My gesture says it all—*What the hell do you want?*

The driver steps out slowly, all six-foot-five of him. Thick arms covered in prison ink and a neck bulging with muscle, and his skin glistens with sweat under the afternoon sun. His hair's buzzed short, and he's got that clean-shaven look that screams he's fresh out of lock-up. Dressed in faded jeans and a threadbare mesh tank, he grins, showing gold caps on his front teeth as he ambles over with an easy swagger, each step deliberate, like he owns my driveway.

He eyes the Cadillac, circling it slowly, hands on his hips. His arms look thick as tree trunks—enough muscle to snap me like a pencil.

Then, he looks at me, visibly confused. "What d'you need the parts for?"

I exhale, relieved but tense. "Are you...Mr. Foster?"

"That's what they call me." He grins wider, eyes gleaming. "Don't make it sound so formal, though. Foster's enough. Ain't my real name anyway."

"Oh. Right." I look him over, taking in the scars, the tattoos. "Good to meet you...Foster."

He props a hand on his hip, eyes narrow. "So, we gonna do this right here in the sun, or you wanna show me what needs fixin' before we're both gray and wrinkled?"

I swallow, my throat suddenly dry. "Yeah. This way."

I lead him into the garage and gesture at the damaged Cadi. He gives it a slow, thorough once-over, running his fingers along the bumper and inspecting every scratch and dent. When he spots the cracked plastic near the fender, he whistles low.

"Not a light tap, huh?" He looks at me with a smirk, his eyes catching the glint of something I'd rather not face. "And you got two of these Cadillacs."

"Wanted to sell this one," I say, shrugging, avoiding his gaze. "But...things happened."

He stares at me for a long second, then lets out a short chuckle. "Whatever you say, bruh."

"Can you handle it?"

"They don't call me Fast Lane for nothing." He flashes a grin, but it's all teeth. His eyes stay deathly cold.

I glance toward the street, noticing the few passersby walking their dogs or heading off somewhere. "So...think we could, uh, keep it on the down-low?"

He scoffs, shaking his head. "Get that other car out of the way so I can back the truck in. Better if the neighbors don't see me unloadin' all this 'custom work.' You feel me?"

My stomach twists, my mind racing. This guy could probably kill me with one hand. And here I am, following orders like an idiot. My shoes are worth more than his truck, and I'm about to lock myself into the garage with him.

"Right," I say, and rush to move the rental out of the way. Once he's inside, I rush back to close the garage door, keeping any prying eyes out.

He's already unloading, propping up parts along the garage wall. None of them are in boxes. I can picture some guy out there mourning his stolen XT6, probably stripped bare in some garage in Boyle Heights.

"You didn't mention these trims were cracked," he says, tapping the plastic above the bumper. "I'll get 'em, but don't be hidin' stuff on me."

"Fine, fine." I clear my throat. "Can you start tomorrow? I'll be here to…you know, help."

"I'll try for tomorrow, but I'm not sure." He scratches his head, giving me a slow, assessing look. "It'll run you twenty-five grand. Cash. Small bills."

I let out a low whistle before I can stop myself. He notices, his face hardening. "We gonna have a problem here?"

"No problem." I force a smile, trying to sound casual. "I'll have it ready tomorrow." I don't know how, but I will. I have to.

His grin returns, still cold as ice. He claps a heavy hand on my shoulder, and it takes everything in me not to flinch. "That's my man! We're in business."

I watch him turn back to the Cadillac, inspecting the grille closely. Then, he pauses, raising an eyebrow. "You missed somethin' here," he says, pointing at the damaged grille. "Some blood right there. Bet there's more under the hood, too."

My stomach churns, a wave of nausea hitting me. I move closer, heart pounding, to see what he's pointing at. "Where?"

"Gotcha." He lets out a low chuckle, clapping his hands together like he just hit the jackpot. "And that makes it fifty grand, Mr. Davis. Now that I know just what kind of fixin' we're doin'."

I stare at him, rage flaring up despite my fear. "Fine. But that's it. Not a penny more, or you'll see I've got street skills, too."

He just laughs, a deep, mocking sound. "Whatever you say, bruh."

Watching him drive off, my mind is racing. There's nothing stopping Fast Lane Foster from bleeding me dry for the rest of my life.

*I'm so screwed.*

# 33

# AMANDA DAVIS

---

I don't know why I said yes.

As if my life wasn't complicated enough without having lunch with my boss. Then, after agreeing, when he wanted to take me to a nicer place in West Hollywood, I was too embarrassed to say no, although I would've been happier to share a quick bite at the diner across the street, where the hospital staff usually goes.

Still wearing scrubs, we stand out among the thinning, mid-afternoon crowd. It's a late lunch, but our shift isn't exactly a nine-to-five. The food is delicious, and his presence is calming and reassuring and just plain pleasant. It's not the thrilling, passionate, desperately-in-love feeling I still recall from my early days with Paul, but thank goodness for that, and why did I think of that in the first place? What's happening also isn't the hostile tension of my most recent years with Paul. It's just plain good...like lunch with a friend should feel like.

That's what Dr. Grant is to me. A work friend.

The conversation is lively at first, as we mostly discuss the cases of the day and tidbits of human behavior we both seem to enjoy dissecting. What that man did when he found out the wife was actually pregnant at 46. How the adult children of the 79-year-old man who just had a stroke reacted to the news.

But then we drift into longer silences and the personal questions I'm dreading. Still, one way to keep them at bay is to ask them, instead of answering.

"What's your biggest challenge these days?" I ask, clinging on to the work theme tooth and nail. Staring at my meal salad as if it holds any answers, I stab a seasoned crouton with my fork and chew on that crunchy goodness slowly, casually.

"In my personal life?" he asks, swallowing the last bit of steak left in his salad bowl. "I'd have to say the dating scene. It's horrendous, and so not my thing. This entire remote, online way to meet people is insane. Depersonalized. It feels transactional and hollowing."

"Ah…I thought you were married," I throw in there, since he opened the door. I seem to recall him wearing a wedding band a few months ago.

"Widowed. Brain aneurysm."

"I'm so sorry," I whisper. I could kick myself right now. "How old was she?"

"Twenty-seven. It was a congenital defect. She was pregnant, and her blood pressure spiked." He plays with the remaining pieces of lettuce in his bowl, pushing them around with his fork. "I lost them both that day."

"I am really sorry." My instinct takes over. I reach over the table and squeeze his hand gently, the way I do with my patients. Then, realizing what I'm doing, I pull away quickly. "I'm sorry," I whisper, feeling my face burning.

He smiles. "How about you? Why am I sensing things aren't exactly that great for LA's most beautiful couple?"

I hate it when people call us that. Since that fundraiser, I've heard it everywhere because, of course, everyone's seen it on television, and they feel compelled to comment. But I'm uncomfortable replying. My answer will be nothing but a well-constructed stack of lies. "Really? Why do you say that?"

"You seem…grim. As if you're grieving, or struggling with some personal issue."

"Ah, I see." I breathe, feeling a bit relieved. "It's very tiring, all the media attention my husband is getting, and my role in his initiatives. But it's for a good cause, and I keep doing it, even if sometimes I—" I stop, a little choked.

He reaches over the table and squeezes my hand. "That's not all, is it?"

Hearing his gentle voice brings the sting of tears to my eyes. "We should go. It's getting late."

"Amanda—"

"Please, Dr. Grant, let's just—"

"It's Michael," he replies with a kind smile.

I pull my hand out of his, regretting it. "Well, Michael...my boss, Dr. Grant, will write me up if I'm late for work," I say, hiding behind humor as if it's a cloak. "Thank you for a wonderful lunch."

I stand up while he rushes to the host's desk to take care of the check. I watch him, noticing things I haven't before. How a few strands of his tousled hair land over his forehead. How the hostess treats him with the right amount of deference, probably in response to his dark blue scrubs. I'm used to women salivating over my husband like he's a piece of meat, hunting him like they're mindless, sexual zombies. It's refreshing to witness a normal interaction.

"Amanda! What an unexpected pleasure." The voice behind those words gives me a start.

I'd recognize the woman's pitch anywhere. It's smooth and perfectly modulated, with deliberate and crisp pronunciation. I turn on my heels as if I've heard the hissing of a snake in the grass.

"Oh, Carly, good to see you."

She kisses the air around my cheeks, and I pretend to enjoy the interaction. Her perfume is vaguely familiar, but this isn't the first time she's hugged me. It's a clingy, floral scent, high-end and memorable.

"Sorry, I'm in hospital garb," I say as an excuse for pulling away, painfully aware of how lame that sounds.

She waves off my concern with the generosity of someone who's always been dressed to the nines and knows it. I meant I was pulling away because of germs, not fashion, but her mind obviously didn't go there.

"And who's this?" she asks, shamelessly sizing up Dr. Grant.

"This is my boss," I say quite coldly, "Dr. Grant."

"Oh, so you're *working*, I guess!" She laughs, her hand lingering in the shake Dr. Grant gives her. "Very nice," she says, the double entendre laid on thick. Then, she winks at me and hugs me again. "Well, I have to run. I'm late for a lineup meeting with *my* boss."

That's Paul, and she knows that I know.

I watch her leave, speechless. I'm not jealous, as Dr. Grant seems to have considered for a moment. He says, "Must be difficult, knowing your husband is surrounded by all these women. But if he's even thinking of looking their way, he's an idiot."

*Oh, he's doing so much more than looking,* I think of saying. But that's not Dr. Grant's problem.

The entire drive back to the hospital, I'm silent in my seat, trying to keep a hint of a pleasant smile on my face and failing. Concern rises up inside me like the tides. What if Carly opens her big mouth and tells Paul I was having lunch with someone, and holding hands if she saw that? What if someone else saw us?

It might push Paul over the edge, and there's no telling what he could do then.

# 34

# PAUL DAVIS

When I get to the station, it's already late, and the editorial meeting has started without me. I'm interrupting the usual dispute over segment lineup. Without making any apologies, I take my seat at the head of the table, and the lively chatter subsides just enough for others to throw some greetings my way while I read the lineup prepared by Carly.

She's nowhere to be seen, which is unusual, but probably for the best because of what I have to say.

Setting the lineup printout on the table, I hold my hands in the air to silence everyone. The arguments subside. "This is boring, people! I'm not going on air with this nonsensical drivel. You're telling me, nothing newsworthy happened in Los Angeles since yesterday? No one was killed? No movie star caught in a DUI? No one wrapped their Lambo around a pole?"

"If you'd been here on time," Latesha says with a smile, "you'd know we're actually arguing over positions three and onward. Carly's typing up the headliner as we speak."

"What's the headliner?" I ask, my interest piqued. Must be something big, if Carly left the meeting to type it up herself.

Latesha's smile is even more annoying than her glares. The perfectly white teeth, the lush lip color, the sparks of narcissistic arrogance in her eyes. "You'll love it," she replies cryptically.

I shrug, refusing to give her the satisfaction of insisting. "And what's our second story?"

"Capsized yacht a mile off of Santa Monica Pier."

I shrug again, and return to flipping through the printed lineup.

"Just wait till you hear whose yacht it is," Aidan whispers, leaning toward me.

I look at my assistant, but refuse to ask the question. He knows better than to wait for me to ask.

"The chief of police was on it," he adds excitedly. "Not with his wife. *And* during business hours."

That's gotten my attention. *Fucking cops.* "Who was he with?"

"Two girls, one barely eighteen. The boat itself was loaned to him without paperwork, from the impound pool. And the chief himself was butt-naked when the Coasties fished him out of the pond."

A grin lands on my face. "Ah," I say, rubbing my hands. "Love it. And *this* takes the second slot? What the hell is that headliner, then? Who died?"

Carly's heels trot in with the rhythm of her excitement as she approaches the conference table.

"It bleeds, it leads, people!" She distributes the one-page headliner copy to everyone seated at the table. "I'm still waiting for second confirmation on the yacht story, and we're good for tonight."

"What are you still waiting for? The Coast Guard should be able to confirm the capsizing incident."

"The capsizing isn't the issue," she replies, leaning against the table low enough to display a first-class view of her cleavage. "Seems the barely-eighteen girl's birthday is next month, moving her from barely to almost, and shifting the chief of police into felony land. *That*, we need to double-confirm."

"Whoa," I react, though my excitement at breaking such piece of juicy news is somewhat dampened by the concern with fact-checking and Raymond's takeover plans. The last thing we need is to make an enemy out of the blue force. "And this is still not the first slot? Why?"

Carly's smile widens as she points to the piece of paper I'm holding. "Read for yourself."

The headline grabs my attention, and blood freezes in my veins. My breath catches, leaving me unable to breathe, think, or even see straight. The words blur on the page, but I can't look away. Each sentence hits like a punch to the gut. "An unsettling mystery... woman's body... Malibu Canyon Road..." My pulse pounds in my ears, drowning out the voices around me in the meeting. I can't even hear the laughter over some half-baked joke about Malibu's never-ending supply of drama. None of it lands.

The page is shaky between my fingers, crinkling slightly. I force myself to breathe, to play it cool, but it's like my body's gone rogue. My hands are clammy, and I can feel the sweat creeping along the back of my neck. I force myself to read every word while my entire being screams silently.

### HEADLINE: Unsolved Hit-and-Run Death on Malibu Canyon Road

#### PAUL:

*Breaking tonight, an unsettling mystery in the hills of Malibu. Authorities are investigating the discovery of a woman's body along Malibu Canyon Road, believed to be the victim of a hit-and-run that likely occurred last week, sometime before last Thursday's storm washed over the area.*

#### REPORTER (at the scene):

*Here on Malibu Canyon Road—known for its sharp turns and steep drop-offs—investigators are piecing together what happened. Evidence at the scene—including fragments from a broken car grille, shattered glass, and blood spatter—suggests the collision happened before the heavy rains swept through last Thursday night.*

*But many questions still remain unanswered... the victim's identity, one of them. Why was she here, on this isolated stretch of road? And why did the driver disappear without a trace?*

**PAUL (VO visuals of Malibu Canyon Road):**
*Detectives are searching for answers, working to understand the full picture behind this tragic incident. Could there be more to the story?*

**REPORTER:**
*For now, officials are asking that anyone who may have noticed anything unusual on Malibu Canyon Road last week come forward. This is a developing story, and we'll continue to provide updates as they emerge.*

"Are you okay?" Carly's hand touches my arm, snapping me back. I nod and look at her, dazed and emerging from the nightmare. She looks genuinely concerned, and it's exactly what I can't have happening. "You look pale," she adds, touching my forehead with the back of her hand as if I'm a child.

I pull away. "I'm okay, just a bit tired. And hungry," I add, shooting Aidan a quick glance. The young man doesn't need more direction. He leaves the room in a hurry. In a moment or two, he'll be back with an assortment of my favorite donuts and a stiff coffee—props to help me survive the day.

I stare at the printout. It's too specific—every detail dragging me closer to the edge. My mind spins with excuses, plausible lies, some kind of explanation I could come up with if they look at me too hard. I tell myself they don't know yet, that they *can't possibly* know. But it's like I'm teetering on a cliff, and one wrong move, one wrong breath, could send me over.

"Do you have a crew at the scene?" I ask Carly.

She nods. "Yup, they left thirty minutes ago. I emailed them the copy. It'll be ready in time, don't worry."

I look at Latesha and wonder if I should let her read the headliner for a change. I'm afraid my throat will turn dry as sand and I'll choke while reading it. Today's options are pure shit: the story of my own crime, and a segment that's going to antagonize the chief of police and a good part of his blue army.

But I can't make any changes to our set routine; that would stand out like a sore thumb. Worse, it would get to Latesha's head and make her even more insufferable than she already is. I'm the lead anchor, so I read the headliner. Always. And it's just a story…it will blow over.

*Will it?*

# 35

# AMANDA DAVIS

I don't catch my breath after the lunch with Dr. Grant—not for hours. Emergencies roll in one after another, leaving me no time to think or try to avoid being alone with him in the break room. There's no chance for a break, and for once, I'm grateful. That lunch was a bad idea, and it's not just because I ran into Carly. It's because I *enjoyed* it. The connection with Dr. Grant feels genuine, like something I haven't felt in a while.

And now, I regret it. I can't help fearing it will make things weird between us at work.

The latest patient is patched up and sent upstairs to the operating room, and it's Sunny's turn to handhold the transfer. I linger in the reception area, where the TV on the wall shows the intro graphics for the evening news. It's tuned to GSB News, as always—everyone here feels they have to support Paul's station. "Paul is part of the family," Dr. Martinez once said.

But now, hearing the muted news theme, I discreetly roll my eyes. Then, when Sunny rushes back from the elevators and puts the volume up, I roll them again. I think she's a bit smitten with my husband. If only she knew.

The graphics fade and the image shifts to the studio. I take a few steps closer, drawn to the screen, and then stop. Something's off. There's a tightness around Paul's mouth. His jaw is clenched, even as he forces a smile and says his opening greeting. His eyes, usually steady and confident, seem a shade darker, flicking over to the teleprompter.

Then, he starts talking. His hands, steepled on the desk in front of him, tremble slightly.

Nervous, I grab the remote from Sunny's hand and push the volume up even more.

"...in the hills of Malibu," Paul's steady voice fills the air. "Authorities are investigating the discovery of a woman's body along Malibu Canyon Road, believed to be the victim of a hit-and-run that likely occurred last week, sometime before last Thursday's storm washed over the area."

I freeze, a chill prickling my skin despite the heat. It doesn't seem real, hearing his steady, composed tone relaying the details of the horrific secret we've been keeping. Each phrase twists like a knife in my stomach. Feeling faint and nauseous, I falter backward until I'm leaning against the reception desk.

The image cuts to the reporter on the scene, and I recognize where he is. I'll never forget that spot. He's standing right where blood pooled at my feet that night.

"Here on Malibu Canyon Road—known for its sharp turns and steep drop-offs—investigators are piecing together what happened," the reporter is saying, while I heave, breathless. "Evidence at the scene—including fragments from a broken car grille, shattered glass, and blood spatter—suggests the collision happened before the heavy rains swept through."

His words blur as my pulse races, and a wave of nausea slams into me, sharp and relentless. It's hard to breathe. My face burns hot, then cold, my hands shaking as I grip the edge of the reception desk, desperate for something solid to hold on to.

Paul's voice returns, paired with some shots of Malibu Canyon Road from the very place it happened. He seems his normal self now, steady and charismatic and with just the right amount of empathy and grimness. My chest tightens with guilt and dread as the man I used to trust calmly recounts our crime like it's any other story.

I barely make it, bending down and reaching blindly for the trash can under the desk just as my stomach heaves. My body betrays me, revolting against the reality I'm not prepared to face, and I retch into the can, weak and exposed. The acrid taste lingers, bile stinging the back of my throat as I try to catch my breath.

Sunny rushes to my side. "Amanda, are you okay?"

I can't look at her. Can't speak yet. I'm still holding on to the edge of the desk, staring at the trash can. She hands me some tissue, then a paper cup filled with water from the cooler, rushed over by Dr. Grant.

Humiliated and shaky, I stand up straight, keeping my eyes lowered. "I must be coming down with something," I whisper. "Sorry, you guys... This is embarrassing."

"You know better than to apologize for the functions of your body, right?" Sunny says, running her hand over my back in a reassuring gesture. Dr. Grant stares at me, but doesn't say anything.

Even after the nausea passes, the panic and shame cling to me, tightening around my throat. I wipe my mouth, my mind spinning, wondering how much longer I can hold myself together in a world where Paul's voice, calm and practiced, conceals the nightmare we share while broadcasting it to everyone. Deep down, I know this is only the beginning—and that terrifies me more than anything else.

Just as Dr. Grant starts telling me I should go home for the day, a thought starts spinning in my mind like a caged animal desperate to break free.

*I have to find a way out of this.*

# 36

# PAUL DAVIS

The second I walk in the door, I see Amanda. She's standing in the hallway, arms folded tightly across her chest, her face pale and her eyes hard. I feel a surge of anger and fear all at once, boiling up before I can even catch my breath. How dares she judge me? She has no right.

We lock eyes, and in a second, we're moving toward each other, whispering in urgent, furious tones, barely containing the tension that's stretched taut between us.

"We can't talk here," she hisses. "Tristan—"

I glance toward the living room, where my son dozed off watching TV while lying on the floor, the sound of cartoons faintly spilling out. We're stuck. There's nowhere to send him—not for a few days, not even for a night. Amanda's father, that hard-assed sea dog, is out at sea, his ship God knows where, and my parents are working around the clock in New York.

"Fine," I say through clenched teeth. "But keep your voice down."

She bites back a retort, and I see her jaw tightening as she struggles to hold it together. Her face is so pale, it's like the life's drained right out of her. And that makes two of us.

"What did you think you were doing?" she whispers fiercely. "Talking about it on live TV?"

She's being irrational and she knows it.

"Do you think I had a choice?" I shoot back. "I can't kill a story when the producers hand it to me. They'd notice! I'm sure other stations had it, too." I run my fingers through my hair.

"It's out there now. And tomorrow, another body will be found, and this crap will be forgotten. This is LA, remember?"

Her eyes throw daggers at me, and her lips are pressed into a hard, thin line.

"Keep telling yourself that," she eventually says. "Remember that cop? The one who stopped next to us on our way home? When he sees the news, don't you think he'll put two and two together?"

The thought slices through me like a knife. "Yeah. There's that...or they'll find something," I say finally, drowning in the wave of anxiety that's swallowing me whole. "They'll comb over that road, every damn inch of it. What if we left something behind? We didn't check—"

"The rain," she cuts in, her voice trembling but steady. "It washed everything away. Remember? It poured for hours. Everything we might've missed...it's gone."

Her words should reassure me, but they don't. They just make the fear sharper, harder to contain. "It's not gone. They found pieces of the grille, and blood. And here?" I ask, voice low. "What if there's something here? They could come knocking at the door any moment with a search warrant."

Her eyes widen as the thought clicks into place. Without another word, she's rushing past me, into the laundry room. I follow, my pulse pounding in my throat. She grabs a bottle of peroxide from the cleaning cabinet, hands shaking, and unscrews the cap. Then, she fits it with the sprayer taken from a bottle of Windex and goes into the garage.

"Amanda, stop!" I say, trying to sound calm. "We went through the carwash that night three times. There was barely any blood on the inside."

"But there was some!" she snaps, spraying peroxide on a rag. "A few drops. We didn't see everything, not in that state, not...not then." She climbs into the Cadillac, spraying the seats and the dashboard, and then scrubbing along the edges of the cracked windshield, watching the peroxide fizz and foam as it settles in the crevices.

"Amanda, enough," I whisper, my own voice fraying at the edges. "We checked everything. The windshield's being replaced. Anything left is...it's nothing."

"They can still find it." She pulls back, her hands trembling as she stares at the spots where the peroxide still bubbles. "Peroxide doesn't foam unless it burns organic matter, like blood or saliva. So, there's still *something*." The silence between us is thick, pressing down until, finally, she says, "What about the clothes?"

The clothes. The shoes. The things we wore that night, stuffed in the wash in a panic. The thought hadn't even crossed my mind. A cold ripple courses through me.

"They were washed," I say, my voice barely a whisper. "That night. You washed everything, remember? Even my underwear."

She stares at me, eyes wide, with fear etched into every line of her face. "Once isn't enough," she says, her voice shaking. "It's never enough." She bolts out of the garage, leaving me frozen in place, and I hear the laundry room door open, the sound of the washing machine lid clanging back. Moments later, she's back from upstairs with an armful of clothing and holding up the pair of shoes I wore that night. She sets everything on the floor, then starts spraying them down with peroxide, her movements frantic. Desperate.

"Amanda, stop!" I whisper, grabbing her hand. "You're going to ruin my shoes. They're Hermès, for fuck's sake. This is too much."

"I don't care!" she says, her voice raw, her eyes glassy with panic. "I don't care if they're ruined! They can't find anything, Paul. Not a drop, not a speck. And blood hides. In seams, in lace endings...it could be anywhere, and they'll find it."

She's being irrational. We should throw everything in the trash, by her logic, and be done with it. It drives me crazy when she turns frantic like this.

She douses the shoes again, squeezing the peroxide until it soaks through the leather, until the soles drip, her hands trembling as she looks for any sign, any trace that we missed. I just watch her, feeling my own fear clawing at me as if every fizzling bubble, every bead of peroxide, carries the weight of what could happen to me.

When she finally stops, she looks up at me with her face ghostly pale. Her hands are soaked, the shoes in her grip barely recognizable, the leather is so stained and drenched. She sets them down on the rubber mat with a long, exhausted sigh.

"Okay," she says, her voice barely a whisper. "That's it. It has to be enough."

The laundry room door is pushed open and gives me a start. Amanda flinches and nearly drops the bottle of peroxide.

"Mom?" It's Tristan, dragging the hems of his pajama pants on the floor and stepping on them, his feet bare. "What are you doing?"

Amanda smiles at him, pale as a sheet. "Laundry, baby. We'll be done in a minute Want a snack?"

"Uh-huh," he says, shifting his weight from one foot to the other, undecided. He looks at us with a wrinkle of concern on his forehead. "I'm hungry."

"Go watch your cartoons. I'll make you something in just a minute," Amanda replies. Her voice sounds so normal, like nothing is wrong.

My wife is the perfect liar.

The door squeaks as it closes. Then, the cartoon sounds resume, a little louder than before.

"I think this is enough," she says after spraying copious amounts of peroxide over the clothes she threw into the washer. She closes the lid, then programs the washer on the longest cycle, adding an extra rinse. She's probably going to run it again and again, just like I did with the Cadi at the carwash.

Nothing feels like enough. Not the rain, not the peroxide, not the scrubbing or the silence. It's as if the fear...as if it's seeped into us, like a stain we can't scrub out, no matter how hard we try. That's what Amanda must be trying so desperately to clean from my destroyed Ralph Lauren tux, only she can't. No one can, though. She's being ridiculous for not seeing that.

And what kills me is that it wasn't my fault. That woman shouldn't have been there at that time of night, dressed in black. Hell, she was just asking to get herself creamed.

We stand there in the laundry room, the faint, acrid smell of peroxide filling the air. We're staring at each other, our breaths shallow and quick. Somewhere down the hall, Tristan's cartoon laughter floats out, a reminder of the life I'm clinging to, of everything I have to lose.

All I can think is that this isn't over. Not by a long shot.

# 37

# AL JAZINSKI

I'm halfway through jotting down notes when Ben Flannagan trails off, his gaze drifting toward the canyon view from his porch. It's almost completely dark, and the winds are picking up, raising dust in small swirls. His house is the closest to the crime scene, due north, but it's a good mile between his place and where the woman was killed. No one south of the scene who we spoke with has seen or heard anything, or remembered what they heard or saw. Witnesses are famously unreliable for a reason: People rarely pay attention.

Flannagan's your typical Malibu type—retired at fifty, tan from a life of leisure, the latest Apple watch glinting on his wrist. The kind of guy who's seen a lot, but still perks up for the excitement of something out of the ordinary.

"Yeah," he says finally, tapping his chin with his index finger. "I saw a few cars heading north on the night of the storm. Pretty fancy ones. It had to be close to midnight or so. I remember because the wind started picking up right after that, and then the rain started, and I was outside, waiting for my son to come home." He shrugs and smiles. "Parents, eh?"

Eckhart and I exchange a quick glance. I raise an eyebrow and jot down *fancy cars northbound, late night.* "Late, huh? Around what time, exactly?"

Flannagan glances back at me, shrugging slightly. "Between eleven and one in the morning, maybe. Could've been later, but I don't remember exactly. Usually, it's quiet as a tomb out here after ten. But there were several, all high-end cars, all speeding. A bunch of people in tuxes, too, from what my boy told me. Famous people."

"Your son saw them?" Eckhart asks.

He nods. "Yeah, my son, Kyle. He was working the drunk driving fundraiser that night, down at the university. Big event—fancy folks from all over Hollywood. He was parking cars, so he got a good look at who was coming and going."

A fundraiser. I make a note, scribbling it on the edge of the notepad. "What time did he finish up that night?"

Flannagan scratches his head, thinking. "He said the event started around six, so I figure he was working well past midnight. He might've seen a few faces you'd recognize—TV people, actors, you know the type. He wouldn't shut up about it for a couple of days, but I didn't pay much attention."

"Mind if I speak with him?"

Flannagan nods toward the house, then shouts for Kyle, who appears a minute later. Dressed in sweatpants and a T-shirt, the kid's tall and lanky, with scruffy hair and a sheepish grin. He looks like he'd rather be anywhere else but here. His eyes dart from Eckhart to me and back, as if we're about to collar him for something.

"Hey, Kyle," I start, keeping my tone casual. "You were working the fundraiser last week?"

"Yeah, all night on Thursday," he says, shoving his hands into his pockets. "Parked cars the whole time. It was at the university campus. Place was packed."

"Anything unusual that night? Did you see anything on the way down?"

He shrugs. "Not really. I drove down Malibu Canyon around five, right before the event started. Everything looked normal. Didn't see any signs of a crash—no broken glass, nothing like that. And I drove back home a little after one. It was pouring. I didn't see anything."

"Any names you remember?" I ask, keeping my pen ready. "Anyone famous?"

"Oh, yeah, tons. You'd recognize half of them." He grins, his face lighting up a little. "That actress who plays in the new legal drama series was there, Kelsie Crichton. You know her, right?" I shake my head, but I'm taking notes. "Oh, and Paul Davis was there—the news anchor and all his team, like his former partner, Carly…Crown, I believe, and the new one, who does the news with him now, the pretty one—Latesha Jones. And some other TV actors, a director or two. And Davis even gave a speech, so everyone was kinda buzzing about it."

"Why were you buzzing about a speech? Those things put me to sleep."

He lets out a quick chortle. "He swore a lot, they said. Too bad we weren't allowed to listen in."

"We?" Eckhart asks.

He shrugs and looks at his feet for a moment. "Parking valets." When he looks up at me, he's a little flushed. "But it was good tips."

I don't let my expression change, even though the name sank like a stone in my gut. "So, Davis gave a speech, huh?"

Kyle nods, his grin widening. "Yeah, he's pretty cool, actually. A lot different from how he seems on TV. He tipped me a twenty."

"Was he drinking?" I ask. "Were other drivers smelling of alcohol?"

He chuckles. "Almost all of them, but no one was crawling to their car on all fours, if you catch my drift. We had a procedure to follow if anyone was inebriated."

I just nod, trying not to give away the spike of adrenaline that's making me itch to get out of here. "Thanks, Kyle. Appreciate the help."

Kyle nods and steps back, then shakes my hand in a rush, his fingers clammy and cold.

Flannagan gives me a half-smile and a wave, but I'm already turning back toward the car, the gears in my mind grinding.

In the car, Eckhart looks at me, eyebrows raised. "Well?" I close the door, staring straight ahead as I let out a deep breath. "Who do you think we should start with?" he asks.

"Paul fucking Davis," I mutter, glancing down at my notes. I hesitate for a moment, knowing I have no particular reason to go after Davis first, but it just feels right. I *want* it to be right, when, perhaps, I should steer clear of him, knowing the damage he can do to me.

But fuck that. The thought of him being behind this is more alluring than my reason can handle. I could be free of him, and wipe that smug smirk off his face with one rattle of my handcuffs.

I do a quick search in the DMV database on my phone. "Davis lives north of here, in Oak Park. And I'd bet my badge he took this road home after the event. The kid said no one was intoxicated, but...there's no way Davis got through a fundraiser without downing a few drinks. No one does."

Eckhart leans back, folding his arms. "So, what's our move? Do we go after your favorite TV host?"

Sarcasm doesn't suit Eckhart as well as he thinks it does, and I almost tell him that. Instead, I shake my head, frustration simmering. Even if I feel like a dog with a big, juicy bone, I'm not going to let my personal bias fuck up an investigation, but if it so happens that Davis is behind this, I'm going to make sure he doesn't slide.

"Not yet. We can't move on him without process, without cause. You know how it works with people like him. We'll need to tread carefully—real carefully. Kid gloves on this guy, Eckhart. He's dangerous, and he's got people watching out for him."

Eckhart snorts, his voice dripping with sarcasm. "Dangerous, huh? I didn't know news anchors were so scary."

"This one is!" I snap back, a little sharper than I meant. I still recall his notes during my interview. He didn't use what he had when he had the chance, and I still don't know why. But I'm sure he wouldn't hesitate to use my wife's history against me if his back was against the wall. I can't share that with my partner, though. "He knows how to spin things, how to work the public. We go in too fast, and he'll have us looking like we're out for blood. We need to dig, get a list of everyone at that event, and maybe some video footage. I want to know exactly when each of the guests left, where they live, and if they took Malibu Canyon Road home that night. Someone must've seen something."

Eckhart glances out the window, his jaw tense as he mulls it over. "So, we play it slow. Real slow. Got it."

"Better than getting our asses handed to us for a hasty arrest," I mutter, drumming my fingers on the steering wheel, wondering what I can tell Eckhart. "This guy's connected. I met him face to face, and I can tell. I don't want to make one wrong move and have him bury us. He's the kind who'd throw a lawsuit our way just for fun. But I do want to take a temperature read...ask him a preliminary question or two. He was the organizer of the event, right? Use that if you need an excuse for starting with him."

He raises an eyebrow. "Sounds like a real son of a bitch."

I let out a bitter laugh. "You have no idea."

Eckhart jots down a few notes on his tablet, glancing at me with a smirk.

"Mind handling him solo tomorrow?" I ask. "I've got a dentist appointment." The lie slips out smooth and easy.

He chuckles, rolling his eyes. "Yeah, right, like I'm gonna buy that. But sure thing, Al, if you have history with his guy. I'll go all soft and gentle. He won't even know what hit him."

I manage a grim smile as we pull away from the curb, the lights of the Flannagan residence vanishing in the rearview mirror. My mind's already churning every lead we need to chase down. The fundraiser, the guest list, the high-end cars that passed by the scene just before the storm hit. The coroner, to give us a definitive time of death.

And the vic's identity. Who was this woman, anyway? And why isn't there anyone looking for her?

# 38

# PAUL DAVIS

An entire weekend flew by, eaten by anxieties and countless hushed arguments with Amanda. She's the picture of mental rigidity, that woman. Her picture should be in the fucking dictionary under the definition for *intransigence*.

Fast Lane Foster showed up Monday morning after standing me up on Saturday, and then on Sunday, too, without as little as a phone call. He parked his crappy Chevy on my driveway and had me take the rental Cadillac out of the garage to make room for his repairs. Now, he's setting down his toolboxes on the garage floor, lining them up against the wall.

"I got almost everything," he says, speaking slowly.

"Almost?" I could strangle him right now.

He has the nerve to scoff at me. "You didn't bother to mention that cracked trim right there, above the bumper." Unfazed, he continues to unload stuff.

His silent toiling triggers yet another fight with my wife.

"—not going to happen!" she hisses, shooting side glances up and down the street. "You can't have that man banging at your car in there all day long. What will the neighbors say? What if they ask what you're working on? Take it to that place in Westwood, late at night, when no one will see you."

We're right outside the garage, the double-door half-lowered to keep prying eyes at bay. I raise my arms in the air, then let them drop as frustration gets the best of me. "I can't drive a damaged car under that many traffic cams and expect to get away with it!" I wish I could yell at her loudly enough to make the windows rattle. "You want me nabbed for this, don't you?" I ask, whispering my rage closer to her face. She doesn't flinch. "Is that what's going on here?"

"No, I just—"

"Hey, I'm gonna split," Fast Lane says, coming out of the garage. "Give you guys some time to square this up."

*Fuck.* I want him working on that car like there's no tomorrow. My dear Amanda never stops fucking things up for me.

Foster leans against the house wall, his bulging bicep inches away from my face. "But I want my money now."

There's no point in arguing. I walk into the garage and return with a thick manila envelope. He takes it and looks inside, then pops an eyebrow and tilts his head as if saying, really?

"You've got twenty-five," I say calmly. "You get the rest when the car's good as new. That was the deal."

I don't like the way muscles are knotting under his skin when he clenches his jaw. He slips the envelope into the back of his worn-out, soiled jeans and mutters an oath. "I'll be here Wednesday first thing. Have your shit figured out, alright? Final warning."

Amanda's staring at him with her mouth slightly open. I'm doing my best to stay cool, but it takes some work. Foster climbs into his Chevy and turns on the engine. Loud, thumping rap music blares from inside the truck.

Amanda squeezes my arm, and I turn to look at her. Meanwhile, a black Ford Explorer pulls to the curb in front of my house. It has red and blue flashers buried it its grille. My breath catches in my throat.

*Fucking hell.*

A man in his thirties, dressed in a cheap gray suit, climbs out and walks over to us, sizing Foster up with keen suspicion in his eyes. Foster's looking at him, too, but then he reverses in a hurry and drives off.

I throw a quick glance over my shoulder. The garage door's halfway down, enough to shield the second Cadillac from view, but the angle could give something away if this guy looks too closely. My pulse quickens.

After throwing Foster's departing Chevy a long look, the man approaches, pulling a badge from his pocket. "Paul Davis?" I swallow hard and nod. "Detective Perry Eckhart, LAPD. Do you have a few minutes?" His voice is casual, but his gaze isn't casual in the least. He looks from me to Amanda, whom he seems to recognize. My nerves ignite with a jolt.

How does he know my wife?

Then his eyes dart to Foster's truck, now halfway down the street and approaching the corner. I find myself hoping that Foster doesn't pick this particular time to roll through the stop sign.

"Detective," I say, putting on my best professional smile. "What can I do for you?"

"We need to ask a few questions about your drive home the night of the fundraiser," he says, nodding toward the Cadi outside the garage. His tone's friendly enough, but there's a glint in his eye—the kind that says he's more observant than he lets on.

"Of course," I say, glancing at Amanda. She's pale, a polite smile pasted on her lips. I step forward, casually positioning myself to block Eckhart's view inside the garage. "I guess you're asking in regard to the woman who was found yesterday, right?"

"Exactly." His demeanor is relaxed and casual, but his eyes tell a different story.

"It was a quiet drive, actually. We left late, and took the Malibu Canyon Road back home."

He nods, taking a few steps closer. I shift slightly, trying to block his advance toward the garage. But he's not looking in that direction. He's checking out the rental Cadillac on the driveway.

"Long drive home," he says, with a slight tilt of his head. "Any trouble on the road? Did you see anything out of the ordinary? Any problems with the rain that night?"

Amanda and I exchange glances. "No, nothing out of the ordinary," I say, keeping my tone even. "We got home around one, I'd say, just before the heavy rain started."

"So, it wasn't raining when you left the venue?" Eckhart studies me, his expression unreadable, and I feel a trickle of sweat down my back.

"No, it wasn't," Amanda says. "I remember clearly, because we waited for a long time for our car to be brought around. We would've been drenched."

The cop takes another step closer to the rental car and looks at it intently, slowly walking around it. "So, this Cadi," he says, pointing at its hood, "is this the one you drove that night?"

"The next morning, too," I reply, a little too quickly. It's as if my brain refuses to lie, and offered this statement instead, because it's true. My stomach tightens, but I keep my face composed. "In fact, if you don't believe me, you can check Golden State's parking video surveillance. They've got footage of me driving it in the next morning, of everyone at our station. And I'm sure the venue had surveillance, too."

He nods slowly, eyes narrowing as he considers it. "Good to know. Might be worth looking into this. Lots of people were there that night."

"Yeah, it was a very successful event," I say, flashing my power smile and feigning excitement. "We raised over five million dollars that night. It's a record for our organization."

"Did you notice anyone driving off impaired?"

"No," I reply too quickly. I want to kick myself.

Eckhart's eyes flick to the car, then back to me, unreadable. "Well, thanks for answering my questions. If you can think of anything, please give me a call." He offers his business card. I take it and slip it into my pocket. Then, we shake hands.

"No problem," I say, relaxing my shoulders a little. "Anything else?"

"No," he replies, his voice hesitant, as if something's holding him back. "These cases, it's always the little things, you know? Something no one thought of."

I smile as sweat runs down my back. "I can only imagine."

He doesn't smile back—just nods once, a little too slowly, as if he's waiting to see if I'll crack under the silence. But I hold my ground, my heart still racing as I maintain my best poker face. Finally, he steps back, glancing one last time at the garage door before turning toward the street. Only the rear end of my wife's Subaru is visible from his vantage point, but the third garage bay has its door closed.

He makes it a few steps down the driveway, but then pauses, turning slightly. "One more thing," he says, catching my gaze. "Your friend there—the guy with the truck. Seemed like an interesting sort. You work with him?"

My pulse spikes, but I give a nonchalant shrug. "Oh, him? He's our handyman," I say, waving it off. "He helps me in the yard every now and then."

Eckhart raises an eyebrow, nodding slowly. "Got it. I'll be in touch if anything else pops up."

I give a tight-lipped smile, nodding back. "Of course, Detective. You know where to find me."

With one last long look, he walks back to his car. I force myself to stay relaxed, arms loose at my sides, even as my mind races. The second he pulls out, I glance over at Amanda, who's been standing beside me with her expression tense.

"That was close," she whispers, voice tight, her eyes still on the driveway as if she expects him to come back.

I nod, swallowing hard. "Yeah. Way too close."

And he had to run into Foster, out of all things. Luck is a motherfucking bitch to me lately. He'll look him up, find out what he's dealing in...and he won't need much else for an arrest warrant. He can probably nail Foster for something or another, and then put the squeeze on him until he spills all about our little deal.

The thought paralyzes me with fear.

We watch until Eckhart's car disappears down the road, but even then, I can't shake the feeling that his eyes are still on us, waiting for a misstep.

He'll be back. I know he will.

This entire thing is unraveling fast. I need to think...

I need a lawyer.

# 39

# PAUL DAVIS

---

After Eckhart's car turns the corner, Amanda and I head into the garage. We're both silent and tense. My gut twists with fear. I can't think of a time I've been so afraid in my entire life. I can't go to prison. I can't even think about what I'll do if they start suspecting me. I'd lose everything I've worked for.

And that cannot fucking happen. Whatever it takes.

I'm quick to close the garage door after we're both inside. Daylight fades with the lowering of the door, and we're soon engulfed in the yellowish light coming from the ceiling fixtures. I'm about to open the door to the laundry room and head inside, where Tristan's cartoons are playing way too loudly in the living room, but Amanda blocks my way. She's livid, her lips pressed into a tight line, and her eyes are widened.

"What the hell were you thinking?" she demands, almost shouting at me. She props her hands on her hips. "You shouldn't have said that!"

I frown, hating how the woman makes me feel, like I'm some dumb fuck. "What the hell are you talking about?"

"The parking vides at the studio!" She pauses for a moment, breathing heavily. "You gave too much, too soon."

I scoff, frustrated as hell. "Everyone knows cops look at video surveillance. It's in every crime show, for fuck's sake."

"Yes, but you offered it really quickly. It means you'd obviously thought about it. Just like a guilty person would."

I feel the blood draining from my face. A weakness creeps up on me, leaving a wave of dread in its wake, and I have to lean against the hood of her Subaru to find my balance.

I force myself to breathe, to think straight, as my eyes shift toward the damaged Cadillac parked in the third garage bay. But I have nothing to worry about. The rental car is identical to mine, down to the tiniest of details. The windows have a slightly darker tint than mine, sure, but who can tell, right? That's why I changed the tires and everything. That Eckhart character will look at the videos, even if he thinks I offered that information up a bit too quickly, and they'll see it's the same damn car, so they'll cross my name off the list. End of story.

I'll be fine.

"And?" I reply, sounding as casual as I can manage. "What's the big deal? They'll see—"

Amanda sighs, a long, pained exhale like she gives Tristan when he screws up and disappoints her. "The parking decal is the big deal, Paul."

My blood turns to ice. "Fuck...I forgot about that."

Amanda shakes her head and heads inside. When she opens the door, sounds from the TV spill over, the cartoon cackling a reflection of how life is treating me now.

"Do you think they'll notice?" I ask quietly, although Tristan has already left for school.

She shrugs and gives me a pitiful look. "I don't know, Paul. All I know is that you can still do the right thing and save yourself—save *us*—from this nightmare. When they *will* notice, it will be too late."

Rage swells inside my chest, suffocating me. I pound my fist against the doorframe. I'm trapped, cornered with no way out.

"All right," I eventually say. "I'll get us a lawyer."

She stares at me with searing contempt. "Today, Paul. Get a lawyer today."

# 40

# AL JAZINSKI

Eckhart leans back in his chair, tablet in hand, scrolling through footage from the fundraiser. His lips press together, his eyes narrowing as he studies each frame. I'm standing at the whiteboard, marker in hand, sketching out on the map I swiped from the cafeteria wall, old style, under Eckhart's disapproving stare. A star for the venue. Malibu Canyon Road there, snaking northbound toward 101. A scattering of numbered addresses around the city marked with red dots—the web of potential suspects getting messier by the minute.

And this is only the people we know of. We can't account for random travelers who might've been driving up Malibu Canyon that night without having attended the fundraiser.

"We've got clear timestamps on most of the big players leaving the fundraiser," Eckhart says, his voice low and focused. "Your man Davis pulled out at 12:15 in his black Cadi. His boss left ten minutes earlier, turning the same way. An actress, right after Davis. Carly Crown, the former news anchor, left at 11:58 in a red Beemer. Two Hollywood producers followed, and—here we go—two of the board members, one heading south, so that one doesn't count. But these are only the people who left late. About a hundred more left between 10 and 11:30."

He angles the tablet so I can see the grainy footage. A line of headlights filters out of the parking lot, one set after another, and it's impossible not to imagine them winding up Malibu Canyon Road under that black sky flickering with lightning.

I jot down the names on the board underneath where I've written *Malibu Canyon Route.* "Seven people," I mutter. "Seven people who took that road north between 11:30 and 12:30, as shown on the traffic camera at the light. And the rain hit at—"

"12:57," Eckhart cuts in. "That's what Weather Services said. Started light, then heavier by one. Moved in from the water."

"So, the window's tight," I say, drawing a line across the timeline. "The crash had to happen before the rain. The coroner said the ground was dry under the vic's body. She was thrown into the ravine before it started." Eckhart raises an eyebrow. "Something to do with insect activity."

"Okay, but how do we know she wasn't killed earlier? At seven, or nine, or whatever?"

I clench my fist until my knuckles crack. "We don't. We're making an assumption here. An earlier crash would've had witnesses. Someone would've seen something. If nothing else, at least the slick of blood on the road."

Eckhart nods, setting the tablet aside. "Let's say it was an accident," he starts, leaning forward. "She's walking along the road, no streetlights, in pitch black. Driver doesn't see her until it's too late."

"They hit her," I pick up the thought, my voice flat. "She's killed on impact. No chance to help. But they stopped. She didn't land in the ravine by herself."

"Right," Eckhart says. "But then, instead of calling it in, they panic. They drag the body off the road and toss her into the ravine. Make it look like a fall, maybe, or just hope no one finds her. That kind of shock—it'd take a few minutes to even think straight."

"Ten minutes? Fifteen?" I pace in front of the board, the marker tapping against my palm. "Long enough for the road to stay clear, but not so long they'd be caught sitting there if someone else came along. At 1:10 or so, when Kyle Flannagan drove home in the pouring rain, everything was over."

"Ooh…I like this. We can look at the time intervals between northbound departures from the venue. See who had the time to do all this without being seen by the next car." He scratches his chin, thinking. "Or maybe they were faster than ten minutes," Eckhart says darkly. "Some people don't freeze in the moment. They act. Get it done. Two minutes?"

I stop pacing, staring at the board. "And then what? They drove home like nothing happened?"

"Exactly," Eckhart says, pointing toward Davis's name. "He left the venue at 12:15. With the drive to the scene, it's 12:26 to 12:30. Right before the rain hit at 12:37. It fits. Sort of."

"Why sort of?"

"Because his car is perfectly fine. He said he drove it to work the next morning. He sounded pretty damn sure of himself."

"And you believed him?" My partner is still young. At my age, I know people lie. A lot. About everything.

"I saw the car myself. It's pristine. Undamaged. I could tell it hasn't been recently fixed. It's got dust on it, all over."

"Damn." I take a deep breath, the knot in my stomach tightening. "Davis lives north of the canyon, but so do other six people in this bunch, and we haven't seen *their* cars. Who's to say all six went straight home from the venue, or some of the earlier hundred or so didn't? Maybe they lingered in Malibu, went for gas or something, and then drove up Canyon Road *after* Davis." As I say the words, I feel a tinge of regret that I can't pin this on that arrogant son of a bitch. "We can't make a move in any direction without proof."

"Then, we get proof," Eckhart says, sitting up straight. "We've got timestamps. Routes. Let's map every guest from that fundraiser who took Malibu Canyon Road that night, and see the time stamps on the other side. There's a hotel up north on the road. I'm willing to bet more than a donut hole that it's got video. Let's see who took too much time to drive up the canyon."

I nod, stepping back to the board, adding more lines and connections. The names pile up: Davis, his boss, Crown and the other producers, that actress, the board member. It's a spiderweb, messy and sprawling, but it's a start.

Eckhart tilts his head, watching me work. "You think it was Davis, don't you?"

I pause, turning to face him. I can be honest with my partner, but only to some extent. "I like him for this, in my gut, but the evidence doesn't back it. He's got the profile—a guy who'd panic, but cover his tracks; someone who lacks empathy and remorse, who damages people for a living on his show and enjoys it. Like everyone else, he's got a lot to lose if this gets out. Still, we got nothing."

Eckhart whistles low. "That never stopped us before."

I nod slowly, capping the marker. "We need the full coroner's report before we push too hard. No assumptions until we know for sure what happened. But at least we have a good time of death."

Eckhart leans back again, running a hand through his hair. "You think it was just bad luck? Wrong place, wrong time?"

I hesitate, staring at the board, and at the lines crisscrossing between the canyon and the city. "Maybe. But bad luck doesn't throw a body into a ravine."

The room falls quiet, with just the faint hum of the air conditioning and the low buzz of Eckhart's computer. I glance at the calendar on the wall. It's already been two weeks since that atmospheric river washed through the city. The longer this case drags on, the more I fear it could turn cold. I can't let that happen. One way or another, we're going to find what we're missing—and when we do, I'll make sure whoever did this doesn't walk away.

And if I have a shred of luck on my side, the perp will prove to be Paul Davis.

# 41

# AMANDA DAVIS

There's no amount of concealer that can hide the black circles under my eyes. Or the swelling from the hour I spent doing chores and crying, keeping the noise soft enough that Tristan wouldn't hear me. I can't hide all that with makeup, not from my father.

I take a break from dabbing and look outside. He's not here yet, but he's never late.

My chest heaves as I hold captive a sob. I haven't seen him in two months, since he set out to sea with his commercial freight ship, *Sea Titan*. These two months have been excruciating. We've spoken a couple of times since the night of the crash, but I couldn't tell him what happened, even if I wanted to. I didn't find the words—or the right time.

When the doorbell rings, I flinch and drop my lipstick into the sink, tracing a smear of red on the white porcelain. I leave it there and rush to the door.

I see Dad's face through the side windows and feel the threat of tears in my eyes. He's lost some weight this time. His cheekbones are more pronounced, and his skin is sunburned. His eyebrows are thick and somewhat untamed, and his unruly white hair longer than I recall. He's probably yet to see his barber.

I swing the door open and rush into his arms. His embrace feels solid and steady, and for a moment, I'm safe again. The scent of his aftershave fills my nose, sharp and comforting all at once. But then I pull back reluctantly. The moment of absolute comfort and safety dissipates, and fear returns with a punch.

"Come on in," I say, stepping out of the way. "I missed you." My voice sounds a little off.

His piercing gaze scans me, his forehead creasing with worry. "Have you, now? You could've fooled me."

His attempt at humor doesn't work. He's worried, and questions are coming. I busy myself in the kitchen, pouring him a large cup of coffee brewed the way he likes it—murky and black.

"How long are you back for?"

He takes a sip of coffee, smacks his lips, then sets the cup down. "A couple of weeks, and then I'm going back to Shanghai."

"That's your route now?" I ask, making myself an espresso. My back is turned, giving me time to regain my composure.

"Yeah, it has been for a while." He takes another sip. "But that's not why I'm here, is it?"

I turn off the espresso machine and give up frothing the milk. I just pour it over the coffee and sit next to him at the counter. "No," I say softly, squeezing my hands together. "I was wondering if you could keep Tristan for a week or so?"

His fingers lift my chin gently. His eyes lock onto mine. "What's going on, Mandy?" His voice is steady, but his concern pierces through.

My eyes burn, and I look away. Only he calls me that.

"Hey, hey," he says gently, wiping a tear that slips down my cheek. "Look at me. What's going on?"

I fill my lungs with air and steady myself. "I...I just need some time, that's all."

He crosses his arms, leaning back as he exhales sharply. "Okay. I'll sit here and pretend I believe that. Whenever you're ready to remember who I am, you can tell me the truth." He tucks a strand of my hair behind my ear while I stare at the coffee cup cradled in my hands. "You can tell me anything, kiddo. You're my little girl. Is he cheating again?"

I shake my head, not trusting myself to speak the lies. After a long moment, I lift my eyes and look at him, knowing he would never judge. Never blame. Still, all I can manage is a thin layer of truth wrapped around the secret I can't share.

"We've been having some…issues."

"Are you two fighting?"

I nod.

"Is it fixable?"

"No…I don't know."

"Grandpa!" Tristan yells from the top of the stairs, then hurtles down, skipping the last step entirely and landing with a thud. I watch as Dad's face softens, and he opens his arms just in time to catch Tristan as he barrels into him.

"Hey, buddy!" Dad says, laughing as he hoists Tristan up. "Miss me?"

Tristan's grin is wide and toothy. "What did you bring me?" he asks, wriggling in Dad's arms.

I watch them, my chest tightening. I can't lose my son. Whatever it takes.

Dad sets Tristan down and pulls a small object from his pocket. Tristan grabs it eagerly, twisting and flipping it in his hands. "What is it?" he asks, his voice full of curiosity.

"It's a compass," Dad explains. "It tells you where North is. Once you know North, what else can you figure out?"

Tristan's eyes light up. "How to get home?"

Dad smiles and pulls him into a bear hug, pressing a hearty kiss onto his cheek. Tristan giggles—wriggling free, but not too fast, like he enjoys the attention more than he'd admit.

"Wanna see what I found?" Tristan asks, digging into his pocket.

The shape and colors of the object make my heart skip. I'm moving before I realize it, but not fast enough. Dad's already holding it—Tristan's prize discovery from the garage floor.

"What's this?" Dad asks, examining the broken Cadillac badge. It's missing a corner, one of the red sections gone. His eyes narrow slightly as he turns it over.

"Found it on the floor," Tristan says proudly. "Cool, huh?"

Dad looks at me, his gaze sharp and searching. "What's going on here?" he asks quietly.

I force myself to smile, holding out my hand. "Tristan, you'll need to give that back. It's not a toy."

Tristan hesitates, his face falling, but he hands it over. I close my fingers around the jagged edges, the sharp corners biting into my palm.

"Go pack your bag, baby," I say, then watch him climb the stairs, crestfallen.

Dad straightens his back, his expression unreadable. "Of course, I'll take him," he says softly. "We'll have lots of fun while you figure out what you need to do about...all this." He gestures vaguely, his meaning crystal clear.

When they leave a few minutes later, it takes everything in me not to cling to both of them. But once the door closes behind them, and Dad's car pulls out of the driveway, I let out a shaky breath.

The hard part is just starting. Paul is meeting with an attorney today. And I already know how that will go. He's going to figure out a way to sell me out.

I need a plan to save myself.

# 42

# PAUL DAVIS

---

*What is wrong with these women?*

The thought rages though my mind as I sit politely and listen to the one-thousand-bucks-an-hour attorney preaching right and wrong to me, sprinkling her talk with legal jargon. I've heard the same spiel from my wife, more than once. What a waste of time and money.

Naomi Hedman is leaning against her desk in her posh office on Santa Monica Boulevard. Her tailored navy suit underscores her hourglass shape. She must have very thin arms, because her jacket is the upper-body equivalent of skinny jeans. A white blouse under that gives her appearance a crisp look. Her cascading brown hair could soften her unsparing demeanor if it weren't for the firm, composed expression on her face. In her eyes, I see her judgment of me, and it isn't pretty.

Also not what I came here for on this bright and early Wednesday morning, way too early for my taste. I've taken the day off to wrap up everything I need to do.

Her keen eyes flicker when a frown ridges my brow. She's quick to stop her senseless, preachy tirade.

"Mr. Davis, let me make this abundantly clear. As long as there's no warrant for your arrest, as long as the police aren't knocking on your door, you can still negotiate this, because you have leverage. Once that's gone…" Hedman gestures dismissively with her manicured hand.

"You've told me that already," I reply impatiently. "Regardless of how well we can negotiate this, I'd be destroyed."

She nods slowly, unconvinced. "Perhaps your reputation would have to suffer, but you might dodge the prison bullet."

I stare at her coldly. "That's what you would do in my place?"

She scoffs quietly. "I would've not fled the scene, knowing the law as I do, but this is not about me. This is about you and your future, Mr. Davis. The future of your family."

Of course, she wants me to surrender and plead the charge down. How else can she bill me for more hours? I don't trust a word she's saying.

"Maybe I didn't express myself clearly, Ms. Hedman. I need an alternative to surrendering. A real option that wouldn't destroy me."

She stares at me in silence for a moment. "What do you mean?"

"Less than ten percent of the hit-and-run cases in California get solved. I won't forfeit a ninety-percent edge just like that. But in case I draw the short straw, I need you to come up with a strategy to immediately contain the damage."

She stares at me in disbelief. "Well, at that time, we could plead the charges down, of course. I'll be by your side the entire—"

"Not what I mean!" I snap angrily. I stand and start pacing her office. There's no point trying to goad her into finding the right answer. "Can I blame this on someone else?"

Her eyes widen. "On whom?"

"My wife, for instance. She was there with me, and helped me, um, do everything that was needed." I stop by the window and stare at the dusk-tinged city scape.

She walks over and leans against the window. "Mr. Davis, do you know the meaning of Schadenfreude?"

"No."

"There's no English equivalent for this German word. When a famous person like yourself is perceived or simply accused of doing something wrong, the same masses that have propelled them to fame and fortune turn against them. *Viciously*. Taking pleasure in bringing them down, in seeing them fail and be dragged through the mud."

"You mean cancel culture?"

"It's more than cancel culture, Mr. Davis. It's a more aggressive form of social dogpiling. It's almost titillating for the masses. The higher up you are, the worse it gets." She crosses her arms at her flat chest. "Don't let this end up in court, Mr. Davis."

I stare at her in disbelief. She doesn't want to help me. It's that simple and obvious. "I don't think they'd have enough to convict," I say, feeling quite confident in my statement.

"If my understanding is correct, the crash happened after an event during which you were seen and recorded downing several drinks. You're a recognizable person, and that will make the bartender's testimony quite interesting. To add some spice to the Schadenfreude, if I remember correctly, you read the news about the incident yourself, on the news, last Friday. Don't imagine that won't come up and get used to paint you as a remorseless, cold individual—perhaps a sociopath."

I can't take another minute of her drivel. "All right, I'll think about it. Until then, can I count on your discretion?"

"You've formally retained my services. You're entitled to attorney-client privilege."

We shake hands, more out of habit than anything. Her fingers are limp and frozen.

"I'll be in touch," I say from the door, not sure that I'll use her if it comes to needing an attorney. I wanted the best there was, the legal shark swimming in the bloody waters of California's entertainment industry. Everyone said this woman was it, the best in handling famous people's errors in judgment.

Well, I'm not impressed. I should've gone with an Ivy League guy. Someone I can really trust. Someone who'd take me seriously.

On the drive home, though, her words keep resonating in my mind. I'm starting to understand how that fancy-named dogpiling she mentioned could happen. It's happened before, to people more famous and more powerful than me, for doing things far less significant, like hitting a pole all coked up, or being accused—not convicted—of inappropriate contact, whatever the hell that is.

As I arrive home, I find Fast Lane Foster in the driveway, sitting on one of the landscaping boulders. It's just him, not his truck. I come to a stop in front of the garage, leaving the door closed, and get out of the car.

"What did he want?" he asks me, his meaty hands propped on his hips. He looks threatening, his face scrunched up in anger. His tattooed skin is covered in sweat—not surprising under the hot midday sun.

"Who?"

"That cop," he says, laughing at my question. "What, you thought I couldn't tell he was five-oh?"

This could go many shades of bad. "Just some questions about an event I attended, that's all."

A lopsided grin stretches his lips. "You mean the fancy fundraiser you attended the night that woman died in a hit-and-run? What a coincidence, right?"

Blood drains from my face. How did he put everything together? I'm speechless. I can't think of anything I could say that wouldn't make it worse.

"When are you going to fix my car?" I ask, my voice steady despite the frantic rhythm of my heart.

"I got the last part in the truck. I can start working later today." He takes a couple of steps closer and grips my arm with an iron-like hold. "What did you tell that cop about me?"

I don't flinch or hesitate. "That you're my handyman, helping out in the backyard."

"You see, we have a problem now, Paul." His hand is still on me, squeezing my shoulder. "He's seen my face. And I don't want no cops in my life, you feel me?"

I nod. "Perfectly."

"I need to disappear, so when they'll come asking questions about you, I won't be tempted to cut myself a deal."

Sweat's dripping down the back of my neck. I tug at my tie, loosening it a little. I can't breathe. This is never going to be over.

"Fix the car," I say in a low whisper. "And you'll get your money."

"A hundred grand," he says, grinning. "I think a hundred large ones could *maybe* be enough to make me move. For now."

"Should I call Larry Chappelle and have him explain to you how things work?" My question is a desperate Hail Mary pass, betting that the slimy lawyer might have some pull with this brute.

"Sure, go right ahead," Foster says, mock-punching me in the arm. "And while you do that, I'll call the local PD and tell them about this client of mine—a kinda weird guy, real sketchy. I'm concerned he might be trying to hide something."

For a moment, we stare at each other without blinking. I see in his blood-shot eyes that I have no recourse.

"Alright," I say eventually. "Fix the damn car like we agreed, and it's a seventy-five thousand payday for you."

He still stares at me, as if trying to figure out if I'm good for my word. Then, he grins and pats me on the back again, and I waver under his heavy hand. When he leaves, he looks left and right as if he's expecting cops to be everywhere.

Maybe he's right. What if they're watching me? The thought chills me to the bone.

And as he walks away with his loose, swaggering gait, I ask myself a disturbing question.

*How the fuck can I get rid of Fast Lane Foster?*

# 43

# AMANDA DAVIS

Standing in the dark, unseen from behind the front room sheers, I watch Paul's interaction with that thug, Foster. If I hold my breath, I can hear the words they speak in low, rushed voices. And I'm terrified. What's to keep this man from blackmailing us for the rest of our lives? I watch him put his hand on my husband, and I gasp, but the contact doesn't go beyond alpha male posturing.

Paul wouldn't stand a chance with this guy, though. He'd break him like a twig.

When the thug walks away, Paul doesn't bring his rental car into the garage. He comes inside the house through the front door, and I'm there waiting for him, fuming.

"Seventy-five grand?" I ask, before he has a chance to say anything. "And how many hundreds after this payment? How could you be so reckless?"

For a moment, he stares at me, slack-jawed. Then, anger rises through him, glinting in his eyes and tightening his jaw.

"What choice do I fucking have, huh? What would you have done in my place? That car needs to be fixed. Pardon me for not taking it to the Cadillac dealership for service."

I bite my lip, wishing I could shut up before I say something I'll regret. "You could've traveled out of state and bought parts here and there. Paid with cash. You could've ordered them on eBay or something, and had them shipped to your parents' address in New York, then driven there to bring everything home. Anything but this." I cross my arms at my chest, breathing heavily. "This man owns us now, Paul," I say, and my voice is shattered. "And he knows it."

"It's not forever," he says gently, taking a couple of steps closer. "The lawyer said the statute of limitations runs out in six years."

"Six years!" To me, it sounds like an eternity. Six years of living with him like this, of being trapped in this nightmare. I just can't... A sob shatters my breath. "How are we going to make it six years, Paul? When my heart stops every time an unfamiliar car drives onto our street?"

He comes closer and opens his arms, but I don't want to be held. Not by him. I pull away, but he doesn't care. He wraps me in his arms and whispers in my ear. "It's going to be okay, baby. You'll see."

My nostrils fill with a scent I recognize. It's a high-end, floral, and unpleasantly sweet perfume that stuck on me like tar on a shoe after Carly hugged me last Friday. I pull back angrily. "Get the hell away from me, you lying sack of shit." He stares at me wide-eyed. "I can smell her on you."

"Amanda, don't," he says, trying to grab my arm, but I slip by, running for the door, my phone clutched tightly in my hand. I don't know where I'm going. I just want to be gone from here, from this house. From him.

The door slams behind me, but I don't stop running. Not until I turn the corner onto Thousand Oaks. I'm breathless and covered in sweat, still dressed in my hospital garb. I don't have my car keys with me, but it doesn't matter. My car is at home, and I'm not going back there. Not tonight.

I take my phone out of my pocket and look at the recent calls. Dad's number is one of the latest. My finger hovers over his name, but doesn't touch the screen. He'd come get me in a minute, but with him, there'd be questions I can't answer and decisions he'd make in my place. And he's got Tristan with him. Seeing me like this would scare my little boy.

Michael Grant's name is right under Dad's, and I tap it. As the phone rings, I lean against a lamp post, still breathing heavily. What am I going to tell him? What am I going to do? Ask him to rescue me from the street corner like I'm some lost puppy?

Maybe not... Maybe just a cup of coffee would be nice, and a friendly face. Some company until I gather my thoughts and decide which way to go. But he doesn't pick up. The call goes straight to voicemail.

I slip the phone back into my pocket and keep walking aimlessly, just knowing I can't go back. After another mile or so, I come to a sports bar I've passed a thousand times. My throat is scorched with thirst. Without thinking much, I go inside and prop myself up on a stool at the counter. The place is abuzz with people, their drunken voices and bouts of laughter mixing with the sports announcers' voices coming from the large TV on the wall. The place smells of acrid, boozy sweat and spilled beer.

"What can I get you?" the bartender asks. I would safely bet my last dollar that he knows exactly what I'm going through. Maybe not every detail, but the look he gives me speaks volumes.

"Beer," I say instead of water, surprising myself. "But only if I can pay with this." I show him my phone.

He nods and fills the glass from the tap, then puts it in front of me on a small coaster. "Bad day?"

I don't reply, just staring at him for a moment before I down half my glass in one breath. "You have no idea," I mutter, breaking eye contact. He gets the message and leaves me alone.

Staring at the slow-moving foam bubbles lining the glass, I drift with my thoughts. Where do I go from here? What can I do? As much as it pains me to admit it, I probably need to rush back home and ask Paul to forgive me for my outburst. Otherwise, he'll freak out and do something stupid. Something that could land us both in prison for years.

I take another gulp of beer, then wipe my mouth with the back of my hand. I'm fighting back tears of frustration, thinking he could blame everything on me and get away with it. Everyone believes what Paul Davis is telling them. Everyone wants to be on his stupid show, and they'd sell their souls for a moment in the limelight. How can I fight this and survive?

"He must be a special brand of idiot."

A man's voice snaps me from my self-pity reverie. It belongs to a well-built man in his mid-thirties, tall and broad-shouldered. He's smiling at me with a glimmer of mischief in his hazel eyes. His black hair is disheveled, and there's a faint shadow of stubble across his jaw, giving him a masculine edge, the kind you see in fashion magazines, although he doesn't seem like the sort.

"Who?" I ask, aware that I'm shamelessly sizing him up.

"The man that brought those tears into your eyes." The tip of his finger wipes a tear off my cheek. I pull away gently, but I don't really want to. I need to escape my reality, even if only for a moment.

There's a magnetic pull about him, something I'm a bit too eager to trust, but beneath the charm, there's something faintly unsettling...a flicker in his eyes or the edge in his grin, a subtle cue I don't quite understand, but decide to write off as the illicitness of the situation.

A beer later, against my better judgment, I leave the bar with a man whose name I don't know.

I'm glad he doesn't know mine, either.

# 44

# AMANDA DAVIS

As I leave the bar holding hands with the handsome stranger, I keep reassuring myself there's nothing to this. I shouldn't feel guilty for wanting to live a little. Paul is cheating on me every single day. Why would it be the end of the world if I spend the night with someone I find attractive? With someone who's willing to treat me right?

He doesn't live far off. The drive is only a few minutes long, putting us on the small streets of Thousand Oaks. I'm tempted to tell him to take me back to the bar, but he seems to have this uncanny ability to read my mind. His hand reaches for mine, and I'm no longer that eager to go home.

He pulls into the double-garage of a small, detached house. The name on the mailbox is Greg Hollen. I find myself wondering if there's a Mrs. Hollen who's going to pick up my scent on her husband, like I did with Paul. But the house seems to belong to a bachelor. No extra décor in the kitchen, and no female toiletries in the bathroom I use to quickly freshen up.

When I'm done, I find him on the living room sofa, watching TV. His leather jacket is abandoned on a chair, his golf shirt taut over his broad chest. As I approach, he stands and wraps me in a fiery embrace that's thrilling at first, with his lips pressing against mine and his hands sliding down my back with a hunger I haven't felt in years. His mouth is warm, his breath tastes like whiskey and something darker, and I kiss him back harder than I should.

The heat between us grows as he spins me around and pushes me against the wall, pinning my wrists above my head, still kissing me. For a moment, it's heady and arousing—almost too much. Then, his grip tightens. Too much.

"Hey," I whisper, trying to free my hands. "That hurts. Let me go."

His smile changes into a spine-chilling grin. His eyes are smoldering. "Come on, you like it a little rough, don't you?"

My stomach churns, the earlier buzz of alcohol fading fast. I shake my head. And try to push him away "No. I said no. Let me go."

He doesn't. Instead, he presses against me harder, his body a wall of brute strength. My heart pounds, panic creeping in. I push back against his chest, but he barely budges. His smile disappears, replaced with a dark glare.

"You came here for this, didn't you?" His voice is low, menacing. "I bet you're not getting enough of this at home." His hand lets go of my wrists and finds my waist instead, digging into my flesh mercilessly.

"I'm leaving." My voice wavers, but I try to push past him.

His hand shoots out, grabbing my arm with bruising force. He blocks the doorway, his broad shoulders filling the frame. "You're not going anywhere," he growls. "I'm not done with you."

Adrenaline surges. I can't make for the door with him in the way. I yank my arm free and dart past him, running up the stairs toward the second floor. My only thought is to get away, to put as much distance as I can between us. My breath comes in sharp bursts as I stumble onto the landing, scanning the darkened hallway for another way out. A bedroom door is ajar, but I barely register it before I hear him pounding up the stairs behind me.

"Where do you think you're going?" he shouts, his voice echoing off the walls. His footsteps are heavy, relentless.

I back away, my chest heaving as he reaches the top of the stairs. His face is twisted in anger, his eyes wild. Before I can react, he lunges at me, grabbing my shoulder and slamming me against the banister. Pain shoots through my side as I cry out, clutching the railing for support.

"No!" I scream, but he doesn't stop. His hand clamps around my throat, squeezing just enough to make me panic. I'm choking, unable to breathe.

Instinct takes over. I thrash, clawing at his arm and trying to break free. My knee finds his groin, and I hit as hard as I can. He yells, loosening his grip for just a second. It's enough.

I shove him with everything I have, using the banister for leverage. He stumbles backward, his arms flailing as he tries to regain his balance.

Then, he's falling.

The sound of his body hitting the stairs is sickening—thud after thud, and a terrifying crack of broken bones until he lands at the bottom, sprawled and deathly still. A pool of blood is widening under his head. My chest heaves as I grip the banister, staring down at him, too shocked to move. The silence that follows is ominous and bloodcurdling, broken only by my ragged breathing.

My knees buckle, and I sink to the floor, still clutching the banister as tears blur my vision. The weight of what's just happened crashes over me, but somewhere in the chaos of my thoughts, a single truth rises to the surface.

*Oh, my God... I killed a man.*

The words fill my mind, echoing in shock and fear with tremors that weaken my body. As reality starts setting in, I gasp silently, covering my mouth with a trembling hand to stifle a sob. Wide-eyed, I stare at the body lying in a motionless heap at the bottom of the stairs, disbelief clinging to me in scattered thoughts and anxious breaths.

*What have I done?*

# 45

# AL JAZINSKI

Someone stunk up the entire precinct heating something in the microwave that smells like feet. Or spoiled cheese. Even my coffee tastes like it now. I throw the whole thing in the trash, paper cup included, and resist the urge to get another one. It would smell the same. I get up from my beat-down, squeaky chair and walk toward the whiteboard.

Eckhart leans back in his seat, tapping his pen against the scratched surface of my desk. His tablet screen is on, but he's not looking at it. Instead, he's grinning in that smug way he does when he thinks he's onto something.

"I gotta admit," he starts, "I like Davis's idea."

Like I didn't feel enough like throwing up. I stop mid-step, halfway between the board and my desk. "What idea?"

Eckhart spins his tablet to face me. It's footage taken in a parking lot, frozen in time, in all its grayscale, pixelated glory. "He suggested we pull the video from the day after the fundraiser. This is from the station's parking lot."

"And?"

"He said it'd show he drove the same car—his black Cadillac—to work the next morning. No dents, no broken glass. It clears him nicely, and it's true."

Son of a bitch. The knot in my stomach tightens. "And he said that, huh? He just offered it? No context?"

"Yeah. None." Eckhart shrugs, leaning forward. "It's not a bad idea. Saves us time, and lets us confirm—"

"Let me stop you right there," I cut in, raising a hand. "This isn't him being helpful. This is him covering his ass. He knows how good it'll look. 'Oh, look at me, my car's spotless, no need to dig further.' Convenient, don't you think?"

Eckhart's smirk fades, replaced by a frown. "Okay, sure. But it was still worth checking. We're trying to eliminate suspects, not play favorites. And his car, I've seen it myself. It did not hit that woman. He's not your guy."

I grab the marker from the board and tap it against my palm, pacing. "It's not just about the car. It's the timing, the demeanor. Davis doesn't suggest something unless he knows it works in his favor. The guy's a pro at spinning the story. What we need is some proof he couldn't manipulate."

"And this footage isn't proof?" Eckhart challenges me, sitting up straighter. "We'll see who drove what, leaving the venue, then getting to work the next morning, and if anything looks off. I guess we can find out quite easily where everyone works, right?"

I sigh, rubbing the bridge of my nose. "Fine. Pull all the damn footage from the venue and everyone's places of employment and waste time on it. But don't imagine it clears Davis."

"How does it not clear him?" Eckhart asks, his voice raised in frustration. "What are you saying? That he damaged the car at one in the morning, and still managed to drive it to work the next day without as much as a scratch on it?"

"I'm saying he was a bit too quick to offer this *solution* to you," I say, making air quotes with my fingers. "You said he offered it. As if he'd spent some time thinking about it. As if he knew we were coming. And that bothers me. Raises a big red flag and waves it in my face."

Eckhart frowns and loosens his narrow tie with a finger. "So, despite all this, he's still a suspect?" he asks, pointing at the tablet.

I shrug and let out a long breath of air. "Damn right, he is. Until we find the perp, or until I hear a satisfying reason why he had his alibi giftwrapped and tied neatly with a bow, waiting for us under the fucking Christmas tree."

"It's not a gift-wrapped alibi, Al. It's him going to his job like he always does, driving the same car he always does. You're not being reasonable."

"Whatever," I mutter, angry with him because he's right.

Eckhart shrugs and picks up his tablet, but there's doubt in his eyes. "It does save us time, you know. We pulled the parking lot footage, and we can see everyone on our list—what they drove, what time they got in. We can expand this to every guest on the list, regardless of where they work. Then, we eliminate them as suspects."

"Yeah," I say, propping my hand on my hip without letting go of the marker. "Everyone except Davis." I groan, rubbing my temples. This entire Davis situation is giving me a headache. Who's to say what the entitled fuck will do if he's cornered? "You take the fun out of police work, you know that? No more banging on doors, no more seeing people sweat and turn ashen. Just files and footage. What a thrill."

Eckhart grins. "It's called efficiency, old man. Welcome to the 21$^{st}$ century."

My middle finger replies with a sharp move.

Eckhart laughs, then smooths out his tie with his hand. The tablet sits upright on the desk in front of him. "Then, there's the other thing about Davis."

I narrow my eyes. "What other thing?"

"I saw a guy at Davis's place," he says, his tone dropping into something more serious. "Someone who doesn't look like he keeps the same company. Didn't I tell you?"

I shake my head in disbelief as my pulse quickens. "No, you seem to leave out critical details. What guy?"

"He was just leaving when I got to Davis's place. I'm willing to bet more than a donut hole that he's done some serious time. Got the ink and muscle and all. I know him from somewhere. Got the tag on his truck."

"Did you run it?" I ask, speaking as calmly as I can possibly manage, when I'd like to shout at my partner to wake the hell up. One day, this kid is going to get killed on the job if he doesn't.

His fingers start tapping on the tablet's screen. "Running it now," he mumbles, and then his eyes become laser-focused on the screen. "Malik Foster, a.k.a. Fast Lane Foster. Whoa…"

I spin back to the board and scrawl the name in big letters next to Davis's. "What's the deal?"

"He's a player. My old partner busted him a while back." Eckhart's face lights up. He leans back and interlaces his fingers behind his head.

He's got something more to say, but he wants me to beg for it. Makes me want to slap him silly. I'm not stooping down to his level.

"Wanna hear for what he was busted?"

My sense of humor is gone. "If you want to stay employed in the LAPD, I'd suggest you spill it pronto."

"You're gonna love this," he says, and then pauses for a moment while I glare at him. "Mostly car rings—stealing, chopping, reselling. Some assault charges, too. I couldn't place him at first, but it's clicked now. You have a scary gut, Al, fucking scary. Your Paul Davis was talking with a chop shop guy."

"So, Foster's not just some random visitor," I say, narrowing my eyes. "He was there for a reason. What's he supplying?"

"Could be anything," Eckhart says. "Parts, maybe. Davis wouldn't have a guy like him hanging around unless he needed something sketchy. I asked him about it. He said Foster's their handyman, helping them in the backyard. But I didn't buy it."

I nod slowly, the pieces clicking into place. "We need to find this Foster character."

"Already put out a BOLO," Eckhart says, finishing typing on the screen of his tablet. "Figured you'd want to talk to him sooner rather than later."

"Damn right," I say, capping the marker and tossing it onto the desk. "Davis is the kind of guy who doesn't scare easy. If

Foster's tied to Davis, we might finally get a crack in his armor. Some leverage. We'll put heat on Foster until he sings like a diva."

Eckhart leans back again, his grin returning. "You think Foster's dumb enough to stick around? Guys like him don't hang out when the heat's on. He knew I was a cop. I know he did."

"Guys like him also don't leave clean," I counter. "He's got a trail. We just need to find it. He's got homies, maybe some broad, perhaps a mother. Someone will know where he's at."

Eckhart nods, but his smirk lingers. "You really got it out for Davis, don't you?"

"Damn right, I do," I snap, turning back to the board. "Everyone screws up eventually. It's our job to find where. For now, all I want is enough stuff for a warrant."

"Sure," Eckhart says, standing and stretching. "But you know what? I don't think Davis is dumb enough to leave blood in his garage or parts lying around. If he's involved, he's already cleaned it up. He might've cleaned it up by the next day when he got to work."

"Maybe," I admit, my voice low. "But if Foster's part of this, there must be something going on. And I intend to find out what."

Eckhart nods, his smirk gone now, replaced by the sharp focus I know he's capable of. "So, what's next?"

"We split this up," I say, grabbing the whiteboard marker and circling the names on the board. "You handle the parking lot footage. I'll follow up on Foster. Let's see where this rabbit hole leads."

Eckhart grins again. "And if the footage comes up clean for everybody?"

I shoot him a look. "Then, we bang on doors, make people sweat, and see who rolls. Someone must've seen something or done something. They always do, and then they lie about it."

He chuckles. "You do love your old-school tactics, don't you?"

I grin back. "What can I say? Nothing beats that."

# 46

# PAUL DAVIS

First, my wife storms out of the house and disappears without a word, leaving me to keep waiting for her to come back. I don't hear anything from her for two hours. Then, she calls, and I can tell she's really upset. Her voice is breaking off in rapid, shaky breaths, but she manages to give me an entire shopping list of things to bring with me. Rubbing alcohol—the 98 percent formulation. Peroxide, the extra-strength version she keeps in the laundry cabinet. A sprayer bottle. Nitrile gloves. And then she gives me an address in Thousand Oaks, and tells me to put the car into the garage when I get there. Says it'll be open for me.

What the fuck?

Who lives there?

*Well, I'm about to find out,* I tell myself as I turn onto the street. The house is a two-story detached, shrouded in darkness, but the garage door opens when I pull onto the driveway. There's another car inside, a Mazda I've never seen before.

I pull into the garage with my lights off, and cut the engine. The garage door goes down behind me, and then the light's turned on. Amanda stands in the doorway, pale and shaking, her hands clasped together.

"What the fuck is going on?" I ask, getting out of the rental Cadi. "Whose house is this?"

"Please," she says, suddenly sobbing, "I—I didn't—"

"Didn't what?" I say, pushing her aside and stepping into the living room.

It's dark inside, except for the faint light coming from a night lamp stuck into a plug by the stairs. I feel for the light switch on the wall and flip it on.

And I gasp.

"Oh, shit," I say, staring at the body lying at my feet. "What did you do?" I ask, turning to Amanda.

She's shaking her head, crying with her mouth open. "I'm sorry, I didn't—it just happened."

Her left wrist is badly bruised, and her throat is reddened with hues of purple. The motherfucker tried to strangle her. But what the hell was she doing in his house?

She better tell me she's been kidnapped.

"Who is this guy, Amanda?"

"I wanted to call the cops!" she says, her voice shattered by sobs. "But I wanted you to be here, because this wasn't my fault. Tristan can't lose us both! I don't know what to do."

"Who is he?" I ask again, unwilling to show her any comfort. A fucking slut. I didn't see that coming.

"Just some guy," she whispers. "I didn't even know his name until I saw it on the mailbox."

*Fuck.* "Is that something you do? Go home with strangers you pick up...where, exactly?"

Her tears dry up instantly, and rage swells her chest. "Don't you fucking dare! Not today, when you reek of Carly's perfume! Don't you dare judge me. I've never done this before, and never thought it possible!"

"Yeah? Really? How about holding hands with your boss over lunch? Was that a first time, too?"

She closes her eyes and turns her head away. A tear trails on her cheek. "Don't," she eventually says. "Are you going to help me or not?"

"Why should I?"

Her eyes are ice cold again, merciless. The woman is more mercurial than a Pacific storm. Calm one moment, unleashing hell the next. Then, calm again.

"Because if you get busted for the hit-and-run, and I for this, Tristan loses both of us."

I shrug, unimpressed. We've gone through the entire "what happens with Tristan" question countless times since the accident.

"And because you owe me," she adds. "I helped you cover yours, didn't I?"

"This is no fucking accident!"

"No, it's not," she admits. "It's self-defense. The question is, do we want cops looking at us right now? At the both of us? Or do you want to help me?"

I give her concern a moment's thought. Then, I realize the opportunity this incident brings. She played herself right into my hands.

"I'll help you," I reply. But it's not out of the goodness of my heart. Not in the least. It's because now I'll have something to hold over her head, to keep her from turning on me. From divorcing me and taking my son if I get into trouble over that stupid accident. I can barely contain a smile. "What do you want me to do?"

"There's a chest freezer over there," she says, pointing at the dining room. "Let's hope there's room in it. But first, let me wrap his head in a plastic bag. Did you bring the stuff I asked you to?"

I get her the bag of supplies from the car, and she slips on a pair of gloves with expert, practiced moves. Next, she pulls a couple of trash bags from a roll she uncovers in a drawer, and pulls them over the guy's head. She's quick in her moves, and bosses me around like she probably does her other nurses at work.

Shoving the guy into the freezer takes some doing, but we manage after moving several trays of meat into the fridge's freezer. Then, she cleans the floor using toilet paper that soaks through with blood, then flushes it all down the drain. The peroxide dissolves the remnants of blood. She lets it soak the lines between the hardboards, spraying it everywhere in a cleaning frenzy. Then, she wipes clean the stairs, handrail, and some banisters, all the way up to the next floor. Downstairs, she finishes up with the bathroom faucets, toilet lever, light switch, and doorknob on both sides.

"Did you touch anything else?"

She doesn't answer. For a moment, she stares at the window, then grabs the alcohol and wipes clean the blinds wand and a couple of slats. "I think we're done here." She goes to the thermostat and adjusts it lower, then picks up the alcohol and peroxide, and puts them back in the bag I brought.

"Is there an alarm system in this house?" I ask, looking around.

"I didn't notice, no. Get in the car and drive out. I'll close the garage door and leave out the front."

I do what she says, and wait for her on the driveway with my lights off and my engine running. She closes the door behind her gently, then presses a button on the electric lock.

The entire drive home, we're silent. She doesn't cry anymore, but she seems to be cold, shivering at times even if it's a warm evening. When we get home, she doesn't speak with me. Doesn't do anything but run into the downstairs bathroom and lock herself up in there.

She's probably crying. I can't tell for sure, with the shower running, but who cares? If she thought I'm not good enough for her anymore, I hope this guy taught her a lesson she'll never forget.

"Thank you, dead man in the freezer, whoever the fuck you are," I say to myself, raising a glass of bourbon in a solitary toast. "You did me a solid today. Now, she can't leave me. Ever. Can't tell the cops about my accident. Can't do anything, really, but try to please me."

I laugh and pour myself another drink. It's been a good day after all.

# 47

## AMANDA DAVIS

I step out of the shower, my skin reddened from the scalding water and the towel shaking in my hands as I rub it over my body. I'm still cold, as if ice is coursing through my veins. Steam clouds the mirror, but I don't need to see my reflection to know how broken I look. I'm trembling from exhaustion, from the adrenaline still flooding through me, and from the weight of what we just did.

What *I* just did.

It's all my fault. *Everything.* And I wasn't ready for any of it.

When I open the bathroom door, Paul is waiting across the hall. He's leaning against the wall with a glass of bourbon in hand, his tie loosened and his shirt unbuttoned at the collar. The smell of alcohol hits me before his words do.

"This was no hit-and-run," he says, his voice dripping with venom and something else I can't quite grasp. Something dark and menacing.

I pull the towel tighter around myself, glaring at him. "No, it wasn't. But it's not my fault, either."

Paul lets out a bitter laugh and steps closer. "Not your fault? You're the one who brought me to some random house to clean up your mess, Amanda. You're the one who went home with him."

The fact that he's right burns through me like red hot poison. "I told you, it wasn't like that!" My voice cracks, and I hate how weak it sounds. "I wasn't—"

"Oh, save it!" he cuts me off, swirling the bourbon in his glass. "You want to act like some saint? Fine. But let's not pretend you weren't looking for trouble when you walked into that bar."

He knows exactly what buttons to push to make me lose my mind. I clutch the edge of the towel, the fabric damp under my fingers.

"You think you know everything, don't you? You think you can stand there and judge me when you stink of Carly's perfume?"

His jaw tightens, and for a moment, I see guilt in his eyes. But it's gone as quickly as it came, replaced by that infuriating smirk.

"This isn't about me," he says, his voice low, dangerous. "This is about you. And what you did. And the body you just stuffed into a freezer."

My stomach twists, bile rising in my throat. I step back, my heels brushing against the cold tile floor. "I didn't have a choice, Paul. He tried to kill me. What was I supposed to do? Let him?"

"Now, there's an idea." His laughter is sharp. Cruel. "No, I get it. You just wanted a quick fuck, didn't you? And now we're both tied into this mess. Another fucking secret to add to the pile."

The air between us crackles with tension, every word cutting deeper, every breath feeling like a struggle. My heart pounds in my chest, my fear mixed with anger that matches the rage in his eyes.

"Now what?" he asks, stepping closer. His voice is quieter, but no less dangerous. "What's the plan, Amanda? You seem to have all the answers. How do you see us surviving this?"

I stare at him, my throat tightening and my vision blurring. "Let me go," I whisper.

He freezes, the glass halfway to his lips. "What?"

"Let me go," I say again, louder this time. "You have enough on me now. Enough to know I'll never tell anyone about the crash. We're even, in some twisted, poetic-justice kind of way. So, just...let me go. Let me keep Tristan, and I'll disappear from your life. You can have your career, your reputation, your freedom. You can see him as often as you'd like. I don't want a single dime from you. Just let me raise my son."

His laugh is icy cold. "You think I'm going to let you walk away? After what you just made me do? Hell no, sweetheart. Think again."

I shake my head, my hands trembling. "I'm serious, Paul. This isn't a marriage anymore. It's a prison. You don't love me, and I don't love you—not anymore. Let's stop pretending. It's as good a time as any."

His eyes darken, and he steps closer, towering over me, pushing me against the wall. His fist crashes against the wall right next to my head, putting a hole in the sheetrock. I flinch, but my eyes stay locked onto his.

He pulls closer to me, until I can feel his breath on my face, scorching, revolting. "Oh, you're not going anywhere. You're going to be the most loyal, faithful, and gracious wife anyone's ever seen. Whenever I feel like fucking, you'll spread your legs and smile for me. And on the twenty-seventh, you're coming with me to the board meeting and making perfectly nice."

I blink, caught off-guard. "What board meeting?"

He smirks, taking another sip of his bourbon. "I saw a note on Ray's desk. Something about vetting me for a new position. It's not official yet, but it's coming. And when it does, you're going to smile and shine like the perfect little wife. Understood?"

My stomach heaves, the room spinning around me. "And if they don't pick you? What then?"

His smirk fades, his grip tightening around the glass. "They will. They'll have no choice. I've made sure of it."

I shake my head, taking a step back. "You're insane."

"Maybe I am," he says, his voice low and cold. "But you're not leaving. Not now. Not ever. And about Carly? Get used to that. She's a better fuck than you've ever been."

The weight of his words press down on me, suffocating me. My mind races, desperate for a way out, but every path feels like a dead-end.

Walking over to the kitchen, Paul finishes his drink and sets the glass down on the counter with a sharp clink. I can see him from the corridor, where I'm leaning against the bathroom wall, exhausted, too tired to move.

"Get some sleep," he says, his voice flat. "You're going to need it."

He climbs upstairs slowly, leaving me alone with my thoughts, my fears, and the crushing reality of what my life has become.

I'll never be free of him. Not if I want to keep my son.

# 48

# AMANDA DAVIS

I couldn't sleep last night. Curled up on the living room sofa and wrapped in a blanket, I dozed off at times only to startle out of sleep with the makings of a scream lodged in my throat. It was almost dawn when I gave up trying to get some rest. Instead, I kept my eyes wide open, staring at the ceiling and going over everything in my head, over and over again.

It all tracks back to the day of the fundraiser.

Sure, I wasn't happy before that day. I was trapped in a bad marriage. I wanted a divorce, and I wasn't making any headway with Paul about it, but I wasn't cornered like I am now. I wasn't looking at doing time in prison, or at losing my son. Still, I can't keep myself from feeling guilty, in more ways than one. For what I did the day of the crash. For not calling the police instead of helping Paul. But, mostly, for yesterday. What the hell was I thinking, picking up a stranger in a bar and going home with him? What did I expect would happen?

Not this, that's for sure.

When I walk into the emergency department, it's a good twenty minutes before the start of my shift. My eyes are dry, but bloodshot and sightly swollen despite the bag of frozen peas I used as a mask. I'm wearing a black turtleneck that does a good job hiding my bruises. I do my best to smile and behave like my normal self, but my thoughts are racing.

What am I going to do? Or, even better yet, what *should* I do? What's the smart way out of this mess?

Sometimes, when I struggle with finding the right answer about how to go forward, I imagine myself watching the scene in a movie and asking myself, what would I tell the heroine she should do? The detaching, calming metaphor of a movie helps me see answers that otherwise elude me.

Only, now I would probably change the channel.

A bitter chuckle escapes my lips as I enter the break room and make for the coffee machine. Someone already brewed a pot, and I'm quick to fill up a cup. It's got a sweet, French vanilla flavor I enjoy.

With the coffee cup in my frozen hands, I take a seat in the weathered armchair. I take small sips, and the hot liquid has the effect I was hoping for. It cleanses my mind and organizes my thoughts.

It was self-defense. I have the bruises to prove it.

And I panicked, just like Paul panicked after the crash. He doesn't have the upper hand on me any more than I have it on him. But what's more important, really, is that he still *needs* me. For his career advancement, for his insatiable quest for power. His need is my leverage, if I play my cards well.

And I need an attorney...someone who can help me navigate this mess. I can't think of anyone I can trust, though. The secrets I'm holding are not the kind you'd share with someone found in an online directory of smiling faces and overpriced suits.

With a long, pained exhale, I must admit that the logical thing to do would be to get a lawyer and call the cops. But the thought terrifies me. Being locked up, even for one day or however many days there'd be until they'd be satisfied I'd acted in was self-defense, is paralyzing. Being away from Tristan even more than I am now, missing him and not being able to do anything about it, is unimaginable.

And what if they don't believe me? It's happened before. Innocent people have been locked up for murders they didn't commit. Cops have quotas to meet every month, idiotic bosses who can rush them through their jobs. Lawyers can screw things up, too.

And Paul... I can't afford to forget he can lie better than anyone I've ever met. He can talk anyone into anything, and he wouldn't hesitate to sell me out, even for a marginal gain. He'd weave such a good story... There would be no coming back from it.

No. I need to be smarter than that.

I finish my coffee and set the cup on the table, then look at the clock. I still have a couple of minutes. I catch myself hoping for a busy day, and then feel remorseful about it, as if my wish is the only force responsible for the inflow of human suffering through our double sliding doors.

A moment later, as I'm rinsing the cup, the door swings open.

"Good morning," Dr. Grant says.

I turn and smile—a quick, shy reaction. "Hey."

The door closes behind him as he draws closer to me. "About yesterday, you caught me in the shower. I didn't see you called until it was almost eleven." His voice is low, but warm. "I'm really sorry, Amanda. Can I make it up to you with lunch?"

I shake my head and dry my hands with a paper towel. "Nothing to make up for, Michael. It's all good." *It's too late now*, I want to say instead. *Much too late.*

I turn to leave, but he reaches out and grabs my hand. "Please—"

Wincing, I pull my hand away, but not before he notices the bruising on my wrist. Ashamed, I tug at the sleeve and cover the bruise. My eyes are riveted to the floor.

"Amanda," he says, his voice barely a whisper. "What happened?"

"Nothing," I say, quick to pull away.

"Let me help you. Please."

"There's nothing you can do, Michael. Nothing happened." I glance at him briefly, then look at the clock. I'm two minutes late for my shift.

"We've seen this here. Every day, we see at least one domestic violence victim," he insists. "We both know how this ends. There's nothing to be ashamed of. Please, I can—"

"There's nothing wrong," I say, holding his gaze firmly. "Just a slip and fall, that's all."

I can see in his eyes that he's not buying it, but he can't do anything about it. He looks at me with unshielded concern and a hint of something I hate more than anything.

*Pity.*

"You might feel you're powerless," he insists gently, "but you do have power in the choices you make. And I'm here for you."

Hearing his words, I realize I know exactly what I have to do. I do have power over Paul, even if he doesn't seem to think so.

When the ambo tone breaks the tense silence between Michael and me, I'm the first to rush out, grabbing a pair of gloves on the way. He joins me by the sliding doors, his demeanor professional and his entire focus on the patient they're rolling in.

"Female, 24, severe abdominal pain radiating to the back," the EMT announces, her tone clipped. "BP 85 over 60, pulse 130, O2 sat 92. Diaphoretic, guarding, possible internal bleed. IV fluids running, one liter in."

"Trauma Two!" Sunny calls from the desk.

The gurney wheels squeak as the EMTs push it through, the patient's moans rising over the controlled chaos. "Sudden onset, mid-epigastric, unrelieved by position," the EMT adds.

We roll the gurney into Trauma Two, and then Dr. Grant counts for transfer.

"Need imaging in here, stat!" he calls. "Give me CBC, CMP, ABG, coag, amylase, LFTs, type and crossmatch."

While Sunny rushes to draw blood, I roll the ultrasound cart into position and squirt some gel over the patient's abdomen. Dr. Grant takes the transducer from my hand and starts the scan. A gray, fuzzy image appears on the screen, but

I'm not looking at that. Transfixed, I'm staring at her tortured face. Her hair is clumped in sweat, strands sticking to her forehead. Her mouth is agape as she gasps for air between cries of pain.

A disturbing thought surfaces from the depths of my memory.

This girl looks just like Marisol.

# 49

# AL JAZINSKI

---

The precinct reeks of bad coffee and wasted lives, but I push through it, landing in front of the whiteboard. I pick up the marker and tap it against my hand as Eckhart scrolls through his tablet, his face set in that smug imitation of Neeson's grin that he wears when he thinks he's ahead of me.

"Any progress?" I ask, my voice sharper than I intend.

He leans back, tossing the tablet onto my desk like it's a winning hand at poker. "Something interesting. Kelsie Crichton—you know, the hot chick who plays in that legal drama on TV? Left the fundraiser in her Mustang. Next day, she's driving a blue Beemer to set."

I stop pacing, narrowing my eyes. "Also hers?"

"Yeah," he says, spinning the chair lazily. "People like her, they got more than one car. Could be nothing. No idea what happened to the Mustang, if anything. Still looking into it." He smiles and reddens a bit. "Wouldn't mind making her sweat a little."

"You dog, you," I mutter, rubbing my temple where the promise of a migraine is starting to bloom. "Of course, you wouldn't mind. Anything else?"

"Raymond Cook—he's the president and CEO of Golden State Broadcasting. Got dropped off in a cab the next morning," Eckhart says, his tone casual, but I can feel the weight of it.

"How did he get to the event?"

Eckhart flips through his notepad. I'm surprised my tech-addicted partner knows what paper is. "Unclear yet. All I could see was a black sedan, but it stopped at the far end of the curb and the view from the camera's obstructed by a tree."

"Interesting. And his car?" I say, letting the marker hover over the board before drawing a line between Cook's name and the fundraiser location, then putting a question mark above it. "What's he usually driving, and where the hell is it?"

Eckhart shrugs, but there's an edge to his voice. "An Audi, and it's not at the station lot. I'll look some more into it. No reports of it getting towed, no crash claims. Just...not there. Could be at the house."

"Yeah, and could be damaged. Hidden in the garage, where we can't go without a fucking warrant." I stare at the board, the lines crisscrossing between names and places, the timeline sketched below in a red line pierced by black, vertical arrows.

"I'll talk to him," Eckhart says. "TV chick, too."

I can't help but roll my eyes. "Yeah, I bet you'll start with her."

"Actually, nope," he says, winking at me and arranging the knot of his tie with exaggerated gestures. "Saving that experience for the evening. Maybe it can last longer, if you know what I mean."

I want to slap him with the LAPD Manual. Instead, I laugh heartily, but my eyes are riveted to the timeline.

"Any news on the vic?" he asks, snapping me back from my unclear thoughts.

"Still no ID," I reply. "Coroner says dental records have been sent out. She's waiting to hear back if there's a match. Prints aren't in any database, either."

Eckhart sighs, his frustration matching mine. "Is the time of death confirmed between midnight and one-thirty?"

"Precisely. The doc mentioned something about rainwater pooling in certain areas and not others, and some critters. But no ID yet."

"She's a ghost."

"Not entirely," I reply, tapping the end of my finger against the timeline that keeps bugging me. "Coroner did find something. Vic was dying of cancer. Advanced stage. She had months left, maybe weeks. And the doc said the advanced illness caused her to be wrong in her preliminary estimate of the vic's age. She was only forty-ish, not fifty-ish." I grip the marker tighter, staring at the timeline. "What the hell was she doing out there in the middle of the woods, at that hour, in that weather? Was she lost? Alzheimer's?"

Eckhart shakes his head. "So far up the mountain? Doesn't fit. She must've been on that road for a reason. It's not like she was hit in a grocery store parking lot."

"Maybe someone put her there," I say quietly, my stomach knotting. Who could leave a frail, dying cancer patient on a deserted road in the middle of the night? Did someone drop her off? Perhaps an Uber? There was no phone or wallet found with the victim. If they were on her, the perp must've taken them or thrown them somewhere, to keep us in the dark. "Let's put some requests for information through the law enforcement portals for Uber, Lyft, the cab companies... Maybe we get lucky. And let's follow up with Crime Scene. I'm hoping they found her phone and wallet."

The room falls silent except for the faint hum of the overhead lights. I glance back at the board, the timeline gnawing at my mind for no clear reason. It's as if I'm forgetting something important. Perhaps another shot of coffee will help me remember.

Last night was tough. Maria wasn't doing well, crying and trying to back out of her decision to go back to rehab. It got me all riled up—the kind of riling that needs lots of scotch to wash off. And now, my mind's not worth shit.

"And Foster?" Eckhart asks, his tone shifting to something darker. "Quite the stretch to assume his visit with Paul Davis wasn't car related."

Tension settles in my shoulders as I look at the scrawled name in bold letters next to Paul Davis's. "He's the key to cracking this open. If we figure out what he was doing at Davis's place, we find out what Davis is hiding. But the son of a bitch is in the wind, and the brass won't approve a unit to sit on Davis's address."

"You think Foster will go back to Davis?"

I shrug. "If he's not done yet with whatever the hell he was doing, yeah, sure. But the lieu won't do it, budgets and all. The bean counters have us by the short hairs."

Eckhart stands, stretching with a groan. "You want me to follow up on the footage? See if we can get a better timeline for the fundraiser crowd? Maybe see some camera feeds from up north, on Agoura, or on 101?"

"Yeah," I say, my voice tight. "Let's look at everyone who took Malibu Canyon Road that night. It could be the perp wasn't a fundraiser guest, and just a random driver." I scratch my forehead with the tip of my index finger. "Oh, and we got another forty-eight hours. If we still got nothing, the lieutenant is pulling us off the case."

"Shit," Eckhart says, grabbing his jacket. "Better get going. I'll get the car."

Before I head out, I give the timeline another look. There's one detail not on the white board: the date of my television interview.

Now, I realize why Paul Davis didn't skewer me on the show that night.

My interview took place on Friday night, the day after the hit-and-run. Davis had me in his sights, but probably decided it wasn't the best time in his life to fuck with a cop, considering what he'd done the night before.

It's the only thing that fits. And it proves—to me—that he's the driver we're looking for.

I add an asterisk to the timeline to mark the day of the interview, and then I stare at Paul Davis's name scribbled in black marker.

*You should've finished me off when you had the chance, motherfucker.*

# 50

# PAUL DAVIS

As I pull into my parking spot at the station, facing the wall, I'm gritting my teeth until my jaw hurts. My knuckles are white on the steering wheel, and fear uncoils in my gut like a rattlesnake.

I can't believe I left Foster alone in my garage.

When he showed up this morning—no phone call, no nothing—he expected me to just get out of the way and let him work on the car by himself. I didn't argue. It would've been pointless. Arguments are meant for people who are willing to reach a compromise, while fucking Foster only threatens maximum prejudice. He's an "or else" kind of guy I can't be rid of fast enough. Maybe that's why they call him Fast Lane Foster. He sure as hell ain't moving that fast when it comes to getting shit done or fixing my car, though.

When I pulled out of the garage, I was glad to see that at least his beat-up truck wasn't there to draw everyone's attention. I don't know how he got to my house, and I don't care. But now he's there, by himself, free to rummage through my drawers and poke his nose everywhere. I don't imagine my two-bit alarm system is any challenge for him.

Who knows what he's going to do?

Then, I had to stop by the bank and get seventy-five grand in cash. I cleared my savings account and dipped into my line of credit. I didn't like the teller's stare one bit, not her questions. Then the manager came, of course. These banks are always quick to take your money, but give it back? It's like you have to earn it all over again. And what business is it of theirs to know what I need it for? It's my fucking money!

It wasn't until my head cleared up a bit that I realized the bank might report the withdrawal to law enforcement. Because we live in a police state, don't we? And now, I can't think of a valid explanation if they come and ask what seventy-five grand of my fucking money bought me. Maybe I'll say I wanted to buy some bitcoin. Donate it somewhere anonymously. Get plastic surgery done. Or something.

*Fuck.*

Meanwhile, Foster could be going through all my stuff, deciding to ask for even more money, because why not?

When I get to the editorial meeting, I'm already ten minutes late. My arrival interrupts lighthearted chatter. I glare at the group critically, as if to ask if they have any sense of responsibility left. Silence turns into a tension that grates against my nerves like nails on a chalkboard.

I sit at the head of the table, fingers drumming against the cold glass surface, my jaw locked tight as I read through the lineup for tonight's news. It's a sloppy, rushed job, to say the least. Aidan's sitting two seats down, hunched over his tablet, looking like a guilty schoolboy who forgot his homework. Carly's leaning back in her chair, arms crossed, putting on the airs of unbothered confidence that she's perfected. When our eyes meet, she flutters her eyelashes and bites her lower lip discreetly, and I know she's craving me.

Too bad I'm not in the mood.

Latesha flips through the rundown, not even looking up, her pen tapping rhythmically against the edge of the table. The two segment producers at the far end avoid eye contact like I'm a ticking time bomb.

"Where's the lead, Aidan?" I snap, letting my voice cut through the room like a whip. The kid flinches, his eyes wide as he fumbles with his printouts, then his tablet.

"I, uh, Carly emailed you the draft last night," he stammers, flipping through screens like that's going to save him. "We're going ahead with the I-15 bridge fire as top story. I thought—"

"You thought wrong," I cut him off, leaning forward. My hand slams against the table for emphasis. The sound echoes off the glass walls, and everyone stiffens. "If I had it, do you think I'd be asking? Or do I need to hold your damn hand to get anything done?"

"Paul." Carly's voice cuts in, smooth and controlled, like she's trying to calm a rabid dog. She leans forward slightly, meeting my glare with that infuriating coolness of hers. "I did send everything last night. Let's focus on the rundown. We can tweak the lead after the meeting."

I swivel my glare toward her, feeling the heat rise in my chest. She knows better than to challenge me in public. "Oh, thank you for your insight, Carly. Didn't realize you were running this meeting now."

"I'm not," she says, calm as ever. "But someone has to keep this productive."

"Productive," I echo, letting out a sharp laugh. "That's rich, coming from you. Last time I checked, you were the one holding this whole shitshow back." I can't stop myself. The irritation, the stress, the weight of everything outside this room—it all pours out.

Carly doesn't flinch, and she doesn't rise to the bait. She just tilts her head, her lips pressing into a thin line. "If you're done," she says evenly, "we have a lineup to plan."

The tension in the room ratchets up another notch, the silence buzzing in my ears. I glance down the table at the producers. One of them is scribbling something in a notepad, the other pretending to read the rundown like his life depends on it. Latesha finally looks up from her papers, her expression carefully neutral, but her eyes say she's enjoying the show.

I'm playing into her hand. *Damn it to fucking hell.*

When I see her pulling out her phone and typing a quick text, I'm even more livid.

I take a deep breath, trying to rein myself in. "Fine," I say, leaning back and rubbing the bridge of my nose. "Aidan, get me all the copy by the end of this meeting. Carly, make sure the field team is ready for the feature on the bridge fire incident. And someone get me a coffee that doesn't taste like yesterday's leftovers."

No one moves for a second. Then, Aidan scrambles to his feet, mumbling something about the break room. Carly raises an eyebrow at me, but doesn't say a word. Latesha goes back to typing text messages on her phone, every item accompanied by the whoosh chime that confirms the send.

I shake my head, frustrated as fuck. This is my circus, my monkeys. And, some days, I swear they're all out to drive me insane.

When I look up, Ray is staring at me from the conference room door. Latesha must've called him. Of course, she did. *Fuck you very much.*

My boss beckons me, and I join him in the hallway. He wraps an arm around my shoulders, just as Aidan slips by with a tall coffee cup in his hand. I take it from him and wave him off.

"Paul, I've been meaning to ask you," he says, his head leaning close to mine to keep things quiet. "Don't you want to take a couple of days off? You've been through a lot."

A chill runs down my spine. I pull away enough to look him in the eye, searching for answers. But he's unreadable. "What do you mean?"

"You know, organizing the fundraiser, the show, everything you do. You're firing on all cylinders, all the time. That can't be easy."

"Oh, that," I say, smiling. "That's not a problem, I'm fine."

He frowns a little, studying me closely. "Then, what's crawling up your ass? Your people are complaining, and you won't need two guesses to know who."

I chuckle, then reply without thinking much. "The cops were at my house. Can you imagine? Over that hit-and-run we covered last week. Seems it happened when all of us were leaving the fundraiser."

Ray laughs and pats my back. "They spoke to me, too. This morning."

"They did?" Relief rushes through me.

"Yeah. Because I took an Uber the morning after the event." He shrugs and chuckles some more. "Apparently, that's cause enough to suspect that my car was damaged in that hit-and-run."

*Wouldn't that be amazing, if they suspected Ray for a while. Or forever, really.*

"Really?" I ask, encouraging him to keep talking.

"Yeah. I told them I always drink at these events, because everyone wants to have one with me. I take limos to and from. And then, the next day, I was too hungover to drive. I told them that." He laughs again and elbows my side. "They went away with their tails tucked between their legs."

"There were two of them?"

"Yeah. One was named Eckhart—a younger guy, and the other one was that cop you interviewed on *The Final Question* a couple of weeks back. Some Polish name—Jazinski maybe?"

My blood turns to ice. This can't be happening. I knew I made an enemy of that cop on the show, when he saw I knew about his wife's DUIs. And now he's working this case? My hand flies to my collar, loosening my tie a little. I can't breathe.

"So, screw LAPD, 'cause they don't know what they're doing," Ray says, smiling. "I need you in your best shape next Thursday evening, at seven-thirty. The extended board wants to formally meet the future national lead anchor of the network. It's our board and the KCLA board of directors in a joint session. Please bring the missus. We want to project the image of a trustworthy voice, of a family man worthy of being invited into people's homes every night at news time. The acquisition vote is early next month. This is the final stretch, buddy."

"Absolutely," I reply enthusiastically. It's the first piece of good news I've heard in a long time. "You can count on me, Ray. We'll make the merger happen."

We shake hands and pat each other's backs. Through the glass walls, Latesha glares at us with undisguised scorn. I smile sweetly at her and watch how it drives her insane.

After the editorial meeting is finally over, I head outside to the parking lot. I want to celebrate the news with a fancy meal, undisturbed by the presence of others. On the way to my car, I pull out my phone to call Amanda, to give her a heads-up about next week. If she needs to get her hair done or whatever, now's the time to book those appointments. She can't be one minute late for this one.

A missed call from her, received about an hour earlier when I was still in the meeting, is paired with a voicemail. I push play and put the phone to my ear.

"Paul, I suggest you listen to what I have to say and pay attention." Her voice is cold on the voicemail, clipped and threatening. "You know I'll keep your secrets, and I know you'll keep mine. We have no other choice. But that's where it ends. I won't be coming to any more business events with you until you sign the divorce papers. I have drafted them for your consideration. They're on the kitchen counter. This divorce can remain our secret, and I will continue to support your career until Tristan comes of age in nine years. Or you can always refuse, in which case you're on your own. Bye, darling. You might want to delete this message, just in case someone looks into your phone activity."

The recording clicks when it reaches the end. I stare at the screen in disbelief. Rage surges through me, burning my insides and clenching my fists. "Fuuuuck!" The bellowing sound of my own voice echoes in the parking garage as I kick a garbage bin with all my strength. It rattles noisily and rolls on the concrete, under my stunned eyes.

But I'm not seeing it. All I'm seeing is the stained, gray surface of the parking floor. It dances in from of my eyes as if it's about to crack open and swallow me whole.

That fucking bitch!

# 51

# AMANDA DAVIS

Sitting on my dad's couch, it's the first time I've felt safe in weeks. Tristan is lying with his head in my lap, his arm around my waist, half-asleep. I don't dare to make the tiniest move, afraid he'll bolt away, and I haven't had enough of him yet. I've missed him too much.

My eyes feel heavy, and I'm tempted to doze off just for a minute, but I can't afford to. Breathing deeply, I will myself awake. Dad's making something in the kitchen. I can hear the familiar clatter of objects and cabinet doors, then the faucet running. It still squeaks when he turns it off. I can't think of a time when it hasn't.

I look around the familiar room. Nothing much has changed over the years, probably because he's gone for months at a time. Mom's picture remains on the same bookshelf, angled just right to see it from the couch where I'm sitting. Another picture, of all three of us, that was taken when I was about twelve, is framed large above the fireplace mantel. The place still smells faintly of cigar smoke and pinecones. Dad collects them on his walks and leaves them in the fireplace to dry out and scent up the room.

Tristan squirms in my arms, and yawns and stretches. Then, he turns face up, grinning at me with his mouth open, and rubs his eyes with his fists. Our cuddle time is over. Realizing it brings a tinge of regret.

"Who wants hot chocolate?" Dad asks, walking into the living room carrying a tray with three large mugs topped with cocoa-powdered whipped cream.

Tristan jumps to his feet and rushes to grab a mug with the eagerness of someone dying of thirst, and maybe hunger, too. "Me!" he squeals, taking the mug to his lips and slurping. Whipped cream clings to his upper lip.

"You're growing a milk mustache, young man," Dad says, laughing at him.

He quickly wipes his mouth with his hand, then licks his fingers.

I roll my eyes. "Excellent manners," I say, smiling as I take the hot chocolate from Dad's hand. "But it's late, Dad. He'll be up all night." I got off work early today, but it's almost seven. Too late for a hot chocolate.

He waves off my concern and takes a seat on the couch next to me. "Bigger problems out there. Let this be the worst of ours."

I take a sip of hot chocolate. It's delicious, with a hint of cinnamon. It reminds me, sweet and painful at the same time, of my childhood, of Christmas vacations spent missing him, of the exotic gifts he used to bring me from the various destinations he traveled to. "It's delicious. I can't believe how much I missed this."

Tristan runs to the TV and turns it on. Without hesitation, he navigates the menus and puts on a Disney movie. Holding the cup close to my face to breathe in the aroma, I put my knees up and turn sideways to look at Dad.

I find him looking at me with an intensity in his eyes that I don't remember seeing in a long time, perhaps not since I told him I was getting married and to whom. He's never liked Paul much. Now, I wish I would've listened.

"What's going on?" he asks, his voice set in that low, intense whisper that has ship crews hold their breath to hear what he has to say.

"Nothing," I say, a bit too quickly, instantly regretting the lie. He deserves so much better than this, but the truth would hurt him more. "We just need to sort through some things."

Tristan turns his head toward me. "When can I come home?"

I thought he wasn't listening. "Soon, baby," I reply, feeling tempted to lie to soothe his fears. "We're cleaning the house and painting the kitchen. You wouldn't like that. It's noisy and smelly."

"Slapping some fresh paint over foundational cracks and nasty crud?" Dad asks, his whisper slow, measured.

I can't help a smile. He always has had a way with words. "Renovating the house, not the marriage, Dad," I say softly, making a gesture toward Tristan.

A deep frown scrunches Dad's tall forehead. "I don't like what he's doing to you. You're gaunt, pale, probably not eating well." He stops for a second, looking at me until I lower my gaze, conceding he's right. "You're stressed out, while he rubs elbows with the muckety-muck, capitalizing on your hard work for his personal gain. A parasite, in my book."

Another moment of deep silence, while I fight back tears. I'm ashamed to look him in the eye.

"I'm not going to ask you if you're happy," he whispers. "I'm not blind. I'm going to ask you, why are staying with him?"

I'm shivering, despite the hot chocolate warming my hands. I take another sip, and then I look at him, noticing the dark circles under his eyes, the weight he's lost, and the way his cheekbones stand out. Behind all that, there's a steel core, a superhuman strength that I've always admired. He's always been my hero.

"I want a divorce," I eventually say, the words spoken so quietly that I can barely hear them. "I've asked him for it, but he won't budge." I look at Tristan, sitting on the floor cross-legged, eyes glued to the screen as he giggles at the colorful, animated chaos. "I can't lose him, Dad." A tremor shoots through me. "I just can't. And Paul promised me I would."

Dad sets his cup down on the table and clasps his hands together in his lap. "This is not the Dark Ages, Mandy. Women have rights. Mothers' rights are protected."

"You don't know him, Dad. He's powerful. He has influence over people, cops, judges...everyone, really. He could easily get custody. He'd negotiate it behind the scenes. Then, he'd move who knows where, just to put distance between Tristan and me. He's told me as much."

Dad's jaw tightens. Now, I'm sorry I said anything. I can't stop worrying I've made things worse. Dad doesn't know everything that's happened. The crash. The man I killed in self-defense. He doesn't know who I am anymore. I don't, either.

I shudder.

"But I'll be fine," I say, breathing deeply. "I'll find a way. Don't worry about me."

Later that night, when I leave Dad's place, I linger over hugging them both, knowing how much I'll miss them. I breathe in Tristan's scent with my eyes closed, hoping it will stay with me for a while, burned into my memory. Then, Dad wraps me in his arms and whispers a few words in my ear.

"You're better than this, Mandy."

He's right. I am.

# 52

# PAUL DAVIS

---

I'm still shaking on my drive home, rattled to the core and angry as fuck. My right fist throbs from the punch I threw against the steering wheel of my car. I might've broken something.

*Damn that woman. Damn her to fucking hell.*

If Amanda thinks I'll be rushing home to sign divorce papers, she's terribly mistaken. But she *will* attend the board meeting, or I'll have another bitch's body to throw in some ravine. I've told her and told her: no one takes my son away from me.

For a while, I drive in the stunned silence of my thoughts. I can't believe I'm actually considering this, but things would be much easier if she had some kind of accident. Perhaps Fast Lane Foster could arrange it. I'm paying him enough as it is, and will probably keep paying him until the day I die. Or until he drops dead like the ripened roadkill that he is.

I check the time on my dashboard and grit my teeth. It's almost eight, and I bet I'll find him still tinkering in the garage, waiting for his pay. Amanda will be sitting on the couch, arms crossed at her chest, fuming because I left Foster by himself at the house. Like I had a fucking choice.

I fish out the burner flip phone from my pocket and retrieve one of the two numbers stored in it. Calling it, I wonder if that piece of shit attorney will dare answer my call.

"Hello?"

I recognize Larry Chapelle's voice, even if it sounds strangled and choppy. He must've soiled his pants already.

"Do you know who this is?" I ask coldly.

"Yes, Mr. Da—"

"No names, please."

"Yes. Sure." A beat. "What can I do for you?"

"You can begin by telling that piece of shit you sent my way that I'm not his fucking cash cow, you hear me?" I'm breathing heavily from the effort I'm making to not rip into him with everything I've got.

"What happened?" he asks, his voice shaky, lowered to a tense whisper.

"He's blackmailing me, that's what's happened. He wants seventy-five grand more, on top of the twenty-five I already paid. Not what we agreed, you and I. You didn't tell me you're going to send someone to blackmail me."

"Y-yes, you're right. I didn't. He wasn't supposed to charge you anything. I'll speak to him and—"

"Today's payday is his last, you hear me? Make sure he gets the message. A hundred Gs is enough for a bunch of parts and a mouth shut forever. More than enough."

A brief silence takes over the open line. I don't even hear Chapelle's breathing.

"Yes, I got it," he replies after a while. His earlier hesitation is gone, as if he's figured out what he has to do to get Foster in line. "It won't happen again."

"That's your personal guarantee?"

"Yes."

The answer is short, concise, and strangely reassuring. I can't think of a single reason why I should believe him, but I do. It's something in the way he's said it.

"Is he done with the work?" Chapelle asks as I'm about to end the call.

"I'll know in a few minutes. If he's not done, he won't get paid."

"I see. Can you please confirm if he's done? A text to this number is enough."

"That, I can do." I let out a long breath of air. "Don't make me call you again."

I end the call as I take the freeway exit, heading home. Foster better know how to spend wisely, because he won't see a dime more from me.

As I'm waiting for a light to turn green, a chime warns me I have a new message.

I open the messenger and curse out loud. My father-in-law's written, *"Paul, it's been a while since we spoke. Let's share a proper meal aboard the Sea Titan—hearty stuff, like sailors eat. Noon next Tuesday, sharp. We're docked at the Port of LA, gate 14. Ask for access with my name. Don't be late."*

*What the fuck?*

I stare at the message, trying to remember the last time Amanda's father and I went for a meal together. What the hell has she been telling him about me? All lies... I can only imagine. But now I have to contain this.

Angry honking snaps me back to my seat, and I drive off, my tires squealing. I use the car's media system to reply to his message, with a simple, unceremonious, "I'll be there."

Because I'll be damned if I shy away from whatever the old fuck has to say. I'm not afraid of him.

When I turn onto my driveway, I see Foster sitting on the boulder, like before. He's grinning as he meets me by my car's door.

"It's all done, my man," he says. "You got my money?"

# 53

# AL JAZINSKI

---

The coroner's office gives me the creeps, like it always does. It smells of bleach and the faint, metallic tang of something unidentified, but I'm not curious to find out what that is. Eckhart and I find Dr. Evans talking with someone who's grieving, probably here to identify a loved one. I don't envy them one bit. I can't count the times I've feared this could happen to me, if Maria makes the wrong choices. Every time she doesn't pick up the phone, or when I come home and she's out who knows where, my overactive imagination paints this exact scene.

We give the coroner a minute to wrap things up. When she's done, she greets us with a wave, her glasses perched on the edge of her nose and her usual no-nonsense expression firmly in place. At forty-five, she's seen more dead bodies than I've seen overtime hours, and her passion and professionalism are only some of the things I admire about her.

"Gentlemen," she says, motioning us inside. "I've got answers for you. Some of them, anyway."

Eckhart and I follow her through the brightly lit hallway into her office, bypassing the viewing room. Good. I don't need to see the victim again, not unless I have to. Evans flips open a folder on her desk, gesturing for us to sit.

"I'll start with what we know," she begins, glancing at her notes. "The time of death: I can place it precisely within a window of twenty minutes. My preliminary estimation is confirmed. She was killed almost instantly upon impact, and the evidence suggests the crash occurred between 12:30 and 12:50 AM last Thursday."

Eckhart raises an eyebrow. "That precise?"

Evans nods. "Rainwater and blood seepage. Her clothing was dry when she died, which means she was hit before the rain started at 12:37. But when she was thrown into the ravine, the rain had just begun, soaking the top layer of her clothing. That's consistent with the time Weather Services reported the rain moving inland. Then, rain carried sand and dirt around her body, but not under it. Additionally, insect activity on the body—specifically, blowfly larvae—indicates a seven-day interval between the time of death and when she was found."

I whistle low. "You never cease to amaze me, Doc."

She shoots me a quick glance. "We were lucky. If it weren't for the rainfall that day, and the drought ever since, the best I could've done was give you a twenty-four-hour interval."

I nod. Being lucky has never hurt a cop. Ever. "What else?"

Evans pushes her glasses up, flipping to another page. "Cause of death was severe head trauma, consistent with a vehicular impact at high speed. She suffered a basilar skull fracture—essentially, the base of her skull shattered from the force of the collision. Instantaneous. She wouldn't have felt a thing."

Eckhart leans forward, his hands steepled. "What kind of speed are we talking?"

"Based on the injuries to her body, the vehicle was traveling at approximately seventy miles per hour. The type of fracture, the extent of damage to the ribcage, spine, and left femur, and the trajectory of her fall all suggest a sedan or SUV." She pauses. "It was clean. No braking, no hesitation before the impact, but forensics was able to tell there was significant braking after. Whoever hit her didn't even slow down before hitting her, but came to a complete stop after."

I exchange a glance with Eckhart. That driver didn't try to avoid her. "They were able to pinpoint the exact spot where she was hit?"

"Yes. Based on residual blood evidence found under the guardrail, we were able to pinpoint where she landed *after* she was hit. Computer modeling did the rest."

"Anything else?" I ask.

Evans flips to the next page. "She was a breast cancer patient, end-stage, undergoing chemo. There was a central venous port in her chest, as well as chemical traces consistent with a specific chemotherapy regimen. Based on the drugs identified, I reached out to hospitals in the area with oncology services." She pulls a printout from the folder and slides it across the desk. "One of them must be missing a patient who matches her general description."

"Missing?" Eckhart asks, frowning. "Did you send her photo out?"

Dr. Evans shakes her head. "That wouldn't help much. She's unrecognizable since the crash. But there are other specifics I was able to share. X-rays of her breasts, race, height, weight, approximate age—this should be enough for a positive ID."

"So, they don't have any idea who's missing from their scheduled treatments? Really?" I let my frustration seep into my voice.

"It's more complicated than that," Evans says, her voice tinged with frustration. "When patients don't show up for treatment, Oncology centers can assume a number of things, including death. Some patients just give up and want to be left alone to die in peace. Others just become too weak to fight. It will take these centers a day or two to give us a positive ID."

I nod, taking mental notes. "What about dental records?"

"Still haven't heard back," she replies. "In the meantime, I'm waiting on a positive ID from the Oncology centers. It shouldn't take long."

Eckhart taps his fingers on the edge of her desk. "Anything else stand out? Something we're missing?"

Evans leans back, folding her arms. "The chemical traces in her port are strong enough to suggest she was undergoing aggressive treatment. This wasn't someone on palliative care. She was still fighting." She pauses, her voice softening. "But her prognosis wouldn't have been good. That's the kind of treatment regimen used for end-stage cases. A month or two, at best."

The room falls quiet. I feel the weight of her words settle over us like a heavy fog. A woman dying of cancer, struck by a car and left in a ravine. It's cruel and heartbreaking on a level I can't even articulate.

Evans clears her throat, breaking the silence. "I also found a faint residue of alcohol on her breath, and traces of prescription painkillers in her system. Neither in quantities to impair her significantly, but enough to suggest she wasn't feeling her best. Why she was out there, in the middle of nowhere, is still a mystery."

"Can we assume suicide by car?" I ask.

Dr. Evans shrugs. "It's your job to assume. I deal in scientific facts only. But if I were to formulate a guess, I'd say yes, definitely a possibility. Malibu Canyon Road at that time of night is very dark and doesn't see a lot of traffic, but the vehicles driving it will be speeding. It'd be a good choice if you were looking to do something like that."

I stand, stretching out the ache in my back. "Thanks, Doc. Keep us posted on the ID."

"I will," she says, standing as well. "I expect to have confirmation soon. A day—two at most."

Eckhart and I walk out into the bright hallway, her final words following us like an echo. As we step outside, the sun feels too warm, too bright.

"She was already dying," Eckhart mutters, almost to himself. "Damn."

"Yeah," I reply, pulling out my notebook and flipping to a fresh page. "But someone decided to throw her in a ditch. That someone deserves a special place in hell."

# 54

# AMANDA DAVIS

Monday mornings, the emergency department is flooded with heart attacks, drug overdoses, and traffic trauma—the staples of people's reactions to starting a new work week. Mondays see an increase of thirteen percent in myocardial infractions compared to the rest of the week's average. That's how much people hate going to work.

Not me, though.

The hospital has become my refuge, a place where Paul can't reach me, and where my shattered marriage and screwed-up life can't consume me. When I'm working on a critical overdose like the one we've just stabilized, there's no time to think, to remember.

Paul didn't sign the divorce papers. Didn't even read them. He behaved just as I expected him to. Made threats. Punched walls. Shouted at me, his face flushing an alarming shade of red, with veins bulging at his temples like he was on the verge of a stroke. I don't know what's scarier: his temper or the fact that he knows he's losing control over me.

It took everything I had to not leave the house, but it's my house, too.

*Going back home to face him was stupid,* I tell myself. *He's not the man you thought he was. Safety first, remember?*

The thought flashes through my mind, bringing a chill to my spine. He wouldn't hurt me...would he?

"Dr. Grant? Amanda? The boss wants you both in her office," Sunny announces from outside the door of Trauma

Three. I don't need to ask who she's talking about. Only Dr. Kenna, the department's chief of staff is called *the boss*.

"We're not done here!" Dr. Grant snaps. His stethoscope is on the patient's chest. "Monitor that rhythm—looks like it's progressing to VT."

"Yes, Doctor," I reply, keeping my eyes on the monitor.

"Whenever you can," Sunny says, shrugging apologetically. She and I make eye contact. I'm asking a silent question, but she shakes her head. She doesn't know what it's about.

A few minutes later, when the patient's up on the second floor and admitted into ICU, Dr. Grant and I walk over to Dr. Kenna's office. There's lingering awkwardness between us, a heavy silence I'm afraid to break.

Dr. Grant opens the door for me, and I step into the boss's office. "You wanted to see us?"

She lifts her eyes from the stack of papers in front of her. "Yes, come on in." I feel a rush of anxiety coursing through me.

My pulse quickens as she flips through a pile of folders and pulls one out. I recognize the color-coded tabs immediately: a patient record.

"The two of you treated Marisol Sosa, correct?"

Hearing her name feels like a physical blow. I exchange a glance with Dr. Grant, who's standing stiffly next to me, hands in his coat pockets. I nod, my throat tightening. "Yes, I remember her," I say. "About three weeks ago, maybe a month."

"The police have been asking about her. Is there anything I should be aware of?" Dr. Kenna asks. Her voice is calm, but her eyes are razor-sharp.

My vision narrows, black spots forming at the edges. My knees feel like jelly. *No, no, no. This can't be happening.* I force myself to breathe, to keep standing.

"Amanda?" Dr. Grant looks at me with concern.

I blink, swallowing the rising panic. "No," I manage to say, my voice trembling. "Just…just a very sad story. Such beautiful girl...and a senseless accident." My voice falters again, but I push through. "There was nothing anyone could do."

The boss looks at me over the rims of her glasses. "I read the notes, but can you elaborate? Give me the background on this."

I look to Dr. Grant, hoping he'll pitch in. My voice is betraying me.

"Marisol was caught in a scaffolding collapse while leaving the mall," he explains, his words precise and deliberate. "The structure gave way, and part of the scaffolding fell directly onto her, causing catastrophic injuries. She had a cervical spine fracture at C5-C6, with severe cord compression and likely incomplete transection. This left her quadriplegic and barely able to breathe on her own."

"I see," Dr. Kenna says, frowning as she scans the chart.

Dr. Grant pauses, glancing at me before continuing. "She was placed on mechanical ventilation, but the injuries were unsurvivable. Her spinal damage alone ensured she'd never regain independent breathing or mobility. She also suffered extensive second- and third-degree burns to over 40% of her body."

"Burns?" the boss presses, her voice a little sharper now. She flips through the case file quickly, probably looking for specifics.

"A paint thinner spill," Dr. Grant clarifies. "The liquid ignited when it came into contact with an exposed electrical cable from the fallen scaffolding. That's what the EMT crew said. Marisol was essentially trapped in a fire. The burns weren't survivable on their own, but the spinal injury was the true cause of death."

My hands are clammy, and I rub them on my scrubs, trying to ground myself. Every word feels like a blow.

"So, nothing for me to lose sleep over?" the boss asks.

Dr. Grant's tone turns firm. "No. Absolutely nothing. We provided every possible intervention; documented every step. Unfortunately, her injuries were incompatible with continuation of life. The mother made the difficult but humane decision to discontinue further treatment that would've prolonged her suffering for a few more days."

"The mother opted to discontinue life-prolonging measures?" the boss asks. I see my own pain reflected in her eyes.

"Yes," Dr. Grant replies.

"She expired within the hour," I add quietly. My voice shakes as memories of Marisol's anguished face flood my mind. Her terrified eyes, her broken body.

Dr. Kenna's eyes meet mine. "Any idea why the police are asking questions?"

All I can do is shake my head.

"No," Dr. Grant replies, firm and unflinching. "There's no reason I can think of. The case was fully documented, and all protocols were followed."

She closes the file and puts it back on top of the stack. There's a moment of silence before the boss speaks again, her tone lighter. "All right, then. Thank you for clarifying. If the police follow up with either of you, let me know immediately."

"Will do," Dr. Grant says, and follows me out of Dr. Kenna's office.

For a while, we walk side by side in silence, heading for the ED. I keep my eyes straight, the long corridor seeming as unfamiliar as if I've never been there before. As if I'm trapped in a maze from which there's no escape.

"You need to talk to me," Dr. Grant says when we're in the elevator, his voice gentle. Understanding.

"I can't." My eyes find his for a split second, but then I look away. "It's nothing that affects our work. Some cases just…get to me." I choke on my words and pause for a moment. I take a deep breath to steady myself. "Marisol's did. It haunts me."

I wish I could tell him the truth, but no one can know what I'm hiding. The police aren't asking about Marisol because of what happened in the hospital.

There's another reason.

# 55

# AMANDA DAVIS

I'm quick to disappear after my shift, before Dr. Grant can corner me and continue a conversation I can't afford to have. I take the elevator to the top floor and sneak into the supply room. No one's there at this hour, and they're probably not going to come by until the start of the next shift.

The room smells of bleach and Pine Sol, and is dimly lit. I don't mind. The door I close gently behind me has a narrow, wired window, and the dim lights will attract less attention. An older computer runs on a small desk, its monitor off. I turn it on, and it takes a moment to light up. The supply inventory system takes up the entire screen. I grab the antiquated mouse and work my way through finding a browser I can use in incognito.

Marisol isn't the only specter that haunts me. Since last Wednesday, I've been meaning to find the right opportunity to learn about who Greg Hollen was. I didn't want to search for him from my phone, or my home computer. There's no privacy anymore... And one day, when the police find his body and start searching for answers, when they trace his last whereabouts and they see me on the bar's surveillance video, I better not be further associated with him in any way.

I type his name into the browser and wait for the results page to load. The computer is quite old, and whirrs loudly as it works. I scroll through the results impatiently, barely registering the wrong ones. A couple of obituaries. Several profiles with his name on LinkedIn, and a few others on social sites. A student at a Florida University. A landscaper in Nebraska. And finally, the one I'm looking for.

I switch over to image results and gasp. The man who still haunts my nightmares is posing in front of a height chart and holding a mugshot board with the insignia of the LAPD. The date is from three years ago.

As I study his face carefully, I almost don't recognize him. The corners of his mouth are lowered, the nose crinkled in an expression of disgust. His eyes bother me the most. I can't believe I thought this man was attractive, even if for a drunken, pissed-off minute. The viciousness that glints in his irises is chilling.

I stare at the face displayed on the old, dusty computer screen, doubting my sanity while trying to think. I need to know more. What he's done, to start with, although I have some idea. If he's done time. For a delusional moment, I'm wondering if I could call Danny Bilger or another one of the cops I know well. But that would be the absolute worst thing I could do.

I search for inmate records on the Los Angeles County Sheriff's Office website instead. It takes a while to find the right place, but I finally find what I'm looking for. And it's a long list. Greg Hollen's criminal record paints the picture of a violent sexual predator, unremorseful and unredeemable.

He started young, at 13, but those records are sealed. Then, he got serious. At 20, he smashed a bottle over a man's head during a bar fight. At 26, he was convicted for sexual battery and rape. With my eyes widened in shock, I switch over to the court system search engine and read the testimony detailing the assault. The victim needed stitches on her face and chest. Her trachea was crushed. She was in the hospital for weeks.

That woman could've been me.

Hollen was sentenced to eight years for that. Not nearly long enough. He got out in six for good behavior, only to be charged again for assault and attempted rape the same year.

Four months ago, he was released again, and he is—was— on probation.

My fingers tremble slightly over the mouse.

Now, I know how his body will be discovered. It won't be a missed rent or mortgage payment, or a power failure thawing his body until the stink makes the neighbors call it in. No... It will be his parole officer, busting through the door when he won't report in as scheduled.

I thought I had a month or two until they find his body.

I'm lucky if I have another week.

# 56

# PAUL DAVIS

These days, I live life one day at a time, and it's killing me. Something else must've happened the night of that damn accident. It's as if the universe got screwed up, and things don't make sense anymore. I told Foster I wanted the car repaired as new, and he tried to screw me over, calling it done without replacing the cracked trim under the headlight. He must think I'm an idiot.

Then, there's my wife and her unbelievable nerve. She thought all she had to do was print some template divorce agreement taken off the internet and make me sign it? Lately, she's not demonstrating a lot of sense. She's got until tomorrow to fall in line, or else I'll get her in line, if I have to drag her by her hair.

Tomorrow, at seven-thirty, the two boards of directors are meeting in a joint session, to meet and vet me for national lead anchor for the future network. In Raymond's own words, Amanda and I are now a brand, LA's "beautiful couple" fighting against impaired driving and making a difference, all under the shimmering, gold-plated logo of Golden State Broadcasting. Making millions while at it. That's the difference I care about. Amanda doesn't know it, but I get a piece of that action, and so does my boss.

And now, this. Another piece of insanity I have to deal with—my father-in-law's invite to lunch. On a normal day, that barnacle bastard and his floating pile of junk wouldn't have made it onto my calendar. As for lunch on a commercial freighter? Ew. I'll probably need a tetanus shot after that.

The skinny man wearing a Port Security uniform grins weirdly when I mention my father-in-law's name. "It's over there." He points a dirty finger toward a large ship that's being unloaded. "The *Sea Titan*."

As if I didn't know.

The barrier rises, and I drive toward the ship. As I approach, the size of it seems surreal. Ship-to-shore cranes dance in front of it, taking containers and dropping them onto trucks. A long line of trucks await their cargo. The ship still has hundreds of them on board.

It's huge, a hulking mass of steel, touched by rust and held together by rivets the size of soda cans. The vessel's name, *Sea Titan*, is drawn in bold, black lettering the size of a small apartment building.

As I pull in next to the steep gangway, I look up and squint into the sunlight, trying to see if the bastard's out there waiting. I can't see anything. When I get out of the car, I shiver under the chilly wind that cuts through my suit jacket.

The gangway is steep and slick with sea spray. The scent of ocean brine clings to everything. I step carefully, holding on to the thick, knotted-rope guardrails as if my life depends on it. It probably does. I look below as I climb, and see the narrow space between the dock and the ship's hull, being pounded mercilessly with every wave. Falling would be an instant death sentence.

At the top, the sea dog himself waits for me, legs spread and feet well-grounded, arms crossed at his chest. The strong breeze ruffles his white beard. He nods and shakes my hand firmly.

"Welcome aboard." There's not a trace of welcome in his eyes or his voice.

"Good to see you, Captain," I say, forcing a smile. "Thanks for the invite."

He doesn't reply. Just stares at me for a brief second before gesturing me to follow him.

He leads me through narrow passageways and up steep, grated stairs that clang under my feet. The crew nods as we pass, some offering tight smiles and others avoiding my gaze altogether. I wonder how much they know about their captain's personal life—about me, the famous son-in-law everyone knows from television news.

The tour is brief but thorough, every detail a reminder we're on his territory. The cavernous cargo hold. The bridge, with its labyrinth of controls and blinking lights. The engine room, a cacophony of grinding metal and idling turbines. It's impressive. Overwhelming, even, and it stinks of salty mildew and grime, and I can't be out of there fast enough. This is so not my thing. But I can't shake the feeling that this isn't about showing off his ship. When he passes by the officers' mess without slowing his roll, I'm sure of it.

Finally, we step out onto the bridge deck, the vast expanse of the Pacific stretching out before us. The clanking, whirring, and thudding of cranes continues on the lower deck. Sunlight glints off the waves, and I have to squint after being inside for a while. I should've brought my sunglasses.

I keep my eyes on the horizon. Looking down gives me vertigo. Must be at least a hundred feet to sea level.

My father-in-law leans against the railing. "Beautiful, isn't it?" he asks, looking at me.

"It is," I reply, though the beauty of it is lost on me right now.

His eyes veer toward the horizon. "Out at sea, we have no room to be sensitive or polite when it comes to garbage." His voice is that low, menacing whisper I hate so much.

I can't understand how his voice can carry over the background noise, but it does. It's spine-chilling.

He pauses for a beat, then continues. "We just weigh it down, so it never resurfaces again to stink up my air. And we throw it overboard. That's how I deal with the nasty, stinking problems in my life. Do you understand me, my dearest Paul?"

My jaw tightens. "I believe I do."

He steps closer, the scent of salt and engine oil clinging to him. "I'm the meanest, fiercest son of a bitch you'll wish you never met." His whispers spread ice into my blood. "This wasn't much of a meal, was it? But I hope you found our conversation inspirational. And perhaps learned something from it."

I don't respond. My mouth is dry, my pulse thudding in my ears. His words hang between us like a storm cloud, filling the air with electricity.

*Is he threatening me?*

He damn sure is. Then, he has the gall to smile—just a flutter on his lips, enough to make sure I get the point. He pats me on my back, while I struggle to find the words to spit in his face.

"I'm expecting my daughter's divorce to be a seamless, smooth affair, and that includes custody," he continues, his tone sharp as a knife. "My grandson should grow up knowing that both his parents are alive and well, don't you think?" His smile widens, fueling my burning rage.

Who the fuck does he think he is? I'll fucking destroy him.

When he gestures me toward the door to the bridge, I follow, but after a couple of steps, I grab his arm to stop him. He turns on his heels. I let go of his arm and grab his uniform lapel instead, then get in his face, close enough to smell the Cuban cigar odor of his breath.

"You might think you're some fucking pirate out here, where this tugboat is your kingdom, but on land, I can make and break you fifty different ways from Sunday. You hear me? Be careful, old man. I got your number."

He doesn't flinch. Eyes locked into mine, he whispers, "I want to see you try calling it."

For a moment, we're frozen like that, breathing each other's searing breaths, my hand clutching his lapel, his eyes drilling into mine, unwavering. Then, I let go.

I open the door with an angry swing and head into the bridge to find my way from there. I can hear him walking behind me, a couple of steps back. He escorts me like that down to the gangway, but stops short of stepping onto it. I don't turn around to look at him. I know what I would see. Him, standing there with his legs slightly apart, unfazed by the slight movement of the ship that makes me queasy. Looking at me as if I'm about to become tomorrow's headliner. *Beloved News Anchor Found Dead Under Mysterious Circumstances.*

*Well, fuck him and the barge he's pushing.*

I grab the rope handrail and hold on as I climb down. My Ferragamo shoes slip on the ridged, metallic surface, making my trip down a treacherous one.

I'm almost down on firm ground when one of the officers I met in passing earlier starts his climb up the gangway. He nods and smiles professionally, then says, "Hope we'll see you again soon."

"Not if I can fucking help it," I mumble after passing, as I get behind the wheel of my rental Cadi. My wheels scream when I take off, heading for the gate.

Looking forward to getting home tonight, after work. It's time Amanda and I have a serious talk. She can't fuck things up for me.

# 57

# AL JAZINSKI

---

Eckhart's been glued to the damn screen for hours now. His office chair creaks every time he leans forward, the tablet in his hand glowing with that grainy black-and-white footage. He's like a dog with a bone, refusing to give up even though we've already chewed the damn thing down to the marrow.

The lieu agreed with him, though. He gave us another few days to find our perp. Eckhart can talk anyone into doing anything. But it's not going to be enough.

Every now and then, he jots down something on his notepad. Time codes, memo notes, and usually with the names of the suspects we're chasing.

I sit back in my chair, watching him out of the corner of my eye. He's got that look—the one where he thinks he's on the verge of something big. I'd like to believe him, but after days of staring at cars and timestamps and parking lot angles, my faith is wearing thin. He's got nothing so far—nothing but excuses for the time he's wasting. It seems that everyone who was there at that event somehow managed to drive their own cars the next day.

Maybe we're just going at this the wrong way.

"So," I say finally, breaking the silence. "Anything new, or are we still living in the land of the almost?"

Eckhart doesn't look up. "Just give me a second." He pauses the footage, then rewinds it, then pauses again. "I swear there's something here."

"There's always *something here*, partner. Trouble is, it's usually not enough to make anything stick."

"No, I mean it," he insists, tapping the screen. "Look at this. See the decal on Davis's windshield?"

When I hear the name, my ears perk up. I walk over to his desk, leaning over to squint at the image. It's blurry as hell, like everything else from that parking lot camera. "Yeah, I see it, like I have like a thousand times. We've already established he drove the same car the next day. And so did, what, twenty-seven of his coworkers?" I can't help being a bit of an asshole over this. This case is four hours short of joining the pile of cold cases stacked on my desk.

Eckhart swipes to another timestamp and a different angle. "Now, look at this. Same car, same decal, but something's off."

I cross my arms, frowning. "Off how?"

He zooms in, pixelating the image even more. "The tint's different. Heavier in this one, lighter in the other. And look at the position of the decal—it's slightly higher now. See it?"

"You get that from this grainy image? You're sure it's not the sun?"

He groans and rolls his chair sideways, then reaches over to another detective's desk, swiping the tablet from her hands without asking for permission.

"Hey!" she snaps. "What the fuck?"

"Just a second, okay?" Eckhart flashes a smile and points at me. "Some people don't get it without the right props."

I prop my hands on my hips. "Really?" I can't believe the nerve on the guy.

He doesn't bother to answer me. He just taps on the other tablet for an endless moment, then sets them down, side by side.

"This is Paul Davis arriving to work on Thursday morning, before the fundraiser," he says, pointing at the tablet on his left. "Note the date stamp. And this is him on Friday morning. Same angle, same camera, same sunny weather."

You have to really try to notice it, but once you do, you can't unsee it. It's there. The darker tint on Paul Davis's Thursday vehicle. The higher, crooked position of the decal he had on Friday morning.

"I see it," I say, scratching my chin. "Parking decals don't usually shift around on their own, but the windshield tint is also lighter. You think he replaced it?"

Eckhart nods, his enthusiasm building. "Exactly. If the windshield got damaged, that could mean there was evidence on it. Blood, maybe. Glass fragments from the impact with the victim."

"Or," I counter, "he replaced it because he got a chip from a rock on the freeway. Happens all the time. The rest of the car is undamaged. You said so yourself. It had dust on it, right?"

"Come on, Al," Eckhart presses. "I thought you wanted to get this guy. You don't think this is worth looking into?"

"It's worth thinking about," I say carefully. "But good luck getting a warrant based on a blurry decal and some tint discrepancies. No judge is signing off on that when the guy in question is a media darling."

Eckhart sits back, deflated. "So, what? We just let it go?"

I shake my head. "No. We don't let it go. We just need a different angle."

"Like what?"

I tap my chin, a grin tugging at the corner of my mouth. "He wasn't alone in that car, was he? Davis has a wife, the other half of their *beautiful couple* shindig." I grab one of the tablets and switch screens to the DMV system, then pull up her record. "Amanda Davis. She was with him that night. I've seen them on TV, and they're in the videos from the venue, leaving together."

"Wait a minute, I know her." Eckhart looks at the DMV picture, enlarging it with his fingers. "We met. Twice. She works at Sunset Valley."

"I know she's a nurse, but—" I scratch my head. "How do you know her?"

"Remember that truck versus sedan hit-and-run the lieutenant had us investigating? She responded to our BOLO. Then, when I went to interview Davis. You were busy that day—I went by myself, and she was there. You think she knows something?"

"Think about it," I say, leaning in. "If Davis was involved in that hit-and-run, she knows. She was there, and she's probably freaking out about it. She's our way in."

"Let's try the hospital first, then the house." He grabs his car keys from the desk. "And if she doesn't say anything?" Eckhart asks, taking his jacket from the back of his seat.

I smile, feeling optimistic for the first time since my interview on *The Final Question* with that prick. "Then, we turn up the heat."

# 58

# AMANDA DAVIS

I took an extra shift last night. I just couldn't go back home; couldn't be alone with Paul. I'm not planning to budge on my decision to stop helping his career unless he comes to his senses about the divorce.

And I know that could push him over the edge.

I don't come home until six-thirty in the morning, tired to the bone, glad I have the day off. He texted me last night, wanting to know where I was. I told him. He wasn't happy. I could tell from the three dots dancing on the screen for a while, then disappearing without a message making it through.

When the garage door opens, I find Paul crouched on the floor, studying the repair job on his car under a powerful flashlight. He's dressed in jeans and an old Metallica T-Shirt, the clothes he usually wears when he's mowing the lawn. I leave the Subaru on the driveway and rush inside, then close the garage door quickly, hopefully before the passing neighbors notice there are two identical Cadillacs in the garage.

"Is it done?" I ask, crossing my arms at my chest. I'm still wearing scrubs, and I'm a bit chilly. Or perhaps his glance freezes my blood.

"It's done. I'm taking it to work today."

I know what that means. "Then, let's get it over with."

Like a well-rehearsed dance, we go through the motions of getting his car ready, in a reversal of what we did that Friday morning after the crash. One by one, he swaps the wheels between the two cars, swearing at each juncture, while I move personal items from the rental into his own.

Clothes. Transponder. Glove box items. Checking the trunk to see if anything's left behind. Looking under the seats. Peeling off the parking decal. Sticking the replacement one on the new windshield, making sure it's straight and level.

"Is this the right spot?" I ask, wondering how I never pay any attention to these things.

He drops the tire iron. It clatters loudly, giving me a start. "Yeah, I think so." He frowns and rubs his forehead, probably trying to remember. I'm angry at him, for not checking while the old windshield was still here. He must've known we have to make this perfectly right.

But then again, neither did I. And I'm just as much to blame as he is.

He's still working on swapping the last tire when he stops in the middle of what he's doing and stares at me for a long moment.

"I'm sorry for being an asshole," he says. His eyes dart from mine to the floor, then sideways. His hands are clasped together, nervously.

I can't think of a time when my husband apologized to me and meant it. I bristle, and take a step back.

"You've been more than supportive with me since that stupid bitch stepped in front of my car that night."

There it is. His viciousness poking its head from behind the unfelt words. His staggering lack of remorse. If I had any confidence that his apology was sincere, it's all gone now.

"Thank you," I reply calmly, resisting the urge to take one more step back. "Let's get this over with, and hope it won't come back to haunt us."

"Yes, boss," he quips, grabbing the tire iron to tighten the lug nuts on the rental. The joke he makes doesn't soften the scathing gaze he throws me. Doesn't make me smile.

I give the cars a final inspection. Everything seems to be in order. As I'm about to head into the house to change before I drop the rental off, I take another look at the two cars. A wave of anxiety washes over me, stifling my breath. It's been three weeks almost, I realize. Three weeks of living through this hell.

And it's not over yet.

The tire iron clatters as he packs it into the toolkit. Then, he places the kit and the jack back into the rental. He's done. He wipes his hands on his jeans and walks over to me.

"When do you want to go?"

"After rush hour. I'll take a shower and eat something first."

He hesitates a little, shifting his weight from one foot to the other, hands propped on his hips. "Um, and you remember, tomorrow at seven-thirty we're meeting with Raymond and the joint boards, right?"

I smile bitterly. That's what the fake apology was for.

"No, Paul, I won't be there. I won't do your board meetings, or any of your career-related events." The glimmer in his eyes turns ice cold. "The last thing you need is more power."

Rage glints in his eyes for a split second before his hand is wrapped around my throat, squeezing. He pushes me against the wall, slamming me hard. It knocks the breath out of my lungs. His fingers hesitate, but don't release their grip.

My eyes drill into his, while my hands remain lowered alongside my body, against my instinct to free myself from the suffocating grip.

"Are you prepared to do time for murder, Paul?" I say, choked, my voice croaking and strangled.

He instantly lets go, as if my skin is burning him. "You tell people lies about me. You're going to ruin both our lives!" He's shouting, his mouth so close to my face that I sense the vibration of his voice against my skin.

"What lies?" I ask, genuinely confused.

He scoffs angrily. "Don't tell me you don't know. What have you been telling that sour sack of sea manure?"

He never liked my father, but he's never called him names to me like that before. *Never.*

"Telling my father that I want a divorce is the truth. You know it." His hand finds my throat again, tentatively. I can see in his eyes the raging battle happening within. If he could get away with it, he would kill me with his bare hands. Right here, right now. "It will make your murder trial that much more interesting," I manage to say.

He lets go and takes a couple of steps back, looking away as if ashamed. But I'm not buying it. He's probably still thinking about how he can get me to attend the meeting tomorrow.

It's not going to fucking happen.

I grab the doorknob for balance as I steady my shattered breath. "If you ever lay hands on me again—" I start, but he cuts me off.

"It won't happen again, I promise." He looks me straight in the eyes, all rage having vanished. A glimmer of something undefined is giving me the chills, but his voice sounds truthful and calm, as if a decision has been made, and I realize what that decision could be.

He's going to cut himself a deal with the cops and sell me out.

# 59

# PAUL DAVIS

---

*Fuck.*

Now, I have to do damage control with Raymond, and it's not gonna be pretty.

It's almost eleven when I enter his office, trying my best to look relaxed and stop grinding my teeth. I'm bringing with me his favorite Starbucks fix, hoping it will appease him when he hears what I'm going to say.

On the drive over, I kept thinking of what possible reasons I could give for my wife's absence from the meeting. I made a commitment, and fuck it, and she makes me break it. I could invent a hospital emergency of sorts, and hope he'll never find out. Death in the family? Won't track. Sick child? Ugh... I'm better off just saying she can't make it. Too many lies are tough to manage.

"Come on in," Ray says, getting up from his desk chair to meet me. I put the coffee cups on his table, then we shake hands. "Take a seat," he says, reaching for the coffee cup with his name on it.

"Thanks." I take a sip from my own brew and find it more bitter than usual. For a moment, we sit in silence, giving in to the pleasure of our shared afternoon habit. "Are the cops done asking you about that stupid hit-and-run?" I ask, doing my best to sound casual.

"I haven't heard from them since I told them I was hungover and didn't drive." He laughs, seemingly impressed with himself. "How about you? Did that beautiful wife of yours drive you home that night?"

I nearly choke on my coffee. "No, I did, but I was fine," I rush to explain. "I didn't have that many. I had to give the final speech and all that."

"Are you ready for tonight?" he asks, his voice teeming with excitement. He leans over the table and mock-punches my shoulder. "It's going to happen! I can feel it."

"Yes, it will," I say, smiling widely while wondering how I'm going to broach the subject.

The intercom buzzes. He springs to his feet and walks over to the desk. He looks twenty years younger, as if the upcoming merger injected new life in his jaded, balding soul.

He pushes a button on his desk phone. "Yes?"

"I have Latesha for you."

He looks at me, then rolls his eyes. "Send her in."

I barely contain an oath. What the fuck does she want now?

The door opens and Latesha walks in, stepping confidently on three-inch heels. Her pant suit fits her body really well. If she weren't such a viper, I'd fuck her once. Maybe twice.

"Hey," she greets Raymond, beaming, and then she notices me, still seated at the small conference table. Her smile wanes. "Oh. Hi, Paul."

"Take a seat," Ray says. "Paul and I were just wrapping something up."

"Cool." She sits across from me and smiles. Her eyes are veering from me to Ray and back, but they settle on him. "Don't mind me."

"So, we're set for tonight?" Ray asks me, referring to the board meeting.

"I'll be there." I pause for a moment, wishing Latesha wasn't in the room. "Amanda won't be able to make it. She sends her apologies...something to do with training with a specialist who's only in town today." Ray's expression shifts, first to disappointment, then frustration. "We're both really sorry, but you can count on me. I'll be there, and we'll make it happen just like we discussed."

Ray presses his lips together and lets out a frustrated sigh. "Damn… I really like that family man vibe about you. They reacted so well to that at the fundraiser. It's just what everyone's looking for."

I curse in my mind. I really hate Amanda right now. Her issues, her threats, every fucking breath she takes. "We'll make it work, Ray, you and me. Amanda works in the emergency department of a hospital. People will understand."

He scratches his shiny scalp. I can see his jaw tightening. "You sure she can't make it?"

I stare at the table's shiny surface for a moment, hoping rage doesn't still glint in my eyes when I look at him. "I'll ask again, but I'm pretty sure."

"But I can," Latesha interjects. "Whatever this is about, I got you covered, Ray."

I glare at her, but she's unfazed.

"Um, I don't know," Ray says. "I've already sent the agenda with Paul's name on it. Perhaps we're better off sticking to what was communicated. I don't believe Amanda's absence will be the deal breaker. It would've been nice to reassert our lead anchor's family values with a strong visual, but—"

"Add my name to the list. I'm happily married, and my husband will make it work, even on short notice. Day or night."

She's leaning over the table as if she's about to climb onto it and crawl to Ray on all fours, ready to suck his dick. From his vantage point, Ray can catch a very satisfying glimpse of her cleavage.

"What does he do? Does it look good on camera, what you two have?"

Latesha's grin widens. She throws me a triumphant glance. "You be the judge of that. He's a fire chief."

I witness, powerlessly, how Raymond's face lights up. Then, the two of them excitedly discuss the upcoming meeting and Latesha's role in it, as if I wasn't even there. It's over before I can think of a way to contain this.

Ray dismisses us both with a gesture, then turns to me and asks, "You're still going to be there, right?"

"Wouldn't miss it for the world," I reply, then walk out the door.

I catch up with Latesha by the elevators, and we share one together. As soon as the doors close, I drill my eyes into hers.

"Slow your fucking roll," I hiss. "I'm not dead yet. I still got claws. This is not your opportunity to have, you hear me?"

She looks at me, visibly amused. "Oh, but it is, my dear Paul. Or else I'll tell the cops you were drunk as a squirting skunk that night when I saw you getting behind the wheel."

I gasp. "Motherfucking, lying bitch! You wouldn't dare."

She laughs in my face. "Oh, wait, perhaps I'll add the fact that you've started parking your car differently since that day? Or that you requested a new parking decal?" She cackles loudly as the elevator slows down. "Marjorie from HR told me that over coffee a couple of days ago. She couldn't think of a reason why you'd need one for the same vehicle. They're built to last."

The elevator comes to a stop. I can't breathe. Can't control the rise of acid in my throat, the urge to scream. I stare at her, slack-jawed, stunned. Then, reality sinks in, and my heart starts racing.

*I'm fucked.*

The doors slide open, and she walks past me, clacking her heels. She pats my arm in passing. "I'm sure you didn't mean it," she says, walking down the corridor, matching my wavering pace. "I'm hearing the poor woman was suicidal." She shrugs and winks at me, right before entering her dressing room. "Too bad you were drunk, though. And you fled the scene."

Her door slams in my face.

I feel my blood draining, building up into a wave that's threatening to drown me from within. The pressure on my chest is unbearable. The only thing I hear is the desperate thumping of my own heart, resonating to the racing thoughts slicing through my mind.

After a moment spent alone in my own dressing room, only one thought remains, clearly taking shape in my mind.

I need to contain this. Right fucking now.

# 60

# AMANDA DAVIS

Returning the rental car goes just as smoothly as I hoped. I'm wearing shades and a ball cap, and smile politely, eager to get out of there. They offer a shuttle to the airport, but I decline. Shuttles have video cameras.

I walk instead, anxiously oblivious to the warm sunshine and perfectly blue sky, looking to put some distance between the car rental office and the place I'll call an Uber from.

But I never get there. A call from Paul interrupts my steady pace.

"Is it done?" he asks, without bothering to greet me.

"Yes." A long breath leaves my lungs.

"Where are you?"

"On my way back. Why?" A chill runs through my veins, prickling my skin with goosebumps. Something must've happened.

"We need to talk. I'll pick you up."

"I'm at Vineland and Oxnard. I'll continue walking south. How long?"

"Not long," he replies, and hangs up.

I swallow my irritation with his behavior. It's as if my time doesn't matter. I'm supposed to wait...how long, exactly, before I give up and call a cab? For a moment, I rehearse in my mind the speech I'm planning to give him about it. But it would be pointless.

He's never going to change.

About fifteen minutes later, he pulls to the curb, and I climb into his car. He drives off without saying a word. He looks tense and pale—scared, even. His hands squeeze the steering wheel tightly. The silence between us is heavy, fueling my anxiety.

"What happened?" I ask eventually.

"People noticed things," he says. "People from work. And they're talking about it."

My heart skips a beat. "What things? The decal?"

"Some bimbo in HR made a comment about it to Latesha, who then said I was drunk leaving the party. Fucking Latesha." He slams his hand into the steering wheel.

"What does she want?"

His jaws clench tightly for a moment. Veins bulge on his temple. "Everything." He turns briefly to look at me. "My job, my position as Ray's number-one, everything I've got. And it's your fault."

*Of course, it is.* Everything that's ever been wrong in my husband's life, he's found a way to blame on me. I'm not in the least surprised he says that. That doesn't mean I have to agree.

"How is it my fault?"

"This wouldn't be an issue if you'd just done as I asked you and showed up for the meet-and-greet tomorrow."

*Oh, bloody hell.*

I'm tempted to yell at him until I lose my voice. But I won't. "Something tells me she noticed you were driving drunk that night—"

"I wasn't drunk!" he shouts, rattling me. It's the shouting in tight, closed spaces that gets to me. My fear and concern turn into resentment.

"I was right there, completely sober, but you just had to drive, didn't you? Stubborn fool," I add under my breath, fighting my tears and losing. What's going to happen to me? To Tristan?

"It was an accident," he adds, sounding unconvinced.

I breathe slowly, steeling my nerves. "What do you want to do?" I ask after a while.

"I don't know," he replies, turning onto our street. "I'll call my lawyer tomorrow. Maybe she can see us first thing."

I turn to look at him, wondering how someone so successful can be so impractical. It's barely noon. "Call her today, Paul. *Today.*"

"Shut up," he says in a low voice, pulling onto our driveway. "No matter what, don't say a word."

I look out the window and freeze. Two men are standing in front of our door. One of them is that cop who was here last week, Eckhart. The other one, an older guy, also looks familiar, but I can't place him.

Paul stops the Cadillac before it reaches the garage door, but leaves that closed. When I get out of the car, my knees feel weak, shaky.

"Detectives," Paul greets them casually, seemingly relaxed. The man's ability to lie never ceases to amaze me. "What can we do for you?"

A badge is flashed briefly. "Detectives Jazinski, Eckhart." The older detective nods at Paul, mumbles a hello to me, and then proceeds to inspect the Cadillac thoroughly. The other one soon joins him, pointing his finger at the hood and then the fender.

"Nice repair job," Jazinski says, freezing the blood in my veins with those three words. "You can't tell a thing."

"What are you talking about?" Paul asks.

"Dust, Mr. Davis." He laughs quietly. There's a glint of glee in the cop's bleary, blood-shot eyes. "Your fenders are dusty, but the hood isn't. You should've taken it through the car wash a couple of times after they fixed it for you."

He reaches behind his back. The rattling of handcuffs twists my stomach into a knot.

"Paul Davis, Amanda Davis, you are both under arrest for the hit-and-run resulting in the death of Esperanza Sosa."

# 61

# AMANDA DAVIS

---

It feels unreal. Paralyzing. The tightening of the cold metal handcuffs around my wrists that sends a jolt of panic through my body, filling me with dread. Eckhart's hand on my head, pressing it down as he shoves me into the back seat of his unmarked SUV. The faint smell of vomit and sweat I sense before tears flood my eyes and stuff my nose.

The two detectives climb into the car, slamming the doors and chatting casually, ignoring us completely.

The low hum of the police SUV's engine fills the silence, broken occasionally by the crackle of the radio. I sit stiffly in the backseat, my wrists aching from the handcuffs biting into my skin.

I look at Paul and can't recognize him. He seems dumbstruck. He's staring straight ahead, his face pale as a sheet and his lower lip quivering slightly. He's breathing heavily, as if he can't get enough air.

"I know the drill," Eckhart says, tapping his fingers on the steering wheel. "Get the warrant served, sweep the house. Bag anything that looks remotely useful."

Jazinski grunts in agreement. "Garage first. That Cadi's priority number one. We'll have it towed straight to impound. CSU can tear it apart."

"Think they'll find anything?" Eckhart asks, his voice tinged with curiosity. "Other than dust?"

"Don't need to," Jazinski replies, leaning back in his seat. "Evidence's tight on the videos. Between that and the fact that it's been recently repaired, we're already covered. But if there's blood, fibers, anything that ties the Cadi to the vic…" He lets out a low whistle. "That's the nail in the coffin."

Eckhart chuckles dryly. "Yeah, well, let's hope they didn't Lysol the whole car."

"Doubt it," Jazinski says. "These types? They always think they're smarter than us. Bet there's something they missed."

My stomach churns at his words. I glance at Paul, who's sitting frozen, his jaw tight. He doesn't look at me.

"Excuse me," I say, "why am *I* being arrested?"

Paul glares at me. He wants me quiet, and he's probably right.

"You're under arrest for suspicion of involvement in a hit-and-run resulting in death." Detective Jazinski makes brief eye contact with me through the rearview mirror.

Eckhart glances back. "Any other questions, you can save for your lawyer."

"Suspicion? Based on what?" I ask, against my better judgment. They read me my rights. I should make use of them.

"Based on evidence, Mrs. Davis. That's all we're saying right now."

My eyes flood with tears, trying not to think of Tristan right now. I can't. It would tear my heart to shreds.

"What about the house?" Eckhart continues his earlier conversation. "What are we looking for?"

"Same story," Jazinski replies. "Shoes, clothes. Anything that could've been worn that night and might have blood on it. Maybe some receipts for cleaning supplies. Hell, even a dry-cleaning tag could be useful. CSU will bag it all."

Eckhart snorts. "Bet their lawyer's already spinning some bullshit defense. 'My clients are just victims of an overzealous investigation.' Blah, blah, blah."

"Yeah, well, let them spin," Jazinski says with a shrug. "Doesn't change what we've got."

A moment of silence passes before Eckhart speaks again. "What's next for these two? Holding cells downtown?"

Paul exhales sharply beside me, his composure cracking for just a moment. I close my eyes, fighting the panic threatening to overwhelm me. A wave of nausea rises as the SUV takes a sharp turn.

Paul's knee touches mine, and I look to him. The conversation happening between the two cops fades as Paul's whispers catch my ear.

"Stop talking," he says. "For fuck's sake, Amanda, just stop. I'll get us a lawyer and we'll sort through this."

"Okay," I reply, but I've lost all confidence. I know he's going to sell me out. I can see it in his eyes. And I'm terrified.

"I swear to God, Amanda, if you say another word, I'll—"

"Hey, shut up back there!" Eckhart snaps. "This ain't some coffee lounge."

"My apologies, Detective," Paul replies calmly. "We were just discussing which lawyer to call. Hers or mine."

# 62

# AL JAZINSKI

---

I lean against the observation glass, arms crossed, staring at Amanda Davis. She's been sitting in the interrogation room for over two hours, her hands folded in her lap, her gaze fixed somewhere on the floor. She's not speaking with her lawyer. Her reflection stares back at me from the one-way mirror, looking pale and haunted.

Her attorney, Dennis Patricio, is a guy I've worked with in the past. He's not terribly pushy, like the overpriced ones are, but he knows his shit and I have to tread carefully. I was surprised she had to call a lawyer's referral service to get him. She wasn't prepared for this. Even if my partner recalled that he talked about another hit-and-run with her at the hospital, and how the passenger could be charged in such cases. She must've known what was coming.

Strange that such a similar situation brought Amanda Davis and my partner together a week ago. A completely random happenstance, like a warning from fate.

And she still didn't get a lawyer.

Well, some people believe in miracles. She must be one of them.

Eckhart munches on a protein bar beside me, his gaze shifting between Amanda's room and the one next door, where Paul Davis lounges like he's waiting for a table at some swanky restaurant. His high-priced attorney sits across from him, this one being a woman whose suit probably costs more than Eckhart's monthly salary. Paul doesn't look the least bit phased. Amanda, though? She's a wreck.

"So," Eckhart says around a mouthful of granola. "Who do you wanna start with?"

I glance over at Paul's room. He's smirking, leaning back in his chair, casually chatting with his lawyer. "Not him. Not yet. He's too slick, too comfortable. We'd just waste our time."

"Figured as much," Eckhart mutters. "The wife, then?"

I nod, tapping the glass with my knuckle. "She's the weak link. Look at her. She's barely holding it together." I turn to Eckhart. "I've got a hunch about her."

"Let's hear it."

I shift my weight, my jaw tightening. "Remember that TV interview? Paul could've skewered me over those excessive force complaints, but he steered clear. Maybe this was the reason. Maybe she's more involved in this mess than we know, and she's about to spill large."

Eckhart raises an eyebrow. "You think she's gonna flip on him?"

"She's got the look of someone who's running out of options. Let's see if we can give her a push."

He nods, crumpling the wrapper of his protein bar and tossing it into the trash. "Alright. I'll keep an eye on Pretty Boy in the meantime."

I step into the interrogation room, closing the door behind me slowly and taking the time to stretch her nerves. Amanda looks up, her eyes darting to the folder in my hand. She's scared, but she's trying to hide it.

"Mrs. Davis," I start, pulling out a chair and sitting across from her. Her lawyer straightens his tie, but stays quiet. "I'm Detective Jazinski. Let's talk."

Her hands grip the edge of the table. "I've already said I have nothing to say."

I ignore her, opening the folder and pulling out two photographs of Malik Foster, a.k.a. Fast Lane Foster. In one, he's floating face down in the waters of Marina del Rey. In the other, he's face up on the coroner's table, a deep gash running across his forehead all the way to his left temple, the edges discolored and ragged. The coroner said it must've been a small axe.

I slide the pictures across the table. Wide-eyed, she glances at them, then quickly looks away, her face losing what little color it had left.

"Do you recognize this man?" I ask, my voice calm, but firm.

She swallows hard, her lawyer leaning in to coach her, but she beats him to it. "No."

"You sure?" I press, my tone sharpening. "Because your husband told my partner he's your handyman, and now he's dead. We think it has something to do with you and your husband."

Her hand flies to her mouth, her breath hitching. "I—I don't know him," she stammers, gesturing nervously. "I swear. Never spoke to him." Her attorney clasps her forearm, and she stills.

I could kick Patricio in the gonads right now. But it's the way this game is played.

I lean forward, lowering my voice. "Mrs. Davis, you're looking at a list of charges that would make your head spin. Accessory after the fact. Evidence tampering. Hit-and-run manslaughter. And now, maybe even accessory to murder. Something tells me this mess isn't your doing. Do you really want to go down for all of that?"

She stares at me without saying a word.

"Perhaps you would've called us, but you were afraid of your husband. Afraid for your life. Is that what happened? Because if you don't collaborate—"

Her lawyer sits up straighter, finally finding his voice. "Detective, if you're trying to intimidate my client—"

"Intimidate?" I scoff, cutting him off. "No, this is just me laying out the facts. Your client is staring down the barrel of some very serious charges. Two people are dead. She's going down hard unless she has something to say that can help her case."

Amanda's hands tremble as she picks up the photographs, staring at them with horror in her eyes, as if Foster might come back to life. Her voice shakes when she finally speaks. "If what you're saying is true," she begins, her eyes still on the picture, "and I could be charged as an accessory—not just for this hit-and-run you keep talking about, but for...this..." She slides the photos back toward me with trembling fingers. "Then I want a deal. On the table. Before I say anything."

I sit back, hiding my satisfaction. "What kind of deal?"

Her lawyer jumps in, his confidence bolstered by her resolve. "Full, unlimited, blanket immunity for all and any actions between the date of the fundraiser and the moment my client was arrested," he says, his voice steady now. "In exchange, we give you Paul Davis, tied up neatly with a bow."

I stare at Amanda, studying her pale face and trembling hands. She's smarter than I gave her credit for. Smarter than her husband, that's for damn sure.

"I'll see what I can do," I say, standing up. "You'd better hope you're worth it."

I leave the room, shutting the door behind me, and find Eckhart waiting in the hallway. He looks at me expectantly.

"Well?" he asks.

"She's ready to talk," I say, a grim smile tugging at my lips. "But only if we give her a free pass. She's throwing Paul under the bus."

Eckhart whistles low, shaking his head. "Wow. That was faster than I thought."

"She's terrified. Foster's murder shook her, and she's not about to take the fall for something she didn't do. It was obvious she didn't know about it." I glance back at the room, my thoughts already spinning. "This is about to get real interesting."

"And Paul Davis?" Eckhart asks.

I grin, itching with anticipation. "He's next."

# 63

# PAUL DAVIS

It's been hours, and we're still waiting.

*Motherfuckers.*

My lawyer couldn't care less at $1,100 per hour. She's reading her email on her phone, rarely looking up from the screen, while I'm losing my fucking mind.

I need to pee so badly. But I'll be damned if I'll beg for a potty break. I bet they do this on purpose, and they're just letting me stew so I make mistakes and say too much. Things they can use against me in court. But they're so wrong... I know better than that.

I wonder what's taking them so long. Are they speaking with Amanda? Is that what's going on? Is she spilling her guts? She can't be that stupid.

"Miss Hedman," I say, and my lawyer looks up from her screen. "Is this normal? Waiting for so long?"

"No." She shifts in her seat, her eyes darting toward the mirror. "It's quite unusual, actually. Especially with certain people. Is there something you're not telling me about your situation?"

I ignore her question. "*Certain*, as in...famous? Or what?"

"More like, represented by a certain class of attorney. Not Legal Aid, if you know what I mean. People who could sue."

"Can we?"

"Sue? Not yet, Mr. Davis. They are well within their rights to hold you for forty-eight hours without charging you, and you've only been here six."

"Fabulous," I grumble, putting my feet up on the scratched, dented table. The room is small and grimy, with scratched, stained walls, and it smells badly. I didn't expect five-star accommodations, but at least some level of decency. And access to a toilet.

When the door finally opens, I jump to my feet. My attorney glares at me, and I sit back down on the small, metallic chair.

It's Jazinski himself, followed by the other cop, Eckhart. They take their seats across the table, and Eckhart drops a case file on the table. It's got a long number stamped in red ink.

"Tell us about the fundraiser, Mr. Davis," Jazinski asks, speaking slowly. "Did you have anything to drink?"

My lawyer nods. I'm cleared to answer.

"You mean alcohol? Yes. I had a couple of drinks, not more."

"Were you drunk when you left?"

"No." My voice sounds firm, sincere, and I gain confidence in myself. "I ate fatty foods at the event, and had one, maybe two drinks the entire evening."

"Beer?"

"Scotch."

"And you weren't even a little buzzed?"

My professional smile appears on my lips. "I had to deliver the closing speech that night. No one forks out the cash at an event like that if the keynote speaker is slurring and unfocused. Especially since my organization is fighting against drunk driving, and raising money to put legislation in place for the cause."

Jazinski and Eckhart exchange quick glances, both nodding slowly.

"How about the road home?" Eckhart asks. "Who drove? Mrs. Davis?"

My eyes dart to my lawyer. She nods her approval. "No. I did."

"And what happened on the way home?" Jazinski asks.

I shrug involuntarily. "Nothing. When we were close to home, the rain started. Heavy."

Hedman's hand lands on my forearm. "My client and I need a break, if you don't mind."

Jazinski glares at her, and he's not the only one. I'm on a roll, selling my story. I can tell they're buying it. And she wants me to stop now?

Jazinski groans, then stands, holding on to the edge of the table for support. "Alright, we'll give you a few minutes. Make it quick."

The door closes behind them with a screechy squeak, and latches with a loud click.

"What the fuck are you doing?" I ask, struggling to keep my voice down.

"Mr. Davis, as your attorney, I can't sit idle and let you perjure yourself. You have the right to remain silent. You can refuse to answer any questions. But if you choose to answer them and perjure yourself, it will lead to more criminal charges filed against you."

My hand flies to my forehead. I stand and start pacing the room, fuming. Then, I turn to her, propping my hands on my hips.

"I could see it in their eyes. They were fishing. They have nothing."

"Mr. Davis, my job is to protect you, but I cannot protect you if you continue down this path. Anything you say needs to be truthful or not said at all. Understood?"

The severity of her words sinks in, chilling my blood. I already lied to them, when I told them nothing happened on the way home.

"But if I refuse to answer, I'll look guilty as fuck," I push back weakly.

"You *are* guilty as fuck, Mr. Davis," she whispers calmly. "Please don't make my job impossible. Shut up, and there will be a time to negotiate this."

"When?"

"When the DA mentions the word 'deal.' Until then, not a word." She looks at me intently, until I nod. Then, she knocks into the two-way glass.

Jazinski opens the door almost immediately, and steps inside. It's just him.

"Alright, where were we?" he says, taking his seat.

"Detective, this line of questioning is not in my client's best interest. I'm invoking his right to remain silent for now, and we will not be making further statements until we've reassessed."

I see his jaw clenching tightly, his eyes darkening. He's fuming, but doesn't say a word. He just leaves the room, and the two of us resume our waiting.

My attorney just confirmed to the cops that I did it. Until now, they could only suspect, but now they know. Otherwise, why would I not want to answer questions about my drive home?

*I'm so fucked.*

# 64

# AL JAZINSKI

Eckhart leans against his desk, chewing on the tip of a pen like it's the last thing he'll ever taste in his life. His eyes are fixed on the whiteboard across from us, where timelines, names, and evidence—or lack thereof—are scrawled in uneven black marker. I sit back in my chair, rubbing the nape of my neck to ease the tension brewing in there. It's going to be a long and frustrating day.

I just got off the phone with forensics, and I can't believe what I just heard.

"They got nothing," I mutter, finally breaking the silence. "Not one drop of blood. Not one damn speck anywhere in that car, inside or out. Clean as a whistle."

Eckhart glances at me, his pen still lodged between his teeth. "How about the shoes? The gala outfits?"

I shake my head. "Nothing. Forensics combed through it all—clothes, shoes, garage floor, the whole nine yards. Nada. They even swabbed their washing machine, every damn corner. Same result."

"Can you imagine what the defense team will do with that?" Eckhart tosses the pen onto the desk. "Fuck. Someone in that family knows how to clean."

"No blood, no DNA, no fibers. The repairs were impeccable, and the electronics were wiped. No GPS data, nothing. Whoever handled that car knew exactly what they were doing."

"What about the list of repairs? Does it match the crash profile?" Eckhart asks, his voice edging toward frustration.

"They said it does. Front grille, windshield, bumper—everything lines up with a high-speed impact. But that proves nothing. Could've been from any incident, any time. They'll deny knowledge of it or refuse to speak, and we'll have no recourse."

Eckhart snorts. "No blood, no trace evidence placing them there. So, what do we have?"

"The evidence collected at the scene, the grille fragments and the red speck of enamel—they are a perfect match to Paul Davis's Cadillac. We have that, circumstantial as it may be. It could've been *any* Cadillac XT6, though. They can't match it to his because of the repairs."

"It's something, but not much. Anything else?"

"A missus who's willing to spill her guts for the right deal. Let's make that deal happen. Seems we don't have much of a choice." I type a quick email to the DA's office, outlining the terms of the deal. "Kinda unexpected for Mrs. Davis to ask for blanket immunity, don't you think? Mobsters do that. Not ED nurses who happened to be in a car crash without even driving the vehicle."

Eckhart shrugs. His bony shoulders poke through his shirt. "People watch too much TV. The curse of our times. But I gotta say, GPS data on that Cadi would've been nice. It would've shown they stopped and spent time at the scene."

"I bet they paid top dollar for that repair job. I wonder where it was done. I'm pretty sure Foster did the repair, but where? In their garage? I hope not...A witness or five would be nice. A traffic cam showing the car was damaged would be even better." I check my email, but it's too soon to see a reply from the DA's office.

"You sure she's going to give us what we need?" He throws the chewed pen into the trash and grabs another. "She seemed genuinely surprised to see Foster's pictures. I don't think she knows anything about that."

"One thing must've led to another. Foster was into chopping cars, right?"

"Right." His voice drags a little as he checks his notes. "Yeah, he was into the whole thing. Stealing, chopping, reselling, the works. Why? What does that scary gut of yours tell you?"

I tilt my head as I think through options. "I bet I know what happened to earn Mr. Foster an axe over the head, if we assume Foster was the repairman for the job."

"So?"

"So, I think he got greedy. He started the repair, found blood, maybe heard about the victim on TV."

"Ah, it makes sense. He asked for more money," he says, and starts digging through the pile of paperwork stacked on his desk. His workspace looks like a teenager's, like a tornado swept through town. A mess of notes, notepads, faxes, case files, and bank statements. I don't know how he can function. "Here it is," he says cheerfully, fishing out some papers from the stack— three printouts stapled together. "Paul Davis's bank statements."

"And you didn't tell me you have this?"

"Telling you now," he replies, in a tone that's supposed to make me calm down, but pisses me off instead. He looks at the statement quickly. "You're not gonna guess," he says, grinning.

I want to punch him in the face. "I don't *want* to guess," I reply coldly. "Do you want to live?"

He shakes his head at me as if to say I'm such a buzzkill, but gives up trying to piss me off even worse. "A week after the crash, Paul withdrew twenty-five large ones from his savings account. Then, another week later, seventy-five more. I think he was being fleeced. You were right. Again."

"Fuck," I whisper, staring at the whiteboard. "I might've been wrong."

"How were you wrong? It's exactly what you said."

"Except Paul *had* the money and was willing to pay it. We're missing something. Unless he grew tired of paying."

A chime from my computer gets my attention. It's the deal from the DA. I open the file, skim it quickly, and then send it to the printer.

"Maybe the missus can point us in the right direction," I say, walking slowly to the printer, giving the old piece of junk the time to grind its labor.

Eckhart looks over at me. "So, you really think Davis did it?"

I lean forward, resting my hand on his desk. "The hit-and-run? I'd bet my house and my cat on it. But the Foster homicide—I'm not so sure."

Eckhart chuckles. "You don't have a cat."

"My wife does, and I hate the little shit. I'd lose the bet just to be rid of it."

He laughs, but it fades quickly. "How the hell did he drive it the next day, then? That's what I can't figure out. You hit someone at seventy miles an hour at midnight, and the next morning, your car's fine? How?"

I shrug. "That's the million-dollar question, isn't it? Did he replace the windshield? Quick repair job because he's Paul-fucking-Davis and knows people? Swap the car? What?"

"He definitely replaced the windshield. The tint was different, and that decal. But he couldn't have done that at three in the morning, right?" Eckhart tilts his head. "So, then, how? You think he rented one just like it? The exact same model? Where would he find that?"

I smirk. "It's LA, partner. Everything's for rent in this town."

# 65

# AMANDA DAVIS

My lawyer's growing antsy. He fidgets in place, then stands and starts pacing the small, dreary interview room. A few minutes later, he settles for a while, working his phone, and then paces some more.

"Do you think it's going to work?" I ask, feeling my throat go parchment-dry. "They do deals like that all the time, right?"

"Yes." Patricio replies. The tone of his voice fills my heart with dread. "But they didn't *offer* the deal. We requested it. It could go either way. Depends on what else they have."

I feel the blood draining from my face. "I see." I wring my hands together, more to keep them from shaking.

He stops next to me and lands a hand on my shoulder. "Let's keep calm. These things are negotiated. We haven't even started yet."

I'm not reassured. Too many things are hanging in the balance. I think of Tristan for a moment, and my eyes sting with tears. Blinking fast, I force myself to think of something else. The dirty dishes I left in the sink this morning, before leaving to return the rental. I do a mental inventory of all my neighbors who have doorbell cameras, wondering if the police are pulling videos, to see who drove the Cadi this morning.

They'll see me driving it. Then, about thirty minutes later, they'll see Paul driving the other one.

I shake my head, then bury my face in my hands. Losing track of time, I focus on my breathing for a while. I need to be calm, focused. And brave.

There's no telling what could happen. God only knows, I never wanted any of this.

The door creaks open, and the older detective walks in. He's holding a thin file folder under his arm.

"Detective," Patricio says, turning his way. "Do we have a deal?"

"We do," Jazinski says, dropping the file on the table.

I feel relieved. I got what I needed. But the finality of the document is not something I can take too easily. I need to be sure. For myself, for all the questions that will flood my mind when this is all over. For my son.

"Before we discuss this, could I please have a minute with my husband?" I ask, surprised to hear my own voice sound so normal.

Both men stare at me.

"That's not how we do things, Mrs. Davis," Jazinski says. "I'd suggest you sign it, and give us your statement. This deal expires in two hours."

"I only need a minute, please. You can be there, and the lawyers can be there, too." I clasp my hands together in a pleading gesture. "Please."

"Your conversation would not be privileged," Jazinski says. "Even if both your attorneys will be present."

"That's fine." A faint smile lands on my lips.

His brow ridges as he's trying to understand my reasons. His hand flies to his forehead, massaging slowly. "Alright, Mrs. Davis. One minute. And please don't make me regret this. I might take your deal and shred it myself."

"Understood," I reply, doubting my own sanity. But it's just something I feel I must do.

Jazinski leads us across the hall to the interrogation room where Paul is being held. He's surprised to see me walk in. His eyes widen in fear, but I walk over to him and wrap my arms around his neck.

"They can't hear a word," I whisper in his ear, so quietly I can't even hear myself. I know he hears me, because his arms wrap around my back, pulling me close, making me shudder. "Are you sorry?"

"What?" His breath touches my ear.

"For any of it…are you sorry?"

His groan of frustration lands in my hair. "For fuck's sake, Amanda, you were there. It was an accident."

"Yeah, it was," I whisper back. "Hang in there. It will soon be over."

I pull away, and he looks at me with fear in his eyes. Unmistakable fear.

"Amanda!" he calls after me when I'm almost at the door. His attorney rushes to shush him.

I turn and smile weakly his way, trying for a reassuring nod. "We'll be alright, Paul. I promise you."

Patricio follows me to the other interrogation room, and the door to Paul's slams behind me, rattling loudly. I flinch. My hands are frozen, and my breaths are shallow.

Moments later, seated at the table, I stare at the immunity deal Jazinski's presented me with. Patricio reads it carefully while I hold my breath.

"That's fine," he says to me, pushing the document in front of me. "You can go ahead and sign."

I start reading it, but the legalese dances in front of my eyes, making little sense. I force myself to slow down, to read everything, to understand it. Shooting my attorney a quick glance, I grab the pen and click it, ready to sign.

"And it's blanket immunity? Does it cover everything and anything?"

Patricio leans over and traces a paragraph with his manicured finger. "See here, where it says, 'The prosecution agrees to grant Amanda Davis full, unlimited immunity from prosecution for any and all actions, events, or omissions,' and so on? That's the blanket statement." He squeezes my hand gently. "It's good, Amanda. You can sign it." He opens the deal to the last page and taps his finger on the signature line.

The tip of the pen hovers, shaking slightly in the air above the dotted line. Once I sign it, there's no turning back. There will be nothing left. No future for Paul and me, no way to avoid what's coming. Tristan will be the son of a convicted felon.

Worst of all, I'll have to testify in court. My son will witness me testifying against his beloved father, and he will never forgive me for it. There's no way I can prevent it; he's determined to be there for his dad. Saying no to that will only make things worse between us. And when he'll hear my testimony, he'll know I'm responsible for putting his father behind bars. For breaking his heart.

But at least he'll grow up with a mother.

All I have to do after I sign is tell the truth, and nothing but the truth. Although perhaps not the *whole* truth. Some secrets are meant to die with me.

The pen scratches the paper as I sign my name, smiling bitterly at the last name Paul gave me. This will be gone, too. Then, I set the pen down and push the papers toward Jazinski.

"Good," he says, checking the signature and putting the document in the folder, then closing it neatly. "Now, I'm listening."

My throat dries up as I'm about to speak. A shudder travels through me, seeding icicles in my blood. A long moment of tense silence passes, but then I clear my throat quietly.

When I speak, my voice sounds strange, as if it belongs to someone else. I start with the thing that's been weighing heaviest on my mind. And I have Paul's recklessness to thank for being able to get free of what happened that night.

"Two weeks after Paul accidentally killed Esperanza Sosa in a crash on the night of the fundraiser, I killed a man."

# 66

# PAUL DAVIS

---

The interrogation room feels colder since Amanda left. What the fuck was that about? Asking if I'm sorry? What should I be sorry about? None of this was my fault.

I bet that's been said in here about a million times before. I stare at the table, scratched and dented, wondering how many lives have been ruined in this room. Mine is probably next.

Naomi Hedman sits beside me, her tablet open and her manicured nails clicking against the screen. She hasn't looked at me since Amanda was here. She doesn't need to. I can tell what she's thinking. That my dear wife has sold me out.

The door opens, and Detective Jazinski walks in first. He looks tired, but I see a spark in his eyes and a spring in his step that set my nerves on edge. He's too damn sure of himself. Eckhart follows, eager, his cocky smile barely restrained. They sit across from us with rushed movements, a thick file getting slapped down on the table.

"Mr. Davis," Jazinski says, leaning back in his chair. "Thanks for sticking around."

"As if I had a choice," I mutter, just loudly enough for my lawyer to hear. She doesn't react. She's like stone, solid and unmovable and cold.

Jazinski opens the folder, glances at it, and then looks me straight in the eye. "Let's talk about your car."

"It's a great car," I say, forcing a smile and feigning indifference. "Smooth ride. Excellent safety ratings."

Hedman sighs audibly. "Mr. Davis will not be answering questions about his vehicle."

"He can remain silent, but I can still talk," Eckhart says, his grin wide and a little too pleased. "You see, your Cadillac? It's been stripped down. Forensics had a field day."

My stomach flips, but I keep my face neutral. "That's funny," I say, leaning back. "I thought it was against the law to destroy private property without due process."

Naomi Hedman interjects. "Was a warrant issued?"

"Of course," Jazinski replies, holding up a piece of paper. "Signed, sealed, delivered. Your client's car is now evidence in an active investigation."

"You mean that hit-and-run you've been talking about?" I ask, playing dumb. "You keep asking all kinds of things, Detective, but I don't see how this has anything to do with me."

"Oh, it has everything to do with you," Jazinski says, leaning forward with his eyes like steel. "The repairs on that car? Impeccable job, by the way. Whoever did it was an artist. But here's the thing: We know exactly what was fixed. The windshield, for example. A replacement job so clean it's almost invisible. Almost."

"Almost," Eckhart echoes, his grin widening. "Then there's the grille, the bumper, the headlights—all matching the profile of a vehicle that hit someone at seventy miles an hour."

I look from Jazinski to Eckhart and back, my mind frozen in disbelief.

Hedman cuts in, her voice firm. "Detectives, if you're attempting to connect these findings to my client without direct evidence, I'm advising him to say nothing further."

"There's evidence," Jazinski adds, speaking slowly, as if he's taking great pleasure in torturing me. "Forensics found debris at the scene, pieces of a grille and a flake of red enamel from a car badge. They fit your Cadillac perfectly."

My mouth goes dry. I try to swallow and nearly choke. "I don't know what you're talking about," I say. "I drove that car to work the next day. Check the station's surveillance footage."

"Oh, we did," Jazinski says, his tone almost bored. "Nice trick, by the way. Swapping out a damaged car for a pristine one in record time. You must've had help."

I glance at my lawyer, but she doesn't look at me. Her eyes are riveted on Jazinski, and concern is furrowing her brow.

"Who helped you, Mr. Davis?"

Hedman raises her hand. "Enough. My client will not be speculating on your theories. Present your evidence, or we're done."

"And then," Jazinski continues, his voice colder now, "you went and did something really stupid."

"Yeah," Eckhart adds, chuckling. "Dumb as hell."

"What the hell are you talking about?" I snap, losing patience.

Jazinski pulls out a photo from the folder and slides it across the table. I recognize the face instantly. It's Foster. Lying face up on a stainless-steel table, bloated, head bashed in, covered with a sheet up to his chin.

The room starts spinning with me—slowly at first, and then faster. I feel my stomach riling up, threatening to unload with my next breath. I grab the edges of the table to steady myself, while in my mind I'm screaming.

*Foster is dead? How the hell did that happen?*

Hedman is giving me a long stare, but doesn't say anything. Her lips are pressed into a tight, thin line.

"You know this guy, don't you?" Jazinski says. "Malik Foster, a.k.a. Fast Lane Foster. Your parts guy. The guy who fixed your car so perfectly, and even wiped the GPS history clean for you."

He pauses for a moment, while my thoughts are racing. They're trying to pin Foster's murder on me.

"Don't lie, Mr. Davis," Jazinski says, leaning back into his chair. "My partner saw him leaving your house last week. You said he was your handyman." He looks me straight in the eye. "Why did you kill him? Was he getting greedy?"

"That's bullshit," I say, my voice rising. "I didn't kill him!"

They laugh. Actually *laugh*. It's the kind of laughter that isn't meant to be funny; it's meant to dig under your skin. To drive you crazy.

"Instant karma, man," Eckhart says, still grinning. "You try to clean up one mess, and another one bites you in the ass."

"I didn't kill him!" I shout now, slamming my hand on the table.

Hedman flinches slightly, and whispers, "Mr. Davis, stop talking now." I just glare at her. I can't afford to follow her advice. I'll get tried for murder if I do.

"I swear to God, I didn't do it! I paid him his money, okay? Seventy-five grand, cash. That's it. Why would I pay him, and then kill him?"

The room goes quiet, the weight of my words sinking in. I realize I've said too much, but it's too late now.

I just confessed to the hit-and-run.

Jazinski raises an eyebrow. "Seventy-five grand? That's a lot of money for a guy you supposedly does your backyard."

"Mr. Davis," Hedman says, putting her manicured hand on my forearm. "I'm urging you, stop talking."

The cops look at one another, then stand and leave. Before the door closes, I hear Jazinski telling Eckhart, "Charge Davis with murder one. We're done here."

I jump to my feet and run to the door. I squeeze the handle and pull, but it won't budge.

"Hey!" I shout as I'm pounding against the metal with both fists. "Hey! I didn't kill him, for fuck's sake! Come back here!"

"Mr. Davis, please sit down!" my lawyer hisses at me. "Do you have any idea what you just did?"

I ignore her and move over to the two-way mirror. I know they're watching from the other room. I bang against the glass and shout, "Hey! You hear me? I didn't kill him, but I know who did!"

Out of breath and scared out of my mind, I let myself drop onto the crappy chair. I'm breathing heavily, panicked and desperate. This can't be the way my life ends. This can't happen.

The door opens and Jazinski returns. He stops by the wall, hands propped on his hips.

"Okay, you got my attention," he says, looking at me as if I'm some piece of trash. "Tell me why I should believe you."

I remember how Chapelle's voice sounded once I told him I was paying Foster that day. Determined. Like he knew he was going to kill him, and he'd never bother me again. He even wanted me to confirm to him when the job was done and paid for. So he'd know exactly when to pounce.

I'm still panting, and when I try to speak, I start coughing. After a moment, I can clear my throat and breathe again. "Someone knew I was paying him the seventy-five grand that day."

"Who?"

I look at Hedman briefly, and she shakes her head, but I keep going. It's my only chance.

"A piece-of-shit lawyer, Larry Chapelle. He's a con artist. Runs a settlement mill, filing lawsuits on behalf of fake disabled people."

Jazinski rolls his eyes. "A model citizen! And how do you know this Chapelle?"

Hedman stands abruptly, sending her chair backward. It clatters against the floor. "Mr. Davis—"

I hesitate, my pulse pounding in my ears. "Chapelle knew everything," I continue, my voice steady now. "He set up the deal for the car parts. You should be talking to him, not me."

Naomi's head snaps up, her eyes wide with surprise. "Mr. Davis!" she says sharply, but I ignore her.

Jazinski nods slowly, looking at me with a glimmer of satisfaction in his eyes. "All right, Mr. Davis, we'll be in touch." He squeezes the door handle, ready to leave, and then chuckles as he's looking back at me. "I bet you weren't expecting us to be in the same room again so soon after that interview on your show, were you, Mr. Davis?"

His comment leaves me slack-jawed and dumbfounded. This was personal. All of it.

That day, during the interview on *The Final Question*, I dropped the notepad with Aidan's notes. Jazinski's wife's DUI, his cover-up. I wasn't sure he saw what was written. Not until now.

He knew I'm aware of his wife's problems and his cover-ups. I'm the next cover-up, the cleanup he needs to do to keep himself out of jail.

He's going to bury me.

As the door slams shut behind him, I collapse back into the chair, my chest heaving. Hedman leans in close, her eyes blazing with anger. "You've just talked yourself into a trial," she hisses. "And we're going to need a miracle."

# 67

# AMANDA DAVIS

*Four months later*

The air is thick in the courtroom. Fine dust particles dance in the light beam coming from the lamp on the judge's bench. He's an intimidating man of at least sixty, hunchbacked and overweight, and probably enduring back pain. A faint smell of Ben Gay comes from his direction. Every few minutes, he shifts in seat, visibly uncomfortable. I can see it clearly from the witness stand.

Well, this ordeal will soon be over. I'm among the last witnesses to take the stand.

I look toward the public seating area, where Tristan is sitting next to Dad. My little boy looks pale, drawn, and I know he's been crying all night. He still won't talk to me, even if Dad keeps whispering in his ear, probably offering the same words of encouragement I still recall him saying to me when I was about his age and heartbroken over Mom's passing. But my son still won't look at me. He keeps staring at his father, the sheen of tears glimmering in his eyes. He's there for him, not me.

Paul is sitting at the defendant's table, wearing one of his charcoal suits. I almost don't recognize him. He hasn't been living at home since his release on bail. He took his attorney's advice and steered clear of me, and I haven't shed a tear about it. He has swung by Tristan's school a couple of times, but hasn't caused a scene. That attorney of his is keeping him on a short leash.

Our eyes meet. It's as if I'm looking into the eyes of a stranger. He's not hateful, nor his usual flavor of arrogant. He's afraid, and trying to hide it. He's pleading with me without saying a word.

The gavel brings the courtroom to order as my thoughts shift to the earlier days of our relationship. When we were so much in love with each other that everything seemed possible, including our very own special brand of ever-after. And now, getting ready to testify against him, I've just sworn to tell the truth, the whole truth, and nothing but the truth, hoping I'll be able to do just that. It depends on the questions they ask.

The prosecutor is a tall, bony woman with skin like Pergament and straw-blond hair cut sharply at shoulder level. She's wearing heels with her figure-hugging suit. They clack loudly on the floor when she approaches me. I brace myself, folding my hands in my lap. I've heard rumors of what she can do.

"Mrs. Davis, please describe, in your own words, what happened on the night of the crash."

I swallow hard. My throat feels like sandpaper, my chest tightening under the weight of a hundred eyes boring into me. Paul's gaze from the defense table is intensifying. I can feel him willing me to say the right things...the things that are most likely to get him an acquittal.

"We were driving home after the fundraiser," I begin, my voice slightly trembling. "It was late, after midnight. The road was dark, winding. It had started to drizzle—just a light mist, really." My eyes dart briefly to Paul. His expression is unreadable, his jaw tight. "She...she stepped right in front of the car."

"Who do you mean by 'she,' Mrs. Davis?"

"The victim," I say, my voice cracking. "Esperanza Sosa."

"Describe what happened for the court."

"She came out of nowhere," I say, my words tumbling out too fast. "She stepped into the road...like she was waiting for something. It was...deliberate."

"What do you mean?"

"She stepped in front of the car right before it struck her. The car's collision avoidance system didn't have time to respond."

"It's your opinion that she was waiting for a car?" the prosecutor presses, her eyebrows raised.

"Yes," I whisper. "A speeding car."

"Who was driving, Mrs. Davis?"

"My husband, Paul Davis."

"The defendant?" she asks, pointing at Paul. I hate these theatrics. But people love them. You can hear a pin drop. Everyone's holding their breaths, including the jurors.

"Yes."

"Was your husband speeding, Mrs. Davis?"

"I'm not sure. I was tired and wasn't my keeping my eyes on his odometer. I never do."

"Was he going fast?"

I hesitate for a moment. "Yes."

"The limit on that stretch of road is fifty-five miles per hour. Is it possible he was going seventy?"

"Again, I'm not sure." From the second row, Detective Jazinski frowns and glares at me.

The prosecutor paces slowly, her heels clicking against the floor. "Seventy miles per hour, in the dark, on a winding road?"

I shrug. "I'm not sure."

"Objection," the defense attorney says. "Asked and answered."

"Sustained," the judge rules, shifting in his seat and grimacing in pain. "Move on, Counselor."

The prosecutor's sharp gaze pierces me. "Did you recognize her at the scene?"

"No," I say, shaking my head firmly. "She was…" My words falter. I glance at the jury, their faces a mixture of pity and scrutiny. "She was unrecognizable."

"As a nurse, did you check her vitals or try to get help?"

"Yes. She'd died on the spot. In retrospect, at that speed, and knowing what I know now about the state of her body after three rounds of chemo-fighting and aggressive, final stage cancer, it's no surprise."

"Was your husband intoxicated that night?"

My eyes meet Paul's. I hesitate, knowing they won't be able to establish his level of inebriation without corroborated testimony. That's what my attorney said. I'm tempted to tell the truth, but I see Tristan's eyes and I waver. "No."

"We heard testimony here today that Paul Davis had several drinks at the event. Is that true?"

"I cannot corroborate testimony I haven't heard. I can tell you that my husband had a couple of drinks in my presence. That's all I can speak to."

I can hear Jasinski's frustrated groan all the way from the witness stand. It doesn't faze me.

The prosecutor's eyes narrow. "Let's clarify. We've heard from witnesses and seen video evidence that Mr. Davis consumed at least five shots of liquor and two beers over the course of the evening. Is that correct?"

"Objection," Naomi Hedman reacts. "Already answered."

"Withdrawn." The DA paces slowly for a moment. "Mrs. Davis, did you know Ms. Sosa personally?"

The question sends a jolt through me. My chest tightens, and I grip the stand railing. "No," I say too quickly. "I didn't."

"Are you aware that the victim's daughter, Marisol Sosa, died in your care?"

The courtroom reels, gasping in unison. The jurors crane their necks to look at me, while I feel I'm not getting enough air.

"Objection, Your Honor!" Naomi Hedman's voice is just as shocked as I feel. "Relevance?"

"I'll rephrase," the DA quickly offers. She steps closer, her gaze unrelenting. "Do you have any thoughts on the coincidence of her stepping in front of your husband's car, specifically? The mother of a former patient who died while in your care?"

"No," I say, shaking my head vehemently. "None. It's just a coincidence. Marisol Sosa succumbed to her injuries in the Emergency Department within two hours of her arrival. It happened a few weeks before that night. An entire team of doctors and nurses worked on her case, not just me."

"And you don't recall meeting her mother, Esperanza Sosa?"

"No, I'm sorry," I say, aware my voice is cracking. "I don't."

The prosecutor stares at me for a long, tense moment, then steps back. She glances at her notes, flipping a page deliberately. "One more question, Mrs. Davis." Her tone softens, going almost gentle, but I know better than to trust it. "After the crash...did your husband express regret or remorse for Esperanza Sosa's death?"

My eyes lock onto Paul's for a moment, and then he closes his, isolating himself from me, from my unspoken question. My heart thumps in my chest as I gasp for air. Memories flood my mind, fueling my racing thoughts. The night of the crash, when he rolled Esperanza's body into the ravine and dared me to stop him. The way he stared at her body, with a look of pure disdain on his face. The way he rubbed his hands together after pushing her over the edge. Calling her an idiot and a bitch, more than once.

I have no reason to lie under oath for this man. Still, I consider it, battling my own demons and guilt. And Tristan's tear-filled, pleading gaze.

"Mrs. Davis?" The DA presses, her voice raised a notch. "Did your husband ever express regret or remorse for the killing of Esperanza Sosa?"

"No," I eventually whisper, on a long, pained breath. He's not worth lying for. "He did not."

"No more questions, Your Honor."

# 68

# PAUL DAVIS

"Ladies and gentlemen of the jury, have you reached a verdict?"

The judge's question turns my stomach into a knot of fraught nerves. I've been waiting in courthouse hallways for almost an entire day, for them to finish deliberating. Naomi seems to think that's a good sign, although she was quick to add that you never know with juries. Some reassurance.

I should've gone with one of the old sharks, not this woman. She could've been harder on my wife. She should've crucified her on the stand. Ripped her to shreds. One of the Ivy Leaguers would've done that. Instead, she was procedural and dignified, and almost elegant in the way she presented the case and her closing argument. Excellent way to lose a trial.

*Fuck.*

But I'm sure the jury has seen though all of it and will return a not guilty verdict. If someone just decides to step in front of your vehicle, you shouldn't have to go to prison for it.

What a fucking mess.

I hold my breath as the bailiff takes a folded piece of paper from the jury foreperson over to the judge. I don't like what I see on the jurors' faces. Contempt, curiosity, even mockery. I was hoping for empathy or camaraderie, and that's when I haven't hoped they'd be a little star-struck, just enough to acquit me.

The jury foreperson, a morbidly obese woman, stands with difficulty, steadying herself by holding on to the railing. "We have, Your Honor."

The judge unfolds the paper and reads it quickly, his glasses perched on the tip of his nose.

"How do you find the defendant, Paul Davis?"

She looks at her notepad, squinting a little. She's probably too vain to wear glasses. She must think she's quite a catch otherwise.

"In the case of the People of the State of California versus Paul Davis, we, the jury, find as follows." She pauses for a moment, looking at the public. "On the charge of vehicular manslaughter, we find the defendant not guilty."

A sharp breath of air leaves my lungs. It's a good sign, but I'm not off the hook yet.

"On the charge of driving under the influence, we find the defendant not guilty."

Another quick, liberating breath, but my hands are cold and clammy, and I can feel the sweat dripping down my back. I was sort of expecting that part. Naomi said they probably won't be able to establish an inebriation level based solely on testimony. I shoot her a quick look and decide that, if she gets me off scot-free, I'll take her to the Bahamas for a weekend and fuck her until she can't walk straight anymore. I know she wants it.

The foreperson shoots me a quick look that chills me. "On the charge of obstruction of justice by concealing evidence and tampering with the vehicle to impede investigation, we find the defendant guilty."

I gasp. "What?" I ask, unable to understand it. My lawyer puts her hand on my forearm.

"Quiet, Mr. Davis."

The foreperson continues, after shooting me another chilling look. "On the charge of felony hit-and-run causing death, we find the defendant guilty."

"Thank you, members of the jury, for your service and your careful consideration of the evidence in this case," the judge says. "Mr. Davis, the jury has returned its verdict. Sentencing in this matter is set for October 14th, at which point the court will determine the appropriate penalties as prescribed by law. In the meantime, you will remain in custody."

The gavel falls, cracking loudly. My head is spinning. This can't be happening. Gasping for air, I turn to look at my attorney.

"What's going on?"

"We'll file an appeal," she says, patting my shoulder for encouragement. "Don't worry, Mr. Davis, we'll fix this. We dodged the vehicular manslaughter and the DUI. That's something. We'll push for leniency at sentencing, and file for an appeal."

I stare at her, still stunned. I can't believe it. Two court officers approach me, and I have an instant urge to run. From across the floor, Detective Jazinski stares at me, the corner of his mouth twitching with a smile.

*Fuck… Oh, motherfucker… I can't go to prison. I just can't.*

One of the court officers grabs my elbow firmly. "Let's go."

I don't have a choice. On my way to the exit, camera flashes blind me. I'll be tomorrow's headliner.

"Just a second, please," Amanda says, rushing toward me. She looks at the court officers, her eyes dry and steady. "Could I please have just a few seconds, to say goodbye?"

What the hell does she want from me? Hasn't she done enough?

The two men look at each other, and then one of them says, "Make it quick."

She has the nerve to wrap her arms around my neck, and whisper in my ear words I can barely hear.

"I'm so sorry, Paul…"

# 69

# AMANDA DAVIS

---

"I'm so sorry, Paul..."

*There are so many things I wish I could tell you right this instant, when we're about to be separated for a while. I wish they'd allow us the time I need to tell you the story of that day.*

*The day Marisol Sosa died.*

*You didn't want to hear about her when I came home that night, overwhelmed with grief and helplessness and guilt. You were still sullen and silent after our argument.*

*Earlier that morning, before work, I'd asked you once more for a divorce, and you were quick and brutal in making your usual threats. "No one takes my son from me," you'd said, even if I had no intention of cutting you off from Tristan. I love my boy too much to see him growing up without his father.*

*That night, you told me to suck it up, and down a stiff drink like everyone else does when they have a shitty day. Those were your words. You told me you were sick of my drama, of bringing all the hospital sob stories home with me. I still recall the bitter tears I'd cried, until you shouted, "Shut the fuck up with this shit!"*

*And so, I did. I never mentioned Marisol Sosa to you again.*

*But now, I feel that I must.*

*She was seventeen, a girl who chose the wrong day to meet her friends at the mall and walk under a scaffolding on her way out. A beautiful girl with dimples in her cheeks when she smiled, and long, wavy brown hair. An ambitious ballet dancer, and an excellent student. Her mother showed me what Marisol used to look like, who she used to be.*

*When I first saw her being rolled in on a gurney, she looked nothing like that. It was moments after the piercing tone of the* ambulance rang in my ears and interrupted my restocking of the crash carts, my morning routine. I was standing by Dr. Grant's side when the gurney burst through the ED doors. The EMTs were moving fast, shouting over one another in tense, urgent tones.

"Marisol Sosa, seventeen-year-old, scaffolding collapse at a construction site as she was leaving the mall. Cervical trauma, suspected cord injury—paralysis in all extremities. Burns to over 40% of her body, second- and third-degree."

Dr. Grant nodded sharply, assessing her. "BP?"

"70 over 40. Barely holding on," the paramedic replied. "Pulse thready at 130. Sat's at 84%. She's been struggling to breathe. We bagged her briefly en route, but she was oxygenating slightly better on her own."

I was already moving, gloves snapping into place as I took position beside Dr. Grant, pushing the gurney into Trauma Three.

"What's the mechanism of injury?" he asked.

"Paint thinner spill," the paramedic replied. "Ignited by exposed electrical wiring from the fallen scaffolding. She was pinned beneath a section of metal while the fire spread."

"Marisol," Dr. Grant called, leaning over her. "Can you hear me?"

Her eyelids fluttered open, but the terror in her eyes was unmistakable. Her lips parted as if to speak, but no sound came out—only a faint wheeze. Her breaths were shallow, quick, and raspy.

"We've got you," I said softly, leaning closer to her ear. "You're safe now. We're going to help you."

We transferred her from the gurney to the trauma bed. Her body was shockingly still, except for her darting, desperate eyes and her gaping mouth. Her skin was mottled and raw, with patches of charred tissue across her neck, arms, and torso. The smell of burnt flesh hung heavy in the air, acrid and metallic, curling into my nose and refusing to leave.

"C-collar in place," someone called.

"Let's roll her," Dr. Grant ordered. "Spinal precautions—one, two, three." We turned her carefully, revealing the full extent of the burns. The team paused for half a second, stunned. Then, we were moving again.

"Get me a central line," Dr. Grant said, reaching for the IV setup. His voice wavered for a moment, but he pushed through. "We need fluids now—ringers, wide open."

"Vitals are crashing," a nurse warned, her tone urgent. "BP's dropping. 60 over palp."

"Push two of epi," Dr. Grant ordered. "And let's get x-rays stat—cervical spine and chest. Call for a CT, but I doubt she'll be stable enough to make it up there."

The monitors beeped wildly as the room burst into a symphony of controlled chaos. I focused on my hands, working the IV as sweat beaded on my forehead.

As soon as the needle was in, I took a step back, trying to shake a disturbing thought.

She's someone's child. And there's no way—

"Sunny, ask someone to locate her mother, stat. I don't know how long—" I choked on my words, while Dr. Grant sent me a quick glance followed by a nod.

"Burn team's on their way," someone said, but it barely registered.

"She's quadriplegic," Dr. Grant muttered, his voice tight. "With this level of cord injury, there's no chance she'll regain any function. We'll have to intubate."

"She's barely perfusing," another nurse warned. "Her extremities are cold."

My throat tightened as I looked at her face. Her eyes were closed now, her lashes clumped together with soot and sweat. She was young—so damn young. Her features, though swollen and bruised, were delicate, almost doll-like. I couldn't stop wondering what she'd looked like before all this. What kind of life she'd had. What kind of dreams she'd been chasing.

"We found the mother," one of the nurses said quietly. "She's on her way. Should be here any minute."

*That was fast. Too fast. "Where is she coming from?"*

*The nurse gave me a grim look. "Third floor. The oncology ward."*

Oh, God.

*I glanced at Dr. Grant, and he nodded. "Let's stabilize her as best we can. Amanda, let's get another ABG, now."*

*"Yes, Doctor." My voice was steadier than I felt, fighting back tears. My hands moved automatically, drawing blood, checking lines, adjusting settings. But my mind was spinning.*

*Minutes passed like hours. Despite every intervention, Marisol's vitals continued to drop. The x-ray confirmed the cervical fracture—C5-C6, with significant cord compression and a possible partial transection. She wasn't going to survive.*

*I was standing at the bedside when her mother arrived. The woman's face crumpled the moment she saw Marisol. Her knees buckled, and she collapsed into a chair, clutching her chest. She was thin and pale, her balding head wrapped in a makeshift turban.*

*"No," she whispered, her voice breaking. "No, no, no. Mi niña... Dios mio..."*

*"Mrs. Sosa," Dr. Grant said gently, but she shook her head, tears streaming down her face.*

*I stepped closer, crouching down to her level. "Mrs. Sosa," I said softly. "We're doing everything we can, but her injuries are very severe."*

*She looked at me with hollow eyes. "Is she in pain?" she asked, her voice trembling.*

*"No," I assured her. "She's sedated and on pain medication. She doesn't feel anything. But—"*

*The words felt like a lie, even though they weren't. I thought of the burns on Marisol's neck and cheeks, on areas above the spinal injury. She must have felt those, at least for a few agonizing minutes. But I couldn't tell her mother that.*

*I was barely there while Dr. Grant explained to Esperanza what had happened to her daughter. She listened, then kissed her daughter's forehead, her thin, pale lips lingering on the girl's skin for a moment. She stroked her hair with a trembling hand. Then, she looked straight at me.*

*"Let her go." She turned her tearful eyes to Dr. Grant. "Por favor, let her go. Don't make her suffer anymore."*

*Dr. Grant's eyes searched hers. "Are you withdrawing consent to treat your daughter?" he asked gently. "Are you instructing us to discontinue life-prolonging measures?"*

*"Whatever it's called to let my baby go painlessly." She sobbed hard, gasping for air, her thin, emaciated shoulders heaving. "This is no life."*

*I was in the room when the machines were turned off, when the ventilator hissed its last breath. I held Mrs. Sosa's hand as Marisol's chest rose and fell one more time.*

*It was over in seconds. Too fast, but too painfully slow.*

*Afterward, shaken to my core, I helped clean the room, wiping away the traces of blood and ash and despair. My hands trembled as I worked, but I didn't stop. I couldn't stop.*

*That night, I came home a wreck, needing you, Paul, even if I didn't want to admit that anymore, not even to myself. You were merciless with me, heartless, brutal and cruel. I cried myself to sleep, the smell of Marisol's burnt flesh still haunting me.*

*The next day, Esperanza Sosa came to see me. She was calm, her eyes dry, her face still...the kind of stillness people have when their minds are made up.*

*"Can I take a minute of your time?" she asked politely.*

*We spent a bit of time at the cafeteria. She showed me pictures of her daughter growing up, how beautiful she used to be, how happy and serene. Dancing in Swan Lake at age ten. Blowing candles out on her twelfth birthday cake. Holding hands with a lanky boy, dressed like a princess, going to the prom just a few months before her accident.*

*In my mind, I still saw her gasping for air, silent screaming, her eyes widened in shock, her hair clumped in sweat and blood on the hospital pillow. As if that reality had replaced everything she'd ever been, erasing it from reality.*

*"I need your help," Esperanza whispered, putting the phone back in her pocket. She reached over the table, squeezing my hand with her frail, cold fingers.*

*I placed my hand on top of hers. "Anything."*

*She remained silent for a while, the cafeteria noises around us fading in the distance as if we were being transported someplace else. "I want to die," she eventually said. "Can you help me make it painless?" She looked me in the eye. "I've had enough pain in this life."*

*"Mrs. Sosa, I—"*

*"I belong with my daughter," she whispered. "Are you a mother?"*

*My throat dried as I tried to reply. All I could do was nod.*

*"Then, you understand." She paused for a moment, looking out the window at the heavy traffic. "I want you to teach me how to die. Where should I go? I could step in front of a car." She squeezed my hand, pleading with her haunting gaze. "It'll be alright. I'm dying anyway, and mi niña is gone already. She's waiting for me."*

*That was the moment you sent a text saying,* "If you can be bothered to extract yourself from the daily sludge of human misery, you need to work with the fundraiser organizers tonight. Make it happen."

*I felt your message like a physical blow. Heartless and cruel like you'd been with me lately, ever since I'd asked you for a divorce. Your text reminded me of the fundraiser I'd—again—agreed to host with you. From where you'd be driving on Malibu Canyon Road, going seventy miles per hour, most likely inebriated.*

*And so I asked that grieving, heartbroken mother, as if in a dream, "What if I could tell you a time and a place where a vehicle would come at you really fast? Where I would be there for you?"*

*I still remember the tears of gratitude that sprang from her eyes as she thanked me.*

*Just so we're clear, my dear Paul, I didn't want you sentenced to prison. I didn't want Tristan growing up without you. I thought it would humble you. Weaken you just enough so you'd let me go.*

*When I came home that night, I was about to call everything off, if you'd just held me. If you'd just listened to me talk about Marisol and how her death had devastated me.*

*You didn't.*

*Then, on the night of the fundraiser, I asked you time and again to let me drive. If you had, things would've been so much different now. But you were as stubborn and as reckless as you've always been.*

*I texted Esperanza on a burner phone a few moments after leaving the venue. I had no idea if she was still going to do it or not. All I'd done was promise her I'd be there for her in her final moments, making sure she wouldn't suffer. The rest was on her.*

*And on you.*

*Why?*

*Because you're so predictable, Paul. I knew you would drink that night, and would adamantly refuse to let me drive. I knew you always sped over that section of road in the woods. And I knew it would be deserted that time of night. All I wanted was for you to get a lesson in humility, while at the same time, Esperanza would find peace at last, freedom for her suffering.*

*You could've done the right thing and called the cops. You could've owned your mistakes and gotten a bitter lesson while skipping jail time. Esperanza was suicidal. With her daughter dying a couple of days earlier, and her cancer slowly killing her, you would've been off the hook, even with a bit of alcohol in your system. That night, I packed with me something to give you to reduce alcohol absorption, in case you made that call. It would've probably landed you within legal limits.*

*Instead, you turned on me...your wife, the mother of your child. Threatened my life, right there, in the rain-soaked woods, with Esperanza's body lying at our feet. And so, I decided to help you bury yourself. The rapist was a curveball from fate, and taught me a lesson. But you, my darling soon-to-be ex, you're going to learn yours the slow and hard way.*

*I wish I could tell you all this, but they only give me time for a few words. I'll make them count.*

I lean closer to his ear and whisper, "I'm so sorry, Paul… But no one takes my son away from me, sweetheart. Get that into your head."

# 70

# AMANDA DAVIS

*About three years later*

The drive to Pasadena is unusually quiet and fast on this early Saturday morning. And I'm in no hurry. Dad and I are taking Tristan to summer camp. He's going to stay there for a week. It's an adventure camp—the kind where they learn to make a fire, build a shelter, and purify drinking water. Although I'm a bit concerned that he's more interested in the snake-handling part of the adventure.

He used to beg me to let him go to camp, but that was before Paul's trial.

And our divorce.

He's been slow getting over his dad being gone, or forgiving me for testifying and for divorcing him. The first year was the worst. He kept shouting and calling me names. I was a traitor to the family, a backstabber, and didn't know what loyalty was. I was a bitch, a liar who hurt his father deeply, and he would never forgive me. Never speak to me again. Of course, his father was a saint who'd been wrongfully accused.

The silent treatment lasted for about two months after the trial. Turns out, the cold virus is a big factor in getting a grieving ten-year-old to speak with his mother again. Then, a science project for school was another ice-breaker. I'd known he'd need time, but I'd never imagined he'd be so slow to forgive.

After about six months from Paul's sentencing, Tristan asked me to take him to see his dad. I cringed at the thought of my son setting foot in a prison, but I took him anyway. Surprisingly, Paul was rather cold with him, maintaining a façade of strength and normalcy that threw my little boy off.

It was the last time we went.

Paul's parole hearing is in two months, and I'm still torn over whether I should tell my son about it, or whether I should testify. Do I want Paul out on parole?

I honestly don't know. Better said, I don't care.

Guilt still haunts me, messing up my sleep and invading my thoughts, just as Marisol's tormented face sometimes does. I'm trying not to think about it.

"Almost there," Dad announces in a cheerful voice. Tristan barely lifts his eyes from his phone. I can see him in the rearview mirror, his head always lowered, missing out on all the beauty of nature. Sometimes, I'm tempted to throw all these devices out the window and never look back.

I pull into the parking lot, next to at least a dozen other cars, and get out of the Subaru. I pop the trunk, and Dad pulls out Tristan's backpack, then gives him a big hug.

"Take care of yourself, sailor," Dad says. His hair is almost completely white, blowing in the gentle breeze.

"Aye, Captain," Tristan replies, patting Dad's back twice in the unspoken signal to let go. Then, he waves to some other boys from his school. I recognize the red-haired, freckled Dylan, his best friend.

It's my turn to say goodbye, and I feel shy out of a sudden, hesitant. What if he rejects me like he's done ever since that day in court? I'm aching to hold my son.

I reach out to smooth his hair, but he pulls back—not too much, just enough to give me the message. He looks more and more like Paul, a younger, innocent, and somewhat sweeter version of the man. The same stunning blue eyes. The same shade of brown hair, smooth as silk.

I open my arms and take a step closer, then hug him closely, closing my eyes and breathing him in.

He's quick to push back. "Come on, Mom, you're embarrassing me," he says, keeping his voice low. "Dylan's mom didn't hug him like he's six."

I stroke his tousled hair. "Have a good time, you hear me?" He turns to leave, and I say, "I love you," while he can still hear me.

He stops in place, turns halfway, waves, and smiles. "Love you, too, Mom."

~~~~~~~~~

**If *A Beautiful Couple* had you totally enthralled and gasping at the twists, then you have to read more unmissable page-turners by Leslie Wolfe!**

**Read on for previews from:**

***The Girl You Killed***
**A shocking yet mysterious crime. A murder trial that polarizes a tightly knit suburban community. A web of secrets, lies, and deceit.**

**\*\*\* and \*\*\***

***Dawn Girl***
**A short-fused FBI Agent who hides a terrible secret. A serial killer you won't see coming. A heart-stopping race to catch him.**

# Thank You!

**A big, heartfelt thank you** for choosing to read my book. If you enjoyed it, please take a moment to leave me a four or five-star review; I would be very grateful. It doesn't need to be more than a couple of words, and it makes a huge difference.

**Join my mailing list** to receive special offers, exclusive bonus content, and news about upcoming new releases. Use the button below, visit www.LeslieWolfe.com to sign up, or email me at LW@WolfeNovels.com.

**Did you enjoy *A Beautiful Couple?*** Your thoughts and feedback are very valuable to me. Please contact me directly through one of the channels listed below. Email works best: LW@WolfeNovels.com.

**If you haven't already**, check out ***Dawn Girl***, a gripping, heart stopping crime thriller and the first book in the Tess Winnett series. If you enjoyed *Criminal Minds*, you'll enjoy *Dawn Girl*. Or, if you're in a mood for something lighter, try ***Las Vegas Girl***; you'll love it!

# A Special Note
## to the Members of the Psychological Thriller Readers Group:

Dear friends,

Your keen attention to detail and sharp critiques have not gone unnoticed. With your insights in mind, I've worked hard to ensure this book doesn't include any accidental breath-holding, unconscious eye-closing, or other inexplicable bodily actions that might defy logic.

I'm proud to say that, thanks to your influence, this book can be wholeheartedly certified as free from any unintentional breath-holding, eyelid-closing, or other rogue actions that defy mindful awareness. Rest assured, all characters in this story have been thoroughly briefed, and they've solemnly sworn to remain fully conscious of their movements at all times.

Consider this my official promise: no one in this book is doing anything without realizing it. #IYKYK

Thank you for reading and for keeping authors on their toes—you've made me better, and my characters more mindful.

With gratitude (and a deep breath taken intentionally),
Leslie

# CONNECT WITH ME!

Amazon store: Amazon.com/LeslieWolfe

Email: LW@WolfeNovels.com

Amazon Author Page: Leslie Wolfe's Author Page

Website: LeslieWolfe.com

Facebook: Facebook.com/WolfeNovels

Instagram: Instagram.com/Wolfe.Leslie

Tiktok: Tiktok.com/@Leslie.Wolfe

Follow Leslie on BookBub: Leslie on Bookbub

# Chapter 1

## A LETTER

They'd taken everything from him.

In a matter of days, Craig Brafford's entire world had been torn apart, pulled inside out, shredded to unrecognizable bits in hues of nightmare.

About half a dozen cops had rummaged through his house looking for who knows what, sparing nothing and breaking stuff out of spite. Now the place was empty, front door unlocked, an invitation for local thugs to loot and occupy as soon as his arrest hit the evening news. He'd begged his lawyer, the widely successful Lamar Goodridge, to swing by and lock it, maybe turn on the alarm system.

"Not my job," the man had answered calmly, his voice low, frozen, loaded with contempt. "You can barely afford my services as it is," he'd added, glancing at the gold watch adorning his wrist. The man charged $900 per hour, and he would've gladly paid for his time, but Mr. Goodridge couldn't let himself be caught giving a crap about one of his clients, or running errands for them.

Humiliated, he'd lowered his head and never mentioned it again, cringing powerlessly at the thought of his beautiful home overtaken by hordes of street filth. Goodridge had taken his case on a retainer that had cleaned Craig's accounts. Regardless, Goodridge still frowned when he looked at him, as if the sight of the inmate clad in an orange jumpsuit was offensive somehow, as if he'd never seen inmates before. Maybe Goodridge was wondering if Craig could pay his legal bills once the ordeal was over. Or perhaps he was trying to guess if his client had done it or not, although Goodridge himself had started their first meeting by saying, "I don't care if you're innocent. Either way, you deserve the best defense money can buy. *Your* money that is. Otherwise…" He let the word trail into silence, accompanied by a shrug and a hand gesture conveying his indifference for all the potentially innocent people who couldn't afford decent legal representation and would lose their freedom for that only reason: not being rich enough. Even if they were innocent.

He was smug, his lawyer. He rarely worked pro bono cases, and when he did, he only represented black defendants, "a tribute to his ancestry," in his own words. His inquisitive eyes drilled into the very fabric of whoever sat across from him, and there was little he didn't see. That was probably why he could charge that much or why he rarely lost a case.

His retainer had left no bail money to be posted; Craig was tapped out. The five-hundred-thousand-dollar bail could've just as well been five million. Too proud and too ashamed to ask for help from affluent people he knew, he braced himself for weeks of confinement. With a swift drop of the judge's gavel, he'd been remanded, his attorney shrugging off his concerns about the time he'd have to spend behind bars awaiting trial.

Then he was hauled over to the Houston Southeast Jail, where he was locked up with the general population.

He'd assumed *innocent until proven guilty* would somehow apply to his time in lockup. He'd been sorely wrong. With the expedience and efficiency of a conveyor belt, the system had stripped him of his remaining dignity, prodding and probing, inflicting physical pain whenever he didn't toe the line, and slapping a number on him without wasting a moment's consideration on his presumed innocence.

He was now prisoner number five-three-three-seven-one-nine.

The number resonated in his mind, the obsessive chorus of an unwritten song he couldn't rid his mind of, the epitome of his lost dignity, of his disappearing identity and his foreclosed freedom. Pale and feeling his insides tied up in a permanent knot of anguish and fear, he'd held his head down and had endured, day after day, waiting, hoping, reciting the unwilling mantra that had ensnared his rebellious brain.

Five-three-three-seven-one-nine.

That's who he was now. He'd unwillingly *become* five-three-three-seven-one-nine, quickly realizing it was far better than fighting back, than rejecting his new reality and its many insults and injuries, all in the name of a precept that only seemed to carry value in movies. There was no innocent until proven guilty. In prison, he was guilty. Nothing else. No one cared while he festered in that hell hole, forgotten by everyone, choking on his anger and shame.

Him, being there... it wasn't supposed to happen. Not to him. Not ever.

Yet three weeks had somehow passed, slowly, while he learned to respond when called "Seven-one-nine" or "inmate." He learned that some of the wardens were just ordinary people making a living, while others thrived on inflicting pain onto the prisoners under their control. Like E. Mellor, the six-foot-four, three-hundred-pound corrections officer with a sadistic glint in his eyes and a grin that stretched his lips over his grinding teeth like a predator's snarl. Mellor sometimes ran his hand over the tip of his rubber stick in an obscene gesture promising nothing good to the inmate who didn't keep his eyes lowered and didn't pay him off. Officer E. Mellor, who knows what the E stood for on his name tag, had taken the last few dollars Craig had on him the day he was remanded and had kept demanding more from the fountain that had already run dry.

That night, at least Mellor was out of sight, the guard pacing the hallways an older Latino, N. Chavez by nametag. His skin was darkened by years of smoking the cheapest stuff available, and his potbelly, stretching the buttons of his shirt to the point of snapping off like spat watermelon seeds, spoke of cirrhosis at some point in the man's near future. Dark circles under his eyes and a stained, grayed-out mustache completed the portrait of the only guard that had not laid a hand on him yet, since he'd been there. The others, Mellor more than any of them, had at least shoved him against the wall or took their rubber sticks to his kidneys in passing, just to show him how things worked. Just for the heck of it.

Garbled radio transmission came from Chavez's lapel, and he quickly responded with a numeric code, then headed straight to Craig's cell with a groan and an expression of frustration on his face.

Craig stood and approached the bars, clutching them with cold, sweaty, trembling fingers.

"Hands," Chavez said, waiting for him to turn around and put his hands through an opening in the bars. Then he slapped a pair of handcuffs on Craig's wrists, the touch of cold metal sending shivers down his spine. "Your lawyer's here to see you," Chavez added.

Craig's eyebrows shot up. "Now?" Goodridge had been there that morning, preparing him for tomorrow's day in court, the first in his trial.

Chavez shrugged. Grabbing his arm, he led him out of the cell and down the hallway toward one of the interview rooms. "What are you in for?"

"I didn't do anything, I swear," he replied, his voice sad, defeated.

A roar of laughter erupted from the cell they were just passing by. "Another innocent man thrown in jail," a guttural voice with a thick Guatemalan accent announced, and soon the entire section was hollering, shouting obscenities, and laughing at his expense.

"No one in here is guilty of anything," Chavez said, sarcasm layered heavy in his voice. "Not even the ones who take plea deals." He shot him a quick look, then shrugged as if deciding not to give a crap about him anymore.

"Murder," he said, lowering his voice. "They're saying I killed—"

"Okay, go in there," Chavez said, shoving him gently into the room.

A man in a tailored suit and expensive shoes stood when he entered.

Craig turned to Chavez. "This isn't my lawyer." Chavez balked at him, then grabbed his radio.

The attorney held his hand up. "Arthur Flanagan, estate attorney," he said, extracting a business card from a holder and handing it to him. Then he popped open the locks on his briefcase and opened it. "I have a letter for you." He took out a thick, bubble-lined envelope and handed it over to Craig.

Chavez took it instead, his gesture quick, determined. "I have to check this before you can see it. Procedure."

The attorney waited, standing, a fresh smell of pricey aftershave regaling his nostrils, reminding Craig of what he used to have and had lost. Estate attorney? What estate? Had one of his parents died?

Chavez pulled the tab and unsealed the envelope.

"Who's this from?" the inmate asked.

The lawyer's eyes darted toward his open briefcase. Maybe he kept a notepad in there. "It's from Andrea Wilmore Brafford," he replied calmly. "It was to be given to you in the event of her death."

His breath caught. He tried to speak, to ask when she had given him that letter, but his throat was parched dry, and only a strangled, raspy whimper came out. He took a step forward and reached for the attorney's arm, but the man stepped back. Chavez grabbed his elbow, and he stopped, frozen in place, feeling the blood draining from his face.

"Take it easy, all right?" Chavez let go of his arm and pulled out a few folded, neatly typed pages. He inspected them quickly, then handed the letter over to him. Before Craig could start reading, the guard looked inside the envelope. "There's something else in here," Chavez said, turning the envelope upside down above his hand and shaking it gently.

A pendant on a silver chain clinked quietly as it fell from the envelope and settled in the guard's hand. When he recognized the blue stones, a wave of nausea hit him hard in the pit of his stomach as the room started to spin with him. *No. That wasn't happening,* his thoughts raced. *It couldn't happen. I still remember what I did. I know what I didn't do.*

"Nice," the guard said, closing his fist around the pendant. "But you can't have this; you know the rules."

"No… no… please, let me touch it for a moment," he pleaded, stuttering, tears rolling down his cheeks. "Let me make sure it's—"

"Okay, for one moment, and that's it," Chavez said, reluctantly opening his palm and letting out a heavy sigh tainted with mustard and onion and cheap tobacco.

Transfixed, he touched the chain with trembling fingers, then ran his thumb over the center stone of the pendant like he'd done it so many times in the past. He swallowed hard, still staring at the small object curled in the guard's chubby palm. It was real. The nightmare was real.

Sweat broke at the roots of his hair and started trickling down his forehead. He raised his handcuffed hands to wipe his brow and noticed the letter he was still holding absentmindedly.

Breath caught inside his chest, he scanned the pages, looking for something that would make sense of it all, that would answer his questions. There was nothing, not until the last page, where the ending paragraph clarified everything for him with a few simple, paralyzing words.

*The girl you killed is watching over you from paradise, lounged on cloud number nine with a Margarita in her hand, hoping you'll have everything you deserve in this life after she's gone. Goodbye, my love. You were the one.*

Blood rushed to his head in a wave of rage, his heart pounding, his fists clenched so hard his knuckles cracked, the last page of the letter crumpled and stained in sweat as it fell to the ground. "No, Andi… no…" he whispered. Eyes staring into emptiness like a wounded, panicked animal, he rushed to the barred door and started pounding against the dirty, wired glass with both fists, the steel handcuffs cutting into his flesh.

"Let me out of here," he shouted. "I didn't kill her, I swear I didn't…" He repeated the phrase over and over, his voice breaking, threatened by tears of rage and powerlessness and despair. The only response he got was from other inmates, banging against steel bars in rhythmic, surreal resonance muffled by the closed door.

"Hey, cut it out," Chavez shouted, but Craig didn't hear him. He kept on pounding against the door, kicking at it, bloodying his knuckles against the scratched metal, pleading and calling for help. Unable to think clearly, he didn't notice the tears streaming down his stained face.

Chavez touched the radio button at his chest. "Need some help in here." Then he collected the pages of the letter scattered on the floor, slid them back into the envelope, and slid the pendant in there before folding the envelope and tucking it inside his chest pocket. "The DA will need to see this. It's evidence."

The guard's words hit him in the chest like a fist, but he kept on banging against the door with all his strength under Chavez's disappointed look and the attorney's disgusted glare until he fell to his knees, drained, sobbing so hard he couldn't breathe. "I didn't do it, I swear," he faltered, choked, gasping for air. "I didn't..."

Chavez walked over to him and grabbed his arm. "Get it together, already. You have court tomorrow."

He looked at the guard through the blur of tears. "You don't understand," he pleaded, grabbing at the man's sleeve. "The pendant, she—" He stopped in time, realizing what he was about to say.

The door opened, and Officer Mellor stepped inside with a glint of excited anticipation in his eyes. "Seven-one-nine, you're coming with me."

*Like The Girl You Killed?*

**Buy it now!**

# Chapter 1

## READY

She made an effort to open her eyes, compelling her heavy eyelids to obey. She swallowed hard, her throat raw and dry, as she urged the wave of nausea to subside. Dizzy and confused, she struggled to gain awareness. Where was she? She felt numb and shaky, unable to move, as if awakening from a deep sleep or a coma. She tried to move her arms, but couldn't. Something kept her immobilized, but didn't hurt her. Or maybe she couldn't feel the pain, not anymore.

Her eyes started to adjust to the darkness, enough to distinguish the man moving quietly in the room. His silhouette flooded her foggy brain with a wave of memories. She gasped, feeling her throat constrict and burning tears rolling down her swollen cheeks.

Her increased awareness sent waves of adrenaline through her body, and she tried desperately to free herself from her restraints. With each useless effort, she panted harder, gasping for air, forcing it into her lungs. Fear put a strong chokehold on her throat and was gaining ground, as she rattled her restraints helplessly, growing weaker with every second. She felt a wave of darkness engulf her, this time the darkness coming from within her weary brain. She fought against that darkness, and battled her own betraying body.

The noises she made got the man's attention.

"I see you're awake. Excellent," the man said, without turning.

She watched him place a syringe on a small, metallic tray. Its handle clinked, followed by another sound, this time the raspy, telling sound of a file cutting through the neck of a glass vial. Then a pop when the man opened the vial. He grabbed the syringe and loaded the liquid from the vial, then carefully removed any air, pushing the piston until several droplets of fluid came out.

Dizziness overtook her, and she closed her eyes for a second.

"Shit," the man mumbled, then opened a drawer and went through it in a hurry.

She felt the needle poke deeply in her thigh, like it was happening to another person. She felt it, but distantly. She perceived a subdued burning sensation where he pushed the fluid into her muscle, then that went away when he pulled the needle out. She closed her weary eyes again, listless against her restraints.

The man cracked open ammonia salts under her nose, and she bounced back into reality at the speed of a lightning strike, aware, alert, and angry. For a second, she fought to free herself, but froze when her eyes focused on the man in front of her.

He held a scalpel, close to her face. In itself, the small, shiny, silver object was capable of bringing formidable healing, as well as immense pain. The difference stood in the hand wielding it. She knew no healing was coming her way; only pain.

"No, no, please…" she pleaded, tears falling freely from her puffy eyes, burning as they rolled down her cheeks. "Please, no. I… I'll do anything."

"I am ready," the man said. He seemed calm, composed, and dispassionate. "Are you ready?"

"No, no, please…" she whimpered.

"Yeah," he said softly, almost whispering, inches away from her face. "Please say no to me. I love that."

She fell quiet, scared out of her mind. This time was different. He was different.

*Like Dawn Girl?*

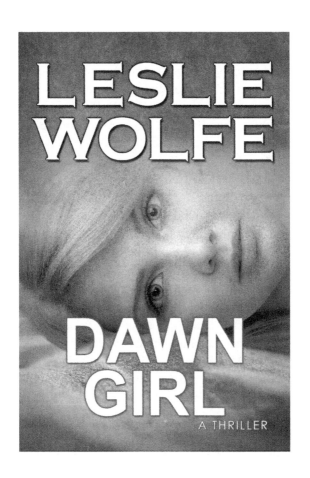

**Buy it now!**

# ABOUT THE AUTHOR

Meet Leslie Wolfe, bestselling author and mastermind behind gripping thrillers that have won the hearts of over a million readers worldwide. She brings a fresh and invigorating touch to the thriller genre, crafting compelling narratives around unforgettable, powerhouse women.

Her books are not only an adrenaline-packed ride, but they're also sprinkled with psychological insights, offering readers an immersive, authentic experience that goes beyond conventional suspense.

You might know her from the Detective Kay Sharp series or have been hooked by Tess Winnett's relentless pursuit of justice. Maybe you've followed the dynamic duo Baxter & Holt through the gritty streets of Las Vegas or plunged into political intrigue with Alex Hoffmann.

Recently, Leslie published *A Beautiful Couple*, a psychological thriller that's pure, unputdownable suspense. This standalone novel will have fans of *The Undoing, The Silent Patient,* and *Little Fires Everywhere* on the edge of their seats.

Whether you're into the mind games of Criminal Minds, love crime thrillers like James Patterson's, or enjoy the heart-pounding tension in Kendra Elliot and Robert Dugoni's mysteries, Leslie's got a thriller series for you. Fans of action-packed writers like Tom Clancy or Lee Child will find plenty to love in her Alex Hoffmann series.

One of Wolfe's latest psychological thrillers, *The Surgeon*, will have you racing through the pages gasping for breath until the final jaw-dropping twist, delighting fans of *Gone Girl* and *The Girl on the Train.*

Discover all of Leslie's works on **Amazon.com/LeslieWolfe.**

Want a sneak peek at what's next? Become an insider for early access to previews of her new novels, each a thrilling ride you won't want to miss.

Amazon store: Amazon.com/LeslieWolfe

Email: LW@WolfeNovels.com

Amazon Page: Leslie Wolfe's Author Page

Website: LeslieWolfe.com

Facebook: Facebook.com/WolfeNovels

Instagram: Instagram.com/Wolfe.Leslie

Tiktok: Tiktok.com/@Leslie.Wolfe

Follow Leslie on BookBub: Leslie on Bookbub

# BOOKS BY LESLIE WOLFE

STANDALONE TITLES

*A Beautiful Couple*
*The Surgeon*
*The Girl You Killed*
*The Hospital*
*If I Go Missing*
*Stories Untold*
*Love, Lies and Murder*

TESS WINNETT SERIES

*Dawn Girl*
*The Watson Girl*
*Glimpse of Death*
*Taker of Lives*
*Not Really Dead*
*Girl With A Rose*
*Mile High Death*
*The Girl They Took*
*The Girl Hunter*

DETECTIVE KAY SHARP SERIES

*The Girl From Silent Lake*
*Beneath Blackwater River*
*The Angel Creek Girls*
*The Girl on Wildfire Ridge*
*Missing Girl at Frozen Falls*

BAXTER & HOLT SERIES

*Las Vegas Girl*
*Casino Girl*
*Las Vegas Crime*

ALEX HOFFMANN SERIES

Executive
Devil's Move
The Backup Asset
The Ghost Pattern
Operation Sunset

For the complete list of books in all available formats, visit:
**Amazon.com/LeslieWolfe**

68780865R00202